FORBIDDEN BY FAITH

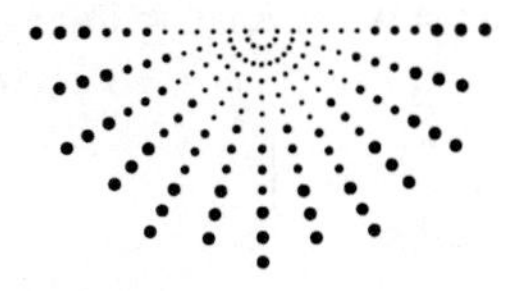

NEGEEN PAPEHN

This book is a work of fiction. Names, characters, places, and incidents either are products of the author's imagination or are used fictitiously. Any resemblance to actual events or locales or persons, living or dead, is entirely coincidental and not intended by the author.

FORBIDDEN BY FAITH
Forbidden Love, Book 1

CITY OWL PRESS
www.cityowlpress.com

Cover Design by Mibl Art and Tina Moss. All stock photos licensed appropriately.

Edited by Amanda Roberts.

For information on subsidiary rights, please contact the publisher at info@cityowlpress.com.

Print Edition ISBN: 978-1-944728-70-0

Digital Edition ISBN: 978-1-944728-71-1

Printed in the United States of America

PRAISE FOR NEGEEN PAPEHN

"FORBIDDEN BY FAITH shows how family, love, and faith can collide, even in this modern age."
– *Romance Author, A. K. Leigh*

"Much more than a love story...full of twists and turns as two lovers navigate their way through one of history's oldest cultural divides."
– *Barry Collier*

"An engaging story of two unlikely people coming together for love. This book is filled with twists and turns. Hard to put down!"
– *Renee Noy*

"A modern Romeo and Juliet. A sexy and gripping story about a perfect love that was never supposed to happen."
– *Alison Ross*

"A little 50 Shades...A little Romeo & Juliet...FORBIDDEN BY FAITH is sure to keep you turning the page. Although after some of the pages, you may need to take a cigarette break (even if you don't smoke!)."
– *Parisa Collier*

"I loved everything! The idea that true love can overcome all challenges, despite tight family bonds, stays with you long after the book is over."
– *Leyla Dastranj*

"This book was my guilty pleasure, a true escape from reality as I got lost in the love story...the author takes the reader on a true journey. I didn't want the book to end!"
– *Azi Amirteymoori*

For Elijah and Noah

PROLOGUE

I push through the doors of the foyer and am hit by the scene unfolding before me. I'm unable to breathe, the air having left my lungs. I feel like I've been kicked in the gut. There's a bar fight at my wedding. I can hear the words in my mind, but I can't comprehend their meaning. I'm standing still while everything moves in slow motion.

I see a table fallen over on its side, glass decorating its edges, remnants of wine creating swirling patterns on the floor. I'm vaguely reminded of a painting I've seen before, but the title escapes me. A flower arrangement has been knocked over, purple petals splattered on the tiles, its beauty now just a memory. Little groups of guests are scattered around, worried looks on their faces. I see them look at me, lean in toward each other, whispering. Some look with sympathy, others with disdain. Directly in front of me, I see a larger crowd. I can't see my way through, but the group is composed of my family. The groom is nowhere to be found.

I hear someone mention my cousin's name, something about a fight. I stand for a moment, baffled, wondering how one person could leave such havoc in his wake. I breathe. I take one more look around, pick up my dress, and head in for battle. I push my way through. The sight of my princess dress in tow parts the crowd like Moses parting the sea. I shove my way in until I am standing directly in front of him.

"What are you doing?" I shout. "What is *wrong* with you?"

My uncle comes up beside me and yells something at his son that I can't comprehend behind the rush of adrenaline and savage anger coursing through my veins. I turn my attention to him.

"*Amoo*, get him out of here!" I demand. Then, I just keep screaming.

Before I know it, I'm yelling in Farsi. Words my grandmother used when we were kids that I'd forgotten I knew. All I'm aware of is the electric burn of anger that's invaded my body.

And just like that, I become airborne. I don't see it coming. I feel two hands circling my waist, whisking me away into the air, through the crowd. I feel the air rustle the edges of my dress as if I'm floating. I'm gently placed on my feet. I look up to see Thomas standing in front of me. It takes me a moment to understand his presence.

He looks at me, kindness filling his eyes when he says, "You're not helping." I reach out for him, but it's too late. He turns, disappearing into the crowd.

There's so much noise, but I don't hear any of it. I can only hear the deafening silence surrounding my shattering heart. I start to cry. What I want to do is get up on a table and scream into the crowd, *Don't you know what I had to go through to get here? Don't you know there are people in this very crowd thinking to themselves that they were right all along? That we were doomed from the start?* But my voice is lost before my thoughts can form around the words. All I keep thinking is, *How can this be happening?*

CHAPTER ONE

I hang up the phone. I really don't feel like getting ready to go to this party, but I already promised Leyla I would, so now I have no choice. She's been dying to introduce me to some of her new UCLA friends. I get dressed in some jeans and a low-cut yellow top, my dark brown waves bouncing against my bare back as I run down the hall.

"I'll be home late, Mom," I yell over my shoulder as I rush out the door.

I make the fifteen-minute drive to Leyla's, trying to work myself into the mood. Shouldn't a single twenty-four-year-old want to go out on a Saturday night? Especially to UCLA, where there would be a prime crop of Persian boys.

Leyla comes running out before I've fully pulled up and jumps into the front seat, breaking me out of my thoughts.

"We're going to have so much fun," she says, beaming at me. "You're going to love these girls." I try to smile at her as we make our way over to the west side.

Once we arrive, Leyla grabs my hand and drags me around the room, introducing me to everyone she knows. Maya, the host, pushes two solo cups full of some fruity concoction into our hands. I can smell the sterile tang of vodka as it touches my lips, feel the familiar burn as it makes its way down my throat. After a few more sips, I begin to feel a tingling sensation in my fingertips, signaling the start of a warm buzz. I smile at the feel of it.

That's when I see him. Out of the corner of my eye, his blue shirt catches my attention. I turn to get a better glimpse. He's beautiful. He's tall, with dark brown hair and a chiseled face. His hazel eyes are the warm color of honey, with flecks of green decorating his pupils.

I discreetly watch him as he makes his way around the room, engaging in one conversation after the next. I notice the gait of his walk, the way he subtly favors his left, the bounce in his step. I watch him run his fingers carelessly through his hair, hear his laugh bellowing from the bottom of his belly, watch the sparkle in his eye as he speaks.

Then, he suddenly turns as if he can feel the weight of my gaze. He looks at me, stalling for only a second, before he smiles. It's the most perfect thing I've ever seen.

I can't help but smile back, maintaining eye contact for a few seconds before I have to look away. I can't meet the intensity of his gaze, feeling a blush creeping up my neck. My heart begins to race, Leyla's words becoming a blur I can't keep up with.

I turn to look at him again, but he's gone. I try to discreetly search for him in the crowd but he's nowhere to be found. It's almost like he's disappeared and I wonder for a moment if I've just dreamed him up. The disappointment hits me like a wave, but I try to hide it, currently locked in a conversation with Leyla and a few other girls I don't really know.

The music begins blaring as the DJ turns up the volume. The girls squeal and Leyla drags me toward the makeshift dance floor in the middle of the living room. I notice the discoloration of the wood where the furniture used to be sitting as I'm swallowed into the crowd of moving bodies.

I don't see the handsome boy anywhere and begin to lose hope. Maybe he's already left the party. The thought disappoints me further, but I brush it off. The night moves on and soon I'm carelessly whirling around to the beat of the song, enveloped in the blanket of my intoxication.

Suddenly, I feel the weight of someone's gaze resting on my shoulders. I look up and find him across the room, staring at me. His head's cocked to the side, a thoughtful expression on his face as he studies me. The room falls silent, the rush of blood through my ears the only thing I can hear. My nerves twist into a knot in the pit of my stomach.

Then, he smiles, that irresistible smile, and just like that, it all melts away. Before I know what I'm doing, I tilt my head, motioning for him to come join me. I'm relieved when he does. He doesn't say a word, just begins to dance. He's so close, I can feel his breath on my hair, the heat radiating off of his skin. I can hardly breathe.

This handsome stranger in front of me could be anyone. I don't know his name, or who he is, but I do know that every time his arm brushes against my body, a surge of electricity runs up my side that nearly knocks me over. I'm mesmerized.

I don't know how many songs we dance to before he asks me if I want to go outside. I can't speak, just nod and follow, locked in his trance. My heart's beating uncontrollably against my chest, making me dizzy. Leyla winks her approval at me as I pass her, but I barely notice. Outside, he finds a quiet spot under a tree and turns to face me.

"Hi, I'm Maziar," he says.

"I'm Sara."

"Nice to meet you, Sara," he replies, pronouncing my name with the soft "A" sound like it should be. Although Sara is a traditional Iranian name, even my friends pronounce it the English way. It makes me smile.

He's twenty-four, like myself, about to start his second year of law school. My first thought is, *Mom is going to love that*. He confirms my suspicions that he's also Iranian, and for a brief second I feel a rush of pleasure course through me—*he's Persian and a lawyer*. But before I can get too excited, I take a deep breath and ask the ever-dreaded question for a Persian girl, "What religion are you?"

To many people, this may seem like a strange thing to ask when you first meet someone. But to an Iranian girl, his answer will dictate whether I ever see him again.

He looks at me, head tilted, eyes crinkled in thought. He's not sure if I'm serious. When I give no indication that I'm joking, he utters the words I so desperately don't want him to say.

"I'm Jewish."

Again, the wave of disappointment hits me like a ton of bricks. I put out my hand to shake his. "It was very nice meeting you," I say, and get ready to walk away...

CHAPTER TWO

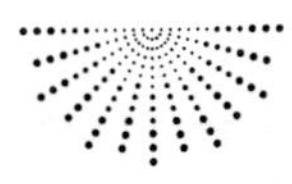

I was born in Hollywood, California, in 1981, at the blue Presbyterian hospital. I know it's blue because Dad points it out every time we drive by. My parents got married in Iran when Dad was twenty-two and Mom was eighteen. They didn't even get to go home together the night of their wedding. Dad was set to leave for the States the following week, and in an attempt to save my mom's virtue, my grandfather refused to let them consummate their marriage until she met him in America. He figured it was better to be safe than sorry, just in case the crazy ordeal didn't work out. You see, my parents' love story deserves its own explanation.

Dad's family owned a school where his mother was the principal. My maternal grandmother was a teacher there. One day Dad and my grandfather, were doing some repairs. Dad took a break to stretch his legs and glanced down the street. There on the sidewalk walking toward him, was Mom. She'd come to keep her mother company on the short walk home. The way Dad describes that moment is pure love at first sight.

He says he saw her and was awestruck by her beauty. "Who is that?" he asked. My grandfather told him, to which he replied, "I'm going to marry her."

In those days in that country, courting had little to do with what we define as dating. Getting acquainted with your future spouse consisted of a few meetings at her house with her parents present, and, if you were really lucky, maybe a group outing to a movie with all of her siblings and cousins. The pairing of a couple also had a lot to do with family status and worth. For this reason, my paternal grandmother was against their union. She did her best to leave no doubt about her disdain for Mom. In the end, their love prevailed, with Dad never giving in to his mother's wishes.

Once the two were married, he made his way to the States to go to school. One year later, when Mom had lost all hope of starting her new life with him, he called for her to come to America. I showed up two years later, with my brother Nima following eighteen months after that.

My parents' life was a struggle, to say the least. Dad worked multiple jobs to make ends meet while he went to school. Mom didn't know anyone and barely knew the language; she had to fend for herself, taking care of us while Dad was away. His family alienated her, making her miserable, which in turn made Dad miserable. It's a miracle they've been married for this long.

Because of Mom's experience with her own in-laws, my parents had always been open-minded about marriage. The only request I could remember them ever having was that I married someone Iranian so he could "speak the language."

Traditional religion did not hold much emphasis in my immediate family. Even though we were Muslim, my parents didn't raise me under its pretenses. They taught me to be spiritual, the religious aspects going as far as believing in God.

If I wanted to go into a Catholic church and light some candles, Mom would tell me to light a few for her too. If I felt like going into a mosque to listen to daily prayers, I could. Our beliefs formed around the commonalities of all religions, letting go of their details.

We were the exception to the rule, however.

Not all families felt the same way, especially in the Iranian culture. Practicing families rarely deviated from the expected, pushing their children to settle down with their own kind. Either Muslim or Jewish, they would rather their children marry someone of the same faith, even if the person was a different race.

CHAPTER THREE

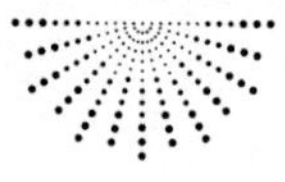

I turned to walk away, but he grabbed my arm. "We're mortal enemies, right?" he said, laughing. Even though we weren't yet, I feared that someday we would be. Realizing I wasn't convinced, he continued, "Hey, wait, I have no problem with your religion."

It wasn't him I was worried about, I explained, but he assured me that his family would be fine. Even so, there was still that nagging voice in the back of my mind telling me I should turn around and run. I'd revisit that little voice frequently in the future and wonder why I'd ignored her.

The rest of the night progressed uneventfully. No new life-altering information was exchanged. Maziar found his friends and we ended up leaving the party to get a bite to eat. We exchanged numbers at the end of the night.

I'd never been the typical Persian girl, groomed all her life to find a husband. My upbringing had been quite the contrary. Mom had seen the struggles of being just someone's wife. She'd spent most of her life rebelling against those restraints. She had pushed me to be a strong, independent woman.

"I never want you to rely on a man, Sara," she'd always say. She wanted my husband to be an addition, not a necessity. While many of my cousins were out prowling the scene in search of a suitable mate, I got accepted to pharmacy school.

When weeks passed and I didn't hear from Maziar, I didn't even notice. The memories of the electricity we shared and his breathtaking smile had faded. When my phone rang with a number I didn't recognize, I almost didn't pick up.

"You don't remember me?" he teased. "I'm your mortal enemy." I could hear him smiling from the other side of the line.

"Oh, yeah, now I remember." I laughed.

We talked for an hour, then made plans to meet that weekend.

Now that I didn't have him in front of me muddling my thoughts with his sex appeal, I realized I didn't know him at all. He could very well be a serial killer who wanted to lure me into his web and make me his next victim. For this reason, I agreed to meet him at the movie theater instead of my house. Public places were more difficult to get kidnapped from, plus it wasn't like I was planning to introduce him to my parents.

When Saturday arrived, I told Nima about Maziar, because someone needed to know who to go after if my body needed to be found. I got to the theater a few minutes earlier than he did, which I thought was a bad start. I chastised myself for not having stayed in the car longer. I also realized he was not a prompt person. Strike one for him. In his defense, I'd come to this date ready to make a list of reasons why he shouldn't make it to date number two.

I was a little worried I wouldn't recognize him. I was equally worried that the dim lights of the party and the alcohol had made him appear to be much better looking than he really was. For this reason, I had Leyla calling me in two hours to give me an escape route if necessary.

Then, he walked into the plaza.

I saw him before he saw me. First off, the lighting and inebriation had done nothing to change his appearance—he was still gorgeous. It looked like he'd just gotten out of the shower, hair damp, casually dressed in a pair of jeans and a T-shirt. The room froze as I stared, the sound of my breath in and out of my chest the only thing I could hear. Then, he saw me.

"Hi," he said. That dazzling smile was stretched across his face as he walked over to me. Point one in his favor.

"Hey," I replied awkwardly, suddenly feeling shy.

Maziar didn't seem to notice, completely comfortable in his skin. He just stood there staring at me as if I were a puzzle he was piecing together. I fidgeted under his gaze. He looked away, the corners of his lips turned up in a grin, knowing he'd made me nervous.

"Shall we?" he asked, gesturing toward the ticket booth. I followed him to the window, waiting while he paid for our tickets. Point two in his favor.

I spent most of the movie trying to catch glimpses of him in the dim light of the theater without getting caught. I was distinctly aware of our arms lying beside each other on the armrest. I could feel the heat radiating off of his, laced with a spark that felt like an electric charge. It was overwhelming. After the movie, he placed his hand on the small of my back, guiding me through the door. I almost melted from his touch. What was with this guy and the effect he had over me?

I'd decided at the beginning of the date that I'd leave after the movie, severing the connection between us before it had a chance to bloom. Even though he'd told me this could work, the voice in my head wouldn't ease up, still giving me the distinct feeling I needed to flee. But once we were outside and he suggested we grab dinner, I heard myself say yes before I could stop. My brain had officially disconnected itself from the rest of me, and now all responses were based purely on emotion. This couldn't end well, yet I'd lost all reason.

We settled on the Cheesecake Factory down the street. The wait was strangely short for a Saturday night, and we were seated quickly. The conversation flowed easily between us, something I'd expected.

Maziar grew up in the Palisades, where he lived with his parents and sister, until he moved away a year ago for school. He currently attended Pepperdine Law School and lived in an apartment nearby. Neither of his last two relationships had been with Jewish girls, which I wanted to take as a good sign. Then, he told me his most recent relationship had ended a week before we met, after two years. Strike two for Maziar.

Again the voice urged me to leave, but I was too intrigued to move.

I couldn't resist the energy passing between us. I felt high on him and I couldn't get enough. I listened to his every word, hung onto his laugh, and melted into his smile. I had lost myself four hours into our first meeting, knowing I'd never find my way back again.

I told him how I'd grown up in the Valley and still lived with my parents and older brother in Encino. I'd just been accepted to pharmacy school at USC and was starting in the fall. He asked me why I'd decided to commute.

"My parents would flip if I moved out on my own. They're a bit old-fashioned that way."

"But don't you want the experience of being independent?" he asked.

"Yeah, maybe, but I'd have to ease them into it. Plus, having someone cook for me and do my laundry when I'm in school sounds kind of nice," I said, resorting to joking, hoping my lack of independence would be charming. Thankfully, he laughed.

As the conversation continued, the topics became more serious. We began discussing our previous relationships, the details of each of our breakups. I suddenly felt compelled to give him another opportunity to walk away, in hopes of avoiding an unnecessary heartache if things indeed went as expected. Jewish and Muslim relationships were uncommon, and all that I knew of had ended in horrible breakups. I couldn't do it.

"So I know you said my not being Jewish isn't a big deal, but honestly, if there's even a chance that your family could be against it, I'd rather we have a nice dinner and leave it at that."

"You really are paranoid, aren't you?" he said, a smirk playing at the corner of his lips.

"No, just practical," I replied, slightly annoyed. "Look, I've been in relationships that don't work out, and I'm sure you agree–they can be brutal. Why start something if we already know that's where it's inevitably heading?"

"Because we have no idea where this is heading," he stated.

"Ugh, I know that!" I said. He was getting the best of me and judging from the look on his face, he knew it. I tried a different approach, attempting to reason with him. "I've had my heart broken before. I really can't do it again," I urged with more desperation than I hoped could be heard in my voice. "So if this is likely going to end the same, then I'd rather we end it here." We didn't know each other yet. We could walk away from this encounter whole, no battle scars, and I'd eventually forget that smile.

But Maziar was relentless, insisting that it wasn't a problem our two religions had been at war for centuries. "My parents will be fine," he said, brushing it off.

I wondered if he was naïve, if indeed this might be strike three for Maziar. But as I looked at him, I couldn't manage to say, "you're out."

I knew this was too heavy a conversation to be having on a first date and I knew it wasn't painting me in a good light. I also knew it was impossible to predict the future. Even so, I still wanted to be assured I wouldn't have my heart torn from my chest.

In hindsight, I realize that there are no guarantees in love and there is always the risk of losing a part of yourself along the way.

* * *

The following weekend, we had plans for our second date. I found myself feeling giddy with excitement as I got ready. We'd been talking every night for the past week, the conversation only ending when one of us had fallen asleep. The more I got to know him, the more I realized I could really like him.

I learned that Maziar had a twenty-six-year-old sister. He thought they had a decent relationship, but I wouldn't consider them close by *my* standards. Neither knew what was going on in the other's life, and from what I understood, they didn't talk much, aside from friendly conversation when passing each other in the hall to their bedrooms.

My brother and I were the polar opposite. We knew everything about each other. If I told my parents a lie about where I was or with whom, my brother knew the truth. He was my person, so it was hard for me to wrap my head around that type of relationship, kind and cordial but each life separate.

Maziar picked me up around noon. I knew nothing of the details aside from it being a little bit of a drive. That's all he would say. My parents were out when he picked me up, which worked out perfectly because I wasn't interested in the plethora of questions they'd ask if they met him.

We drove north for about an hour. Soon the scenery changed, surrounding us with a lush green landscape. He exited onto a long, curved bridge standing over a large ravine. It was nestled between two great hills on either side. The bridge had prominent archways every few feet, giving it a mystical air. It was gorgeous. To the right, I could see a lake. Maziar pulled off toward it.

He'd packed us a picnic and stowed a few fishing rods in his trunk. We walked down to the water's edge and threw down a blanket. We nestled close to each other. He opened the basket to reveal sandwiches, a platter of cheese, and a bottle of wine. I felt a warmth begin to stir in the pit of my stomach, followed by a flutter of butterflies.

The rest of the afternoon was spent in a comfortable familiarity, as if Maziar and I had been together for years, not just days. The conversation rolled off our tongues with ease, never falling victim to awkward silences. We laughed, the kind that starts from your toes and ends in the pit of your belly. We fit in a way I'd never experienced with another human being before.

He had a thing for fishing and was determined to teach me how it was done. I was pitiful. Even though he'd shown me how to throw out the line a handful of times, I still couldn't manage it without tangling the string. Instead of becoming irritated with my incompetence, he laughed.

Surprisingly, we actually caught a fish, or at least Maziar did while I stood behind him and squealed as he brought the slimy, flapping creature out of the water. I watched him gently grab it, speaking softly as if he were trying to soothe the fish in its last moments. There was a kindness in the way he removed the hook, in the way he held the animal in his hands. Its body jerked relentlessly, but he never rushed the process, allowing nature to fulfill her destiny as she wished.

Suddenly, I couldn't bear to watch. "Please throw it back in. I don't want it to die." He looked up at me for a few moments, then, without a word, he placed the fish gently back into the lake. We stood side by side watching it swim away, the sound of our breath mingled with the lapping of the water. "I'm sorry," I said, unsure if I was apologizing for the fish or ruining the trip altogether.

"For what?" he replied, still staring at the water.

"For making you set it free."

He turned and faced me, his hazel eyes catching the light of the sun, and smiled. I watched the lines around his lids crinkle, melting my anxiety.

"I love that you made me let it go."

On the drive back, the sun was setting, and the sky was illuminated into a canvas of pinks, purples, and oranges. The colors swirled around each other, creating puffs of sherbet-colored clouds you could almost taste.

Maziar pulled over so we could properly adore its beauty. We both got out of the car, standing side by side in the stillness of the dusk. His hand lightly brushed mine, and I felt the familiar surge of electricity course through my veins. I lost all restraint, reaching out and grabbing hold.

Maziar turned toward me. When I faced him, I saw the warmth and longing in his eyes. My breath caught in my throat. He put his hand on my cheek and slowly leaned in to place his lips against mine. My heart beat rapidly against my chest as I felt my body melt into his. I don't know how long we stood there in our embrace, but when we parted, we both did so reluctantly.

I could have spent the rest of my life in that moment, kissing him.

CHAPTER FOUR

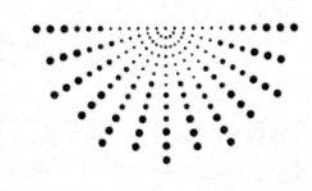

We spent all our free time together, and when we weren't together, we were on the phone. I was infatuated with him. He was like heroin coursing through my veins and when he wasn't with me, I felt like I needed another hit. The electrical frequency between us just grew with each encounter, and I found it hard to keep myself from craving his touch. I wanted to hold his hand, sit really close, feel the heat off his body every time he was near me. The relationship itself felt easier than any I'd ever experienced. We slid into being a couple as if we were always meant to be together. He felt like he made up a piece of me, like we'd done this before in lifetimes past.

He felt like home.

As the days went on, I started to focus less on the future and fall deeper in love. The academic year had begun, but any chance I got, I made my way over to his apartment. We'd play house, lost in the make-believe of living together, where only the two of us mattered, if only for a moment.

Two months in, I was finally ready to broach the topic of our relationship with my parents. Up until then, they didn't know that when I went out, I was going with Maziar. The benefit of having Leyla as a best friend was that she always covered for me. It wasn't that I thought they wouldn't like him, it was that I knew Mom would freak out when she found out he was Jewish. She had told me numerous times that she didn't want me to be disliked and disregarded by my husband's family as she had been.

"Life is hard enough as it is. Why add more complications to the situation?" she'd say.

I still hadn't forgotten that this relationship was built on forbidden ground, and even though I basked in the beauty of what we had, the voice in my head wouldn't let me be completely comfortable. I was always waiting for the other shoe to drop.

One Friday night after I'd gotten home from my last class, we sat down to have dinner together as we normally did before my brother and I headed out for the night. As we talked about our day, the anxiety continued to weigh down on me, to the point that I felt a panic attack about to come on. I couldn't stay quiet any longer, so I just blurted it out, in the middle of Dad's sentence about the ridiculous politics at his work.

"I've been dating a guy for a few months," I said. They all froze and looked at me as if I were speaking a foreign language. "He's Persian," I continued. Mom had a hint of a smile playing at the corner of her lips. Feeling guilty for allowing her to start to build a perfect future for me in her head, I quickly added, "And he's Jewish."

Complete silence followed. Mom dropped her fork. The clanking of the metal against her plate radiated off the walls, magnifying the sound. She looked at me as if she wasn't sure whether to yell or cry.

"It's totally okay. It's not a big deal for him or his family," I said. She didn't move, making me sweat.

In an attempt to alleviate the heaviness in the room, Nima tried to lighten up the mood and started to ask me details about him.

"What's his name? Where did you meet him?"

"His name is Maziar, and I met him a few months ago when I was out with my friends," I replied.

"Cool. What does he do?" He tried to keep the conversation moving along, not allowing Mom time to attack. I was grateful.

"He goes to Pepperdine law school." I glanced over at her, hoping the information I had just shared would soften the blow. It did nothing, as she continued to stare at me, shocked and angry.

I couldn't tell her that I'd already fallen in love with him, and I was doomed if what he told me wasn't the truth, that in fact his family wouldn't be okay with this union. I couldn't tell her that I was rapidly losing sleep over it, during the nights when I didn't have his arms to quiet the storm and make me forget. I couldn't say any of this, because then Mom would shatter. Whether she showed it or not, I would have broken her heart.

"We want to meet him," Dad said. "Bring him over next Sunday night." Just like that, he was to come over the following weekend for dinner.

Wednesday rolled around and I had sufficiently avoided Mom's calls. School made it easy to dodge her, only interacting for a few minutes in the mornings before I headed to class. I had just gotten out of a biology when my phone began to buzz again in my pocket. I stared at her picture flashing on my screen, the dark, short bob framing her face like two delicate hands, her warm brown eyes, scrunched up in laughter, realizing I couldn't avoid her forever. The longer I waited to deal with her questions, the worse her attitude would be with Maziar when he came over. I picked up.

"Hi, Mom," I said, in as chipper a voice as possible.

"Hi, *azizam*, where are you?"

"I just got out of class. Why?" I asked.

"I wanted to talk to you. Do you have a minute?"

"Okay," I replied. I should have lied.

"I wanted to talk to you about the boy you told us about. Why didn't you tell me you were dating him? You always share that stuff with me, Sara."

I could hear the hurt in my mom's voice, causing regret to settle on my insides. I took too long to reply, unsure of what I could say to salvage her feelings. When I provided no answers, she continued.

"Sara, I know you like him, but haven't I told you enough about what I had to go through with your dad? You know this isn't a good idea. Have you met his family? Are they okay with this relationship?"

She threw her questions at me like darts, pent up over the past few days when I'd ignored her. I had to take a minute to think, the panic making it tough to get my bearings. I knew I needed to sound convincing when I said there was nothing to worry about, despite the fact that I didn't fully believe it myself.

"No, I haven't, but he says they don't care." A lame answer, but what else could I say? The truth was that I had no idea if they really had issues with my being Muslim, but I had let the notion of walking away go when I'd realized how I'd felt about Maziar. I was all in now, praying what he was telling me was the truth.

"Sara, I don't think this is a good idea," she said again, as if I hadn't heard her the first time.

"Mom, it will be just fine. Wait until you meet him. You'll see. You're going to love him, I promise," I urged. "I have to go into class now. I don't want to be late." I didn't have class, but I needed to get off the phone before she had a chance to say anything else.

"Okay, *azizam*," she replied, hesitantly. I knew she wasn't finished with this conversation, but I was hoping that meeting Maziar would somewhat calm her nerves on the topic. "Have a good class."

"Thanks. I love you," I said.

"Love you, too."

When Saturday came, I was rendered useless. I could barely breathe, let alone do anything of substance. Mom stared at me with her ominous eyes as I did my best to feign being tired from a long week of school. I wasn't fooling anyone.

It was seven o'clock when the doorbell rang; Maziar was on time. Dad was a very prompt person, to the point where it could be seen as a flaw, so being punctual definitely gave Maziar some brownie points with him. I sighed with relief, needing all the backup I could get against Mom's disapproval of the situation.

I opened the door to find Maziar smiling down at me. His presence was calming, and for a moment, I forgot that I was worried. There was no way they wouldn't love him. He was just so damn lovable.

He came inside and shook hands with my dad. He then handed a bouquet of tulips and a cake over to my mom, simultaneously commenting on how beautiful the house was. In the Iranian culture, you never showed up empty-handed. Maziar seemed to hold a PhD in the art of Persian schmoozing, which surprised me. He laid the compliments on thick, and before I knew it, Mom's hard defenses had softened and she was beaming at him.

Dad began with his interrogation as soon as we sat down to dinner. "So, Maziar, Sara tells me you're at Pepperdine. How do you like it?"

"I'm really enjoying it, *Aghah* Abbas."

"Have you decided on what you're going to specialize in?"

"No, not yet," he said, then threw in, "but I have a few areas I'm leaning toward."

"How about your parents? What do they do?"

"My mother used to run a daycare center when we were younger, but she's home now. My father and uncle have a lighting business. They work with hospitals and large companies."

The conversation continued in this manner, Dad rapidly asking his questions while Maziar did his best to answer appropriately. He responded with the ease of someone who was speaking to an old friend, never breaking his stride. Although Mom liked him, she remained uninvolved, her apprehension of the situation still very much present.

"Maziar, you seem like a nice young man," Dad said. I held my breath, knowing what was coming. He continued, "But you have to understand that my wife and I are a little concerned with where you see this relationship going. We do have some differences that could cause problems." I appreciated how Dad tried to remain as respectful as he could while asking if my being Muslim was an issue.

"Our religions aren't going to be a concern, *Aghah* Abbas. Sara and I have talked about it. My family will be fine," Maziar answered, getting straight to the root of the problem.

I finally exhaled.

Afterward, the conversation lightened, the elephant in the room having been addressed and slaughtered, for the time being. There were little bubbles of hope floating around, as everyone relaxed simultaneously. Nima started cracking jokes, and before I knew it, we were all laughing and enjoying ourselves. After Maziar left, neither of my parents could deny liking him. Mom still had her concerns, but they were far less prominent than when the night began.

That's how Maziar became part of my family. But truth be told, it wasn't my family I was worried about.

CHAPTER FIVE

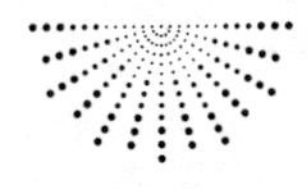

Maziar was the yin to my yang, the up to my down. He was my other half and I knew it deep down to the core of me. It had been a few months now and we still hadn't made love. I could feel the need to attain that ultimate closeness with him boiling over inside me.

There was a law school event the following weekend. I'd woven an elaborate set of lies so I could spend three days with Maziar. That Saturday morning, I tried to contain my giddiness so as not to tip my parents off. I may have been a twenty-four-year-old in graduate school, but as far as my Iranian parents were concerned, I still needed to leave the door open when my boyfriend visited. It was definitely unacceptable to be heading over to his house to sleep in his bed all weekend.

As I drove over to his place, I couldn't contain my excitement. It amazed me how I could still feel such outrageous butterflies just at the thought of seeing him. I had packed a sexy, lavender, lace bra and its matching bottoms to wear underneath my slinky black dress. I'd decided that tonight would be *the night*. I had no clue if he would reciprocate the offer, but I was too excited and nervous to worry about it. All I could think about was seeing him. It had been too long since I'd had my drug.

I pulled up to his apartment building and he came outside to greet me. He kissed me as he helped me with my bag. We ate lunch, and then spent the remainder of the afternoon lying on the couch watching television until it was time to get ready.

I was just putting the finishing touches on my outfit when he walked out dressed and ready to go. I had to remind myself to keep my mouth shut because my jaw wanted to hit the floor. This was the first time I'd seen him dressed up, and I was in awe of the specimen before me. To say he was handsome would not do him justice. He was wearing a fitted black Hugo Boss suit with a deep green shirt that pulled the green out of his eyes and a thin black tie. I had to pinch myself.

This was actually my life, and this man was really mine.

I was going to meet his law school friends for the first time and I was nervous. I wanted to make a good impression. We were the last to arrive, so he introduced me to everyone all at once. My heart was pounding in my chest and my hands felt clammy.

The girls were quick to initiate me into their club, though, and it wasn't long before they were sharing all of Maziar's law school bloopers. As the night moved on, I felt myself begin to relax. We spent the better part of the evening laughing hysterically; I was thoroughly enjoying myself.

The alcohol was plentiful. About halfway through the night, we witnessed a lover's quarrel between his friend and her date. They were early on in their relationship as well, and apparently she found it unacceptable that he stared at every beautiful woman who walked by. I barely knew her, but we spent the remainder of the evening consoling her. As I watched Maziar offer a tender side of himself to his wounded friend, the love swelled inside me. A few hours later, we dropped her off at home and headed back to his place. I couldn't wait to get him inside.

We didn't make it through the door before I was pulling off his jacket and unbuttoning his shirt. The path to his bedroom became a passionate tangle of clothing and limbs. When we finally made it to his room, the dance slowed and he gently laid me down on his bed. Little by little, he etched a path of kisses up my body until he made it to my lips. He brushed his lips softly against mine and pulled back to look down at me for a moment. He looked like he was drinking in the details of my face, committing every contour, every freckle, and every mark into his memory. For the first time he was wide open, and I could see straight into his soul.

"I love you," he said, more to himself than me, as if he were surprised by the realization of his own feelings.

"I love you, too," I whispered, a knot suddenly lodged in my throat.

"What is it? What's wrong?" I could see the concern etched on his face.

"I hate that you've said those words to another woman before."

He paused for a moment, looking at me thoughtfully before he spoke. "But I've never meant them as much as I mean them now."

I stared at him and could see the truth in his words. I knew with an infinite certainty, that from now on, I only wanted him to look at me with those eyes, to say those words only to me, and mean it. I leaned in, pulling his face to mine. I kissed his lips with a shuddering intensity, as if I'd been starving all my life for his touch. I wrapped my legs around his waist, closing the space between us. We moved with an unspoken rhythm, one our bodies seemed to know by heart. He'd take me to the brink, slow down, then build me up all over again. When we finally reached the peak, the earth shattered beneath us and we came crashing down onto the pillows together.

Later, as I was lying in his arms, I knew that this man had ruined me. I would never be able to get myself out of the tangle he'd created, and the truth was I never wanted to.

CHAPTER SIX

Before I knew it, it was our sixth-month anniversary. We were having so much fun together that every day we spent in each other's presence felt like its own celebration. For this reason, I wasn't expecting us to do anything considerable in honor of the day. But Maziar had other plans.

He called me at seven thirty in the morning. "Good morning, Sunshine."

"Ugh, what time is it? Are you dying? Because there is no reason other than that to be woken up this early on a Saturday morning," I grumbled.

"I need you to get up and be ready in a half-hour. Dress casual, preferably in workout clothes."

"Why?" I asked, my eyelids still closed behind the heat of sleep.

"I want to take you somewhere," he said. "Please get up." I could hear the excitement in his voice, breaking down my defenses.

"Okay." I reluctantly rolled out of bed.

He showed up at my door thirty minutes later with two coffees in hand, smiling like a child.

"We'd better have some epic plans, to have me up this early," I teased.

"Trust me. You're going to love it," he said as he handed me a coffee and opened the car door for me.

It was a beautiful morning. The sun was peeking out from behind a coverlet of gray clouds. Pieces of blue sky could be seen scattered between the tufts of gray like a hidden promise.

About twenty minutes later, Maziar pulled over onto a dirt shoulder. I looked around, realizing we were at some sort of hiking trail. I sat there for a minute, baffled as to why he would think this was something I would enjoy doing. Did he not know me at all? I was a Persian girl, and therefore my genetics deterred me from all things pertaining to nature and bugs. He saw the disgusted look on my face.

"Humor me, Sara, just for a few minutes before you write this whole thing off," he begged playfully. "I really want you to see this."

"Okay, I'll try," I said, forcing a smile.

He started down the trail, helping me as we went. It was easy at first, but then the path narrowed and became more winding. I stopped being annoyed that I was hiking and began to worry we'd get stuck, never to be found again. I'd watched more documentaries on hikers being lost in the wilderness than was good for me. He assured me it was just a little farther up the trail.

Once we got closer, I could suddenly hear the sound of running water. We ducked through an opening in the path with low-hanging branches. When we came out on the other side, it felt like we'd stepped into an alternate world.

There was a stream surrounded by a canopy of trees. The vibrant greens mixing with the crystal blue water and the blanket of small, purple flowers running along the stream's edge made me feel like I'd entered a secret garden made for fairies.

Our vantage point was above, allowing the scene to unfold in its entirety. Adjacent to the stream was an old jeep that appeared to have been abandoned years ago. Something about its presence made the place even more magical. I knew the jeep held an abundance of stories it protected in its silence, of travelers come and gone on this very spot. I'd like to think some of them were star-crossed lovers like us. I wondered for a moment what stories it could tell.

"I used to come here when I was younger, when I needed to escape. It helped me think," he said, staring out at the water below us.

"It feels like a different world," I replied.

"I know," he said. "I've never showed it to anyone before." He stared at me, wide-eyed and bashful, as if sharing his little haven made him vulnerable. I was moved to be the first to see inside his secret garden.

Suddenly, I felt a little drop of water hit my cheek. I looked up and realized it had started drizzling. I closed my eyes, letting the raindrops wash over me. The stream felt alive, as if I could feel its energy vibrating through me. I let its spirit fill me.

All at once I became very aware of Maziar's proximity to me and I opened my eyes to find him standing a few inches away, just staring. He stepped a little closer and leaned in. When his lips touched mine, it felt like fireworks exploded around us.

"Wow," I whispered.

It felt like the energy that ran through our bodies united with each other and with the magic of this place. He put his hands around my waist and pulled me in.

Then we danced.

There was no music, just the sound of the stream and the birds. We stood there swaying to their rhythm, drenched from the rain, without a care in the world. I looked at him, in the backdrop of the garden, committing every detail of the moment to my memory. I memorized his face, all the details of the way he was looking at me. I never wanted to forget.

Once we were really wet, and the cold was seeping into our bones, we ran back up the trail as fast as we could, laughing the entire way. We sat in the car for a few minutes, talking and warming up. As I looked at him while he spoke, I realized I never wanted another day to go by without him. I wasn't sure if it was possible to love someone so much it hurt, but that was how I felt about Maziar.

In hindsight, I wonder if the pain was some premonition of the hurt to come.

The rest of our celebration consisted of hot showers, good food, and a bottle of wine we shared between us. We ended the night at his apartment watching a movie. His arms were wrapped tightly around me as I floated away into a world of forgotten dreams.

I couldn't remember a time when I was any happier.

CHAPTER SEVEN

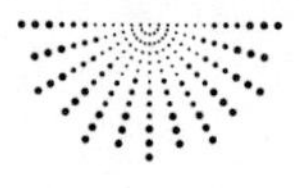

A few weeks later, we headed to a party at Maziar's friend Pasha's house. He and Maziar had been friends since birth; their mothers were neighbors in Iran. As if that wasn't nerve-wracking enough, Maziar's sister Bita would also be there.

Despite being together for months, this would be the first time I was meeting her. I'd wanted to push the issue, urge him to introduce me to his family earlier, but I was terrified of the outcome. Instead, I pretended like I didn't care, until I even believed it.

I sat in the car on the drive to Brentwood with my leg tapping furiously against the floor. I felt anxious and nauseated, wanting nothing more than to jump out at the next stoplight. I wasn't given much time to put the plan in motion before we pulled into the driveway.

To say Pasha lived in a big house was an understatement. It looked more like a manor, taking up a quarter of the block, with tall white pillars and statues of lions at the entryway. The driveway was made of cobblestone, giving the impression that we were somewhere in Rome rather than Los Angeles.

The valet moved cars around the crowd as if we were stuck in a jigsaw puzzle. As I waited for the attendants to make their way over to us, I realized I was surrounded by girls who looked like models on a Nordstrom's runway. I felt depressingly underdressed in my mint-green sundress. I suddenly had the urge to reach across the center console and punch Maziar for not preparing me properly for the event.

When we finally walked toward the massive front door, my anger was quickly replaced by panic. I felt way over my head, wanting to turn and run back out of the cast-iron gates, straight home. I didn't get time to formulate an escape plan because as soon as we stepped onto the stoop the doors swung open and Pasha appeared as if from thin air.

"Hi," he said, his melodic voice reminding me of wind chimes.

He stood over six feet tall, with a moderate build that showed off his statuesque figure from underneath his teal button-up shirt. His muscles bulged every which way, reminding me of the perfect distribution of hills and valleys. He had an air of confidence that just rolled off of him but didn't hold a hint of arrogance. Something about him made you desperately want him to like you. When he smiled, he went from intimidating to gentle, making me feel more at ease.

Maziar took me in and introduced me to his friends. Everyone was nice and genuinely interested in meeting me. I was aware they were all Jewish, but they seemed to care very little that I wasn't. One of the guys, Emanuel, had brought his girlfriend, Azi, with him. I felt a connection to her instantly, creating my first ally in the web we unknowingly were building.

Just as I started to forget my discomfort, Bita showed up. She walked in like a princess entering her debutante ball. She reeked of self-indulgence and arrogance. She came in with two of her friends. They stopped at the entryway, scanning the room, appearing like C-list actresses striking a pose for the paparazzi. I would like to say no one noticed them, but that wasn't true. The room did take notice, everyone stopping to stare in their direction, whether in awe or disdain.

Bita was dressed from head to toe in name-brand attire, with her Birkin bag slung over her shoulder. Her friends looked like clones. My first thought was that she was the typical Persian girl I'd always found so ridiculous. My second thought was that I found her intimidating.

I wondered how it was possible she was even related to Maziar. I knew that he came from money, but to what extent, I wasn't sure. We didn't really talk about it. He was so down-to-earth and easygoing that it was easy to forget his family was wealthy.

She spotted him in the crowd and made her way over to us, stopping every few feet to say hello to one person or kiss the cheeks of another, the customary Iranian way for greeting friends. The closer she got, the more prominent her beauty became, until she stood in front of us in all her glory. Her dark green eyes reminded me of Kaa from *The Jungle Book*, hypnotizing me if I stared too long. Her cheekbones sat high on her face, contoured to perfection by her makeup. Her eyelashes were so long they swept her eyebrows every time she blinked.

I felt completely inferior.

"Hey," she said to her brother as she gave him a hug, ignoring me at first. Then, as if she'd just noticed his arm wrapped around my waist, she casually swept her eyes across my dress. The inferiority just worsened.

"So this is the infamous Sara, I assume?" There was a patronizing tone to her voice as she said my name.

"Yes, this is Sara, my *girlfriend*," Maziar said with more aggression than she seemed to appreciate, her eyes crinkling like she'd just tasted something bitter. She quickly regained her composure, allowing her emotions to linger only moments across her face.

Bita didn't stay long, moving on to people she found more interesting. Regardless of where she was though, I was aware of her presence, making me feel uncomfortable again. Her novelty began to wear off, replaced by the irritation taking shape in the pit of my stomach.

Later in the evening, I happened to glance in her direction, catching her in a flirtatious conversation with a guy I hadn't been introduced to. He was tall, skin browned by the sun, wavy blond hair nonchalantly falling around his face. He had piercing blue eyes that glowed from across the room. He looked like her personal Abercrombie model as she playfully drew circles on his chest while she spoke. He definitely wasn't Iranian.

"Who's that with Bita?" I asked, leaning in toward Azi.

"That's Scott. She's dating him."

"Huh, interesting," I mumbled to myself, filing the information away in my mind.

I felt Maziar tap my shoulder. "I'm going to go to the bathroom. I'll be right back. You good?"

"Yes," I said, apprehensively watching him walk away. Something about being alone in a room with his sister screamed danger to me.

"I need to go find Emanuel," Azi said as soon as Maziar turned the corner. "He's been playing pool for hours. Knowing him, he's gambling away his inheritance." She smiled. "I'll be right back."

I suddenly found myself utterly alone. My heart began to race and my hands became clammy. I walked to the bar to get a drink, hoping the alcohol would calm my nerves. I chastised myself for acting so ridiculous. I could do this; I could be alone in this crowd for a few minutes.

As I grabbed my drink, I turned to find Bita standing behind me. Gone was her placid expression of earlier, replace by venom burning in her eyes. I was certain she'd waited all night for Maziar to leave long enough for her to get me alone. She reminded me of a scorpion, her tail swaying as she got ready to strike. I refused to let her know she made me nervous, so I passively stared back at her.

"I hear you're not Jewish," she said.

"You heard right," I responded, not missing a beat even though her comment caught me off-guard.

"You're wasting your time, you know that right? You must not be very bright," she said, an evil smirk plastered across her face.

"I beg your pardon?"

She actually laughed then. It reminded me of Maleficent in *Sleeping Beauty*, the laugh of someone teetering on insanity. "Being with my brother is pointless. It's not like it's going anywhere."

"And why is that?" I replied, consumed by a veil of anger so thick I could barely see straight.

"Because you're not Jewish." She said it in a very matter-of-fact tone, as if that were explanation enough.

I was fuming, my entire body beginning to shake. I was about to launch myself at her to scratch up her pretty Botox-filled face when

Maziar appeared beside me. He knew something had just happened between us, even if he didn't know the details. He placed his hand on my arm to steady me, then turned icily toward his sister. First shock, then fear flashed across Bita's face.

"What are you two talking about?" he asked, his eyes intently focused on her.

"Nothing," she said. "Sara and I were just getting acquainted, that's all." Then she flashed her smile at him before making her way over to her friends.

"Are you okay?" Maziar asked, once she was gone. I was so angry I couldn't even answer, which was explanation enough for him. He grabbed my hand. "We're leaving."

"No," I said, yanking it away. "We're staying." I refused to let Bita win.

An hour later, he dragged me out of the door.

"Okay, talk to me," he said, once we were in the car.

I shook my head, more at myself than at him. "I..." I said, but didn't continue.

He waited patiently beside me, keeping me in the corner of his eye. I knew I needed to give him an answer, but I just couldn't find the words. The anger was still burning through my veins, the despair in quiet pursuit.

"I don't want to talk about it," I finally said, and to my surprise, he didn't press any further. He just drove me home in the silence the night had created.

I was full of hatred toward his sister, but more so than that, I was encompassed with the fear of knowing that I had been right about us. We were doomed, a cliché ending just as I'd expected.

When he pulled up to the house, I opened the door before he'd fully stopped, needing to put distance between us. I didn't glance over my shoulder as I muttered, "Goodbye."

I heard the faint sound of his response, but I was halfway up the drive and couldn't make it out. I didn't turn to look at him as I put the key in the lock or after I walked through the door, but I knew he waited in the darkness of his car. I was too overwhelmed to worry about his feelings, at a loss for the words or energy needed to deal.

Hours later, when I still lay staring at my ceiling, I kept replaying the conversation I'd had with Bita in my head, all the while coming up with witty comments I wished I had made.

* * *

The next day, Maziar insisted I tell him what had happened with his sister. I briefly gave him the Cliff Notes of our conversation, not allowing him to push me any further. He apologized for Bita's behavior and tried to assure me she was of very little concern. I didn't believe him, but I desperately wanted to, because the alternative was too much to bear. That little nagging voice had made its way back, with the pressing dedication of a Persian mother. At times, I wanted to resort to banging my head against the wall just to shut her up.

I couldn't help but let Maziar convince me that I had it all wrong, that in fact his family was only a minor blip in our story. I hung onto his words as if they were my life jacket, with the strength of sheer desperation. I knew better, but for once I didn't want to be right.

Life, however, had different plans. It would teach me that ignoring my intuition would only lead to disaster.

CHAPTER EIGHT

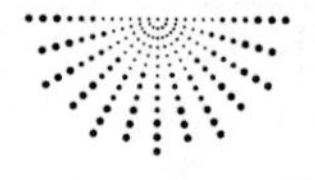

I knew that Hanukkah was an important Jewish holiday and referred to as the eight-day Festival of Lights, but I didn't know much else. There were so many instances in which I felt like we were failing in this relationship, that I didn't want to make my lack of knowledge another reason. I did some research.

Centuries ago, the Holy Land of Israel was ruled by Antiochus III, King of Syria. At the beginning of his reign he was favorable towards the Jews, but after losing a battle to the Romans, he became a tyrant. A believer in paganism, he was adamantly against religions and began suppressing all Jewish laws. Worship became forbidden, all the scrolls of the Torah were confiscated and burned, and they were no longer allowed to circumcise their children, rest on the Sabbath, or keep kosher. An old Jewish priest and his faithful followers refused to adhere to the king's demands and left for the hills of Judea. Antiochus attempted to wipe them out, and although he outnumbered them, the Jews were victorious, reclaiming their Holy Temple in Jerusalem.

When they sought to light the temple's menorah, they found that there was only a single day's supply of oil. Miraculously, this oil somehow burned for eight days. Thus, began the tradition of lighting a candle each night on the menorah, for each of the eight days.

Maziar had told me that his family celebrated the holiday by rotating parties at different houses each year, for the first and last nights. This year, the first night was at his parents' house. For some reason completely baffling to me, Maziar kept insisting that I join them. I had barely managed to get over the trauma of the encounter with his sister.

At this point, I'd had minimal interaction with his parents, consisting mainly of a greeting at the door if I was picking Maziar up from the house. They were never rude, as is not the way of our culture, but very proper, and icy cold. They showed little interest in knowing the woman their son was dating.

"I don't think it's a good idea, Maziar. They barely talk to me. They don't even like me! Why would they want me there?"

"They don't know you yet, Sara, that's all. It'll be fine. It's just dinner."

He talked me in circles, countering all my concerns. I left each conversation wondering if it truly was all in my head.

A Hanukkah celebration, however, was more than a simple dinner. If Maziar was wrong, I'd endure a night of guarded stares and disdainful expressions with an audience of strangers. This was not an event I could escape from without major repercussions.

Maziar continued to insist. I knew he was hoping that things would go better this time, leaving me less hopeless about us. Eventually, after speaking with Leyla, I gave in.

"Don't you think it's better to know what you're up against now, so you can set up your defenses?" she asked.

"I guess," I replied hesitantly. The truth was that I was afraid of what I would find, that my fears would only be confirmed by the interaction. I could feel it in the pit of my stomach, knew this would be an all-out war.

"It's going to be okay," Leyla said, trying to give me a reassuring smile.

I wished I believed her.

* * *

The night of the party, I spent over an hour trying to figure out my outfit. I wanted to look beautiful, naïvely hoping it would make them like me. Finally, I settled on a pair of black pants and a forest green top that lay loosely at my hips. My dark brown hair fell in curls around my shoulders, softening my features.

"You look beautiful," Mom said as I walked into the kitchen.

"Are you sure?" I asked.

"Maziar is lucky to have you," Dad replied in confirmation.

My parents were ecstatic that I was finally included in one of Maziar's family gatherings. They'd been worried that my lack of involvement was an indication that he wasn't serious about settling down with me. When I'd told Mom about tonight, she'd interpreted it as moving in the right direction, which, to a Persian mother, meant toward marriage. I felt a pang of sadness when I realized they had no clue what I'd gotten myself into.

Forty minutes later, I pulled up to his parents' house. I forced myself to get out, even though my legs didn't want to move. I made my way over to the door, taking a few deep breaths to gather the courage to ring the doorbell. Mom had armed me with flowers and baked goods, so his family would know she'd succeeded in teaching me manners. I was hoping it was a good enough peace offering to get me through the night. Maziar opened the door a few seconds later. I was so grateful that it wasn't Bita or his mother greeting me that I almost threw myself into his arms. Looking like a hussy ten seconds into the night was a bad idea, though, so I stopped myself.

The entryway opened up into a foyer with a winding staircase to the second floor. To the right was a large living space with fancy Louis XIV furniture, couches and chairs with high backs, framed by decadently carved wood. This type of furniture was common in Iranian households. Directly in front, the foyer bled into a large hallway that led into the family room. To the left of that was their dining room, and a little farther it opened up into the massive chef's kitchen. I didn't know how to cook, which was a definite flaw on my Iranian wife resume, but if I did, I would have loved that kitchen.

There were people everywhere. He started to introduce me to each person as we walked through the house. There were about twenty-five members of his family there. He then took me into the kitchen where his mother, Naghmeh, was plating appetizers. She greeted me with her usual polite, cold demeanor. I gave her my offerings and was grateful that Maziar didn't linger very long. His father, Parviz, was sitting in the den with a few of the other men. He was much easier to bear, polite but distant, nowhere near as intimidating as Maziar's mother. I could almost swear I felt a fleeting kindness behind his deep green eyes.

Once I had been introduced to everyone, Maziar got us drinks, and we went outside where the younger crowd was socializing. That's where I met his cousin, Neda. Immediately I could see she was not like the others. She had a different air about her. She wasn't decked out in name brands, but instead, her entire outfit looked like something that could be bought at Banana Republic. Her dark brown hair was up in a ballerina bun and she wore big silver hoops. Her fingers were filled with an eclectic collection of fashionable Bohemian rings, adorned with stones of various colors and sizes. Her tanned skin complemented her baby blue eyes. She was stunning.

She smiled when she saw us, motioning to the empty seats beside her.

"Hi, I'm Neda," she said brightly. "Maziar's told me so much about you." Her energy was infectious.

I needed a safe place amongst strangers, and Neda provided it. She came with an ease I found welcoming. She instantly opened up, sharing memories of their childhood with me. I found myself laughing comfortably beside her. She made me feel like I was just Sara, not Sara the Muslim girl dating Maziar the Jewish boy.

I spent the rest of the night sandwiched protectively between them. When dinner approached and we were called in for the Hanukkah festivities, Neda and Maziar flanked me like soldiers, seating us on the opposite side of the table from his mother and sister. It became apparent that Maziar had filled Neda in on the situation by the way she was staring at Bita.

"Ignore her," Neda whispered as she noticed the daggers Bita sent my way.

The festivities began, and I sat silently watching. At first, it appeared unorganized, but I realized quickly that everyone, other than myself, knew exactly what was going on. Suddenly they all stood up and faced the menorahs. There were at least five of them, one for each of the smaller family units. The men put on their kippot, small velvet skull caps, before the children lit the shamash, the middle candle.

"I don't need this," Maziar whispered, handing me a prayer sheet. He had it memorized.

They all began chanting three prayers in Hebrew, followed by a beautiful song. Once they were finished, the women started setting the table while the younger children played with their dreidels. Even though I felt uncomfortable, I got up with Neda and helped.

It's customary for female family and friends to help the hostess set and clear the table. I was neither, but desperately needed to make a good impression. Staying seated wouldn't help. I was met with stares, some layered with curiosity, some bordering on contempt. I took a breath and held my head high, pretending I didn't notice. When we sat back down, I welcomed the false security between Maziar and Neda.

As I looked over at Bita, I suddenly remembered the distinct moment before an earthquake, when the faint sound of a thundering train could be heard, signaling its arrival. When our eyes met, I could hear the distant rumble.

"Sara, you doing okay?" she asked, a bogus expression of concern on her face. "I know this is all new."

I was caught off guard and still trying to come up with a response when Maziar jumped in.

"She's just fine," he said, anger exuding from his eyes.

The table had fallen silent, everyone watching the exchange between siblings. Some looked confused. Others, who understood where she was going, just stared.

Maziar's aunt, Lily *Khanoom*, suddenly spoke. "What does she mean, Maziar? Does her family not celebrate the holiday?" She seemed genuinely lost.

He'd been backed into a corner. He now had to tell his entire family what I just realized we seemed to be trying to hide. I don't know where the courage came from, but I looked at Maziar's worried face and felt the urge to protect him. Someone was getting crucified tonight. Better it be me.

"I'm not Jewish, Lily *Khanoom*; my family is Muslim," I said, addressing his aunt directly, too afraid to look around the table.

Lily's mouth dropped open. I braced myself for the thunder. Her husband, Bijan *Khan*, the eldest brother on his father's side, looked up at Maziar. I had spoken, but he ignored it, speaking directly to his nephew.

"What is the meaning of this? You know our ways. Fun is okay, but this is not," he said, waving his arm in my direction.

Neda jumped in. "And why not, *Amoo*? We don't live in the time when you were young. We live here in America. Different types of people interact every day, and some even fall in love."

Bijan *Khan* finally looked at me. "I'm sure you are a wonderful girl, *aziz*, but this is just our way. Everyone must stick to their own; it's easier. I'm sure your parents feel the same way."

Naghmeh had been staring at us, and I could feel the icicles forming on my skin. Before I was able to interject about how my parents had no issues with Maziar being Jewish, she spoke up, unable to hold her tongue any longer.

"Love? What is this nonsense about love, Maziar? I told you it was okay to bring her, but I will not tolerate hearing this ridiculousness at my table."

My heart sank.

"This is not the time nor place for this conversation," Parviz said. "It is the holiday. We are to be happy and festive. My daughter spoke out of turn and should not have." He glared at Bita and she sank back in her seat. "These kids are young. What do they know of real love and real futures?" He waved his hand, dismissing our relationship as child's play. "Let's go back to enjoying the evening and leave these things for another night."

Like that, it was dropped. Everyone slowly looked away and went back to their previous conversations.

"I need to go to the bathroom," I whispered urgently, to no one in particular.

"Okay," Neda said, immediately standing up.

Maziar grabbed my hand as I turned to leave, his worried face looking up at me. I couldn't bring myself to break him any further, so I squeezed his hand. It was the only comfort I could give.

"Can you wait for me?" I pleaded to Neda, outside the bathroom door.

"I'm not going anywhere; I'll be right here. Take all the time you need," she said confidently.

Once inside, I sat with my back to the door, head in my hands, trying to pinch back the tears. I refused to give them the satisfaction of knowing they'd successfully wounded the Muslim girl.

I don't know how long I stayed in the bathroom, but true to her word, Neda was outside waiting for me when I came out. She grabbed my hand and silently guided me back to the table, daring her family to cross her. I had no doubt she would jump to my defense if I needed it. No one said a word.

Anger began to consume me as I was greeted with cold, pitying stares. Who did these people think they were? They didn't have the right to lessen my worth based on their prejudices. I came from a well-respected, upstanding family. I was a good girl. I was in graduate school, making something of myself so I would never have to rely on a man to pay my way. I was smart, and I worked hard to be me. Being Muslim was only a part of me, one that I was proud of.

How dare they?

By the time we got to the table, I'd gone from anger to outright rage, all directed toward Maziar's sister. She had done this, and I was determined to make her pay. I kept my features steady, looking unaffected by what had happened. I would make them believe I didn't actually care. I turned and smiled at Bita, who I knew would already be staring. I saw her confusion before she could recompose herself, and I wondered if she could hear the rumble.

"Bita, how is your friend? You know, the blond guy you were at the party with the other night?" I said, my voice oozing sweetness like molasses. "Scott, right? He's your boyfriend, isn't he?"

Again the table went silent, but this time they weren't staring at me. Then, like an avalanche, she was bombarded with questions. As I'd hoped, the family had no idea that Bita was dating anyone. They also had no clue he wasn't Persian, a detail I knew would be a problem in this family.

Maziar looked at me, shocked. He hadn't thought I'd throw his sister under the bus. He hadn't expected me to retaliate, a fact I found irritating. I could see he was disappointed, but I didn't care. I was thoroughly disappointed in him and this entire night. I was going to enjoy my revenge without his guilt.

Bita stared daggers at me as I sat back and smiled.

* * *

Maziar tried to give me grief over what I'd said to his sister, but it was short-lived. He could see that the anger had wrapped its ugly tendrils around my body, and pushing me would only lead to an explosion neither of us wanted. He knew that part of me held him responsible for making me face our reality by forcing me to go the party. So he let it go.

Denial proved to be a wonderful asset. I brewed long enough to realize I didn't like the outcome I was heading toward, so instead, I found my way back into the comfy cloud of denial. It allowed me the luxury of hiding the truth behind what I wanted it to be: that Maziar and I would be okay.

CHAPTER NINE

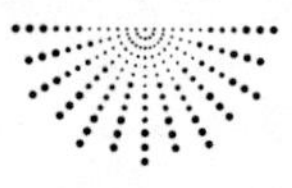

Norooz, meaning the New Day, is the name of the Persian New Year. It marks the first day of spring, or the equinox, the beginning of the year on the Iranian calendar. *Norooz* is celebrated by people of diverse ethnic and religious backgrounds. Although it is observed by both Muslim and Jewish Iranians, due to the New Year celebration of Rosh Hashanah, Muslim Iranians traditionally celebrate Nooroz to a greater extent.

For *Norooz*, a traditional ceremonial table display is set up, called the *sofreh*. The *sofreh* is set with the holy book of your faith, a bowl of goldfish representing life, painted eggs for fertility, and seven traditional foods starting with the letter "s" in Farsi. For instance, *sabzeh,* wheat sprouts, symbolizes renewal, *seeb*, apple, represents health and beauty, and *sonbol*, hyacinth, represents spring.

The date and time fluctuate yearly based on the Iranian calendar, dictated by the equinox. It usually falls somewhere around March 20th. The exact hour toggles between the middle of the night and the afternoon.

Some years, we have to get up at three in the morning to celebrate. Although inconvenient, it is an important holiday for my family, and we loyally adhere to its rituals. In my home, everyone has to wear at least one new article of clothing, sit around the *sofreh* together a half-hour before the New Year, and pray. Afterward, we exchange gifts.

This year, *Norooz* was at 3:15 in the afternoon. The tradition was that each individual family would ring in the New Year on their own, and then everyone would congregate at our house to exchange gifts and have dinner.

Mom invited Maziar and his family to join us. Maziar graciously accepted the invitation and declined for his parents, giving the excuse that they had previous commitments. I knew better, but it was easier to pretend.

Maziar would be meeting my extended family for the first time, and more importantly, my grandmother. This was huge, especially for my mom to be the one orchestrating it. She knew her mother opposed my relationship. Similar to Maziar's parents, my grandmother was unable to see past the traditions she was raised with. But Maziar had somehow won Mom over, giving her the courage to challenge the matriarch.

I had the urge to stop her, knowing this battle was pointless. She had no idea a disaster was lurking around the corner, but I did. However, admitting it would also mean admitting defeat, and I wasn't ready for that yet. So instead, I said nothing.

He showed up at four in the afternoon, again armed with flowers and pastries.

"*Aede mobarak, Shireen khanoom*," he said, as he handed over his gifts, making Mom blush beneath his gaze.

He looked very handsome in a pair of dark blue jeans and a navy blue blazer. When he leaned in to kiss my cheek, I could smell the familiar scent of his shampoo mingling with his cologne. I inhaled, allowing it to fill my lungs with comfort.

When we stepped into the living room, my normally loud and obnoxious family fell silent, as if a mute button had been hit. All heads turned toward us. Maziar, however, was a master at commanding a room and didn't skip a beat as he whipped out his amazing smile. My *mamanbozorg*, grandmother, was the first to speak.

"This must be the famous Maziar we've heard so much about," Grandmother said, dryly.

I felt myself wince at her tone, the anxiety building in my stomach. I dreaded a repeat performance of Hanukkah.

My cousin Nasim looked hesitantly between her and Maziar, as anxious as I suddenly felt. She glanced at Ellie, the more assertive of the two sisters, for a way to alleviate the tension that was quickly building in the room. One comment from *Mamanbozorg* and the night had already taken a turn.

"Hi, Maziar," Ellie said, as if on cue. "It's great to finally meet you. Sara has told us a lot about you." She was smiling broadly at him as she made her way across the room.

"Like the fact that you're Jewish," my cousin Ardeshir stated loudly.

The room fell more silent than I thought possible. Ellie was staring at her brother in warning, Nasim was still looking back and forth between us with a worried look on her face, and Ardeshir smiled wickedly from the corner. I was about to pummel him when Maziar reached out and placed his hand on my arm to calm me.

"Let's not be rude, Ardeshir. I taught you kids better than that," *Mamanbozorg* said coolly, the warning hidden beneath her words.

He scowled in his seat, reprimanded like a child.

"*Salom, Shahla khanoom*," Maziar said, without sparing Ardeshir a glance. He sailed smoothly toward her, unaffected by her judgments. He wrapped her tiny hand in his, leaning in to kiss both her cheeks in greeting.

My grandmother stared at him passively, no doubt sizing him up. Even though Maziar seemed undeterred by her disapproval, I could feel the rings of perspiration forming beneath my arms, the sheen of stress invading my forehead. I hadn't noticed Mom walk in. She was standing across the room, angrily staring at my cousin.

"Sara, why don't you kids go outside until dinner? You guys are too young to have to endure us old ladies and our opinions," she said, looking at her mother. "And, Ardeshir, we don't speak to our guests that way."

"Sorry, *khaleh*," my cousin replied begrudgingly, as he stood up.

Ellie grabbed Maziar's arm, still smiling, and guided him outside. "Come on, Sara," she ordered.

Mom squeezed my shoulder as I passed, signaling that it would be okay. I had a hard time believing her, but I did my best not to allow my family to see how they'd upset me.

Once away from my grandmother's disapproving eyes, the tension began to dissipate. Maziar took it all in stride. He never flinched, just turned on his charm. He even included Ardeshir in the conversation. Soon, everyone was eating out of his hand, as usual. I wondered how he was able to do that, to turn everything around in his favor somehow.

Ellie smiled at me encouragingly from across the table, trying to be a pillar of strength in the storm. I wanted to be like Maziar, able to ignore the way both our families had failed in seeing past their prejudices, but I couldn't. No matter how badly I wanted Maziar to win my grandmother over, I knew he hadn't, adding only one more obstacle to the mountain of reasons this couldn't work out.

Mamanbozorg was the head of our family. It was only a matter of time before my relationship became the constant topic of debate among everyone. What if they somehow succeeded in convincing my mom that our relationship was wrong? My parents were my only allies. I'd have no hope left if that were destroyed.

I knew we were doomed, no matter how nonchalant Maziar pretended to be. We would eventually have to face the truth, and when we did, I'd have my heart broken into so many pieces I would never fully recover. Yet I couldn't find the strength to walk away, so I just kept hanging on, praying for a miracle.

Mamanbozorg remained at her post, looking disapprovingly in our direction every time we came inside. I tried to ignore it the best I could. Ellie kept refilling my wine glass, trying to veil the truth in a haze of intoxication. By the third drink, she'd successfully dulled my feelings until I could barely feel the knot in the pit of my stomach.

Maziar sailed through the night marvelously, despite my family. He did his best to charm the women and join the men. My parents helped him navigate through, wanting as much as I did for him to be accepted. I knew Mom dreaded the disapproval of my grandmother, fearing how difficult things could get if she didn't like him.

When I walked Maziar to his car at the end of the night, he didn't say a word about how my family had acted.

"I had a great time, Sara. Thank you for inviting me."

"You don't have to say that, Maziar. I know it was horrible," I replied, unable to meet his gaze.

He reached out and lifted my chin so he could look into my eyes. "No, it wasn't," he said, gently kissing my lips. "Before I forget, I've got something for you." He leaned into the driver's seat and pulled out a small box.

It was wrapped in lavender paper with white silhouettes of butterflies printed on it. A white bow sat neatly in the middle of the square. He was staring at me with anticipation as I pulled it open, exposing a black box. A thin, rose gold chain was nestled inside its velvet walls. It had a delicate heart pendant the size of my thumbnail attached to it, twinkling between my fingers as it caught the light of the streetlamps.

"Look on the back," he urged.

I turned the pendant around and saw that Maziar had inscribed our names. The simplicity of it hurt. To him, we were just Maziar and Sara, two halves of a whole. But to everyone else, it was so much more complicated than that.

"I love it," I whispered.

"I love you," he said as he leaned in to clasp the chain around my neck.

I stood on the curb and watched Maziar drive away, disappearing into the night. When I could no longer see his taillights, I walked back inside to face my family. My hand was wrapped possessively around the pendant, trying to find strength in its cool metal.

My grandmother was sitting next to my aunt, both whispering furiously at Mom.

"Don't you remember what happened to Farzaneh's son?" my aunt asked. "Their families still can't be in the same room without fighting. And they already have a baby. It's so difficult, for everyone. She cries all the time."

"Things like this don't work. It's been proven, *Shireen*. There's a reason why we've been at war for so many years. It's not a coincidence," my grandmother added, shaking her head in disapproval. I wasn't sure whether it was me or Mom she was more disappointed in.

I didn't need to hear the rest, their message abundantly clear, emphasized by the pull of their eyebrows and the harsh look in their eyes. They stopped speaking when they noticed me.

"Sara, come here so we can talk to you," my grandmother commanded, patting the empty spot next to her on the couch.

I just stared at the old woman I loved, with the deep grooves around her eyes, more prominent now as she frowned at me, and felt deflated. She'd disappointed me, the betrayal more than I could bear, and now I had nothing left to say to her.

"I'm tired, *Mamanbozorg*," I said. "I'm going to bed."

I could hear them all gasp as I turned and walked down the hall. I had blatantly disregarded her opinion. But if she couldn't find it inside herself to be compromising, I couldn't find it within me to care.

CHAPTER TEN

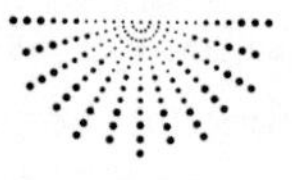

Second semester was halfway over, and midterms were rapidly approaching. Maziar and I had been studying so much that it left us little time together. Months ago, I would have found the distance devastating. Now, strangely, I felt relieved. I needed a break from the rampant and distressing thoughts of our relationship always circling my mind. Studying provided just that reprieve.

Our tests began a week apart, allotting me a small window of time before Maziar was done. One of the pharmacy fraternities was throwing an end-of-finals party. Since Maziar was studying, I'd agreed to go. It had been months since I'd partied with my friends.

I got ready at Sandra's house, since she lived nearest to the school. She was single, dolled up, and looking beautiful. I found myself needing to feel beautiful again. It had been a long time since I'd stared at my reflection in the mirror, feeling anything other than exhausted, my weary eyes looking back at me.

I dressed in black lace shorts and a hot pink top. I wore heels, accentuating the definition of my legs. When I looked in the mirror, I actually felt sexy. The dark circles under my eyes and the wrinkles of worry on my forehead had disappeared thanks to the magic of makeup.

My skin had a glow I hadn't seen for weeks, and a smile stretched across my face, one I'd forgotten I had.

* * *

The fraternity rented one of the large, old colonial homes that were located a few blocks away from the main campus, in what was referred to as Fraternity Row. When we arrived, it seemed as though the entire school was there, strewn across the lawn. Everyone was armed with a red solo cup, filled to the brim with some kind of liquid elixir. Some were leaning against the rails or sitting on the steps, already too intoxicated to be able to hold their own weight.

Our friends were already there when we walked in. We made our way over to them and Thomas and Abby went to get us drinks. I leaned against the wall, observing the crowd as I waited for them to return. Everywhere I looked, I saw people carelessly enjoying themselves. I was envious.

I was deep in thought when I felt someone brush his hand lightly over my shoulder. I turned to find Ben standing beside me.

"You doing okay, doll?" he asked.

"I'm fine; why?" I said, distracted by his electric-blue eyes.

"You just seemed too deep in thought for this kind of party." He smiled, showing off his dimples.

Mom had told me that if a pregnant woman wanted her child to have dimples, she had to put two small crabapples inside her cheeks and bite down. It was an old Iranian wives' tale, but I couldn't help but wonder if Ben's mom had eaten crabapples.

I realized I'd never really noticed how good-looking Ben was before. He was tall, his six feet making my five-foot-five seem childlike. His dirty blond hair was messy, contradicting his neatly cropped body, the muscles pulled tightly beneath his T-shirt, creating a road map I wanted to trace. On his left arm I could see a tattoo peeking out from the edge of his sleeve, but couldn't make out what it was.

I didn't realize he was watching me until our eyes met. He looked confused and intrigued at the same time. I hardly noticed I'd been caught, too busy checking him out as I wondered how it would feel to kiss his lips, if they'd be soft and smooth or rough and weathered.

Suddenly, Thomas and Abby returned with drinks, startling me back to reality. Thankful for the distraction, I took a long sip. Long Island Iced Tea. Its contents burned a path down my throat, bringing me closer to the escape I was seeking tonight. One I was determined to find at the bottom of my cup.

There was a DJ blaring music in the backyard. I could feel its vibrations beneath my feet as Sandra guided me to the dance floor. As I whirled around I tried to steal glances at Ben, who was leaning against the fence talking to Thomas. He was looking at me, too, our eyes locking momentarily before I turned away. I wanted to grab his hand and make him dance with me, but I didn't. I wasn't sure where these thoughts were coming from, but I knew if I didn't stop myself, I'd wake up with regrets in the morning.

There was an ease I felt with Ben that seemed oddly natural, and somewhat unnerving. It reminded me in ways of how I felt about Maziar. I began to wonder if there really was only one soul mate for each person, or if souls were actually made up of pieces, each one being able to connect with a different individual. Maybe who you ended up with had less to do with who was "the one" and more to do with timing and the one you found at that moment.

Somewhere around one in the morning, we headed home. As I lay on Sandra's couch staring at the ceiling, I found myself tangled in thoughts of Ben instead of Maziar. For the first time, I allowed myself to see the possibility of a different outcome.

CHAPTER ELEVEN

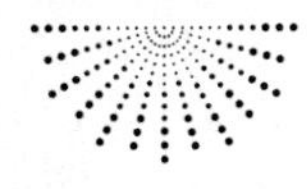

Life continued to move forward, taking Maziar and me with it. Although I toyed with the idea of another man, of a relationship less complicated than ours, the moments were fleeting. The love I felt for Maziar was undeniable, so I still couldn't find the strength to leave. Soon, I began to ignore all the reasons threatening to tear us apart, convincing myself that they didn't exist, until, eventually, I began to believe it.

My parents did the same. Mom ignored my grandmother's relentless complaints, choosing to believe that Maziar's family was as accepting as they were. But one year into the relationship, she became suspicious, worried why they still hadn't met. I was questioned frequently about the infamous dinner, each time with Mom's eyes staring holes into my excuses. She knew nothing of the past few horrific interactions I'd had with Maziar's family. I'd kept them secret, knowing that if she were to find out the truth, she'd want me to break up with him.

Maziar and I frequently discussed our parents meeting because it was inevitable. He always acted nonchalant, as if it were a simple task to orchestrate, but he never followed through. No plans were made; no dates set.

One morning, when we were lying in bed at his apartment, I decided to broach the topic of "where we stand." I needed some stability in the direction we were heading, an anchor I could hold onto. I was hoping he'd be honest, come up with a plan on how we were going to deal with his parents. Up until then, all he'd ever said was that it would be fine.

Neda and I had become friends. She was the only one telling me the truth, filling me in on the drama on their home front. Maziar was confiding in her, so she would tell me things he couldn't. Because of her, I knew the situation was much worse than he was letting on.

I was determined to get Maziar to talk.

"Have you asked your parents about doing dinner with mine?" I asked as we lay in bed. My hand rested on his chest, and I felt the muscles beneath my fingers tense. Even though I knew his reaction wasn't good, I had to know the truth. I couldn't pretend things were okay any longer, not with Mom's questions. I forced myself to move forward.

"I was thinking we could go to that Italian restaurant we love."

"I talked to my mom, but they're so busy this month. We couldn't come up with a date," he said immediately, his face a passive mask. When I didn't respond, he continued, "We're going to sit down later and come up with a good night."

I felt the irritation boil up inside me. I knew he was lying. His nostrils flared when he didn't tell the truth. They were flaring now.

"That's surprising. I didn't know your parents were that social," I replied dryly, daring him to lie to me again.

"They aren't usually. Just an off month, I guess," he answered, as he caressed my arm with his fingertips. He leaned in and gently kissed my neck. "I don't want to talk about my parents. I can think of better things to do."

He wrapped his arms around me and tried to pull me close. It took so much restraint to stop him. I wanted to get lost in his embrace instead of face this potentially fatal conversation. In the pit of my stomach I knew what was coming, every fiber of my being screaming for me to stop. I needed more time. I didn't know how I was going to walk away from him when he finally said what I'd known all along.

How would I make it through this horrific collision of my heart? The answer was simple, I wouldn't. He was going to break me, and I would never recover.

I sat up in bed to disconnect from him physically. I needed to think, the electrical current between us was making it hard to do so. My back was to him when I spoke.

"Why is it so hard to set up a dinner, Maziar?"

He didn't answer. His silence consumed me, crushing me under its weight. My ears filled with the furious thumping of my heart like a base drum. When he finally spoke, it felt like his words were coming through water, dulled and hard to hear.

"They refuse to meet your parents. My mom says it's a waste of time since we won't be getting married." He sat there frozen, waiting for the avalanche to fall.

His words felt like a punch to the gut, making me sick to my stomach. I ran to the bathroom and threw up. Then, I began to cry, as the year of hoping for a miracle crumbled around me. It wasn't like I hadn't expected this, but to hear him finally say it made it real.

"Sara, let me in. Please," he said, standing behind the locked door.

I could hear the pain in his voice, but instead of feeling sympathy, it just made me furious. The anger surged through my body like a bolt of hot lightning. How dare he take me down this path after I'd told him not to? How could he do this to me?

I stood up and opened the door, watching fear spread across his face at the state I was in. At that moment, there was a part of me that truly hated him for doing this to me, and he could see it.

"How could you?" I asked. "I told you I didn't want to start this if your parents were against it, but you didn't listen! You kept saying it was all going to be okay, but it isn't, is it, Maziar?"

"Sara, let me explain," he begged.

"No! I don't want to hear it. There's nothing for you to explain. Your family are

close minded jerks, and there's no changing that. And you're an asshole for knowing it and doing this to me anyway!" I screamed through my tears, my words drenched in the anger I felt.

"Sara, please stop. Let's sit down and talk about this," he urged, as I hastily packed my bag.

"No!" I yelled again. I could only see red now, the desire to leave him with a deep, gashing wound suffocating me. I looked straight at him and steadied my gaze, locking eyes with his. "I *hate* you for doing this to me," I said, in an oddly calm tone, out of place in the moment. I watched his face crumble, inflicting the last fatal blow.

It didn't matter that each step sent daggers into my soul. I forced myself to put one foot in front of the other, determined to make it to my car. I pushed past him, but he grabbed my hand, stopping me. I looked at him with such vehemence in my eyes that he stood speechless. Then, he let go. I turned and walked out. He had broken me, but I was going to be the one who left him.

I made it two blocks before I had to pull over because I could no longer see through the tears. I sobbed until I couldn't cry anymore. Then, I just sat there and stared into the darkness, clutching my body in an attempt to shelter it from the excruciating pain tearing through me.

I had known this would happen all along. I wanted to hate Maziar, to blame him for everything going wrong. I wanted it to be his fault that our relationship had broken. But I knew it wasn't. I knew I was to blame as well, for refusing to accept our circumstances, even if I couldn't admit it.

I finally pulled myself together and drove home. It was late enough that my parents were already asleep, allowing me to sneak into my room undetected. I lay on my bed, wrapping my body around the pillows in an attempt to cushion the blow.

The heat of my broken heart tore through me each time my heart banged against my chest. I felt like my lungs were constricting, as if each breath took an enormous amount of strength to inhale. The end was finally here, and now that the truth was staring me in the face, I could do nothing to ignore it.

CHAPTER TWELVE

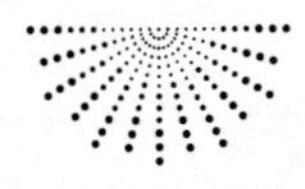

I spent the next three days hiding in bed, too broken to face the world. I feigned the stomach flu, which wasn't too difficult because I regularly got sick at the thought of having lost Maziar forever. My mom was concerned but knew not to push me. Maybe the crazy, wide-eyed look of a trapped animal she saw in my face tipped her off. Whatever the reason, I appreciated being left to my own devices.

Maziar had been calling and texting consistently. On day three, I finally picked up. I knew it was a bad idea. I was already so weak and defeated that I'd have no defenses against him. I guess that's the human flaw, giving into your weaknesses even when they aren't good for you. But I was a full-fledged addict, and I desperately needed another hit.

"Hey," he said, his voice washing over me like sunshine after a storm.

"Hi," was all I could muster up in return.

"Sara, we need to talk. Please meet me somewhere...anywhere. Please."

"Maziar, I can't. There's nothing else to say," I said, deflated.

"You're wrong. There's *so* much more to say, baby. Please."

I don't know if it was the fact that I'd waited days to hear his voice, or the fact that when he said "baby" it created a direct line into my heart. I don't know if it was the desperation I could hear in his words, or that I just wanted any reason to see him again. I knew I should've said no, that seeing him would only kill me, but instead I heard myself say, "Okay."

We made plans to meet at Starbucks at seven. With the crowd, I'd be forced to keep my composure and wouldn't be able to have a breakdown. I wasn't interested in showing him what he'd really done to me.

I foolishly held on to the fairytale notion that maybe he'd somehow convinced his parents to love me overnight. I knew it was farfetched, but I was desperate for this nightmare to be just that, a dream I could wake up from.

I hung up the phone and stared at the ceiling for a while. When it was time for me to get ready, my body felt like lead, weighing me down into the mattress. I pushed against the cushion with all my strength, heaving myself off the bed. With the power of sheer will, I forced myself to shower. I stared at my makeup, knowing I needed to use it. I had dark rings around my eyes from the lack of sleep, and my face looked gaunt from not having eaten for days. I had no energy. I finally gave up and just threw my hair up in a bun.

When I walked in, I saw him sitting in the far back corner, in as secluded a spot as he could find. I stopped for a moment to catch my breath. A deep surge of pain was threatening to knock me down. The room began to spin. I steadied myself by leaning against the wall. As I watched him, I noticed his disheveled hair and the same dark circles around his eyes.

When he saw me, he stood up, awkwardly fidgeting in his spot, the muscles in his legs twitching to approach me but too unsure to make a move. I made it to the table before he could decide what to do. He reached out to hug me. I knew I would shatter if I let him touch me, so I grabbed his arm midair and slid down into my seat.

For a long time, we just looked at each other, neither one knowing how to put into words the plethora of emotions we were feeling. I had never seen Maziar look so sad. It was that true, deep sadness you felt down into your bones, when you'd been forced to make a sacrifice you didn't want to. That was what we were being pushed to do. For no other reason than old traditions, he was being torn from my life, and it felt like I was being crushed into nothing but dust.

I knew deep down that I would walk away from this never being the same. Again, that surge of pain washed over me, and I almost hunched over in my seat, grabbing my chest. I had to close my eyes and breathe. When I looked back up at him, I could see tears running down his face. That was when I came undone. I could no longer hold onto to my composure, and I just began to cry, fiercely sobbing with all disregard for the people around me. I sat there crying as if I'd just been delivered tragic news. In a sense, I had.

When he came over to my side of the table to hold me, I didn't stop him. Instead, I turned and buried my face in his neck, trying desperately to freeze us in time. I clutched onto his shoulders, frantically searching my mind for a solution. But I came up empty. There was no way out of this darkness.

Maziar helped me up, and we went to go sit in his car. I tried to get myself together, realizing that tears couldn't help us. The situation we found ourselves in was now our reality, and no amount of sadness could change that. Regardless, the pain in my chest was unbearable. I lay in the passenger seat, staring at nothing, until he spoke.

"I've been fighting with my parents for months, but they won't budge. I don't know if they're ever going to come around," he said quietly.

I turned, catching a tear rolling silently down his cheek.

"Why did you do it, then?" I said, turning to stare out the window again. I couldn't watch him break down any longer. It was too much.

"Do what?" he asked.

"Tell me they'd be okay with it, even though you knew they wouldn't." I needed to know.

He didn't say anything at first, just looked out the windshield at the people walking by. Without turning towards me, he said, "Can I be honest?"

"I wish you would be."

"I didn't know we'd get this far. When I met you, I had no idea I'd end up falling in love with you."

"So you decided to take the chance because you were attracted to me?" I asked, trying to wrap my head around what he was saying. I knew I should be angry, but I didn't have anything left to give to that enormous emotion. I was just numb.

"I know it was selfish. And I know it was stupid. If I could go back, Sara, and do it all over again, I would have walked away just to save you from all of this. I swear." He turned reaching for my hand. His eyes were pleading for me to understand. "I couldn't walk away. There was something about you, I've never felt that way about someone right when I met them. It was like I was being pulled to you. I know it's no excuse."

I couldn't deny the connection between us, but I knew it wasn't a good enough reason to take me down this path and break my heart. I tried desperately to find the hate I knew I should be feeling, but I was just so tired I couldn't manage it.

"Don't leave."

"What?" I asked, looking at him in confusion. How was I supposed to stay, now that I knew his parents were against us?

"Please don't leave. We can figure this out. I know we can," he begged.

I knew that was a lie, that there was no way forward from here. We couldn't stay in denial any longer, pretending things would somehow work themselves out. Ultimately, he'd have to choose and I knew it was an impossible choice to ask of him. No matter what I thought of his parents, they were still the people who had raised him. His mother was the one who'd spent sleepless nights with him when he was sick, who'd nurtured every wound, every loss, and every heartbreak he had felt until this moment. His father was the one who'd never missed a soccer game, played basketball with him in the backyard, and taken him to buy his first car. To walk away from his foundation would only lead to destruction later. Despite what he'd done, I loved him too much to let him do that.

I leaned in this time, wrapping my arms around him, letting him get lost in my embrace. I don't know how long we stayed that way. Then, he looked into my eyes, with that look that was only mine, and he kissed me. We got lost in each other, in the darkness, one last time.

When it was over, neither of us wanted to be the first to walk away. Finally, when I realized that this wasn't helping us, I untangled myself and grabbed my stuff. He looked terrified. I put my hand gently against his cheek and he leaned into it.

"I love you, forever," I said, then got out of his car and walked away.

I didn't cry. The pain cut straight into my soul, and tears would no longer do it justice.

CHAPTER THIRTEEN

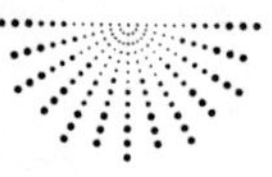

It had been two months since I last saw Maziar in that parking lot. Sixty-one days since I saw his beautiful face, heard his voice, or felt his touch. The weeks after we separated were a dark blur. One day led into the next, and I went through the motions on autopilot. I stayed in my room and only left when absolutely necessary.

My parents were both sad and angry when I finally told them why Maziar was no longer coming around. Being an Iranian mother, Mom desperately wanted to say, "I told you so." Surprisingly, she somehow refrained. I think she was more worried about the state I was in than in being right.

After the second week of holding myself hostage in my bedroom, my parents called on Leyla for help. She came over and dragged me out of the house, despite my protests. When I realized fighting would be useless, I just plastered on a smile and pretended I was having a good time, secretly praying for the comfort of my dark room.

I would never have gotten out of bed again if it were entirely up to me. Unfortunately, I still had the matter of school to deal with. At first, I felt like it was a huge burden I couldn't bear, along with my broken heart. Later, I came to realize it was my only salvation.

I began throwing myself into my studies. Day and night I lost myself in chemical equations and complicated math problems. It gave me something other than Maziar to focus on. The dedication put me in the top five percent of the class when the year ended.

After the first year, we were all required to start an internship in a pharmacy. We would travel to these locations in pairs. Everyone wanted to be placed in one of the larger chain companies, in hopes of showing off their skills and securing permanent placement after graduation. Finishing in the top tier of my class created opportunities. I was assigned to the CVS in the Palisades. I should have been excited; everyone was competing for that location, but I felt weary being that close to Maziar's family.

Ben came up to me after we'd been given our assignments. He stood eyeing me for a moment, as if he were deciding on the best way to approach a wounded animal.

"Hey, Sara. How are you?" he said cautiously.

For a minute, I wasn't sure if he was asking me how I felt in general or if he was referring to my failed relationship. My friends all knew about the breakup with Maziar. I hated the pity in their eyes when they looked at me, as if I were some broken bird. I was broken; I knew that, but I didn't want everyone to see it.

"I'm okay," I replied, not even bothering to ask how he was in return. I wasn't in the mood for conversation. Somewhere in the loss of my heart, I had somehow lost the ability to be human.

Realizing I would contribute nothing else, he said, "That's cool. What location did you get?" He tilted his head so he could see the card in my hand.

"I got Pacific Palisades," I said, moving the card so he could see. "How about you?"

"I got the same place," he said and grinned.

I felt a strange stir in my stomach as I noticed his smile. His lower lip slightly drooped at the right corner, as if he weren't sure if he should slip into a frown. His dimples were deep and gave him a boyish appearance. It made me feel comfortable when he smiled.

There was a warmth about him that felt like fingers wrapped around a hot cup of tea on a cold day. It was calming. I couldn't help but return the gesture. It had been so long since I'd really smiled that the movement of my facial muscles felt foreign.

"It's going to be nice to have a familiar face there when we have no clue what we're doing," he laughed. His chuckle felt like it started at his toes. It was infectious; I couldn't help but laugh too.

I felt a cozy comfort begin at the tips of my fingers, making its way up through my arms. Slowly, it began to chip away at the cold pain of the past few weeks. Desperate to keep it going, I said, "I was about to grab some lunch. Want to join me?"

"Sure," he replied, still smiling.

We settled on the café at the other end of the quad. As we walked over, I was reminded of salt and pepper shakers –his light skin and hair clashing with my olive tone and dark brown curls.

We began debating the difficulty of our anatomy class final, then moved on to weekend plans that had come and gone. I'd been absent from most of the recent ones, so Ben gave me all the highlights and bloopers. I was laughing by the time we reached the café doors, and it felt wonderful.

He never once mentioned Maziar or the breakup. Ben had always seemed to have the ability to know when to, and when not to, broach certain topics with me. It felt unfamiliar to connect with someone other than Maziar this way. I could feel myself pulling toward it, craving simple human contact.

Ben and I spent most of the following days together, discussing simple things. Their lack of importance felt safe and soothing after spending so much time worrying about life-altering events. I began to laugh and smile again. I started to feel something other than the mindless numb state I'd spent so many months in. I started to feel human.

To say there was nothing more to us than friendship would have been a lie. Ben had become my new lifeline. He helped me find the parts of myself that hadn't yet been destroyed. He held my hand while I picked myself up and started to rebuild the pieces scattered around me.

I was so preoccupied with what I was getting from Ben that I neglected to realize that I was quickly putting myself deeper into his heart. The voice in the back of my mind kept telling me I would hurt him, but selfishly, I ignored her. That vulgar need to feel again was driving me forward without any inhibitions or fears of the outcome to follow. I was moving on pure, primitive motivation. I needed this, and I needed Ben, and I just didn't care what that did to him.

CHAPTER FOURTEEN

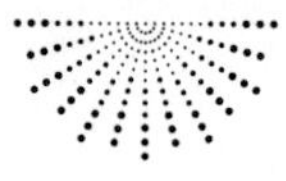

The first day of our internships started at seven in the morning. We had to check in with the pharmacist for a walk-through and to discuss what would be expected of us. Our goal for the program was to get exposure and training on how to take patient prescriptions and input them into the computer, answer doctor calls, and counsel patients on the different medications. If it was slow enough, the pharmacist would let us assist her while she filled the actual scripts.

Even though Ben lived downtown, he insisted on picking me up for our first day. He was very much going out of his way coming to Encino, but I couldn't talk him out of it. I hadn't really tried, having lost sleep over worrying about my proximity to Maziar's family. Something about walking in together felt safer.

The irony that I had pulled an internship in the Palisades had not fallen short on me. I wasn't sure what pharmacy they used, but I couldn't help but pray it wasn't this one. Maziar would be home for the summer and running into him would surely end in disaster for me. I desperately wanted to see him, which was all the more reason why I couldn't. I had just begun to reconstruct myself. I knew that seeing him would open up my healing wounds. I had lost nights of sleep over the possibilities, and now the day was here. I didn't want to face it alone.

My parents had voiced their concerns over Ben when they realized the two of us were spending time together. I had tried to keep our relationship hidden, but they began to notice the late-night calls, the frequent pick-ups, and my new found giggle. They were worried I had walked out of one impossible situation to only find another.

I began to realize that my parents weren't as open-minded as I'd believed they were. It was fine if Ben and I were just friends, but the potential of anything more frightened them. They weren't willing to entertain the idea of my dating anyone who wasn't Iranian. Mom had stood up to my grandmother for Maziar, but it was blatantly obvious she wouldn't do that with Ben. I loved them, but their limitations angered me.

Nothing romantic had evolved between Ben and me, but they didn't care. They played the angle of concern, pretending they were worried about his feelings, but I wasn't falling for it. They were worried about how my relationship with Ben went against their beliefs. They worried what people would think.

I had just walked away from one battle and wasn't ready to go into another one. Nothing had happened between Ben and me yet. Even though I knew better, I continued to deny where we were headed. I insisted they were overreacting and ignored their relentless comments.

On our first day of the internship, Ben showed up at 6:15. He had even stopped at Starbucks to get us coffee. He'd known to order me a soy latte with one sweetener. I believed it was a testament to how close two people were if they could order for each other. It didn't seem like a big deal, but I found it comforting that Ben had taken the time to notice my details.

We pulled into the parking lot and he looked over at me. "You ready to do this, doll?" he asked, knowing my concerns. I'd spent many nights confiding in Ben.

"I'm fine," I reassured him.

* * *

The managing pharmacist was named Setareh Darbanoo, but everyone referred to her as Seti. I was immediately wary of dealing with an Iranian pharmacist. They were known to be snobby and somewhat bitchy, but when I met Seti, she seemed the opposite. She greeted us with a warm smile and shook our hands. She gave us a quick tour of the pharmacy and briefly explained what our duties would be.

"Today," she said, "you'll be observing so you can get the feel for things. Tomorrow we'll start you on some hands on stuff."

She was in her early thirties. She was short, about five-foot-two and very petite. She compensated for her height by always wearing a pair of fashionable high heels. She had jet black hair extending halfway down her back in gorgeous, thick beach waves. It was apparent that she'd had a nose job, the arch too perfect to be natural. I found myself unconsciously running my finger over my own nose, feeling its slight imperfection as the small bump rose beneath my finger tip. I suddenly felt mediocre in comparison.

Her beautiful, big, gray eyes just added insult to injury. They were such a unique color, framed by her dark, thick lashes and perfectly shaped eyebrows, that they were all you saw when you looked at her. She would be considered lovely by everyone's standards. But her physical appearance was not her best attribute. She was friendly and kind; you could see it in how she cared for her patients, never getting frustrated by the many questions they asked her. And she was ridiculously witty and funny. When we didn't have any patients around, she cracked jokes and engaged in playful banter with the employees. I liked her.

The first day was pretty uneventful. There was a constant flow of patients, but nothing too overwhelming. Seti had Ben and me rotating through different positions so we could get a sense of how things worked. We were stationed on opposite sides of the clinic. I could feel his gaze settle on me from across the room, and was greeted by his warm smile each time I looked up. I'd look away, grinning at the sudden appearance of butterflies in my stomach.

When we were released for lunch, we walked out to find the sun shining brightly. Ben was wearing a navy blue polo shirt that stood out against his tanned skin. The tattoo peeking out from his sleeve caught my eye. This time I didn't stop myself as I reached out to move the fabric back. I felt him tense at my touch, heard the breath catch in his throat. I was by no means out of love with Maziar and knew that I couldn't give myself fully to anyone. It didn't stop me from touching him just then, even though I could see the ripple of goosebumps run across his flesh.

His skin felt warm under my fingertips as I pulled back his sleeve. At first glance I saw the lines of a tribal tattoo, but the closer I looked, I realized they formed a shape. I pulled his shirt up a little farther to get a better look. The image transformed into a phoenix, a magical creature in Greek mythology. Its head was bent down and laid at the top of his shoulder. It was a side view of the creature, as if it were lying up against his arm. Two massive wings were behind it, wrapping partly around his bicep, as its tail curved up underneath its body, resting above his elbow. The entire image was outlined by a lattice of dark, thick, black tribal lines. It was masculine and powerful.

I ran my fingers over it, locked in an intimate moment with the creature. I noticed a date written underneath the line that created the tip of its tail. I stopped and looked up at Ben. He was staring at me with this indescribable intensity. I had almost forgotten he was there, so involved was I in my seductive exchange with the bird.

"What does this date mean?" I asked, running my hand over the "July sixteenth."

"It's the date my grandfather passed away," he said. I grew quiet, not knowing what to say as he continued, "My parents got a divorce when I was three, and I never saw my dad. My grandfather stepped in and took his place." Ben's mother remarried when he was eight and Ben had a great relationship with his stepdad, but his grandfather was a constant presence in his life. "He got prostate cancer and died four years ago. I wanted to get something in his memory."

"Why a phoenix?" I asked.

"Because it symbolizes renewal. In Greek mythology, the phoenix never dies. It rises from the ashes of its predecessor. I want to believe that my grandfather will rise again somehow. Even if our paths never cross, I still find it comforting."

I felt tears swell up in my eyes at the beauty and innocence in his belief. It was both heartwarming and heartbreaking at the same time. I had to blink a few times to keep from crying. Ben just smiled and hugged me. There was no romance in it, just appreciation for sympathizing with him.

"We need to eat," he said, changing the subject.

We walked over to the complex across the street and headed into the deli. He opened the door for me and placed his hand on the small of my back to guide me through it. I felt a warmth radiate from his hand and spread across my body. It wasn't the electricity I felt with Maziar's touch, but something different. It was just as comforting because it felt familiar and patient. It came from a core deeper than romance and passion. It started from a pillar of friendship and trust that had somehow twisted like a DNA helix and evolved into something more.

For the first time since my breakup, my thoughts of Ben weren't convoluted and confused by my feelings for Maziar. They had gained their own independence, and now what I felt for these two men ran side by side in separate paths. I knew if I were to follow one road, I would lose the other.

I wasn't yet ready to decide which path I would take.

CHAPTER FIFTEEN

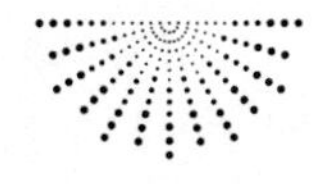

A month had passed, and we were well into our internship. Ben still insisted on coming to Encino each morning, but I'd convinced him to let me drive every other day. He reluctantly agreed, being too chivalrous to go willingly. I had also convinced him to abandon the early Starbucks runs for twenty more minutes of sleep. Instead, we visited a drive-thru for our morning coffee.

We had fallen into a comfortable routine together. Morning coffee, carpool to work, lunch together, work some more, then carpool home. Some nights we said goodbye and parted ways, others we would grab dinner first, or see a movie, or meet up with our friends. Everyone assumed we were together, but we just kept coasting as we were, avoiding titles. My parents had grown very worried. They continuously complained about my relationship with Ben. But I'd decided I no longer cared.

I had generally been the spitting image of what they'd envisioned their daughter to be. I'd done well in school and was becoming a pharmacist, one of four career options they'd insisted on. All Iranian parents wanted their children to become doctors, lawyers, dentists, or pharmacists. Those encompassed all acceptable choices. I had given them that.

I could fluently read and write Farsi, a big deal since I was born in the States. I didn't smoke or do drugs and only drank on occasion. I wasn't promiscuous, not that they had any idea I wasn't still a virgin. I rarely rebelled against them, and I was a rule-follower almost to a fault, my friends making fun of me because I would become uncomfortable at the smallest misstep.

As far as I was concerned, I had given them enough to brag about to their friends. They had no valid complaints. I'd handed them ninety percent of me, molding myself to their expectations. I refused, however, to allow them to dictate whom I would be with. That ten percent belonged to me, and they would just have to deal with it.

On Monday, Ben came to my house in the morning as usual. We headed out, getting our coffee on the way. We talked and laughed, sang along to our favorite songs, then sat in the comfortable silence between us. The universe gave me no indication that this day would be the first of many to rock my core again.

We smiled as we walked into the pharmacy, threw on our white coats, and started the day. I was on phones, dealing with doctor calls. Ben was a few feet away from me at the window for prescription drop-offs. This combination of positions allowed us to talk during our down time, which we loved. It made the day go by faster.

The afternoon rush was always the busiest time of day. The phone started to ring almost immediately. I was on my fifth call when I heard her voice. Although I was distracted, I recognized it immediately. The high-pitched singsong voice of the serpent was hard to forget.

The room froze as it always did, and all I could hear was the sound of my heart pounding in my ears like a steel drum. My back was to Ben but I knew she was at his window. The nurse on the line was rambling on about a patient, but I caught nothing of the conversation. Seti was facing me and must have noticed my skin pale because she looked confused. I told the nurse I would call her back and abruptly hung up. I gave Seti a look of desperation before I slowly turned in my chair.

Bita was already looking at me, her green eyes sharp and mocking.

She had recognized me from the back. Her she-devil stare was full of hatred. I returned it easily, my own anger bubbling under the surface.

"I didn't know you worked here. How convenient that must be for you. Did you do it on purpose to mess with my family even more?"

Recognition flashed across Ben's eyes and he immediately placed her. He'd never met Bita, but I had told him enough about her for him to know who she was. He went to speak, no doubt to defend me, but I gave him a guarded glance. He stopped himself, waiting on my move. I had to take a breath to calm myself down, the need to claw her face fiercely teasing me. I stood up and moved closer to the window, so I could speak quietly.

"I don't care about you or your family," I said, the anger shaking through my limbs as I held onto the counter. "I'm working here, otherwise I would have plenty more to say. But for now, I'll ask you to take your disappointing self as far away from me as possible. I refuse to be harassed by you any further."

What I really wanted to do was to tell her and her whole family to jump off a cliff. Whatever havoc they'd dealt with in my wake was less than what they deserved. But I would surely have gotten fired from my internship for that. I would probably get in trouble for the little I had already said. I loosened my grip on the counter, my knuckles white with fury.

"Is everything okay over here?" Seti asked, suddenly appearing beside me.

"Everything's fine," Ben said, before I could respond. "I just had a question about the prescription and Sara was helping."

He crushed Bita under the weight of his stare. She smirked, readying herself for the challenge. The anger burned behind Ben's eyes, the muscle in his jaw twitching. She noticed and hesitated for a fraction of a second. Seti stared at Bita expectantly. I prepared to launch myself across the counter.

"We're good," Bita finally said, then walked away.

My legs began to wobble as I watched her leave. I felt like I was standing in a pool of Jell-O. Seti must have sensed my imminent breakdown.

"Sara, why don't you go to the stockroom and refill the supplies?" she said.

I nodded, heading toward the back. Ben grabbed my hand as I walked by. I looked up at him, drinking in his strength, then quickly walked away. I began to cry as soon as I walked through the stockroom doors. I was furious, and caught off-guard, causing feelings for Maziar I'd shoved away to come back up to the surface. I was trying to gather the supplies through the tears blocking my vision when Seti walked in. I froze in all my pathetic glory.

"Want to tell me what just happened out there? Because I know Ben was lying. Judging from how your friend was staring at you, I'm assuming there's definitely some unpleasant history there."

I stood there dumbfounded.

"I just want to make sure you're okay. You're not getting in trouble," she said.

Next thing I knew I was vomiting up Maziar's story in a hurried urgency, pausing only to take a breath in between sentences. Seti listened, never interrupting me. Once I was done, I looked at her through red-rimmed eyes, waiting for her response. She stayed quiet for a minute as she digested the slew of information I'd just thrown at her.

"Wow, that really sucks," she finally said.

We both burst out laughing. She had the uncanny ability to lighten even the most morbid of moods.

"No, but seriously, I'm sorry this has all happened to you. It really is sad, but you're going to have to keep it together if she comes back. Do you think you can do that?" I nodded. "Okay, good. Now go and wash your face and come back out to work."

She smiled at me, wrapping me up in a warm hug. I imagine this would be how it felt if I'd grown up with a sister. I was back answering phones five minutes later.

Ben kept looking over at me, trying to make sure I was all right. He was facing a line of patients out of the door. I could see that it was killing him that he couldn't come over and talk to me. I tried to give him reassuring glances every time we made eye contact, but I knew he was worried.

The afternoon rush was a hidden blessing. It kept me too busy to obsess over my run-in with Bita. Before I knew it, it was six o'clock and we were done for the day. We closed up our stations and headed out the door. The minute we made it to the car, Ben grabbed me and pulled me into his arms, holding me tight. He didn't say anything, but I could hear his words anyway.

I couldn't speak. I didn't want to break down in the arms of one guy who cared for me about another guy I couldn't stop loving. It felt so unfair that Ben would have to witness what happened today, to have my unresolved feelings for Maziar thrown in his face. I just put my arms around him and squeezed back.

It took strength to allow himself to have feelings for someone broken like me. He gave me comfort, despite my affection for someone else. I appreciated who he was even more that day. This would not be the first, nor last time, I would witness Ben's unfailing character.

A few weeks later, Bita returned with her entourage. It was her attempt at a power play to intimidate me. I had spent too many nights hating her to care how large a following she brought in. This time, Seti and Ben were on point. Before I even knew it, Seti walked over to my position at the window and pulled me into refills with her, placing Ben in my spot. He flashed a playful, malicious smile at me on my way out.

When I realized Bita was standing in line, I just laughed. Her face contorted into a pile of angered wrinkles, the portions that were not paralyzed by her regular Botox injections. She quickly attempted to regain her composure, but I'd already seen her irritation. This angered her further, which only made it that much more enjoyable for me. I turned and willingly walked away, not looking back. I had no desire to deal with the serpent.

CHAPTER SIXTEEN

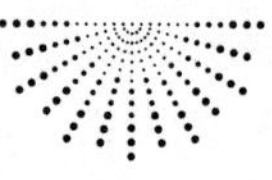

With August came my birthday. I hadn't wanted to do anything to celebrate, but it seemed as though everyone had other plans. Ben and Leyla had worked together to coordinate a night at a karaoke bar. Neda was taking me out to brunch earlier that day.

Neda and I had kept in touch, even after my relationship with Maziar had ended. We'd tried at first to pretend nothing had changed, but the remnants of the breakup had loomed over our heads with its discomfort. Slowly our coffee dates dwindled into biweekly courtesy phone calls.

She'd called me a few days before my birthday, convincing me to let her take me out. I reluctantly agreed. There was a part of me that was nervous to be in the same space as her again. In my mind, Neda was synonymous with Maziar. She was the only part of him I hadn't lost, and something about being so close to her, now that my life had started making sense again, gave me anxiety. It felt as if seeing her would somehow bring everything I'd rebuilt crashing down.

Saturday morning came sooner than I'd hoped. I'd been up since 6:30 tossing and turning, unable to get back to sleep. The butterflies in my stomach were making me sick and I was desperate to cancel on her but I couldn't come up with a viable excuse.

There was a part of me, though, that hoped she had mentioned it to Maziar, and he was lying in bed sleepless, worrying over me too. But I knew deep down that Neda wouldn't have told him. I don't think he would have been comfortable with us remaining in contact, so I doubted he even knew we were still friends.

I'd settled on a pair of light blue jeans and a loose beige V-neck shirt. Maziar's necklace still sat nestled in the center of my chest, as it always did. I reluctantly took it off for fear she would discover how I was pathetically hanging on to some nonexistent hope. Mom watched intently, perched on the edge of my bed, as I undid the clasp.

"Don't mention Maziar at all when you're with her," she advised.

"I know. You've already said that a hundred times, Mom!" I said, frustrated. I was already nervous about this date. She was just making it worse.

"I know, *azizam*, just making sure," she said and smiled. "You just don't want him to know how hard getting over him was."

I felt my cheeks flush with irritation. She'd been sitting on my bed for the past hour lecturing me on how I should keep my feelings concealed. She felt it would be the best form of revenge.

"I'm over him, *Maman*! I have no reason to talk about him."

She eyed me thoughtfully, then just looked away, making it clear I wasn't fooling anyone.

Persian women were a special breed, possessing certain ironclad strength. They never showed weakness. Too much emotion was equivalent to weakness. There were no conversations, no hashing things out, and no working through problems. Absolutely no one considered therapy, unless they were clinically insane. An Iranian woman just put on a calm face and slapped you with the silent treatment. Unfortunately, I was sure I would fail my mom and the whole of Persian women; I wouldn't be able to successfully convince anyone that I didn't care.

I came out of my room when Neda arrived. She turned toward me, all smiles and bubbles as usual. She looked beautiful, with the familiar bohemian air dancing about her. Neda had one of those captivating personalities that made you want to be around her. She exuded strength and self-assurance, but at the same time, she was humble and kind. She was the person you found yourself confiding your life story to, and would have no clue how exactly you got to spilling all your secrets.

As we waited to be seated, I felt awkward and fidgety. I bounced back and forth on the tips of my toes as if my feet were resting on hot coals. I wanted to crawl out of my skin.

Neda watched me dancing about. She reached out and placed her hand on my shoulder, startling me.

"You okay, Sara?" she asked concerned.

"I'm fine," I said, my voice sounding unnaturally high-pitched to my own ears. She looked at me, unconvinced.

"What do you want to know?"

"Nothing," I blurted out quickly.

"That's a lie and you know it. We might as well address it now and get it over with so we can actually enjoy ourselves."

We were interrupted by the hostess telling us our table was ready. As I followed her, I could feel the anxiety building inside me. I wanted desperately to know if Maziar had moved on, but I wasn't sure if I'd be able to deal with the magnitude of that information. I was deep in thought when we reached our table, almost tumbling over the hostess when she stopped. Luckily, I was able to grab the back of a chair and steady myself before falling. I still managed to score a few annoyed glances from the neighboring patrons.

I couldn't make eye contact with Neda for fear that she could see the broken pieces her cousin had left behind. I busied myself with sugar and cream, absently stirring the coffee the waitress placed in front of me. Again she reached out and put her hand on mine, steadying my methodical movement. I looked up at her.

"He still thinks about you," she said. She hesitated a moment before adding, "But he's moved on."

My breath caught in my throat. Was it just me, or was the room moving side to side like we were on a boat? I closed my eyes, trying to steady the swaying.

"What do you mean he's moved on? He has a girlfriend now?" I asked, eyes still closed, holding my breath as I hung onto her next words.

"No, he doesn't have a girlfriend, but he's dating," she replied. When I looked at her, I could see sympathy, and even pity, in her face. Then, she threw in, "Nothing serious or anything," as if that made it less of a blow.

It had finally happened; I'd become that pathetic person. The one who was left behind and still held on like a foolish child. The person everyone looked at with pity and eventually boredom. How'd I let myself get here? How did I end up being a stupid girl, allowing myself to embark on a journey I knew would leave me in its dust?

Neda took a deep breath, as if she were gathering her own courage to speak.

"But Sara, you need to move on. He fought with *Amoo* and *Zanamoo* as hard as he could, but they wouldn't budge. I think he just realized it wouldn't work and is trying to move on with his life. You know I love him, but he's not good for you anymore."

She squeezed my hand, and my mind was suddenly flooded with thoughts of Ben. I wanted to be near him, have him throw his arms around me, make me feel like the world revolved around me. I wanted to see him look at me the way he always did, making me feel like I was the only person in the universe who mattered.

"Move on, Sara. Don't waste any more time waiting around for him," she urged.

I knew she loved Maziar fiercely, which made what she was saying even worse. Maziar would have interpreted this conversation as a betrayal; he would never forgive her. But she said it anyway, because she was my friend, and because she truly believed we were over.

"Thank you. I appreciate you being honest with me."

* * *

When I got home, I dragged my body to my room, the weight of the world resting on my shoulders. I wasn't plagued with the pain I would have thought I'd feel after finding out that Maziar had moved on. I didn't feel overwhelmed with anger. I just simply felt bone-tired, the kind that was emanating from the deepest parts of me, and radiating out like a blanket threatening to smother me to death. I wanted to lie down and sleep for an eternity. I walked into my room and closed the door, falling face first onto my pillows.

I vaguely remember Mom coming in a few times asking me if I was ill. I mumbled an incoherent response and shooed her away. When I finally awoke, the day had turned to night, and someone had thrown a blanket on me. I felt peaceful wrapped up in the cocoon of the covers and rolled over to go back to sleep when I glanced at the clock on my wall. It read six. I sat up with a jolt, realizing Leyla would be picking me up in an hour.

I heard my phone buzz on the nightstand. I'd missed three calls from Leyla, two from Ben, and a handful of text messages from both. They knew I had brunch with Neda this morning. They probably both thought my silence was an indication that it had gone badly. I quickly sent them messages saying I'd fallen asleep, then jumped in the shower.

Leyla showed up at my house at seven, despite my pleas for extra time. She thought it would be more productive for her to sit on my bed staring with disapproving eyes at my tardiness. I couldn't decide what to wear, and she was making me more nervous pointing out every minute that passed on the clock.

"Just put something on, Sara! We're going to be so late!" she begged.

I threw my hands up in defeat and settled on a pair of dark blue jeans and a white blouse. I threw on Maziar's necklace out of habit, but hid it beneath a few others, trying to make myself feel less ridiculous. He'd moved on. The thought suddenly pressed down on my mind, but before I had a chance to dwell on it, Leyla dragged me out the door. I couldn't help but laugh that I was being scolded for being late to my own party.

We got to the karaoke bar twenty minutes later. It was small and quaint, with a stage at the far right facing a flat screen that showed all the lyrics to the chosen song. To the left of the stage were bins, each filled with various props that could be used during the performances.

Currently, there was a middle-aged man, wearing a big Afro wig, singing obnoxiously to "I Will Survive" by Gloria Gaynor. His singing was miserable, but he had half the place yelling at the top of their lungs along with him, and the other half laughing hysterically. It seemed to be a success.

Leyla came up behind me and grabbed my arm. I turned toward her and saw that my friends had taken over the three tables at the far left wall. They were talking, each with a drink in hand. Ben was sitting in the middle, slightly turned toward his right, engaged in a conversation with Sandra. I couldn't hear what they were saying, but she was giggling.

He was radiating with charm, something I'd realized he had no clue he possessed. He didn't seem to notice how women naturally flocked to him. He was oblivious to the fact that he was gorgeous, making him that much more appealing.

Leyla guided us toward the table, and everyone broke out in a cheer once they'd realized I had arrived. I laughed at their goofiness, obviously further in on drinks than I'd estimated. I had some catching up to do.

"Happy birthday, doll," Ben said when I made my way over to him.

I smiled, batting my eyes like a lovesick puppy. What was I doing?

My parents didn't know Ben would be at the karaoke bar. Their protests had become more frequent and exponentially more irritating. Even though something seemed to be happening between us, I hadn't admitted it to them. They'd become relentless with their "worries" about Ben, so when they'd asked if he would be there, I'd lied.

Ben had grown up in Minnetonka, Minnesota, a small suburban city in Hennepin County. His mom was a schoolteacher and his stepdad a CPA. He was one of three brothers, each two years apart. Ben was the middle child.

He grew up playing baseball and was good enough to get a full scholarship to Stanford, where he played for four years. He studied hard and got a 4.0 GPA, landing him at USC pharmacy school. He'd never had anything handed to him, and the life he was creating for himself he'd done on his own. He was humble. I loved that about him.

Ben's best friend, Josh, was visiting for the weekend. I suddenly noticed him sitting to Ben's right. They had grown up together, living on the same block from the age of six. They were in the same first grade class. Josh had started school a few weeks late and Ben was designated as Josh's buddy. It sparked a lifelong friendship.

Sandra was sitting next to him. I noticed the subtle way she leaned in toward Josh as he spoke. It was obvious they were into each other because neither noticed me until Ben reached out and tapped Josh's shoulder. They both looked up.

"Hi," Sandra squealed, standing up to hug me.

"Hey, Sara. It's so nice to finally meet you," Josh said, over her shoulder.

Everyone scooted down to give me a seat next to Ben. He pulled out the chair for me like the gentleman that he was. Josh bought the table a round of shots and my first vodka tonic. Abby was busily snapping photos, and Maya had consumed enough liquid courage that she was now trying to drag Leyla up on stage with her to do their own rendition of Whitney Houston's "I Want to Dance with Somebody." Ben had his arm draped over the back of my chair, locked in an intense conversation over a baseball game with Thomas.

I realized I was surrounded by all of my favorite people. Even though Maziar was missing, every single person there would have done anything for me. For the first time in months, I felt blessed. I knew Ben was one of those blessings.

The night turned out to be a hot mess of outlandish renditions of famous eighties and nineties songs. As soon as we all had enough alcohol in our systems to dull our fears, we went up in various combinations to perform our favorites. My favorite performance of the night was when Ben and the boys got up to sing their version of Silk's hit, "Freak Me." It felt like we were caught in a clothed interpretation of a *Magic Mike* movie. We all lost our voices as we cheered them on. Ben had a group of groupies desperate for his attention in the front row, but he never took his eyes off me, leaving my skin tingling with excitement. When they were done, the house gave them a standing ovation.

Leyla leaned in and whispered, "If you don't go after that, then I will."

I laughed, knowing there was some truth to her statement. She smiled at me as she planted the seed of Ben a little further into my mind.

CHAPTER SEVENTEEN

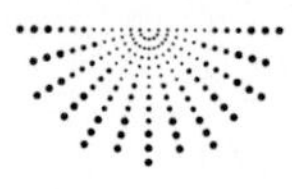

Our summer internship was approaching its end, and there was a certain sadness in the air at work. We'd all become friends and saying goodbye seemed impossible.

It was Friday, and Seti came over to where Ben and I were restocking supplies.

"You two free tonight? We're all going for sushi after work. You guys want to come?"

Ben and I were still carpooling, so our after-work decision had to be united. He looked at me, raising an eyebrow in question.

"I'm good to go if you are, Ben," I replied.

"We're in, then," he said, smiling, flashing his dimples at Seti as she flushed under his gaze.

Once the day was over, I ran to the bathroom to freshen up. I was still wearing Maziar's necklace around my neck. I watched in the mirror as it twinkled against the fluorescent lights overhead. My hand involuntarily reached up for it, rubbing its smooth, cold surface between my fingertips. I didn't know why I kept wearing it even though things were over between us. It comforted me somehow, as if it were a magical talisman connecting the two of us through its existence.

When I stepped back outside, I could see Ben leaning up against the pharmacy counter waiting for me. I took in the shape of him, the curves of each muscle smoothly bleeding into the next as if he were a statue carved to perfection. My breath caught in my chest as I felt butterfly wings flapping in my stomach.

"You ready?" he asked as I approached him, gently touching my wrist. I felt my skin burn where his fingers rested, lingering long after he'd removed them.

"Yes," I said, smiling, as he guided me out the door. We made it to the restaurant a few minutes later.

It was on the smaller side with long rows of tables running along both right and left walls and smaller tables filling up the middle. We spotted the others sitting at a table next to the sushi bar and headed over to them. They'd already ordered their first round of drinks, so Ben and I quickly looked over the menu. I ordered a key lime martini and Ben settled on sake.

I was halfway into my second martini, feeling the familiar warmth of intoxication inside my belly. Its haze had settled on my thoughts and I found myself uninhibitedly staring at Ben. He was truly gorgeous with those piercing blue eyes.

He was deep in conversation with Seti and hadn't noticed me looking at him. I watched his lips as they formed around his words, suddenly feeling the need to press my own lips up against them. I wondered if they tasted like sake. He felt the weight of my gaze and turned toward me. He flashed me his crooked smile. It was infectious, and I found myself giggling in return.

My buzz had rid me of my restraints. It felt good to feel excited again, to revel in someone's desire for me. My hand was resting on the table, so he reached out to squeeze it, a sign of affection he frequently used. This time though, I held on. He looked down at our intertwined fingers, surprised, then looked up, searching my eyes for an answer to the riddle I'd just placed before him. I held his gaze, smiling broadly. He looked at me for a few moments as if he expected me to change my mind. But I left my fingers wrapped around his, giving him the confidence he needed. He held onto my hand and returned to his conversation with Seti.

Unfortunately, there's always an uncharacteristic calm before an explosion. Ben heard it before I did. I was too far into my intoxication to pick up on the subtle sounds of my surroundings. I saw his body stiffen, then his gaze move toward the door. His fingers tightened around mine protectively. Fear slowly crept up my sides, knowing something was wrong. My brain was too sluggish from the alcohol to comprehend what was happening. I sat there, confused, until I heard it. I felt my heart drop.

Maziar's voice carried through the crowd like the methodical hum of a bee's wings. At first, I just stopped breathing. I had to be imagining it, like the hundreds of other times I'd thought I heard or saw him. Then, I looked up at Ben and saw the worry resting in those heartbreaking eyes and knew he was really there.

I instinctively let go of Ben's hand and saw the disappointment flash across his face, but it didn't register. I was too preoccupied with my own feelings. I slowly turned in my seat, desperate to confirm I wasn't hallucinating.

I recognized Pasha immediately. He had his head back, laughing loudly at something someone had said. His arm was draped around a tall, thin, blonde girl with a short, black miniskirt and a very flattering top, accentuating her fake assets. I didn't recognize her, but that wasn't surprising. Pasha frequently changed up his flavor of the month.

I saw Emanuel and Azi standing to his left. I was suddenly hit with a pang of jealousy at seeing Azi with all of Maziar's friends. I wanted to cry. She unconsciously looked in my direction and froze with shock. Then, she smiled kindly, but it didn't reach her eyes.

I had suddenly found myself in some unfathomable nightmare.

I scanned the group, looking from one person to the next, searching for Maziar. He was blocked by the semi-circle the others had formed. I silently sent a prayer that he was there alone. I begged God to save me from having to see him with someone else.

The hostess approached them to say their table was ready. As the group started to disperse, Maziar came into view and, much to my dismay, I saw that his arm was draped around someone. I didn't recognize her. She was a few inches taller than me, coming up to his forehead. She was lanky and tall where I was short and petite. She reminded me of a supermodel. Her light brown hair fell midway down her back, complemented by her dark chocolate brown eyes. They stood out against the lightness of her skin. She was leaning into Maziar's shoulder, smiling happily, as she listened to the conversation going on in front of her.

The hate I felt for her consumed me. I couldn't think. I couldn't breathe. I wanted to launch myself across the restaurant and pummel her. At the same time, I desperately wanted the floor to open up and swallow me whole, whisking me away from the hell I'd suddenly found myself in.

As I tried to figure out what to do, he looked over at me. The color drained from his face. His muscles stiffened with recognition, but he managed to maintain his casual attitude so as to not alert his date to my presence. He just stared at me, trying to have a silent conversation I couldn't understand.

Azi saw the exchange between us. In what I assumed was her attempt at helping, she walked up to Maziar's date and asked her to go to the bathroom. She was clueless to what was happening, so she agreed.

I suddenly stood up. I couldn't be there any longer, the walls closing in on me; I was suffocating. I looked over and realized both Ben and Seti were staring at me. I couldn't find the words for an explanation.

"I need to go outside," I said. "I'll be right back." I pushed my chair out before either of them had a chance to offer to come with me. I squeezed Ben's hand as I turned for the door in an impotent attempt at alleviating the tension.

Maziar's friends had already started toward their table, so they were no longer barricading the entrance. He stood halfway between his table and the front door, stuck in a profound moment of crossroads.

I ran through the entrance of the restaurant and halfway down the block, not caring how pathetic I looked to anyone watching. There was a bus bench, and I reached for it, trying to steady my shaking body. I tried to slow my breathing, afraid I'd hyperventilate. I was shaking all over. I moved to the front of the bench and sat down before I collapsed onto the sidewalk. I put my face in my hands and started to cry. My heart felt like it was breaking all over again.

Part of me was certain that Maziar would run out after me. But he didn't. A few minutes later, I felt a hand rest on my shoulder. I felt the heat radiate through my arm and knew it was Ben before I turned around.

"Are you okay?" he asked as I looked up at him.

I could see the conflict he was facing. He wanted to help me because he cared for me, but at the same time he wanted to hate me for not being over Maziar. I had no words of comfort to offer him. I just placed my hand on his wrist and pulled him around the bench to sit next to me. He put his arm around me, not saying a word, letting me deal with the war raging inside me. There was a tenderness in his embrace I knew I wasn't worthy of.

I ached for Maziar and the part of me that still loved him when I desperately didn't want to. I fought the tears that wanted to fall, because he didn't run out after me. I knew he was over me, and I could think of nothing more heartbreaking than that. Then, I thought of Ben and how I'd kept us in limbo for months because I was too terrified to take the next step with him. I knew he deserved better than me, but I didn't want to lose him. All the while he sat patiently beside me, in the quiet cool of the evening, each of us lost in the avalanche of what tonight had done to us.

"I can't go back inside," I said.

"Okay, I'll go deal with the check. Then, we can leave."

He was standing to go when I reached out and grabbed his arm. I stood up and pulled him in, throwing my arms tightly around his neck. He wrapped his arms around my waist, and we just stood there, letting the breeze blow away the remnants of the evening.

"Thank you," I said, "for being so amazing."

I pulled back and looked into his eyes so he could see the truth behind my words. He smiled a halfhearted smile, all he could manage after the emotional beating he'd taken. I leaned in and kissed his cheek, my lips brushing against the corner of his mouth. Then, I sat down on the bench, staring at the cracks in the concrete, listening to the shuffling of his feet as he walked away.

I wanted badly to kiss him, to get lost in the way he felt about me. I wanted to feel Ben's body up against mine, to escape from the pain I was feeling into the bliss of two bodies ignited together. I wanted to lie curled up next to his warmth, his arms wrapped tightly around me. I wanted his safety.

He deserved for me to love him as much as he loved me. He deserved to have all of me and not just the little viable pieces that were left behind in this hollow shell of my body. He deserved the world. I wanted to love Ben.

Seti came out and walked over to sit next to me. I was staring out at the street, watching an old napkin swirl around the concrete in a dance with the wind. She put her arm on my leg and just watched it with me for a while.

"I'm sorry for running out and making a scene," I finally said.

"It's fine. No one other than me noticed."

"Good."

"So that was Maziar," she said, more as a fact than as a question.

"Did he look like he cared that he'd seen me?" I asked, holding my breath. I'd run out so quickly that I had no idea what his reaction to seeing me was.

"He watched you leave and you could tell he wasn't sure if he should come out after you or not. The guy he was standing with leaned in and said something. Maziar shook his head. I couldn't hear them. His date came out of the bathroom and grabbed his arm. Then, they walked over to the table," she said, looking at me sadly. "He did seem distracted, though, and kept glancing back at the door. He kept looking at Ben, too."

I wanted to believe that Maziar was tormented by the idea of Ben and me together. I wanted him to feel how I felt when I saw him with her. I let myself take his distraction as a small win.

"But he didn't bother coming out after me," I said, tears threatening my resolve. I pushed them back, refusing to let Maziar make me weak.

"I'm sorry," was all Seti could offer.

We sat in the silence of the cool evening, no words left to say. Ben came out a few minutes later, holding his keys.

"Ready to go?"

"Yeah, I'm ready," I said, hugging Seti goodbye.

Ben and I walked side by side toward the car. I leaned in and playfully bumped him, trying to lighten the heavy mood. He looked at me and smiled, but it never reached the corners of his eyes. I felt pain ache in my heart at how I'd made him feel inadequate tonight. He witnessed a confirmation of my unresolved feelings for Maziar, and in turn interpreted it as a lack of feelings for him. But, that wasn't true. I did have feelings for him, despite my feelings for Maziar. I was suddenly desperate to make him see that.

I wasn't over Maziar, but I couldn't lose Ben.

We got in his car, and he started to drive. For the first time, there was an awkward silence between us. It was uncomfortable and out of place. I started to feel anxious as I sensed Ben pulling away from me. The panic crushed me under its weight as I realized I could be losing him. I had lost Maziar; that was determined with finality tonight. I could not bear to lose Ben as well.

"Will you go somewhere with me?" I asked, the pleading heavy in my voice.

"Sure," he said with a sigh; apparently his patience had run thin.

My heart began to pound against my chest. He inched closer to his window, visibly retreating away from me. I wanted to scream at the top of my lungs and tell him he couldn't leave me too.

"Where did you want to go?" he said, even though he seemed uninterested in going anywhere with me.

I told him to exit on Hayvenhurst, making a right up into the canyons. We drove for a few minutes, turning onto Mullholland Boulevard. The road became winding, weaving in and out of residential areas along the mountainside. As we got closer, the homes began to spread out and become less noticeable.

At the top of the hill sat a church. It was a large white building with a gray tiled roof. It didn't have the large arches familiar from most churches, but a more traditionally shaped roof. I imagined that the large stained-glass window in front projected a rainbow of colors onto the pews when the sunlight shined through. My favorite part was the red doors.

It sat on the edge of a cliff, overlooking the mountains. There were parking spots along the side that looked out onto the view. I guided

Ben to the far corner, farthest away from the church. We parked under an alcove of trees. From here, all the lights of the city below glittered in silence.

Ben turned the car off but didn't face me. He just continued staring out the window. I didn't know what to say, or how to begin to explain the conundrum of emotions I was feeling. I could still feel my heart beating wildly against my chest. I took a deep breath, realizing this was it.

I was now in the moment where I would have to decide on which path I was going to take, or I'd lose them both. I wasn't sure if I could ever stop loving Maziar, but I knew I couldn't lose Ben. He had been my anchor, my strength. He'd forced me to move forward when I couldn't. He had held my hand and guided me through the storm. There was a place in my heart for him, and I knew that with unfailing certainty.

"Ben, I'm so sorry," I said, turning to face him, but he wouldn't look at me.

"For what? You haven't done anything." He sounded defeated, devoid of the brightness I was so accustomed to seeing in him.

"I know tonight was terrible. I hate that you had to see it. I hate that you saw me like that."

He looked at me then, the pain in his eyes expressing the broken heart he was feeling. I reached out and grabbed his hand.

"Don't," he said, pulling it away. He sounded tired. His pain was etched into his features, like roads drawn on a map that I'd created.

"Please don't leave me," I said, silently pleading with my eyes.

"Why shouldn't I leave you? Is it because you don't want to be alone, or is it because it's me you want to be with?" he asked angrily, catching me off guard.

I could see him struggling to maintain his composure, straining against his own restraints. I knew he had every right to hate me, but I desperately didn't want him to. I cared about Ben. His unwavering loyalty had kept him in my life through my relationship with Maziar, patiently waiting for his chance. Tonight, I'd seen that Maziar was no longer mine to hold onto. He hadn't even cared enough to come after me.

But Ben had.

It was depressing to think that Maziar could go from being my everything to becoming nothing as we both faded into memories. But, as sad as I found that to be, the reality of it was that he was gone. I'd waited four months for him. I'd given him one hundred and twenty-two days to come back to me, and in that time, I hadn't heard from him at all. His life had moved on without me while mine stood at a standstill. I was done waiting for him.

I had this amazing guy standing before me, desperate for me to love him. He could have his pick of girls. Women threw themselves at him everywhere we went, but he only had eyes for me. I could love him. I deserved to love someone like him.

I placed my hand on his face, felt his resolve waver up against my palm. He leaned in slightly, absorbing the little comfort the moment allotted him.

"I'm not afraid of being alone. It would probably be easier for me to never love another human being again," I said, staring into the deep blue ocean of his eyes. "If I stay alone, I wouldn't take the risk of getting hurt." I moved closer to him, my face inches away from his. This time he didn't pull away. "So it's you I don't want to lose, not the possibility of being alone."

I could see his pulse racing in his neck. I leaned in, placing my lips up against his. I had thought of this moment so many times in the past few months. I felt an explosion occur between us, wrapped up in warmth and covered by my need for him. He slipped his hand behind my head and wrapped his fingers in my hair. His mouth moved up against mine in a rhythm that was unfamiliar, but natural, both at the same time. He slipped his other hand around my waist and in one fluid motion pulled me from my seat onto his lap. I wrapped my arms around his neck, pushed my body into him. He held on to me tightly, as if he were afraid I would fly away.

We explored each other's lips, neck, the tender skin beneath our ears. Our hands ran over the fabric of our clothing, wanting desperately to tear it away, but refraining. Our bodies guided our emotions up to the surface where they could no longer remain quiet. I wrapped myself around him, trying to eliminate any doubt left between us.

We sat intertwined in the front seat together and stared out the window afterward, enjoying the backdrop to our very first moment in the story of us. The weight of the evening had dissipated, bringing with it a new lightness in the air. My back leaned against his chest and I could feel the rhythmic rise and fall of his breath. It was soothing.

As I looked out onto the city lights, I realized I was moving away from the life I'd imagined with Maziar and into one I hadn't imagined before. It was both terrifying and exhilarating. I leaned forward and wrapped my fingers around the clasp of my necklace, removing it from my neck. I slid it inside my pocket.

A smile spread across Ben's face, this time reaching his eyes.

CHAPTER EIGHTEEN

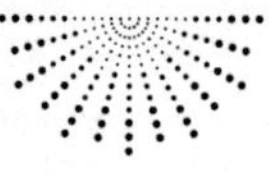

The end of August brought with it the end of our internships. We were sad to go, but Seti had hinted that we should look her up once we graduated. We were hopeful that we would work with her again.

I had decided that I would move in with Sandra for the coming school year. I hadn't discussed it yet with my parents and was nervous about talking to them. In the Iranian culture, it was generally accepted that women remained in their parents' households until they were married. There were exceptions, as with anything, such as moving out for school, but those were usually in scenarios where the school was located in another state or too far away to make the drive daily. My forty-five-minute drive to USC would not be long enough to adequately tip the scale in my favor. At least not for my parents.

There were only two weeks left until the new semester began and I was running out of time. I needed to start packing and doing it in secret would be impossible. I needed to face the dreaded conversation soon.

I decided I would broach the topic that coming Friday night at our family dinner. I had already spoken to my brother weeks before, so he knew my plans.

"You should totally move out. It just makes sense," Nima said.

As it was, there were some nights I would stay at school late, studying. By the time I made the drive, I would get home well past midnight, only to wake up and do it all over again in the morning. That was the angle I was going to take with my parents. I was glad my brother was on board. I would need him in my corner once Mom exploded with rage.

Friday showed up faster than I had wanted it to. Mom had made *khoresht bademjoon*, eggplant stew, a popular Iranian dish that was poured over white rice. It was my favorite. I was sure the woman had some sort of sixth sense. I was convinced she had made it in an attempt to guilt me out of moving. Nima and I exchanged glances as the same thought crossed both our minds. He smirked while I panicked.

Dad came in from the den where he'd been watching television. I helped Mom bring in the last of the food and we all gathered around the table. Dad started in on his usual questions of how we were and what was going on with school and so on. I sat in my seat, sick to my stomach with nerves, trying to gather the courage to tell them what I had planned. Nima looked over at my horrified expression and thought he would help me out.

In between big spoonfuls of *khoresht*, he blurted out, "Sara is planning on moving to downtown in two weeks."

I almost spit out my food, caught between coughing and choking. Mom turned on me with an angry fierceness in her eyes. Dad saw this and just shook his head, like he'd had enough of my Friday night outbursts of life-changing information.

"What is he talking about, Sara?" Mom asked.

I took a sip of water from the glass she'd placed in front of me earlier, stalling. My throat felt morbidly dry.

"Well, I'm about to start my second year, and my schedule is going to get busier. The commute is killing me, *Maman*. I just thought if I was living closer to school, I could use that time for studying instead of wasting it in my car."

"She's right, Mom," Nima interjected. "It's a far drive to school from here. Sometimes she isn't even home until past midnight."

I gave my brother a look of gratitude for having my back. Mom looked at Nima like she was about to say something, but then decided not to. Dad jumped in, not giving her any time to rethink her silence.

"Where do you plan on living, Sara?" he asked.

He was practical when making decisions. He wanted to know all the details before making up his mind. Mom was quite the opposite; she took little time to think things through but rather made instant decisions based on her current emotions.

"Sandra's roommate just graduated and moved out. She has an extra bedroom now, so I thought I'd move in there," I said.

"You're just trying to move out to be closer to that boy," Mom threw in angrily.

I looked at her, the apprehension I felt moments ago quickly replaced by my own anger. I was so sick of her constant intrusion on my life, always judging my decisions. I was itching to tell her off. Nima reached out placing his hand on my shoulder to calm me down. Nothing good would come of losing my temper.

"No, it's not because I want to live closer to that boy," I replied, not breaking eye contact with her. "Just in case you forgot, that boy has a name. It's Ben. He's a really nice guy and you're being unfair. I'm twenty-five years old. I should be able to date whoever I want. I wish you guys would understand that. But my moving has nothing to do with him and everything to do with school." With that, I got up and walked away. I couldn't be around my mom any longer. I was tired of her "plans for me" and had no interest in hearing about how I was messing them up for her.

I threw myself down on my bed and covered my eyes. I could hear the heated discussion still going on at the table. I couldn't make out all the words, but I could hear the rise and fall of their voices. My brother was coming to my defense. Nima was the level-headed one whose opinions were always respected by my parents. Where I was erratic and emotional, he was calm and rational. I could hear him reasoning with Dad. I was angry and didn't want to hear any more of their conversation, so I threw on my headphones.

"Burning House" by Cam came on. I'd listened to it at least a hundred times when Maziar and I had just broken up. Almost six months later, it still made me want to cry. We were stuck in a burning house even before we began our relationship and it seemed like we spent the entire time struggling to get ourselves out before we burned along with it. In the end, we were consumed by the flames, despite our battle to survive.

I lay on my bed, quietly staring at the ceiling, wondering if I'd ever fully get over him. Would I ever be able to remember our relationship as what used to be and not what could have been? I wasn't sure. I'd moved on, but I couldn't quite break free; there was always some invisible rope anchoring me to him despite my protests.

I felt like a horrible person as I lay thinking of Maziar while I was dating Ben. It wasn't fair; I knew that much. But my life couldn't stay frozen any longer. I had made my decision. I was moving on. I just needed to figure out how to get my feelings under control. I constantly felt confused and it was exhausting.

As I was wrapped up in my emotional maze, headphones on, I missed the soft knock on the door. I saw it slowly open, catching my attention. I pulled the headphones off as Dad walked in.

He sat down next to me on the bed. I scooted up against the pillows so I was facing him. He put his hand on my leg and looked at me with the warm, strong eyes I was used to seeing from Dad. He always had a way of making me feel safe. I never felt afraid that I would ever disappoint him, even if he was angry with me. It was just a matter of us not seeing eye to eye and not that I was failing him.

Mom, on the other hand, always made me feel inadequate, like I was falling short by not doing things exactly as she wanted. Maybe it was a mother-daughter thing, or a Persian mother thing, but it resulted in guilt and anxiety, both of which I had no interest in feeling.

"Do you really want to move out? You would be on your own. Your mom wouldn't be there to help cook or clean for you. Can you do it all, especially while you're in school?" Dad asked.

"Yes," I said, confidently.

He looked at me, his eyes glossing over as if he was no longer seeing me. It felt like he'd taken a trip back in time. After a few moments, he leaned in and kissed my forehead.

"Okay," was all he said.

I sat staring at the door he'd just walked out of, wondering if my parents had actually given me permission to move out. A few minutes later, Nima came in, grinning, confirming that I had indeed not imagined things.

I was moving in two weeks.

* * *

Mom gave me the best silent treatment she had in her arsenal for the following week as she watched Dad, Nima and me pack up my things. I could see how difficult this was for her but I couldn't let it sway me. I stood my ground.

The day of moving had finally arrived. My brother helped my dad pack up the car and we headed downtown. Mom stayed behind with the lame excuse of cleaning but I could see her wiping her tears away as we drove out of sight. Although we weren't able to find common ground lately, I knew she looked at me as her confidante. Now I was leaving her behind, to fend for herself among the savages.

Once we got to the apartment, my friends were waiting to help move me in. Dad greeted Ben cordially but remained distant. Ben pretended not to notice, continuing to put his best foot forward.

With so many people the process took only two hours, the stairs being the only obstacle slowing us down. After all my boxes were in and Dad had put together my bed frame, I walked my family downstairs so they could head home.

I stood there with a heavy heart, knowing I'd taken another step further away from them. I hadn't thought it would be so difficult for me to grow up. Despite our conflicts, I loved and depended on them. They were my rock, the single constant force in my life. I was, in a way, saying goodbye to that. I was taking the next step in being an adult, claiming my independence.

I started to cry as soon as my dad hugged me. He held me for a few moments while my tears wet his shoulder. He leaned back so he could see my face and wiped them away with his big, rugged hands, the same hands that had picked me up and cleaned off bruises so many times as I was growing up.

"This isn't goodbye, *eshgham*. This is just see you later."

"I know," I said in between tiny sobs.

"We are only a short drive away, and you can come home any time you feel like you need to. Dry your tears now and go back upstairs. It's time to start this beautiful new adventure," he said.

He pulled away from me then, standing aside so my brother could say goodbye. I wanted to reach out and grab him, wrap my arms around his neck like I did when I was little. I wanted to beg him to take me home again. But I didn't.

Nima came in next, wrapping me in his strong arms. He was my person, my best friend since the beginning of time. I feared being away from him the most.

"Call me. I'm a phone call away," he said as he squeezed me tighter. "You're going to do great, I promise," he whispered into my ear, and then kissed my cheek.

"Pick up the phone when I call you," I begged.

"I will," he said, smiling reassuringly.

I stood on the curb and watched as they drove away. I remained there long after they were gone, holding onto my sadness. The distance would be difficult for me.

Ben came up behind me, placing his hand around my waist and startling me out of my thoughts.

"I'm sorry," he whispered in my ear.

I smiled, leaning into his chest so he could hold me tighter. I stood on my tiptoes, turning to kiss him. He returned my kiss, slow and patient, mirroring the depth of his feelings for me. I welcomed it, losing myself for a moment.

Everyone stayed to help me unpack and put my stuff away. Then, they all left to grab dinner. Ben and I remained behind. He went to go get us pizza while I finished up the last few things. He returned twenty minutes later with food and a bottle of wine. We pulled up one of the boxes that had not yet been opened and created a little dining table, eating amongst a castle of bubble wrap.

"I'm really excited that you're here," he said, tapping his plastic cup of wine against mine.

"Thanks," I replied, "I'm happy too. A little nervous, but happy."

Once we'd done all we could for the night, we both crawled onto my bed and collapsed on the covers, too tired to pull them aside and climb in. After a few minutes, I opened my eyes and glanced at Ben. He was staring up at the ceiling, off in a faraway land of daydreams. I closed the space between us, grabbing his hand in mine. I started to slowly play with his fingers.

He turned onto his side, facing me. I matched his movement. We stared at each other, neither of us speaking. There was a passion in Ben's eyes that was unfamiliar and new, one that my body responded to with understanding. I scooted over the few inches left between us and slipped my arm around his neck. I brought his head down toward mine and kissed him in the dim glow of the streetlights outside my window.

He gently placed his hand on my waist, playing with the frayed edges of my T-shirt. Hesitantly, he slipped it beneath the fabric, touching my skin. He drew seductive patterns with his fingers, making an urge swell deep inside me. His need was fierce and tangible, like I could reach into the air surrounding us and grab onto it. He was a gentleman, though, and despite the restraint it took on his part, he would not be the one to take the lead in this dance. He held his desire at bay, waiting for my move.

I was struggling between my physical need for him and my emotional unpreparedness of having sex with someone new. The heat between my legs urged me to move forward but my heart sent warning flares up all around me. Despite the alarms, I couldn't resist touching him. I pushed my body tightly up against his, pulling his shirt over his head. Our hands began exploring each other's bodies, our lips leaving hot trails of lust all over each other's skin.

It was apparent where this dance would lead, and my mind screamed louder that I wasn't ready. I pulled away from Ben, disconnecting the surge of power between us. He stared at me, startled and confused, the rejection stinging like a slap in the face. I gently pushed him onto his back and straddled him. Rejection was quickly replaced by intrigue, the direction I'd hoped it would take us.

I stared at him, slowly unbuttoning his pants, his eyes widening with anticipation. I leaned over, playfully placing kisses on his lower stomach. He slightly withered under my touch, trying to maintain his composure.

I gently slipped him inside my mouth. He let out a moan and exhaled. I could feel his pleasure hardening with each stroke, and when he couldn't take it any longer, he indulged in the explosion that followed. His body relaxed into the mattress, and I lay back, content that I had convincingly avoided ruining another moment.

Later that night, as I lay with my head on his chest, he twisted my curls between his fingers, lulling me into a peaceful sleep. He told me stories of when he was younger. I felt a calmness envelop me, one that I hadn't felt in months. I fell asleep somewhere in the story of Ben and Josh taking his stepdad's car out for a joyride.

I dreamed of the sun and the beach that night, of the waves of the ocean. And sitting beside me was Ben. Maziar was nowhere to be found.

CHAPTER NINETEEN

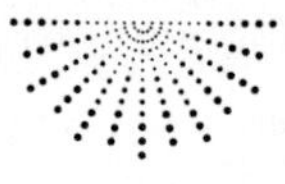

The second school year brought with it the chaotic rhythm of lectures and studying. Time felt like it was moving faster than it should. Our first set of midterms had already arrived, taking place the week before Thanksgiving break. Ben was planning a trip home for the holidays, and had mentioned that he wanted me to join him in Minnesota. This was a serious step in our relationship, and although I was apprehensive about taking it, I could appreciate that he was excited for me to meet his family.

Josh and Sandra had been talking since my birthday. He'd come to visit her a few times since then. When they were together, he couldn't take his eyes off her, and their two bodies danced around each other like they were meant to occupy the same space in the universe. Josh had asked Sandra to join him for Thanksgiving as well. She'd already said yes.

I knew my parents wouldn't agree to the trip. The struggle between us had continued, only worsening as my relationship with Ben deepened. Now that I had moved out, Mom felt the loss of her control even more, and it angered her. I'd contemplated lying as I'd done so many times before, but the idea of getting on an airplane without telling them where I was going felt dangerous. There were so many possibilities that could go wrong. I didn't want to risk it.

My midterms had ended on Tuesday and I went straight home afterward. It was the first weekend in over a month that I had actually spent with my family. My workload at school had become tedious and finding time to make the trek to Encino was proving to be more difficult than I'd anticipated. Also, the constant tension that could be felt in the confines of their walls had become progressively less appealing week after week.

Mom's silent treatment had weakened, but when we spoke, I was still faced with curt responses and constant disapproval. I no longer discussed my relationship with her, and it drove her mad. I missed the closeness we'd had, but I couldn't allow her to control me with the same prejudices I'd faced with Maziar's family. I'd drawn a line in the sand and I wasn't crossing it for anyone, Mom included.

When I walked through the door an hour later, I could hear her bustling around in the kitchen. Dad was sitting on the couch, deep within one of his books. I glanced over at him and realized that he had aged. His hair had grayed around the temples and was thinning on top. He had prominent wrinkles around his eyes now that crinkled even more as he looked up and smiled at me. I felt a deep sadness at the thought of my parents' mortality, something I didn't think of often, but had started to notice more frequently.

I went over to him and threw my arms around his neck. I kissed his cheeks over and over as if he were the child. He stood up and hugged me back, swaying back and forth when I didn't let go. We danced to the music of our heartbeats, in time with the tapping of his foot, around the living room like we used to do when I was little. It didn't matter how old I was—I always looked at Dad through the eyes of someone looking at her hero. There was nothing I didn't think he could do or situation I didn't think he could fix.

I knew he didn't share the same view as Mom regarding Ben, but he was stuck in an impossible situation between the two of us. Even if he could see past the fact that Ben wasn't Iranian, she wouldn't let him.

He squeezed me a little tighter and kissed my head as I snuggled up to him. He finally let go of me and sat back down on the couch, shooing me into the kitchen to help Mom with lunch so he could get back to his "studying." I took one last look at him reading, letting the warmth of his love fill me with the strength I needed for the discussion I was about to embark on. I walked into the kitchen.

Mom was crying from the onions she'd grated into the red mixing bowl in front of her. She was making *kotlet*, small oval-shaped patties, that she was frying in the large oiled skillet beside her. I automatically walked over to the pile of tomatoes and lettuce next to the sink and started to run them under the faucet. Once they were washed, I started slicing the tomatoes and arranging them on the large white ceramic platter sitting on the counter. I moved on to the lettuce next and did the same, creating a festive dish of reds and greens that reminded me of Christmas.

Kotlet is another traditional Iranian dish. It's made from a mixture of ground beef, onions, potatoes, and egg. The mixture is taken and shaped into thin oval-shaped patties, no bigger than the size of a palm, and fried to a crispy brown perfection. They can be eaten plain or can be made into pita sandwiches with the trimmings I was in the process of chopping up.

Mom and I worked in the quiet, comfortable silence of the kitchen for a few minutes. I reached out and grabbed the jar of pickles, twisting the lid off.

"How were your tests?" she asked.

"They were okay. The last one was a bit hard, but I think I did well over all," I replied, keeping my eyes trained on the pickle jar.

"Did all your friends go home for the break?" By "friends," I knew she was referring to Ben. Now that she had started on the topic, I figured it was a good time to cross the bridge to Minnesota.

"Some of them did; some didn't." I paused gathering my thoughts and what was left of my dwindling courage.

"What is it you want to talk to me about?" she asked.

I snapped my head up and looked at her with what I assumed was an expression of shock. I began to wonder if Mom actually did have a phone line into our brains. I knew it was impossible, but my convictions had started to falter with her uncanny ability to be two steps ahead of us. Mind-reading seemed to be the only viable explanation.

"Okay, Mom, don't say no until you hear me out," I said with less confidence than I'd wanted.

"Hmm, that doesn't sound good," she said never taking her eyes off the frying pan.

"Ben went home for the holiday break." I stopped, waiting to see if a spatula was going to fly across the room at the mention of his name. When one didn't come, I continued. "He wants me to go to Minnesota to meet his family. He's been telling them about me for the past three months and they would like to meet me."

"And?" she said, turning to look at me. The venom hung on the edge of her response and I used it to propel me forward.

"And...I want to go." I stood my ground, my gaze as stubborn as hers.

"You want me to tell you it's okay to go stay with your boyfriend, in another state, so you can meet his family? Have you lost your mind?"

Her voice had risen a few octaves, causing Dad to come wandering into the kitchen to see what the commotion was about.

"No, Mom, I'm not asking you to let me go to Minnesota to stay with my boyfriend for the weekend," I said, rolling my eyes in disdain. "Sandra is also going and we're planning on staying in a hotel nearby, together. Anyway, it's not like I need to fly across the country to spend time alone with him. I live down the street. You're being ridiculous."

As soon as the words left my mouth, I immediately regretted them. I had just called Mom ridiculous. She turned on me, with the feral look of an animal about to claw her way through a pack of wolves. I physically cowered, taking a step back. Dad jumped in to keep the situation from getting further heated.

"What about Thanksgiving? You wouldn't be spending it with the family?" Dad asked, his hand on Mom's shoulder, trying to calm her. It didn't work.

"No, I would. I was going to fly out on Friday."

"I don't understand why you insist on continuing this nonsense with this boy!" she screamed at me.

"Nonsense? I don't know what I have to do for you to realize this isn't some childish crush. I know you think I shouldn't be with Ben, but you have no valid reasons for it," I replied as calmly as the moment would allow me to.

"He's not Persian. What more of a reason do you need?" she said, as if it were obvious.

As the weight of Mom's words sank in, I felt like I had suddenly woken up. I began to realize that the world was riddled by prejudices, deep-rooted in culture and tradition. They'd become so woven into the intricacies of people's upbringing that they had faded into the background, no longer seen but ever present. My family was no exception.

"That's not a good enough reason! He's a great guy, but you wouldn't know that because you're too busy holding onto your foolish ideas to see it." I yelled, unable to contain my anger any longer. Dad went to speak but I held my hand up to stop him. "Maziar's family judged me the same way you're judging Ben, and it wasn't fair. You agreed that it was wrong. Don't you see you're being the exact same way?"

"Sara, calm down," he said. "No one is being prejudiced. We can just see a future you can't and the difficulties you will face with Ben. We want what's best for you."

"I don't think so, Dad. You guys want me to stay in your pretty little box so no one thinks badly of you. Well, I'm sorry you can't see past yourselves. But this is my life, and I'm going to do what I want. You can stay the hypocrites you're being, or you can get over your hang-ups and get to know him. Either way, it doesn't change anything."

"So you're telling us you're going to Minnesota," Mom said, horrified.

"Yes, I believe I am," I said, as confidently as I could.

Mom was fuming, Dad was crumbling, and I just stared at them unwaveringly. The anger that fueled my determination came from further back than the moment we were standing in. It stood for all the times I was too weak to stand against Maziar's family. I held my ground, refusing to allow anyone to turn me into the broken bird I had once been, losing more than I deserved. That included my parents.

I knew they were paying for sins that weren't all theirs, but I didn't care. As far as I was concerned, they were being just as bad as Maziar's parents had been. He hadn't been able to choose me, but I was going to be stronger than him. I was going to choose Ben.

"I will stay for Thanksgiving so you can save face in front of the family. That drama wouldn't help any of us. But then I'm going to Minnesota."

Both my parents stared at me, draped in disbelief as I turned around and walked out of the room. Once I was in the safety of my bedroom, I grabbed my laptop and bought my ticket, not allowing myself time to regret my position.

By the time Dad came to my room, I was on my bed reading a book. He knocked softly before he opened the door. I looked up hesitantly, but he smiled in an attempt to make me less uneasy.

"Hi, Dad."

He sat down and squeezed my knee.

"So I talked to your mother. She really doesn't want you to go," he said.

"I know."

"You know, Sara, we really do love you and just want the best for you. I know it doesn't look that way right now, but it's the truth," he urged.

"Ben's a really good guy, Dad," I replied, trying to keep the desperation out of my voice. The weight of their disapproval lay heavy on my shoulders.

"He may be, but he's just not the right guy," he said.

"How do you know that? You don't even know him," I protested. I could feel the frustration building again.

"He just doesn't fit into our life, that's all."

"Ugh! You guys are such hypocrites. Why can't you see that?"

He didn't respond at first, the silence surrounding us like a heavy cloak. I knew I'd embarked on a road that could lead to losing my parents. Although the prospect terrified me, I was too stubborn to back down. He reached out and squeezed my knee again as he stood up. He looked at me. The pain from the space I was creating between us was visible in his eyes.

"We aren't Maziar's parents," he said, as he walked out the door.

Long after he left, I stared into space trying to calm the new sense of panic that had started taking over. Had I made the right choice? I was having a great time with Ben, and I loved him, but I didn't feel any certainty in our future. I didn't know if I could see happily ever after with him. Was it worth losing my parents over?

I honestly wasn't sure.

* * *

Thanksgiving came and went. Mom avoided me as much as possible without making it obvious to the family. My grandmother spent the better part of the night complaining that I had gotten too skinny, then chastised my mom for not cooking and freezing enough food for me to take back to my apartment when I visited. Mom proceeded to defend her maternal duties by placing the blame back on me, claiming it was because I didn't make regular visits home. This debate continued throughout the night. It was triggered every time I passed by my grandmother, as if my silhouette was reminding her that I'd been starving the past few months. I tried to avoid her. Even though I was angry with Mom, I didn't want her to have to deal with my grandmother's persistent nagging. I knew what it felt like to be judged.

When the night was over, I helped clean up in the silence she demanded. She wouldn't look at me, acting as if I didn't exist. I matched her attitude, walking around as if it didn't bother me, even though it did. Dad and Nima tried to navigate between us as peacefully as possible, staying neutral.

I had an early flight so I excused myself, retiring to the safety of my bedroom. I crawled into bed, beckoning sleep to save me from the anxiety of the day. When it finally came, I went willingly.

Morning came sooner than I'd expected, and I dragged myself out of bed in the dark hours before the world was awake. I looked at myself in the mirror, feeling despair at the swollen, sleep-deprived eyes staring back at me.

Nima had offered to take me to the airport, but when I came out of my room, dragging my small suitcase behind me, I saw Dad sitting on the couch drinking a freshly brewed cup of *chayee*. I could hear Mom's movements in the kitchen.

I was expecting Nima, so I was taken aback for a moment when Dad was there to greet me. He looked deep in thought until the shuffle of my feet broke him out of his revere. He smiled at me wearily.

"You ready to go?" he asked.

"Yes," I responded, "but I thought Nima was taking me."

"He was, but it was a late night and he was really tired. You know me; I get up early no matter what time I sleep, so I told him I would take you."

"Okay," I said, silently cursing my brother.

Making the drive alone with my dad, as he dropped me off at the airport to fly off to a rendezvous with my Caucasian boyfriend, seemed like the worst kind of torture humanly possible. Where Mom was all about denial, Dad was all about facing reality head-on.

Mom came out of the kitchen with tea in one hand and a feta cheese and pita sandwich in the other. Even though she was angry at me, she still made sure to feed me. No doubt she was partly worried that my weight would only be one more thing *mamanbozorg* would hold over her head once she'd found out about Ben. Mom had hoped things between us would fizzle and I'd have moved on by now. Since that didn't seem likely, it was inevitable that my grandmother would find out, and when that happened, all hell would break loose.

The scowl on her face scrunched her dark eyebrows together, giving her the appearance of a Frida Kahlo painting. She placed the food on the table, then turned and walked back into the kitchen, ignoring me. She wanted to leave little doubt of her disapproval of my decision. I had no energy to engage her, so I sat silently on the couch, finishing my breakfast as quickly as I could. I picked up the cups and put them in the kitchen when I was done. I didn't say goodbye as I followed Dad to the car.

My life had become a series of never-ending arguments with Mom, and I had become too weary to engage in them any further. She would continue to throw her tantrums, but I would try my best to brush them off. It was too exhausting to feel like a constant disappointment.

Dad and I sat in a humble silence for the first ten minutes, enjoying a rare moment of peace before he spoke.

"Sara, I know you're a grown woman. It may seem like your mother and I don't realize it, but that's just because we'll always look at you as our little girl regardless of how old you get." He sighed, staring out the window, the recent struggles taking their toll. "But even so, I know you're an adult and you make your own decisions. You're a smart girl; you always have been, so I don't worry about you too much. But because I'm your father, it's my job to tell you to be careful. Make the right choices, because sometimes you end up having to live with the wrong ones forever."

Was he talking about getting pregnant or was he just referring to my choice of boyfriend? It was too early in the morning to solve his riddles.

"Okay," was all I could think to say.

He reached out and patted my leg, content with my response.

I turned my head, staring at the scenery flashing across my window for the remainder of the drive while Dad listened to his news radio. He didn't say anything else regarding "choices" or my relationship. I was grateful for his silence.

* * *

I walked toward the airport terminal. Now that I was actually on my way to Minnetonka, the reality of its significance washed over me like a current. I was actually doing this. I was walking further away from one relationship and deeper into another. It felt like I was embarking on a weekend that was pushing me into a reality that I could no longer easily walk away from. Meeting Ben's parents somehow felt like it was solidifying our relationship, making it more real. I knew I acted sure about us when I fought with my parents, but truthfully, I wasn't as confident as I pretended to be.

When we were off the ground, the stewardess came down the aisles taking drink orders. To calm my nerves, I asked for a glass of wine and pulled out my e-reader. I had a direct flight, so I spent the next five-and-a-half hours drinking two glasses of wine, eating four packets of peanuts, and reading. I must have dozed off because the captain's voice startled me awake as he announced the plane's descent.

I stood in the cattle line to exit the airplane with my heart pounding wildly against my chest. I was feeling a mixture of dread and excitement, a combination that frequently left me utterly confused in its wake. I wanted badly to see Ben, but I was terrified of the significance this weekend held. I tried desperately to clear my thoughts of the fear, to push Maziar and my parents as far back in my mind as possible.

Moving forward in my relationship with Ben meant I was moving further away from Maziar. I was truly tired of the constant emotional battle wreaking havoc on my heart. I didn't know why I couldn't just let him go. It made me feel stupid and weak, and I hated it.

Then I had my parents. For the first time in my life, I'd blatantly refused to listen to them, choosing to make a decision they were clearly against. I didn't know how we'd find our way back from here. I was on untouched ground, and I found it terrifying.

As I was stuck in thought, I didn't realize I'd walked out into the terminal. I heard my name and was snapped back into reality. I looked up to find Ben ten feet in front of me, smiling brightly.

It was cold in Minnesota, somewhere in the high twenties, much colder than my California skin was used to. Ben was dressed in a pair of loose, dark blue jeans and a green puffer jacket. It gave his normally crystal-blue eyes an aqua tint, reminding me of my favorite crayon in the Crayola box. His dark brown beanie sat snug on his head, the ends of his hair curling out from underneath.

In moments like these, I was hit with the magnitude of my attraction to him, and he just took my breath away. The anxieties of the morning melted into nonexistence in those few seconds of uninterrupted eye contact. We were locked in an unspoken conversation, becoming unaware of the crowd around us as he gave me his crooked smile. My heart was still frantically beating against my chest, but this time with the anticipation of spending the next few days with him.

I stood there locked in our trance for a few more seconds as my own smile broke across my face. Then, I ran to him, launching myself into his arms. He caught me with ease, holding me close to his body. I breathed in his scent of soap and deodorant, letting them fill me up as I became drunk on him.

Lost in his embrace, I didn't realize that Sandra and Josh had come up behind us. I heard Sandra squeal my name, and Ben pulled back to allow her in. I reluctantly let go, wanting just a few more minutes to get my fix. I could feel the beginning tickles of an addiction take form, and I welcomed it, needing a new drug to get hooked on.

Sandra threw her arms around me, all smiles and giggles, and I could feel the happiness exuding off of her from just from being near Josh. They orbited around each other like planets to the sun, caught in the pull of gravity toward one another. There was no doubt that they were made for each other. Just looking at them, I could hear the distant sound of wedding bells and see their white picket fence, two kids, and a dog.

What I had told my parents regarding the weekend was mostly true. Sandra was coming to Minnesota to visit Josh and meet his family. However, Josh had his own place and Sandra would be staying with him. There was a hotel room at the inn registered under my name, but I would be staying there alone. I figured seventy-five percent of the truth was good enough to share with them. Ben and I spent most nights in one of our two beds anyway, so I didn't really see it being any different if we spent a few nights together in another state.

Ben led us outside, and as the automatic double doors opened, I was hit with the fierce cold wind of the world around us, sending goosebumps all over my skin. I stumbled, not expecting it to be so frigid. The iciness of the wind made the tip of my nose feel like it was solidifying into icicles. I had to stop for a moment to gather my bearings.

Ben looked at me and laughed. "You'll get used to it," he said.

The cold was already freezing my hands and causing an ache to roll through my fingers like only the chill of a real fall could do. It was actually painful, more so than I would have imagined it could be. My thin sweater and equally useless scarf weren't doing the trick and I began to rethink my weekend wardrobe.

It was close to lunchtime when we left the airport, and I was starving. We pulled into a quaint little diner about twenty minutes later. It had a worn-in vibe that could only be found in a small town where the locals frequented the same places. Its brown and beige booths lined the walls, their leather dulled and less vibrant than I'd imagine they were in its heyday. The kitchen was nestled behind an old-fashioned bar with round leather stools. I imagined teenagers drinking malts while leaning up against it, socializing after school. The whole place looked like it belonged in a movie.

The boys took a booth to the right and Sandra and I slid in next to them. The waitress appeared moments later to take our order. She was an older woman, probably in her mid-fifties, with short blond hair that swept across her shoulders. She had light blue eyes, the color of a pale ocean, and dimples when she smiled. The name on her tag read Kelly.

"How are your parents, boys?" she asked immediately.

"They're good, Mrs. Wyatt," Ben replied politely.

"How are Jess and James?" Josh asked.

"They're great. James is home for the holidays, but Jess wasn't able to come. She has an internship that she had to stay for. But she'll be here for Christmas," she said while looking at Ben.

He smiled nervously at her. The entire exchange felt odd but I couldn't pinpoint why.

Then, she asked for our orders and left. I turned toward Ben in confusion.

"Jess and James are twins; they went to high school with us. James is at Harvard Law School now, and Jess goes to John Hopkins for medical school," he said.

"Jess is Ben's ex-girlfriend," Josh added, earning a glare from Ben.

It suddenly made sense. Ben had told me about Jessie. She was his first everything. His first love, first time, and his first heartbreak. After high school, they'd decided a long-distance relationship was unrealistic, so they ended things despite being in love.

This seemed to be the sad truth about life. We created moments with people who became our world, every breath hanging on their existence, every heartbeat singing their name. Until one day, the world shifted beneath us, and we got lost within its consequences, destined to be just two humans living life simultaneously, becoming nothing more than a distant memory of the meaning we used to have for each other.

Ben didn't harp long on his past with Jessie, being that he'd just picked up his current girlfriend from the airport. But I could see a remote longing when he spoke her name. I would be hypocritical if I judged him for it, so I didn't. Maziar was an ever present energy, wrapping his tentacles around every corner of my life. I was in no position to be angered by a subtle moment of desire that crossed Ben's eyes when he spoke of his ex.

An hour later we were heading to the hotel. I was staying at a small inn five minutes from Ben's house. He had parked his car at the hotel that morning before picking me up from the airport, so he would have a way to get home once Josh dropped us off. I was supposed to be at his house in a few hours for the big girlfriend reveal party.

"I'm going to head home. I'll be back at five to pick you up," he said kissing my forehead. "You should take a nap."

He leaned down and gently placed his lips against mine, our kiss moving like the waves of the ocean, calm and quiet at first, then stronger and more determined. I wrapped my arms around his neck, pulling his body closer to mine. His hands ran up the back of my shirt, his fingers sending chills throughout my body.

The world seemed to shift and something in me awakened. A desire I hadn't felt in forever burned to life. Maybe it was that I was miles away from home where my past didn't exist, or maybe it was that I'd missed him the past week, but either way, I wanted more. But before I could urge us further, he pulled away, disconnecting his body from mine. I was left disappointed and malnourished.

I looked up at him, confused. He laughed at me when I puckered my lips into a frown.

"Oh, don't do that. You're tired and need to get some rest. Tonight is a big deal and I need you awake. I'm about to walk you into a circus. I need you to be ready," he said, still smiling.

"Boo. You're such a party pooper. I can think of other ways to relieve myself of some stress." I giggled as I ran my fingers up his chest.

He pulled me back in again and placed his chin on my head. He held me close. I could feel the rhythm of his heartbeat against my chest. It was like a calming lullaby.

"You know I want nothing more than to be with you. But there is plenty of time for that. Right now I need you to rest," he ordered gently.

The melodic tone of his voice was reminding me of how sleepy I actually was. I conceded to putting our escapade on hold and let him say goodbye. I closed the door behind him and leaned against it for a moment. Up until now, thoughts of sex with Ben were fleeting and terrifying. I always felt uncertain, not allowing me to take that next step with him. Just a few moments ago, though, it was different.

I knew before I made this trip to Minnesota that we were at a crossroads. We would either take the next step in our relationship or it would just be left to wither and disintegrate into nothing. I hadn't been sure what direction I'd wanted it to go when I boarded the plane this morning. Now I did.

It felt strangely freeing to allow myself the simple pleasure of moving forward with Ben. I might not have broken all the bonds that bound me to Maziar, but at that moment, I realized I had broken at least one.

CHAPTER TWENTY

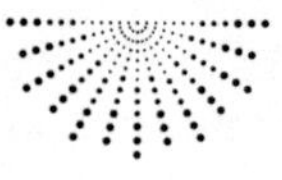

When Ben showed up at five, I was still running around in circles trying to get ready. I was nervous about meeting his family and wanted desperately for them to like me. I couldn't choose an outfit, unhappy with everything I'd packed. I was having a fullblown girlie breakdown when he knocked on the door. I opened it and immediately placed my head on his chest.

"What's wrong?" he asked, concerned.

"I look like crap. That's what's wrong," I pouted.

"Are you kidding me? You look gorgeous. Besides, my family is very laid-back. They won't care what you're wearing," he said reassuringly. "Just grab your bag so we can go."

It was freezing outside. I felt awkward in my black leggings, afraid I looked like an idiot who was inappropriately dressed for the weather. I pulled my burgundy jacket in tighter, wrapping my big cheetah scarf closer to my neck against the frigid air. My Middle Eastern hair had decided to choose this moment to rebel against the cold, damp weather of the city, falling down my back in frizzy waves. I felt very self-conscious.

Ben was still in the same jeans but now had on a white button-up shirt with a gray knitted cardigan over it. He'd replaced the brown beanie with a gray one, making his eyes appear more gray than blue. He always looked like he'd walked off a magazine cover. With my insecurities in overdrive, I was stuck between the desire to rip off his clothing and the furious need to beat him to death.

The drive to his house was only five minutes, much shorter than I needed to get my nerves under control. I unsuccessfully tried to calm my shaking hands, breathing slowly against the furious beating of my heart. I was so traumatized from meeting Maziar's family that I was terrified of experiencing another disapproval. Even though I knew Ben's family had none of the prejudices of Maziar's, I still couldn't help but be scared that history would somehow repeat itself.

We pulled up to his house and he turned off the ignition. My hand shot out and grabbed his arm before he could open the door.

"I'm not ready yet. I need a minute," I pleaded.

He must have seen the fear in my eyes because he put my hand in his and said, "Okay, you tell me when you're ready to get out." Then, he turned and faced the windshield, giving me privacy with my emotions.

Ben's house was beautiful. It was one of six houses that sat along a roundabout in a circle facing one another. Each house had a large wide lawn with a walkway leading from the driveway to the front door. His was light gray with dark gray tiles on the roof, the windows bordered by white shutters. There was intricate stonework adorning the walkway. The front door was a beautiful dark mahogany color, accented against the grays. It was the kind of house you wanted to raise a family in.

Knowing I couldn't hide forever, I turned toward Ben, squeezing his hand.

"I'm ready," I muttered nervously.

"Okay" he said, a smile stretched across his face.

There were no lines of disapproval around his eyes. No deep grooves of frustration at the edges of his lips. He was letting me take my time. I knew deep down that I really didn't deserve him. For all of his determination and stability, I was filled with anxiety and confusion. Where he was wholeheartedly sure of us, I still questioned our relationship, or more so myself in it.

I knew I loved him. I just wasn't sure if it was the all-consuming, make-you-crazy sort of love. Maybe love could come in different forms, and I had experienced the whirlwind kind of love with Maziar but was now experiencing the calm, cool kind of love with Ben. On the other hand, maybe I wasn't in love with him the way I should be. I continuously tried to gauge my feelings for him. What I needed to do was stop questioning and comparing. The past only seemed to clutter my judgment.

Ben walked around the car and opened my door like the gentleman that he was, breaking me out of my thoughts. He held my hand as he led me into the house. We stepped down onto a foyer of dark brown travertine. To the right was a formal living room and dining area. The living room had a beautiful cathedral ceiling, lined with dark wood beams housing a large chandelier made of wrought iron with pillar candles. To the left was a winding staircase that led to the second floor.

We moved farther into the house down a hall. The wall suddenly opened up to a large set of windows that let in a rush of natural light, giving the area a celestial glow. A large deck was outside, overlooking the tall trees, all turning the immaculate oranges and reds of the season, and a small lake that bordered the backyard of the houses. I could clearly imagine nights around the fire pit when Ben was little, hot chocolate in one hand and laughter filling the air.

As we walked into the kitchen, I could hear his family talking. They turned and looked at us, barely skipping a beat before launching into greetings. No one stared at me coldly or seemed to be judging me. On the contrary, they were all welcoming. Ben introduced me to his mother, June, and his stepfather, Frank. June reached out and threw her arms around me, squeezing me tightly.

"I'm so happy to finally meet you," she said. "Ben's told me so much about you." Her tone was kind and motherly. I couldn't help but smile with relief against her shoulder.

Ben introduced me to his older brother, Jeff, and his wife, Kate. They had two little boys, Nathan and Zachary, neither concerned with me in the least. They immediately launched themselves at Ben, climbing up his body like a jungle gym as he swung them around, dropping them onto the couch in a fit of giggles.

Ben's youngest brother Michael was there with his girlfriend, Jenny. They approached me simultaneously, their movements almost synchronized when they reached out to grab my hand. They were high school sweethearts. Although they were two years younger than us, they'd lived together since they'd graduated. I found it interesting that, despite Michael's age, his parents clearly treated him like an adult while mine still treated me like a child. I couldn't imagine June trying to tell any of her children how to live their lives. I was envious.

Within minutes of my arrival we were sitting around the kitchen island, drinking wine and munching on the elaborate spread June had placed before us. They asked me questions about my family, and I replied honestly, never feeling the pressure that was so common when meeting an Iranian family. I wasn't afraid I would answer incorrectly, making me less desirable in their eyes.

I could feel the ease with which Ben integrated into his surroundings. He was just as much a part of their tight unit as the rest of them were, despite the geographical distance. They moved in an unfamiliar harmony, almost as if they were all riding on the same wave. I found it fascinating.

When it was time for dinner, I got up and helped June set the table as my upbringing demanded. It was decorated with festive china, browns and oranges spread across the table, circling a centerpiece of red and yellow flowers. Everyone helped, the women carrying the food while the men refilled the alcohol.

June had made a second Thanksgiving meal. There was turkey with cranberry sauce, mashed potatoes, gravy, green beans, stuffing, and homemade biscuits. It was the epitome of what Thanksgiving should look like.

In our home, we had a meal that was a hybrid between the traditional holiday foods and Iranian dishes. We'd have the turkey and cranberry sauce, but there would also be rice and Persian stews. The sides depended on the younger generation, divvied up between the cousins. None of us had the cooking skills of June. Our renditions sadly paled by comparison. Now that I had experienced what a real

Thanksgiving meal tasted like, I was ruined forever. I made sure to tell her, making her blush with the compliment.

Once the meal was over, everyone else helped clean up while Frank tended to the fire pit. When I walked out onto the deck, the sky was filled to the brim with stars. It reminded me of a jar full of fireflies. Not that I'd ever seen a jar full of fireflies, being that I was a native of California. Nonetheless, it was how I imagined it to be.

June brought each of us a plate piled high with pie and whipped cream. I was rapidly approaching a food coma, definitely gaining weight from this meal alone. If I were back home, I'd have declined. All the women would watch disapprovingly at the consumption of such unnecessary calories. It was a constant topic of conversation in my family. Pointing out those who had "let themselves go" while trying to figure out the secret behind those who had "lost so much weight."

We all nestled down around the fire, desserts in hand, talking well into the night. Before I knew it, it was midnight. The little ones had already fallen asleep on the couch while watching a movie. Kate tapped Jeff's leg, telling him it was time to go, setting off the chain reaction of goodbyes to follow.

"Did you have a good time tonight? My family wasn't too overbearing or anything, were they?" Ben asked on the drive back to the hotel.

"No, not at all. I loved them. It was great. They're really fantastic, Ben," I said, squeezing his hand.

"I'm glad," he said, with a childlike grin stretched across his face. "I know they loved you, too."

A few minutes later, I stood at the hotel room door rummaging through my bag for the card key. I wasn't sure if he was staying the night and was afraid to ask. He stood just inches away from me, his breath tickling the back of my neck, making it difficult to focus on the task at hand. His fingers were resting on my hip and he began to gently rub them in a circular motion. A wave of desire rushed through me, its heat radiating the entire length of me. I opened the door, flustered as I stepped inside. He followed me in.

I placed my bag down on the table and turned to face him. He was putting his keys and wallet on the nightstand. I came up behind him, gently touching his shoulder. I felt him stiffen beneath my fingers. I ran my hand lightly down his back, softly nudging him to turn around. He looked at me apprehensively. Never taking my eyes off of him, I slowly shook off his cardigan, then pulled his shirt over his head, letting each article of clothing fall where it landed.

I ran my fingertips over the definition of his anatomy, tracing the outlines of his muscles. I heard his breath catch in his throat, could see the goosebumps spread over his flesh. I placed my mouth on his chest and painted a trail of kisses up to his neck, where I lingered. He exhaled as I made my way to his mouth. I started to kiss him, nibbling on his lower lip teasingly. When I looked up at him again, I could see fire burning in his eyes. I could feel his restraint bending, like an animal wanting to be uncaged. It ignited my desires further.

He grabbed the belt of my jacket and slowly undid the tie. His fingers grazed my shoulders as he pushed it off my body, allowing it to fall to the floor. Then, he slipped his hand under my shirt and in one fluid movement pulled it over my head. He playfully ran his fingertips across my bra, teasing my nipples with his thumb. A low moan of pleasure escaped through my lips, encouraging him forward.

He began kissing me, first my lips, then my neck and collarbone. He'd unfastened my bra and now it was lying on the pile of clothing we'd created on the floor beside us. His hands cupped my breast and when he touched me, I shuddered. I could hardly breathe.

We stood together, naked and vulnerable in the dim glow of the lights shining through the window. He looked at me questioningly, watching my face for any hints that he should stop. He let his hand linger on my waist as if he wasn't sure how to proceed. I closed the distance between us, pushing my body up against his. He lifted me up as if I were a rag doll and took me over to the bed. I wrapped my legs around him, feeling his arousal hard against my thigh. He gently lay me down, lowering his body on top of mine.

"Are you sure you want to do this?" he asked, his words heavy with wanting.

"I do," I said as I wrapped my arms around his neck, pulling him closer.

"I don't want you to do it because you think I want you to."

"Shhh," I mumbled as I put my lips on his.

Our bodies instantly aligned, our movements natural and familiar as if we were the harmony in a line of music. With his lips and hands, he began to slowly put my broken pieces back together, making me whole again. Under his guidance, I found parts of me I had thought I'd lost forever. I felt as if I were flying as he gently took me to the point of despair. When I thought our bodies couldn't take much more, we shattered together onto the bed, surrounded by the intoxication of making love. We fell asleep in a tangle of limbs and sweat in the exhaustion that followed. As I balanced on the edge of sleep, I could've sworn I heard him whisper that he loved me.

Lying beside him, I realized that love was a kind of faith, a belief in the person you were with and the person you were when you were with them. I didn't know where things would go, but what I did know was that I believed in Ben.

CHAPTER TWENTY-ONE

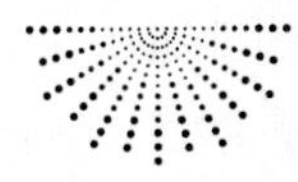

In the weeks that followed Minnesota, a pleasant aura surrounded my relationship with Ben. The emotions readily passed between us and a sense of comfort cocooned us. We moved in sync, complementing each other as opposed to the push-and-pull visible before.

There was already talk between us of my heading to Minnesota for another visit with Ben's family during the winter break. I hadn't discussed it with my parents yet, but I'd cross that bridge when it became necessary.

Exams turned into a whirlwind of late nights, sleep deprivation, coffee, and protein bars as we crammed as much information into our brains as humanly possible. Our group linked arms in strength, encouraging and pushing each other to keep moving forward day after day. The two weeks seemed endless, one day blurring into the next. By the time we reached our last exam, no one could remember when they'd had a full night's sleep or a warm meal. When it was finally over, Ben and I dragged ourselves to his apartment. We collapsed onto his bed and were asleep before our heads touched the pillows.

When I awoke, the sun had already set, draping the room in darkness. I could tell Ben was still asleep by the heaviness of his breathing. I turned over and grabbed my phone. It was seven in the evening. I was hungry, but my body still craved sleep, so I cuddled up against his side again and closed my eyes. I fell back into a peaceful slumber.

The next time I woke up, it was six in the morning and Ben was gone. I lay there for a few minutes admiring the streaks of light shining through the window shades, throwing wing-like patterns onto the comforter. I felt like I was surrounded by a sea of butterflies.

I finally rolled out of bed and made my way to the kitchen where I could hear the subtle clatter of pots and pans. It was still very early in the morning and the world had yet to fully awake. The apartment was lit with a blue glow from the sun's ascent into the sky. I stood in the hallway, admiring Ben's silhouette in the kitchen. He appeared to be making breakfast.

I cleared my throat to signal my arrival and he turned around. He stood there shirtless, with only his sweats on. They hung low on his hips and I could see the indentation of the muscles there. I walked up to him, wearing only his T-shirt, and wrapped my arms around his waist. I placed my head on his chest and listened to the rhythmic thumping of his heart against my ear.

"Good morning," I said, smiling against him.

"Good morning, doll. Sleep well?" he asked.

"I love when you call me that."

"I know." He smiled. "You hungry?"

"I'm starving," I replied, suddenly aware of the grumbling in my stomach.

"Okay, sit. I'm making us breakfast. There's fresh coffee in the pot," he said, pointing toward the counter with his wooden spoon.

I poured myself a cup, inhaling the warm aroma of coffee beans, and hopped up onto the counter, not wanting to make the short distance to the table. From this vantage point I could enjoy my coffee and the fantastic view. Ben finished making us his feast and we shuffled over to the table to eat.

"What kind of wedding would you want?" he asked suddenly, as he took a bite of his eggs. His nonchalant demeanor made me uneasy, the question catching me off guard.

"What do you mean?" I stuttered, syrup dripping off the bite of pancake I held midway to my mouth.

"I mean would you want a traditional Muslim wedding, or, like, a nondenominational one?" he said.

It was a valid question but I hadn't thought that far into our future, which I realized was odd since I was now on relationship number two with a non-Muslim man. Equally strange was the fact that I'd never discussed this with Maziar either, and marriage had felt definite with him.

"I think I'd want the traditional," I said after a few moments. "I mean, I'm not religious, but it feels more cultural to me. Plus, my mom's been planning my wedding since I was born. I don't want to take that away from her."

"I think my mom would want a church wedding too," he added, thoughtfully.

"Nobody said we couldn't have both."

"Would your parents be cool with that, though?"

I thought about what he was asking, and the truth was, I wasn't sure what they'd be okay with. But either way, in the end the decision was mine. They'd just have to deal with it.

"I guess they'd have to be," I said.

"Okay," he replied. Then, he leaned over the table and kissed me.

A few hours later, Sandra called to tell us we were going to the Sky Bar on Sunset Boulevard.

* * *

The venue was outside, located around the pool of the Mondrian hotel. The far wall surrounding the area was made up of repeated wall-sized windows, each providing a private nook with a spectacular view of the city lights. We set ourselves up in an unoccupied section.

Ben bought our first round of drinks, handing each of us a vodka tonic. I took a sip and leaned back on the pillows, indulging at the end of another long term. The boys pulled up chairs, and we planted ourselves for the next few hours. We were all warm and fuzzy, wrapped up in conversation, when the world tilted on its axis once again.

I was sipping on my third vodka tonic, laughing at Thomas' story, when I randomly glanced up at the entrance. Walking in at that very moment was Neda. I froze, drink halfway to my lips, staring. I couldn't breathe for fear of who would be following in behind her.

The color must have drained from my face because Ben reached out and asked, "Are you okay? Are you feeling sick?"

I couldn't speak as I continued to watch in horror. Azi and Emanuel appeared on her tail. And then, within the span of a heartbeat, there was him.

Maziar.

He wasn't looking in our direction but Neda was scanning the crowd. She saw us and a broad smile stretched across her face. She had the blurry look of drunkenness dancing in her eyes, and I realized she had lost all common sense as she headed straight for us. I immediately looked at Ben, hoping he could see the apology in my eyes before our world exploded

Neda made it to us within seconds. Azi followed quickly behind her, the boys taking up the rear. Neda squealed as she launched herself into my arms. I stood there shocked, paralyzed from the rush of fear coursing through my veins. Azi was staring at me with worried eyes. She had played out the scenario in her mind as well, and was now ready to attempt damage control.

Maziar stood with his hands in his pockets, head tilted slightly to the left, a smile playing at the corner of his lips. He was staring at me with the intensity that only Maziar possessed, completely oblivious to everyone watching us. I felt naked and exposed.

My heart had stopped beating and I'd stopped breathing. Words that had been left unsaid for months threatened to find their way to my lips. The memories of goodbye came rushing back to me and I had to look away, no longer being able to engage in our silent conversation.

Ben coolly stared at Maziar, but I could see his hatred in the tightening of his muscles and the fists by his sides. He had witnessed our wordless exchange and I wondered if some of that hatred wasn't for me as well. I wanted to reach out for him, but Neda was still wrapped around me like an octopus. Ben looked toward me, almost disgusted, then grabbed his drink and left. Thomas followed, his expression mimicking the worry I felt in my bones.

Once Neda detached herself, Azi stepped up and hugged me.

"It's been too long, my friend," she said.

"I know," I replied.

"I've missed you."

"Me too."

"I'm sorry," she whispered into my ear, too quiet for anyone else to hear.

She pulled back and our eyes locked in understanding. Emanuel said hello and gave me a quick hug, his discomfort oozing off his body. He, like the rest of us, wasn't sure how to proceed.

Suddenly, as if the world had split in two, Maziar stood before me. Our surroundings quieted, fading into silence. Everything felt like it was moving in slow motion. I could see nothing else but him. I knew I should turn away, break the connection, and put distance between us, but I couldn't. I was rooted to the ground, cemented in the moment. Maziar was my kryptonite and I wasn't strong enough to withstand him.

He took a few steps closer until we were inches apart. I sucked in my breath, becoming intoxicated on his proximity.

At some point Sandra had moved in next to me. She squeezed my arm in a feeble effort to snap me back to my senses. It didn't work. I couldn't even breathe, let alone think about the consequences that were inevitable to follow. All I could do was focus on not collapsing beneath the avalanche of emotions burying me. Maziar hadn't broken his eye contact, hadn't taken a second to acknowledge the people around us. He was intently set on me, like an animal circling his prey.

"Hi," he said calmly.

I hadn't heard his voice for almost a year; I had forgotten the way it pulled at my heart like the loveliest of melodies. His simple hello felt like a knife cutting through my chest, leaving me for dead yet again.

"Hi," I replied shakily.

"It's really good to see you, Sara."

I just looked at him, trying to comprehend what was happening. Everything about his demeanor and the way he spoke signaled that nothing had changed, even though it had. I felt confused as he took another step in, muddling my thoughts further. His lips were inches away from me now as he completely disregarded our audience.

"I really miss you," he said, quiet enough for only me to hear.

I suddenly felt like I'd been kicked in the gut. He reached out and grabbed my hand, his fingers snapping me out of my trance. I yanked it away, offended at his presumption. I couldn't do this; I couldn't let him manipulate me again.

He stood startled as I eyed him angrily. How dare he expect it to be that easy? As if I'd been waiting around for him to realize he'd made a mistake. Did he think all he needed to do was tell me he missed me and I'd be putty in his hands? I would not be that stupid girl again. I would not be taken back into the depths of hell that easily.

"Don't," I snapped.

I pulled free from Sandra and stepped around him. I needed to leave, to get out of his space. It was threatening to drown me.

Neda was standing behind him and grabbed my arm. I loved her, but at that moment I didn't have anything to say to her. She should have ignored me, should have taken them all to the opposite side of the club. She should have left me in the happy little life I'd built around myself. Instead, she'd wrapped a bomb around my waist and detonated it, bringing my reality down around me in a pile of waste and rubble. I pulled away from her as well.

I was trying to find a path away from them all. Suddenly the crowd thinned and standing directly in front of me was Ben. My beautiful Ben. The angel who had rescued me and helped me find myself again. The lovely soul I had now crushed for the hundredth time.

He'd seen the entire exchange, had seen Maziar mere inches away from my face, sensed my heart stop as the world faded around me. He'd seen my feelings for a man I had long ago promised I'd forgotten. This man who loved me stood there angry and broken.

I reached out for him, the desperation of what was happening clawing me from the inside out. He turned and pulled away, making his way to the exit. I hurried behind him, terrified he was leaving me. He was at the door before I was close enough to grab his arm.

"Don't," he said, anger blazing in his eyes.

"Please," I whispered, my last desperate plea.

"I can't do this anymore, Sara. I have to get out of here. Can you make your way back with Sandra?" he asked.

I stood baffled that even now, when I was the cause of his imminent demise, he was still concerned about me. I just nodded. I could see how badly I'd disappointed him, but before I could try to explain, he turned and walked away.

I watched him go, knowing that this was the beginning of the end.

I walked back to where my friends sat, all stunned from what had just happened. I was relieved that Maziar was nowhere in sight. I was too deflated to deal with him. I grabbed my things.

"Sandra, I need to go."

"Okay," she replied, hurriedly grabbing her stuff.

"Bye," I said to everyone and no one in particular. My friends were too shaken to reply, and I was too devoid of the energy necessary to reassure them.

Halfway to the exit, I heard the familiar melody sing my name again, stopping me in my tracks. I wanted to run, to head for the doors and never look back, but I couldn't. There was a part of me that longed to be near him, to smell that familiar scent of his cologne, to feel the heat of his body wrap itself around me. I slowly turned.

"Sara," he said, unable to keep the pleading out of his voice.

"What is it, Maziar?"

"Please don't leave. I need to talk to you," he stammered.

"Why? What do you need to say to me? And why tonight?" I asked.

"I'm sorry. For so many things. I don't know why it's taken me this long. But please let me talk to you," he said, his words weighing down the air around us, wrapping us in its darkness.

I stood there feeling as if I'd left my body, now perched on the ceiling, watching the scene unfolding below. Here I was, standing in front of Maziar for the first time in what felt like an eternity. He was begging me to hear what he had to say. I'd dreamed of this moment so many times, had played this scene out in my head over and over again. It was finally here, and it was devastating. I didn't feel the happiness I'd thought I would. Instead, I felt tired, so weary I could barely stand. And I felt sad, so very, very sad, that this was what we'd become.

I realized it didn't matter what he wanted to tell me. There was nothing left for us but a bunch of memories and wasted time. He had hurt me, breaking the most intricate parts of who I was. Now, I had broken Ben, an innocent bystander in this ridiculous struggle. I didn't have any energy left to deal with the story of us. It had ended a year ago. It was time I put it into the ground, mourned, and moved on.

"I can't do this, Maziar," I said. "I just can't. I'm sorry."

I turned and Sandra grabbed my hand. She got us a taxi and opened the door so I could slide inside. She followed, closing it behind her. I gave myself the luxury of one more glance toward the man who had broken my heart so long ago.

The man I was now leaving behind.

* * *

I stepped in front of Ben's door and stood there, frozen. I knew he wouldn't want to see me, but the idea of waiting until morning to have the inevitable conversation was killing me. He would be flying to Minnesota and I couldn't bear it if he left with everything unresolved. I had no idea what I was going to say to him, how I was going to make things right, but I needed to try. I was moving forward on pure survival, my primal instincts in full force. The tangled web I'd created around myself was strangling me in the silence of those I had lost tonight.

I reached out and knocked on the door. It was close to one in the morning and I had no idea if he was even awake. He hadn't responded to any of my texts. I waited for what felt like a lifetime before hearing the shuffle of feet down the hall. He opened the door and stood there staring at me with a blank expression that only showed how exhausted he was from dealing with this situation. Neither of us spoke. After a moment he stepped aside and let me in.

Ben walked over to the living room and sat down on the couch. Sitting in front of him was a bottle of scotch and a glass, half the contents of the bottle already missing. He reached out for the cup, staring at me coolly as he took a sip. I sat across from him wracking my brain for something to say.

"I'm sorry," I finally offered.

"I know," he replied, his eyes filled with disappointment.

Too overwhelmed to contain my emotions, I began to cry. For the first time since I had known Ben, he didn't get up to console me. He just sat there watching me. He took another sip, averting his eyes to the floor in disinterest. I began to panic.

"What happens now?"

"I don't know, doll," he said plainly, still watching me cry.

"Do you want to break up? Are we over?" I asked, once I was able to speak again.

He sat there working on his drink, thinking. It felt like an eternity before he spoke.

"I don't know what I want right now, to be honest. I saw how you looked at him tonight. Can you really tell me that you feel nothing for Maziar? That you truly belong to me?"

I wanted to say I was over Maziar, to say I was all in, but I'd be lying. Besides, Ben already knew the answer. Instead, I said nothing.

"I think I should take the next few weeks to think about what it is that I really want and what compromises I can actually live with. I think you should go home and do the same thing. We can't stay like this, Sara. I can't worry about running into Maziar all the time and what feelings you'll have when we do. It's too hard and I'm just too tired."

I wanted to kick and scream, tell him I wouldn't lose him, tell him I loved him and only him, but I couldn't. The reality was that I had no idea what I wanted anymore. I loved Ben, and I was overwhelmed with the fear of losing him. But at the same time, I knew I wasn't over Maziar. And, truthfully, I wasn't sure I ever would be. Ben didn't deserve to be second best, he deserved to be someone's one and only.

"Okay," I said, my response consumed by the bitter silence that followed.

Eventually I got up. I didn't know what I was supposed to do, but all I could think to do was leave. He got up with me and walked over to where I was standing.

I tried to memorize the blue of his eyes, the lines that outlined his face, the way his hair was spiked every which way. I reached out and touched his cheek, feeling the tenderness within him. He put his hand on top of mine and I couldn't stop the tears from silently falling. He reached out and wiped them away, still trying to save me. Then, he pulled me into him and held me close. I placed my head on his chest and let the rhythm of his heart quiet my storm. I breathed him in, holding on to his scent as a lifeline. I held him tighter, terrified of letting go.

"I really do love you, Ben. I don't know how we even got here," I whispered into his chest.

"I know. I love you too," he said, no longer able to hide behind the façade of his disinterest.

He leaned in and kissed me then–the gentlest kiss, filled with the mourning we were doing for the loss of each other. The intensity increased and I matched him with a fierceness of my own. My body pushed up against his, my hands running up his shirt, pulling him closer. I wanted to melt into him, to escape this Earth and become part of him. We tore at each other's clothes and, before we could blink, they were thrown in a pile on the floor. He kissed me fiercely, as if he was trying to survive. He lifted me up and I wrapped my legs around his waist. He took me into the bedroom and laid me on the bed. His tenderness returned as he looked down on me from the edge, as if he realized this could be the last time we would ever be together again.

He gently eased his body on top of mine and made love to me that night, the pain and sadness we both felt smothering every kiss, every touch, invading every moment. I feared I would break into a million pieces, melting away into the sheets, to be lost forever. Who knew what we would be in the morning, but in that moment all I knew was that I needed him.

I didn't linger in bed with him afterward. The longer I stayed, the more I would miss him later. I went to the living room and got dressed. He trailed behind me a few minutes later in his sweats. I turned to face him.

"Goodbye, Ben."

"Bye, Sara."

I left his apartment and walked the block to my house in slow motion. My mind was a muddled mess of thoughts swirling in all directions and I could hardly breathe past the fear in my chest. Sandra came rushing out of her room when she heard me open the door. I just looked at her and started to cry. I slid to the floor of our living room, fierce sobs vibrating off the walls. I could no longer hold the pain confined within the small space of my body. It wanted to be freed, to rush into every corner around me, claiming my life as its own.

Sandra sat on the floor with her arms around me and let me cry as she cried along with me. At some point in the night, when I no longer had tears to shed, or a voice to cry out with, she guided me to my bedroom. I was exhausted, too broken to do anything but sleep, gladly surrendering to its darkness when it came for me.

CHAPTER TWENTY-TWO

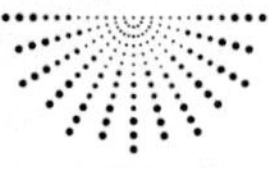

The next morning brought with it the familiar dread upon waking up. That stomach-knotting panic that reminded me what had happened the night before wasn't a dream. I was supposed to get up and get my things together so I could head home, but I could do nothing but lie there. I stared up at the light shining through my curtains, the butterfly swirls it threw all over my walls. I was reminded of the morning before when I lay in Ben's bed. Had it really just been twenty-four hours ago when my life felt so perfect?

I heard a soft knock on my door.

"Come in," I said.

"Hey, how are you doing? Feeling any better?" Sandra was looking at me with a mix of worry and sadness. I could even see pity. I hated that part the most. I couldn't stand the look everyone gave me every time my life fell apart. I knew they were just concerned, but it made me feel like some sort of failure.

"I'm fine," I said.

She could sense I wasn't in the mood to talk, so she left, closing the door gently behind her. I rolled over and grabbed my phone off the nightstand. Staring back at me were five missed text messages. One was from Nima, asking me what time I would be home. Then, there were four from Maziar.

I stared, stunned. His name looked foreign on my screen and I had to blink a few times to make sure I wasn't dreaming. With shaky hands I opened them up.

12:45 Sara, I need to talk to you. Can you please call me? I hate how things happened tonight.

12:55 Sara, I'm coming over. I have to see you.

1:20 I'm outside. Please come out. PLEASE.

1:45 Sara, don't hate me.

I bolted up in bed like I'd been struck by lightning. Maziar had come over to my house? What?

First off, how the hell did he know where I lived? I'd moved into my apartment long after our breakup. Neda. She must have given him my address. The way things had gone down, she wouldn't have tried to stand up to him if he demanded it from her. He was probably as angry with her as I was. The idea of Maziar being a psycho stalker didn't seem plausible.

That left the question: what was Maziar thinking? Why was he suddenly so adamant to talk to me? An entire year had passed and there had been nothing but crickets. Why now? I didn't understand where all this urgency was coming from.

I began to feel as if I were stuck in a tornado, everything flashing by so fast that I couldn't make anything out. I had four pleading text messages from my ex-boyfriend and none from my current boyfriend. Everything felt ridiculously backward.

All of a sudden my phone began to ring, flashing Maziar's picture on my screen. I held the phone for a half a second before throwing it across the bed like it had spontaneously burst into flames. I felt panic rise in my throat, as if I were going to be sick. I just stared at the phone, watching it ring in succession until the call went to voicemail.

The shock of it all had yet to fade and I couldn't make out a single thought spinning in my head. I was very confused.

A few seconds later, I heard the familiar ping of a message. He'd sent me another text.

8:30 Sara, I need to see you. Please. I will meet you anywhere...

I jumped out of bed and quickly packed my overnight bag. I had no time to get ready, so I pulled a sweatshirt over my head and bunched my hair in a bun as I ran out the door. I needed to get out of here. I needed to think. I needed to go home. I really didn't know what I needed. All I knew was that there was a chance that Maziar might come back and I wasn't ready to see him.

I came out of my room and startled Sandra. She dropped her bag with a little yelp.

"I'm sorry," I said, apologetically.

"Are you okay?" she asked.

"Yes...no...I don't know."

"Start spilling," she demanded, pulling out a chair and gesturing toward the one across from her. "I know you think you don't want to talk about it, but something is wrong. Keeping it to yourself isn't helping."

I felt like I had no idea what was actually going on, so how was I supposed to put it into words? But I knew Sandra was right. I could feel myself ready to explode into a million pieces if I didn't make sense of it soon.

I sat down and began retelling her the events of the night before with Ben.

"He didn't walk you home when it was that late at night?" she asked, appalled.

I started to laugh and she looked at me like I'd officially lost my mind.

"I just told you that I think Ben was saying that he's done with me, and even though he didn't officially break up with me, that seems to be where he's headed. He then followed it up with some great sex, which confused the hell out of me. And all you're worried about is that he didn't walk me home? That's kind of funny."

We both started laughing. It felt good to find humor in the depressing circumstances of the situation.

"Maziar has been texting me since last night," I blurted out. Sandra froze mid-chuckle. "He actually ended up outside our apartment, begging me to come out."

"He didn't!" she responded, as baffled as I felt.

"Yup, he did. He called me again this morning. He said he wants to see me."

"You talked to him?" she half-asked, half-shrieked.

"No. I let it go to voicemail. He texted me after I didn't pick up."

"Well, it was obvious that he still has feelings for you," she said thoughtfully. "Anyone watching could see it. And honestly, it was also obvious you had them back."

"Yeah, but I didn't do anything! I didn't know they would be there or that Maziar would decide that last night would be the night he wanted to talk to me," I countered in desperation. I hadn't caused this; fate had.

"All I'm saying is that I get why Ben's mad. I'd be pissed too."

Yes, I couldn't deny that something had happened between Maziar and me, but I didn't go looking for it. I wasn't seeking Maziar out or trying to have some heartfelt conversation with him. I understood why Ben was angry, but it wasn't as if he'd had no idea what Maziar had meant to me or how hard it was for me to get over him. He'd also decided to walk away and give Maziar an open opportunity to approach me. What he should have done was take my hand and walk us both away, getting me out of the inevitable mess that was sure to follow.

Sandra and I sat there for an hour, both our trips home on pause while we tried to hash out all the different scenarios regarding what Maziar wanted to talk about. Then, we discussed Ben and whether I should try to reach out to him or leave him alone, if no contact this morning was a really bad sign, and if I should be angry about how things went down last night at his apartment.

"Do you really want to know what I think?" she asked.

"Of course I do," I replied. I was tired, thoroughly exhausted from the drama that had become my life, and desperately in need of some guidance.

"I really think you should talk to Maziar. Ben told you to figure out what you wanted. You've been waiting for this opportunity since you guys broke up. And now it's here. I'm not saying get back together with him, and I'm not even saying stay with Ben, but you deserve some closure and I think this may be your chance to get it. You don't know what Maziar has to say. Maybe he just wants to say sorry. Maybe what he has to say will make it easier for you to finally walk away. I mean really walk away, Sara. You and Ben, or you and anyone for that matter, don't stand a chance with your feelings for Maziar still bottled up inside you."

I knew Sandra was right. I dreaded seeing Maziar again, afraid I wouldn't be able to be strong. What if he wanted to get back together? Nothing had changed since we'd broken up. His family hadn't magically become supportive of inter-religious marriages, they hadn't suddenly upped and moved away to another country where we wouldn't have their constant interference, and he hadn't decided to disown them and sever all ties. Nor had either of us converted. Maziar was still the Jew and Sara was still the Muslim. There was no new pathway forged that would allow us to survive this time. Which meant I would have to be strong enough to walk away from the idea of us once again. I didn't know if I could do that.

"You're going to be okay," Sandra said, hugging me. "Call me with any new updates on your soap opera," she teased as she headed out the door.

After she had left, I threw everything into my car and made the forty-five-minute drive home in silence, allowing myself time to separate my thoughts and make sense of what I was feeling. I desperately needed to talk to Dad. He'd have a rational approach on how to handle the Maziar situation.

When I opened the door to my house, I was hit with the familiar smells of home. Mom was in the kitchen cooking away, the aroma of food filling my nostrils with nostalgia. I stood there in the doorway, listening to her absentmindedly singing, and I felt a deep ache in my chest. We hadn't been the same since my trip to Minnesota, with a deep chasm created by my rebellion. Time had introduced a truce between us, but I could still feel her distance when she spoke to me. I missed her.

I made my way into the kitchen, lightly tapping on the door frame to avoid startling her. She turned and looked at me.

"Hi, *Maman*," I said.

"Hi," she responded. "Did you just get here?"

"Yup. Anyone else home?"

She was staring at me, more intently than felt comfortable.

"No, your brother went over to a friend's and Dad went out to get some stuff from Home Depot."

"Oh, okay," I said, disappointed.

"They should both be home soon, though."

"Okay," I repeated, lingering in the doorway.

Mom was impeccable at reading me. I was trying to avoid eye contact in hopes that she wouldn't see all the emotions behind them. I also didn't want to be alone. The room, though, was filled with the weight of our broken relationship and tears burned the backs of my eyes because of it. I stood staring at the floor, afraid to take the first step, but desperate not to leave. Then, I heard her pull out a chair at the table.

"Sit," she demanded.

There was no disobeying her. I walked over and sat down. I had wanted to talk to my dad—he was easier, far less intimidating and judgmental. I silently sent a prayer that he would show up soon.

I looked up apprehensively as Mom eyed me from across the table. She said nothing, just stood up and walked over to the cabinet, taking out two glass teacups. She went over to the kettle brewing on the stove and filled them. She grabbed a box of chocolates sitting on top of the microwave and came to sit down across from me. She handed me one of the cups and took one for herself, then opened the lid of the chocolates and placed them in the middle.

"*Chayee* makes everything better," she said. Her voice had softened, pulling at my heartstrings. "What's going on, *azizam*? You look very worried."

She hadn't called me that since Minnesota, and the tears began to involuntarily roll down my cheeks. I had the urge to place my head on her chest while she hugged me and played with my hair, like when I was younger.

"This looks serious," she said with a familiar tenderness I hadn't seen from her in weeks. We'd been so cluttered with our struggle that I'd forgotten the connection I used to feel between us. I could feel it now, and I hurt with how much I'd missed it.

"Okay, tell me what's going on," she urged. She saw me hesitate and reached out across the table and squeezed my hand. "You can tell me. I love you. That's all that matters."

Before I knew it, the events of the past twenty-four hours came toppling out of me. I told her everything, leaving out only the part about Ben and I making love. She listened and held my hand as I tried to put my confusion into words, trying her best to remain unbiased as I spoke about Ben. In the end, she didn't seem as shocked about Maziar as I'd expected.

"First, stop crying," she said, handing me a tissue. "I know you feel bad about the way everything has happened and I know you feel guilty about hurting Ben's feelings. But this is life. Things get complicated and confusing. Feelings aren't always clear. You fall in love and then out of love. And it just goes around and around until you finally settle down. Ben isn't stupid. He knew you hadn't fully gotten over Maziar, but he pursued you anyway. Is it sad that he now has his heart broken? Of course. But what's happened has happened, and you can't just sit around crying about it. That doesn't help anyone."

Mom's abruptness would usually have me on edge and I would've found it insulting, but not this time. She was telling me the truth, being straightforward with it. There was no sign of contempt for Ben or Maziar, or any judgments of me.

I realized she was essentially telling me to stop whining and man up, which in truth was exactly what I needed to do. I started to laugh and she quickly joined me. I saw Mom relax, and I realized she, too, was feeling the apprehension of our relationship.

"Has Maziar called or texted you since this morning?" she asked.

"I'm not sure," I said. I had thrown my phone into my bag after putting it on silent, because I hadn't wanted to hear it ring anymore.

"Well, go get it," she said, waving me out the door. I suddenly had a vision of two girlfriends discussing a boy over cups of tea.

There were two more messages from Maziar and still none from Ben.

9:45 Sara, I know you're getting these texts. My phone shows that you've read them, which means you're just avoiding me. I understand that, but I still need to talk to you, and I'm not giving up that easily.

11:00 Please call me back.

"What do I do?" I asked her.

She took another minute to think. This newfound calm in her was very different from her normal, quick responses. I found this new, improved version a little unnerving.

"Well, what do you want to do? Do you think talking to Maziar will help, or just make things worse? He seems to be a bit determined. I have the feeling it's only a matter of time before he shows up here." She smiled: the idea of Maziar sitting outside the house, waiting, was somehow comical.

"I honestly don't know if it would make it better or worse," I said.

"In that case, take some time to think about it. A few days won't make a big difference. If he really does want to talk to you this badly, he'll be there a few days from now too. And if not, then his feelings aren't true and you're better off not bothering with him again anyway."

I smiled at her.

"What?" she said.

"When did you become such a relationship expert?" I teased.

I sat with Mom in the kitchen for the next few hours as she bustled this way and that, cooking dinner. I helped her chop and stir, and when it was time to sit down with my family, I helped her set the table and serve the food. Dad and Nima had come home shortly after our conversation had ended.

Where months ago I would have run off with one of them, today, I stayed rooted in my seat. The two of us talked about anything and everyone we could think of, smiling and giggling like old girlfriends. At some point, Dad stood in the doorway watching us. I could see that the peace between Mom and me was a huge relief for him. He didn't interrupt, just winked and walked away, not wanting to affect the magic that was taking place in the kitchen.

CHAPTER TWENTY-THREE

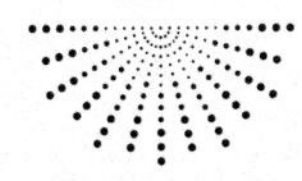

It rained for the next few days, and I welcomed its gloominess. It mimicked the current mood I was in. Its wetness also provided the perfect cover to cancel all plans that Leyla had made for me.

Maziar had been true to his word, persistently text-messaging me every day. At first, he pleaded, begging me to meet him. After a few days, though, he changed his tactics, sending me random messages about his day. He would tell me where he'd gone, what he'd seen that made him think of me. He would recall various moments we'd spent in this coffee shop or that restaurant. Soon the dread of his messages dwindled as he pulled me back into our memories. His strategy was clever.

I was sitting on my bed painting my nails when I heard the familiar ping of my phone.

1:45 I just drove by Lure and remembered the oysters we loved. Meet me
for dinner tonight?

I don't know what changed inside me, but I suddenly needed to see him. I'd been stalling for days, worried I wouldn't be strong enough to walk away once I heard him out. But if I truly wanted to sever all ties with Maziar, I had to eliminate any possibilities of a future with him. Before I had time to rethink my decision, I texted him back.

12:00 Okay. What time?

12:01 7:30?

12:02 Sure.

12:02 Should I pick you up?

12:02 No. Will meet you there.

12:03 Okay...can't wait.

I stared at the phone, stunned that I'd just agreed to meet him. I started to feel a familiar panic rise in the pit of my stomach. Ben hadn't contacted me since he left for Minnesota. It had been five days. I knew it was a bad sign, but we hadn't officially broken up, and the limbo I found us in was nerve-wracking. It made me feel guilty that I was meeting Maziar, as if somehow it would be considered cheating if I was willingly in the same place as him. Although I was determined to use this encounter to separate myself from Maziar once and for all, I was scared my defenses would be weak against his kryptonite.

I ran out of my room and found my parents sitting on the couch, Dad with his most recent book on one end, Mom with her magazine on the other. Her legs were stretched out toward him and his hand rested on her ankles. They reminded me of an old black-and-white photograph, making me wish I had a camera to capture the moment. I startled them when I came rushing in.

"What is it, Sara?" Dad asked, concerned.

"I told Maziar I'd meet him for dinner tonight," I blurted out, looking at Mom.

"Good," she replied, smiling.

"You don't think it's a mistake? Am I only going to end up screwing myself by seeing him?"

"Why would you be doing that?" Dad asked. "You want to see what he has to say, right? It's just dinner and just a conversation. Nothing changes when you leave if you don't want it to."

That was the problem. It sounded so simple, but what if I wanted something to change? And if I didn't, would I be strong enough to make that choice?

My parents spent the next twenty minutes helping me compartmentalize my feelings on the situation, arming me with the strength to stand up against Maziar's forces.

"Don't get emotional, Sara. If he knows how nervous you are, he will have all the power," Mom advised. "You always want to keep men guessing."

"Just remember, this is what life's about. Falling in love, then getting your heart broken. Then doing it all over again," Dad added. "It builds character, *eshgham*. You will be better for it despite how it goes."

Afterward, I went back to my bedroom and proceeded to continue panicking. I called Sandra and then Leyla, telling them what I'd done. They were encouraging, both agreeing I needed to see him. They were waiting on standby for my call when it was all over.

As six o'clock rolled around, I shakily dragged myself off the bed and forced myself into the shower. I thought long and hard beneath the scalding water, trying to figure out how I felt. I was confused, my love for both Maziar and Ben tangled and twisted into a heaping mess I could no longer undo.

I walked out into the living room an hour later.

"You look beautiful, Sara. That red sweater deepens the brown in your eyes," Mom said, as she wrapped her arms around me. "You're worth the world, *azizam*. Don't you forget it," she whispered.

"I'm nervous, Mom."

"I know," she replied, squeezing me tighter. "But don't forget, he's just a boy."

He's just a boy, I repeated to myself as I walked out the door, terrified. I slid inside my car, placing the key in the ignition. I listened to the hum of the engine bursting to life, its rhythmic purr somehow soothing my frazzled nerves.

As I stared out the windshield, trying to gather my courage, I heard my phone ping with a message. I rummaged through my purse and almost dropped the phone when I saw Ben's name flash on my screen. I hadn't heard from him in a week, but it would be just my luck for things to happen in this exact order. As I sat in my car to go meet Maziar, he had decided to send me a message. The irony of it was ridiculous.

7:10 Hey. Sorry I haven't called. I'm not ready to talk yet. I wanted to check in on you though.

I didn't want to respond. I didn't want to tell him I was going to see Maziar. It was hard enough to deal with tonight as it was, but having to own the guilt over how it made Ben feel was something I wanted to evade at all costs. At the same time, I knew that avoiding him would make things worse. I'd been so wrapped up in meeting Maziar that I hadn't thought much about Ben. I decided to respond but stay as vague as I could, in hopes he wouldn't question me further. I didn't want to lie.

7:13 I'm doing okay. Are you good?

7:15 I'm okay. Been with the family mostly. Going out with some friends in a few minutes but I wanted to text you first.

7:16 Thanks. Have a good time with your friends.

7:18 Thanks. Talk soon?

7:19 Sure.

I waited another few minutes to see if any more messages came through, but they didn't. I knew his disinterest in my whereabouts wasn't a good sign, but I couldn't spend tonight stressing over it. I already had an impossible task in front of me and I needed to focus on one life-altering event at a time. I pushed Ben to the back of my mind. For now, I needed to make it to the restaurant and deal with Maziar.

I walked in twenty minutes later, glancing around the room in search of him. I described him to the hostess and she walked me to the back corner, toward a booth I couldn't see from the door. There, sitting on the bench facing me, was Maziar.

His black sweater accentuated the deep, dark pupils of his eyes, in contrast to the honey hues of his irises. I was mesmerized for a moment, forgetting how to breathe. He stood up hesitantly, moving toward me. There was a lapse in my reflexes as my senses were overwhelmed by his proximity. He took it as an invitation to move in farther. Before I knew what was happening, he had his arms wrapped around me.

In those few seconds he held me, all my senses came alive. I was fiercely aware of his hand resting on my lower back, the electricity burning through my skin. He had pulled in close and I could feel the rise and fall of his chest as his breath made my hair sway. And his smell. I was intoxicated by the fragrance of his cologne mixed in with the scent of his body.

I closed my eyes and afforded myself a few seconds to forget where I was. I allowed myself to be transported into our past, when I was his and he was mine. My heart hurt with a pain that surprised me. It felt like an anchor was pulling me toward the ocean's floor and I had to force myself to physically disconnect from him. He reluctantly let go, pausing a few seconds to stare into my eyes before letting his arms drop to his sides.

"Hi," he said.

"Hey," I responded, feeling as if the greeting were too small for the momentousness of the situation.

"I'm so glad you decided to come tonight. It's really good seeing you, Sara."

I stared at him, wondering why I was even here. What was he trying to do, other than ruin the life I'd been able to create without him?

"Why?" I asked. He looked at me as if my question confused him.

"Honestly, Maziar, I have no idea what's going on right now. I can't figure out why you brought me here after all this time."

I hadn't expected to be so bold. I even shocked myself a little as I heard the words coming out of my mouth. The truth was that I didn't have the strength, or energy, to toy with small talk. I needed to know what this was all about, to gain some clarity on the twisted triangle I found myself in, and I didn't want to waste any time.

"I've wanted to talk to you for a long time," he said, dropping his gaze, the weight too heavy to bear on his shoulders. He loosely held his fingers around his cocktail, lightly tapping the glass as he spoke.

"At first, I stayed away because I couldn't see you. I'd wanted to but it was too hard. I knew it would be tough for you as well. I blamed myself for how things ended. I really did want to try to make it as easy as possible for you, Sara." He looked up at me sadly as he continued. "Then, I saw you at the restaurant. I wanted to talk to you, to tell you she meant nothing, but it seemed stupid after all that time. I wasn't even sure if you cared." The last came out in a whisper. I could see the pain in his beautiful eyes, as vivid as the day he had first watched me walk away from him.

"I saw what seeing me did to you, and when you ran outside, I wanted to run after you. I just couldn't, because I didn't know what I would say. Telling you how sorry I was while I was with someone else just felt wrong. I kept watching the door, hoping you'd come back. Then, I saw Ben get up and go out after you. I thought the two of you were together. I didn't want to make a bigger mess than I already had, so I left you alone."

The images of that night cluttered my mind as I relived the moments of my heart shattering when I saw Maziar with another girl.

"I've thought about that night a hundred times, Sara, about–if I were given the chance to do it again–what I would do differently."

"What would you have done?" I asked quietly, my voice fighting around the knot in my throat.

He reached out and held the fingers of my right hand that lay limply on the table between us. I glanced down at them, feeling a strangeness I'd never imagined I'd feel with Maziar.

"I would have run after you. I would have talked to you, told you that I still wasn't over you, that she meant nothing. I would have told you that I thought about you every day." He stared at me with an intensity that stopped the air from passing through my lungs. "I would tell you how much I missed you and that every day away from you has felt like an eternity in hell for me. I'm still in love with you, Sara."

I had waited, for what felt like a lifetime, to hear Maziar say those words to me. In that moment, though, I realized that some things were just better left unsaid. Whether Maziar still loved me didn't change a thing. Our circumstances remained the same. It was inevitable that we would be doomed no matter how many times we embarked on this path together. I tried to push away from my emotions, to disconnect myself from my heart and focus with my head. I'd come here tonight to end this thing that continued to linger between us. I needed to remember that.

"What do you want from me?" I asked, unable to keep the pleading edge out of my voice.

He took a long look at me. He held my hand tighter, realizing I was about to flutter away. His despair, like high beams, blinded me.

"I want you back."

I hadn't let myself hope he would say that to me tonight. I thought if he didn't, the disappointment would be unbearable. I realized that hearing him say he wanted us, and knowing that it was impossible, was more than disappointing. It was utterly devastating. I slowly exhaled, no longer able to hold the sadness at bay. He reached out and held onto both my hands, desperation alight in his eyes.

He was pleading with me to stay, to give us another chance, in the silence that was exchanged between us. I just looked at him, taking in the lines and contours of his face, memorizing them the best I could. He knew my answer before I even spoke.

"How would we do this again, Maziar? Nothing has changed. We didn't break up because one of us was flawed. We didn't have a fight. Neither of us was unfaithful, or hurtful, or abusive. We broke up due to our circumstances, and those haven't changed."

"Sara, please," he pleaded, not concerned with how frantic he looked.

I could see his pain and it just added to my own. Once again, I found myself to be the voice of reason in our impossible situation. I was the one who had to muster up the strength and walk away. I didn't know where I would find the energy to leave this seat, let alone leave Maziar behind again.

"Maziar, don't do that. Don't make this seem like this is a choice and I'm not choosing you. There isn't a choice here; don't you see that? Have your parents miraculously changed their minds about us?"

"No," he said and stared back down at the table.

I reached out and put my hand under his chin to get him to look at me. He grabbed my palm and placed it on the side of his face, leaning into it like he used to. He closed his eyes, taking a trip back into our past, finding the comfort in me that I had once provided him. I gave him a few seconds in the serenity of our memories before I pulled my hand away, needing to sever the connection between us. I had to stay focused and I couldn't do that with him touching me.

"We can't do this again. We'd only end up right back here," I said.

"I know."

A tenderness surrounded us, wrapping us in the blanket of its deception. We stared at each other, knowing we'd reached the end again. The hostess walked up to our table, stumbling to a stop when she realized she'd interrupted something pivotal. We were too lost to notice. She quietly cleared her throat, trying to get our attention.

I blinked a few times and wiped the stray tear that had made its way past my hold. Maziar smiled at me, the kind of smile that told me that, even though we couldn't be together, he loved me. I knew we would love each other past this moment and this day. Maybe we would love each other for a lifetime, even after we had each created futures with other people.

He turned toward the waitress and she quickly muttered her apologies.

"Can I get another vodka tonic, please? And a glass of wine for the lady?" he asked. I nodded. The waitress took our order and hurried away.

"This didn't go exactly how I'd planned," he said, with a half-smile. "I wish there were a way to make this work. It's just so damn unfair. What if I just disown them and walk away? I'm almost done with school. As soon as I pass the bar, I can get a job and an apartment and we could be free of them."

The innocence in him was comforting. But things were more complicated than that, even if he didn't want to see it.

"I don't think that would work," I answered.

"Why not?" he asked, still desperate for a solution. He genuinely believed he could break ties with them. He loved me enough to sacrifice his world for me, but I couldn't let him do that.

"Well, for one thing, do you really *want* to never talk to your family again? That's a tough thing to do. You don't agree with them, but you still love them." He was about to say something but I raised my hand to quiet him. "There would be so much you would miss. Even if you could see past the life you grew up in and the people you call home, just because you love me, I can't be everything for you. Someday, I won't be enough and you'll resent me. Maybe even end up hating me."

"I could never hate you, Sara," he whispered.

"I can't take that chance," I said wearily. "I would rather be without you, knowing you are somewhere thinking of me, than be with you and see the pain and anger of losing your family when you look at me. You think you'd be fine, but no one person can be everything to another. In the end, your family would still be what breaks us up."

Maziar just looked at me, but I could see the fight had left him. He knew, just as well as I did, that there wasn't much hope left for the two of us. I wanted to be happy that he'd finally accepted it, that we could both walk away now, but I couldn't help the nagging pain that had taken over my heart. My body ached with it and I had to keep the panic from consuming me. This was really over. It played on repeat in my mind, shoving a dagger further into my heart each time I thought it.

"Maybe we can't be together, but I'm happy that we were once. I don't regret any of it, Sara. I love you. I always have."

I'd waited a lifetime to hear him say he loved me, but as the words left his lips, I became undone. I felt my heart shatter into tiny pieces raining around me, leaving a gaping hole where Maziar had once been. That part of me would be gone forever after I left this restaurant, and no matter how life proceeded, it could never be filled again. I would walk away tonight less of a person than I'd been when I'd walked in.

I'd lost a part of me that Maziar would have in his safekeeping forever.

We finished our drinks. I never asked him about the girl at the restaurant and he never asked me about Ben. We both knew life had moved on, but the details of it didn't matter to either of us. Our war wounds had been ripped open and we were both bleeding out onto the table. We were just focusing on surviving.

On the drive home, my mind replayed the night over and over again. Everything Maziar had said, how he relentlessly held my hand across the table, the loving embrace we shared for the few minutes before we said our goodbye. I wanted to commit every second of it to my memory, never to forget. I could still smell his cologne on my sweater, rubbed into the fabric after he held me. The smell was intoxicating, and even more so, devastating. I began to cry, alone with all the haunting memories. It broke my heart to know that I'd walked away from the love of my life and that Maziar and I would soon be a distant memory in the story of us.

I pulled over and let myself cry. When I was done, I just stared out the window. I hurt all over, and the only person who could make it stop was driving home to the Palisades. The unfairness of life had brutally taught me lessons I hadn't asked to learn.

I called Leyla and told her I was coming over. I didn't want to be alone, and I needed to be with someone who understood how horrible this was for me. I'd made it to her front door when I heard my phone ring with a text message. I took a deep breath, afraid that it would be from Ben, or Maziar, either of which I couldn't handle at the moment. I pulled my phone out and opened the screen. It was from Maziar.

12:00 I already miss you...

* * *

Within the first few days following the dinner, Maziar sent me messages about how unfair things were and how difficult life without each other would be. He did most of the talking, while I listened. I'd made the decision to walk away, so I didn't respond, but I also couldn't bring myself to tell him to stop texting. The finality of our last conversation had me swimming in the sadness of losing him again. If I had any hopes of surviving, I had to avoid the avalanche of pain that would surely follow if I opened up the lines of communication.

Eventually, the messages dwindled, leaving only silence within the air space between us. I spent the first few days of that silence constantly holding my breath, waiting for my phone to flash his name. When it never came, I convinced myself it was better to have no contact. Regardless of what either of us felt, we were both aware that the future between us was dim, anything exchanged only prolonging the inevitable breaking away we would have to do.

CHAPTER TWENTY-FOUR

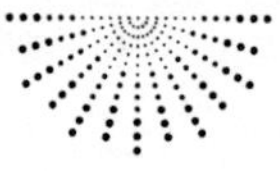

I spent the remainder of the break at home with my family, and when I wasn't with them, I spent my time with Leyla. Ben hadn't reached out to contact me again after his initial message. Then, three days before school started, he sent me a text saying he would be home the following evening. He asked if we could talk.

I'd been thinking of what I wanted to say to him since I'd last seen Maziar. I didn't know much, but what I did know was that Maziar was no longer a viable option for me. I knew that any attempt to rekindle our relationship would only lead to its demise. I couldn't wait around on the hope of a chance that things would transform somehow. I couldn't wait for his family to stop hating me.

I still loved him–I knew that, too–but it didn't matter in the bigger picture. I could love him forever and it wouldn't convince his parents that we were good for each other. I had to make peace with our situation. I knew we would probably love each other, in some capacity, for the rest of our lives. He would always be my "what if" and "if things were different" but he would never be mine again. Life would propel us forward and we would each find love with someone new. They would probably never know the details of our past together, never seeing the pieces of our hearts we'd lost to one another. He would be the love of my soul forever, but I would put it away, keeping it my secret. I didn't know if I believed in other lives, but if they truly did exist, I prayed that in our next life we would find each other again and have then what we couldn't have now. Until then, I would move on.

Sandra had made a trip to Minnesota to visit Josh, taking a few extra days off from school to be with him, which meant I was alone when I got to the apartment. Waiting by myself until Ben made it home drove me crazy. To keep myself busy, I went on a cleaning spree while blasting my headphones, trying to drown out my thoughts. I kept replaying my last conversations with Ben and Maziar over and over in my head.

I never used to believe it was possible to love two people at the same time, but I'd come to realize that I was wrong. I loved them both. I loved them differently, but I loved them all the same. I was madly in love with Maziar, the kind that twisted itself around the air I breathed, into every cell inside my body. His was the kind of love that consumed my whole world. Ben's love was less volatile, more constant. His was not all-consuming but all-encompassing, like gentle hands that held me together when I wanted to fall apart. The kind that was a beacon of light in the darkest of days, the one I looked for and ran toward to keep me safe.

Neither love was better than the other, each fulfilling different needs I had. If the world were a perfect place, and I could be with either of them, I would have chosen Maziar. His love was a drug my heart couldn't resist, the addiction I would spend the rest of my life fighting. But life wasn't flawless, and complications were imminent.

I wasn't sure if choosing Ben because I couldn't choose Maziar made me a horrible person. On the same note, if I had never met Maziar, I could have lived the rest of my life happy with Ben by my side. I didn't know if walking away from Ben just because part of me wanted Maziar was really my only choice.

Maybe part of me was using Ben, being unfair to him by moving forward in our relationship when I still loved another. I would love Maziar forever, though, and loving two people would be my destiny no matter who I was with. I loved Ben. We had built something meaningful between us. I wasn't going to walk away from that because it might be making me a selfish person not to. People did far worse things than stay with a boyfriend they loved while still not fully over another. At least that's what I spent the day trying to convince myself of.

I made the one-block walk to Ben's house at six. I moved slowly, still struggling with my feelings, trying to figure out what I needed to say. When I got to his door, I stood there, frozen, terrified of what awaited me on the other side. It had been close to a month that we hadn't seen or talked to each other. I knew it would be awkward at first, but I prayed it would be short-lived. I finally forced myself to knock.

After a few seconds, I heard the shuffling of feet and the door swung open. Ben suddenly appeared, staring down at me, his eyes reflecting the green off his shirt like emeralds. He gave me his crooked smile, but there was a weariness behind it that only compounded my uneasiness. I slowly let out my breath, not realizing I'd been holding it.

"Hi," I said.

"Hey, doll," he replied.

How I'd missed those words. I walked up to him and put my arms around his waist, pulling him close. He was hesitant at first, but I didn't budge, not allowing him the chance to push me away. Slowly, he wrapped his arms around me.

I closed my eyes, relishing the warmth his body radiated in my direction. I had missed the safety I felt when he was with me. His stability and dependability added order to the chaos that always brewed inside me.

But something was wrong. There was an unfamiliar stiffness to his grip on me, a hesitation that felt heavy like a thick winter blanket. I felt the knots forming in the pit of my stomach in response. I tried to hold him closer, fighting against the urge to panic.

Ben severed the connection between us and pulled away, putting a few feet of distance where his body had just been. I suddenly felt cold without him there to shelter me. He said nothing as he walked toward the couches. I followed, each step feeling like I was dragging myself through a pool of thick maple syrup. When I made it to the living room, he stood to the side, waiting for me to find a seat. I moved past him and sat down. He took the seat across from me.

The anxiety began to build, and I couldn't stop the panic that had set in. I noticed Ben didn't look well; he was pale and had dark circles under his eyes. He had an unsettled look about him that I hadn't seen before, leaving me feeling on edge and confused.

"Thanks for coming over. I'm sorry I didn't call you. I should have. That was wrong of me."

"It's okay. I get it," I stammered, nervously. The tension was killing me.

"No, it wasn't okay, but I just couldn't talk to you. I was trying to figure things out."

He looked so uncomfortable in his skin sitting there that I started to speak, not knowing what else to do.

"Ben, don't apologize. The night at the club was really bad. I hate that was how we left things before you went to Minnesota. I'm not proud of what you saw, but that's over now. I've thought about it a lot and my future doesn't include Maziar. We had a past together and I just couldn't ignore him that night. It seemed wrong. But I wish we had just left together before things got worse."

I was rambling now, searching for the right words to say to take us back to how we were before all of this. He had stopped looking at me and was now staring at the floor. I wasn't sure he was even listening.

"Ben, I'm hoping we could go back to how things were, before they got twisted and messed up. I really want to try to fix things between us," I pleaded. He didn't respond. "Please say something."

"I don't know if I believe that," he said.

"Believe what?" I whispered, already knowing what he was going to say.

"That you're actually done with Maziar. You've said that before, Sara, and look at us now. I believed you then, but I shouldn't have. I don't know if I can put myself through all of that again."

The panic rose in my throat, threatening to make me sick on the living room floor. Ben was slipping away; I could see it as clear as a cloudless sky. He was retreating further and further away from me, trying to find somewhere safe where I couldn't hurt him anymore.

I was losing him.

This wasn't how the conversation was supposed to go. I was going to tell him I was over Maziar. He was supposed to reach out and pull me into his arms, kissing the top of my head, telling me he loved me. Instead, he thought I was crying wolf, no longer able to find any trust in my words.

"I understand how it feels to have someone in your past. To feel an irrational loyalty to them because of what you shared once. You're not the only one with a first love."

His body looked tired and worn, but his eyes burned with anger and pain. I fidgeted under the intensity of his gaze.

"Jessie tried to sleep with me," he said.

He sat there looking at me, letting the words balance between us, allowing them to imprint in my mind. When he offered no further explanation, I found my voice and demanded it.

"And?"

He allowed for a few more moments of agonizing silence before he spoke. I had to remind myself to stay rooted to my seat, wanting to hurl myself across the table at him.

"It doesn't feel so good when you aren't sure if the person you're with is faithful to you or not, does it, Sara?"

"I didn't cheat on you!" I yelled, my face flushed with anger.

Ben remained calm, irritating me further.

"You might as well have. I saw how you looked at him. It was obvious that you still love him. I think I could deal with you sleeping with him easier than you still having feelings for him."

Suddenly, the fight seeped out of me. Ben was right. The potential of him cheating on me with Jessie was easier to bear than the idea of him still loving her.

"Did you sleep with her?" I asked, my desperation visible in the way I sat on the edge of my seat.

"No," he said, and looked away. "I didn't sleep with her."

I exhaled, having held my breath for the worst. A flutter of relief flapped around my chest. Ben stared out the window at a little boy riding his bike down the street.

"There are moments when I think I should have. Then we wouldn't be sitting here trying to figure out what we're going to do about us," he said, watching the boy ride in circles.

My eyes filled with tears, knowing I'd finally made Ben regret having ever been with me.

"Don't say that, Ben," I pleaded.

When he looked at me again, his eyes mirrored the pain in my own. I began to cry, unable to hold back my tears any longer. What had I done?

"Sara, please don't," he said, his words catching in his throat. "Please," he whispered when I couldn't stop myself.

Before I knew what I was doing, I closed the space between us, throwing my arms around him. At first, he resisted, trying to remain unaffected. But his defenses were flawed and slowly his body melted into mine. He reached over and pulled me onto his lap, putting his arms around me, diminishing any space left between us. I wrapped my legs around him, overcome with the need to absorb his safety as I held on.

"Please don't leave," I whispered into his ear. "I love you."

He came undone then, unable to balance the burden of the past few weeks any longer.

"Sara, I can't be hurt again," he pleaded.

"I know," I replied. "I'm not going to hurt you. I want you and no one else, Ben. Please, give us another chance."

He quietly searched my eyes for the truth. Then, he reached up and wrapped his hand in my hair, pulling my head toward him as our lips slammed together in urgency. My lips parted, giving him passage, wanting desperately to feel his mouth on mine as I kissed him deeply. I could think of nothing other than how badly I needed him, how I needed to create that closeness that existed between us.

He hastily unbuttoned my shirt, slipping his hand inside and cupping my breast, his fingers grazing over my nipple. I gasped as his desire melted onto my skin. We made love on the couch, clumsy and hurried in our movements, desperate for its magic to erase the tragedy of the past few weeks from our memories. And when we reached the pinnacle of our dance, we both shuddered against the pillows together. He held onto me, burying his head in my neck.

I relaxed into his embrace as Maziar began to fade into the background and Ben made his way to the forefront of my mind. Wrapped in the cocoon of his love, I was able to find peace again for the first time in weeks.

CHAPTER TWENTY-FIVE

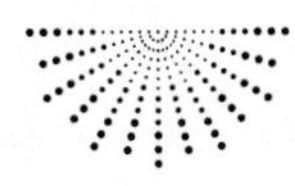

The end of the school year was rapidly approaching and the freedom of another summer to tool around without the responsibilities of school had us all buzzing with impatience. The end of the year also brought with it Neda's birthday.

She was turning twenty-six and had decided she was going to throw herself a big birthday bash at her house in the Palisades. Her family owned a large estate that sat on top of the hill, overlooking a breathtaking view of the city lights and ocean. I'd been there multiple times since Maziar and I had broken up. However, this would be the first time that we would both be there together.

I was beyond nervous about seeing him again. We hadn't spoken since the night at the restaurant. Since then, Ben and I had continued on the journey of rebuilding our relationship. It had been five months and things were good. They were better than good; they were great. We had fallen back into our familiarity. At first, he was apprehensive, building a protective wall between us. I remained patient, knowing he needed time to trust me again. He'd finally let go and let me back in.

When I approached him about the party, he nonchalantly agreed to go, but my gut knew this would be an unspoken test, one that I would surely need to pass. If I showed the slightest sign of wavering, our glass tower would come toppling down, leaving us by its wayside.

If I was honest, there was a part of me that wanted to see Maziar, the part I had put to sleep and locked away months ago. I knew things were over and I wasn't toying with the idea of a future between us, but my heart ached to see his face, watch his eyes light up when he spoke, hear the deep rumble of his laugh. I didn't share my feelings with anyone, not even Leyla, fearing that if I said them out loud, they would take shape, becoming a monster I couldn't control. I needed to stay strong, remain passive, show Ben he was my only. I needed to keep my feelings locked away so they couldn't hurt any of us anymore.

I had driven home Friday night to be with my family for the weekend. We had our customary family dinner, followed by a backgammon tournament. When I'd finally gone to bed, I'd spent most of the night tossing and turning, trying to play out the different scenarios that could happen when I saw Maziar. I had no clue if he was seeing anybody. He could very well show up with a girl on his arm. Although that would be hard to see, it would be the easiest of scenarios for both of us. I felt like Neda would have warned me if that were the case, and I wondered if she'd told him that I would be showing up with Ben.

At eight in the morning, I gave up hope on getting any real sleep and rolled out of bed. I grabbed my headphones, kissed Mom goodbye, and went for a long run. I'd become accustomed to pushing my body to its furthest limits, relishing the physical pain that distracted me from the thoughts and emotions wearing me down.

When I got home, she was sitting at the kitchen table with two hot cups of tea, waiting for me. This had become our new Saturday morning ritual. I would wake up and go for a run while Mom fed the men. Then, we would have some girl time, just the two of us, over our cups of hot *chayee* and scrambled eggs.

When I entered the kitchen, the smell of butter filled my nose, making me nostalgic for my youth. Mom's eggs were always the best. Only she could make the room fill with that heavenly smell. It always transported me to when I was a child, filling me with a sense of comfort I equated only with her.

"Hi, *azizam*. How was your run?" she asked.

"It was good."

"I don't know how you can do so much running. If you're going to do it every day, you have to eat more. Your grandmother is going to think I'm starving you!" she said. I laughed at her, a grown woman still afraid of her mother's disapproval.

I supposed we all spent our lives seeking our mother's approval, regardless of our age. I wasn't sure if that was just a child-parent thing or a Persian thing. Either way, it was a destiny that seemed to hover over us all.

She placed the eggs and pita bread in front of us and took her seat across from me.

"Your *khaleh* called this morning to tell me that Ellie got engaged last night. Pouyah took your uncle out last week for coffee to officially ask his permission to marry her," she said. Ellie had been set up with him a year ago by one of my aunt's friends.

No Persian girl was a stranger to the tedious matchmaking of her female relatives. There was always someone's nephew, grandson, or neighbor, off to medical school or law school, that your mother, aunt, or grandmother was singling out for you as a potential mate. They were like ants scurrying up an ant hill, trying to be the first to sink their claws into the next "great catch." I was always being solicited by the women in my family to set up one blind date after another. At get-togethers, someone was always pointing this boy, or that boy, out to my cousins and me. It was the Iranian way, to broker pairings in hopes of saving daughters from becoming old maids. If we were still single at the ripe old age of thirty-two, all hope was lost among them. It was frustrating but fascinating to watch the women scoping out the young men for their daughters. They had it down to an art.

Mom had gotten better where Ben was concerned. We had gone to dinner with my parents a few times and they were always cordial. I knew she didn't put much weight on our relationship, though, secretly hoping that we would break up. Luckily, she was smart enough to know that outwardly fighting me on it, or being rude to him, would cause our fragile truce to break down again. The closeness between us had just started reestablishing itself, becoming each other's confidantes again. Neither of us wanted to do anything to mess that up.

Mamanbozorg, however, had become even more relentless in her crusade to teach me the ill of my ways. In her mind, I'd completely failed her. Ben was not only Christian, but also Caucasian, nowhere near what she required in my mate. It had put a large rift between us, our relationship no longer what it used to be.

"Sara, I wanted to seriously talk to you about something that has me worried."

I had to suppress the moan threatening to escape. I hated these "serious" talks Mom always wanted to have with me. They were inevitably about how I was lacking in one way or another.

I braced myself for what she was going to say, reminding myself not to react. I'd found it easier to just listen and seem like I agreed rather than trying to defend my choices. In the end, I still made my own decisions, but letting my parents think they had some say in it saved me some heartache.

"I'm concerned about you going to Neda's birthday tonight. I'm pretty certain that Maziar is going to be there, since she's his cousin. I'm just worried that seeing him again may not be the best decision for you right now," she said.

"Why?" I asked, trying to sound nonchalant.

She looked at me, motherly worry evident in her eyes. She knew that Maziar was a very sensitive subject for me, and I could see she was trying to tiptoe around her words in an attempt to avoid setting me off. Were my feelings for him so transparent that even Mom wasn't convinced that I was over him? If that were the case, then I'd fail miserably tonight. Ben would see right through me.

"I'm worried that you'll see him and end up upset again. You've been doing so well lately without him. You know that he isn't any good for you. Maziar is a good boy but his family doesn't want you and you deserve better than that."

She recited one of my grandmother's sayings, "*Hamoon ash, hamoon kaseh*," which translated into "the same stew, the same bowl." It meant that no matter how many times I went back to Maziar, it would result in the same outcome. Nothing would have changed.

"Don't worry, Mom. I'm going to be fine. Maziar and I probably won't even talk. Plus, Ben will be there with me. I doubt we'll even end up in the same room. We'll be avoiding each other," I said, with more confidence than I felt. "Seeing him won't be a big deal."

"That's the other thing. You saw what happened the last time the three of you ran into each other. I really don't want you to be stuck in all that drama again."

"I'll be fine," I said, brushing her off.

"Okay," she said, the doubt obvious.

She popped a sugar cube into her mouth and went back to drinking her tea. Neither of us brought the party up again, but Maziar loomed in the kitchen for the rest of our breakfast. Once we were done, I went to my room and threw myself on the bed. It was bad enough that I was nervous about seeing him while I was with Ben, but now I had to worry about disappointing my mom as well.

At about six thirty, I started getting ready. By the time I got dressed, my room looked like a bomb had exploded in my closet. We were in the throes of spring and the weather was warm, so I settled on a long, turquoise maxi dress that tied at my waist. I had a thin gold chain on with a single pearl pendant that sat in the dip of my neck. My hand nervously played with it.

I stood in front of the mirror and looked at the person reflected back at me. Time had changed her from the naïve girl who thought love was filled with rose petals and rainbows to the cautious, tired one standing before me. I used to think that I would meet my Prince Charming and he would sweep me off my feet into a life of happiness and hope like in fairy tales. Now, I knew that life was much more complicated. I was heading out to stand across the yard from one man while on the arm of another, and I loved them both. My head knew that I was treading on thin ice, and if the floor beneath me were to shatter, I would find myself trapped in its freezing water.

I couldn't go back there. Each time I returned to the place that held dreams of Maziar, I came back a little more broken, my resolve even more weakened than the time before. I was now living a different story, one that had Ben as the lead. I hung onto his image tightly, reminding myself that I was happy.

The drive over to Neda's was a quiet one. I was lost in anxiety, Ben deep in thought, neither of us sure of how the night would unfold. Leyla was with us, sitting as quietly as she could in the back seat, trying to be invisible. I was so preoccupied with the possible scenarios of the evening that I was startled when Ben turned the car off.

"You ready?" he asked, as he looked at me stoically.

"Of course," I chirped, trying to convince both of us I was totally fine. I kept telling myself I could do this. I could see Maziar again.

I took one last deep breath and stepped out into the unknown of the night. On shaky legs I walked to the front door, grasping Neda's gift with such conviction that my fingers were crushing its edges. The door was wide open, beckoning her guests to the warmth of its confines. I reached out and held Ben's hand before we went inside.

We were greeted with a crowd of close to fifty people, bodies jammed into the front room of the house like sardines. I was stuck in a terrified haze as my eyes quickly darted back and forth, searching. The crowd parted slightly and I spotted Neda at the far end. She was standing at the sliding door leading into her backyard. I could see the ceiling of twinkle lights beyond the glass, sparkling magically in the night. The light was framing her body, giving her the appearance of glowing. She saw us approaching before we reached her, and her eyes lit up like they always did when she saw me.

"Sara!" she squealed in her usual Neda fashion.

She threw her arms around me and squeezed me with genuine affection. Then, she introduced us to the friends she was talking to and we engaged in a few minutes of socializing. Neda placed her arm around my waist while Ben was talking to one of her friends, pulling me closer to her.

"He's out back," she whispered into my ear, then winked and walked away to greet the newest arrivals.

Leyla turned and asked us if we wanted to get a drink. The bar was situated in the backyard. I tried to deter her with my eyes, but she was too busy gawking at the boy in front of her to notice. My stomach churned with nerves as Ben grabbed my hand, following Leyla outside.

I quickly scanned the yard; it didn't take me long to spot him. He stood across the way, by the fruit trees lining the back wall. He was talking to a few of Neda's friends. They looked familiar, but I couldn't place them.

We stopped in front of the bar. Ben walked up to order our drinks, and I allowed myself a second to look at Maziar. Every time I saw him, it still felt like the first time. My heart would beat furiously and I'd get lightheaded as my body synced with his. I would feel the familiar gravitational pull from across the room. This time was no different.

He was in a pair of dark blue jeans and my favorite pair of gray Converse shoes. I couldn't help but wonder if he'd worn them knowing I'd be here. He looked more tanned than before, his skin glowing against his light green T-shirt, his dark hair looking more stark in contrast. He'd grown his facial hair out; it was now a scruffy, cropped beard. It made him look older.

He must have felt me staring because he suddenly looked in my direction. Our eyes locked, and I felt the magnetism urging me in his direction. He stared at me, making my heart pound against my rib cage, trying to burst free from my chest.

Ben had the drinks and was turning toward me. I saw his movement from the corner of my eye. I forced myself to look away from Maziar. I was not going to have a repeat of the club. I reminded myself that I was with Ben. It was time to stand by my choice. Maziar was better kept as a memory.

He politely excused himself from the conversation and I breathed a sigh of relief as he started toward the house. He disappeared into the crowd of the living room. I told myself that if I could just keep us on opposite sides of the party all night, I'd be okay.

"You okay, doll?" Ben asked, as he handed me my drink.

"Yup, I'm fine." I tried to keep my tone nonchalant and light.

The night continued with an unspoken agreement between Maziar and me. We existed in opposite hemispheres, avoiding each other. I stole a few glances at him from the corner of my eye even though I knew I shouldn't. I watched him dazzle a beautiful blonde with his irresistible charm, debate with a group of guys over a recent basketball game, and lend a tender ear to Neda as they discussed something that appeared serious. All the while, I leaned into Ben, hung on to his words, held his hand, continuously proving myself.

Later in the evening, I went inside to use the bathroom. I saw Maziar talking to a few people in the backyard and figured it was safe. But as I opened the door to head back outside, I stopped abruptly in my tracks. He stood there, leaning against the wall, waiting for me.

I started to panic, realizing there was no way to leave without walking past him. I froze, trying to think. He looked at me and our eyes locked. Everything started to move in slow motion, my thoughts becoming fuzzy and incoherent. I knew I should push past him, make my way back out to Ben, but I couldn't get my feet to obey.

"Hi, Sara," he said, his voice as familiar as my own.

"Hi," I managed.

"So, what? Are we just going to ignore each other? Pretending you don't see me, is that how you're playing this now?" He immediately laid into me, the aggression in his voice harsh and unyielding. My throat dried shut making it difficult to speak. My lack of response irritated him further. "Oh, that's nice, Sara. Now we're not even talking."

I wasn't expecting anger. I shook my head trying to clear my thoughts, confused at his reaction to me. "Why are you so upset?" I asked.

"Are you serious? You've been ignoring me all night." He ran his hand through his hair, causing it to look disheveled. "I get you're here with your boyfriend, but...shit, you can't even say hello?" I could see his eyes soften. Along with anger, there was the hurt of being ignored.

I felt his pain pull at the edges of my heart, increasing the pressure in my chest. I forced myself to push past it. The only emotion we needed right now was anger. I could work with anger; it would drive a wedge even further between us. Although it broke my heart to have him hate me, it would ensure that he wouldn't try to reach out to me again. I was terrified of blowing up the little remaining between us, but I knew it was necessary for our survival. We needed to be free of each other, with no paths left to create any hope of finding our way back.

"What would be the point, Maziar?" I asked. "We don't have anything left to say. At least, I don't have anything left to say."

I tried to keep my face calm as I watched my disinterest throw daggers at him. I kept reminding myself this was necessary; I'd chosen Ben.

"Look, I'm sorry I didn't say hi, but I honestly don't think we should pretend to be friends, because we aren't. It's just easier for everyone if we stay out of each other's way."

"What are you saying, Sara? Is this because of Ben? He doesn't want to you to talk to me? Is that it?" he asked, accusingly.

I wanted to reach out to him, to shelter him from the pain I could visibly see I was causing. I wanted to tell him I was lying, that I did want to speak to him and that I wished there was a way to be in each other's lives. Instead, I went in for the kill.

"No, Maziar. It's because I don't want to talk to you."

I saw my words crush him before the strength of his anger took over. The hard set of his eyes returned and his face flushed with it. Before he could speak, Ben walked into the hallway. He glanced back and forth between us, sensing the tension.

"You doing okay, doll?" he asked, cautiously eyeing Maziar.

I turned toward him, acting as if Maziar no longer existed. "I'm fine. Let's go outside, babe," I said, confidently.

Without glancing back, I made my way over to Ben and put my arm around his waist, guiding him outside. He turned and looked at me, the shock of my reaction rendering him speechless. I seemed strong, unaffected, slightly bored even, by what had just happened. On the inside, though, I was bleeding.

I spent the remainder of the night attached to Ben's side. If his arm wasn't around me, I was holding his hand. I intently listened to what he said, laughed at his jokes, remained interested. I didn't scan the crowd looking for Maziar, but I knew he was nearby. I could feel the energy of his gaze boring through me.

I kept reminding myself that I'd moved on, that we needed to sever all ties, obliterate any possibility of a way back. It was the only way to let go. I needed to focus on my relationship, on moving forward. Ben deserved that.

I needed to leave Maziar behind.

I deserved that.

* * *

Ben pulled up to the front of the house and turned off the car. The house was dark, my family having gone to sleep hours ago. It was close to two in the morning, the street peaceful and quiet.

He turned toward me. I could see him from the corner of my eye but I continued to stare at the flickering street lamp in front of me. Breaking Maziar's heart had left me bone-tired, too exhausted to broach the topic of how it had made Ben feel.

When I didn't turn toward him, he reached out and ran his thumb gently down my cheek.

"You okay, doll?"

"I'm fine, babe. Just tired," I replied, with a weary smile.

He slipped his hand behind my head and pulled me toward him. He softly placed his lips against mine and kissed me. I could feel a tenderness in them that wrapped itself around me, keeping me from falling apart. His warmth filled me as he continued to run his lips across mine. I inhaled his familiar smell, allowed myself to get lost in the comfort that was Ben.

When he finally pulled away, he stared into my eyes and said, "I love you."

There was a new-found strength in his words. He didn't need to say it, but I knew that he'd seen me choose him tonight, erasing the insecurities that he had felt before. I smiled, knowing I'd eased his mind. At least I'd done that much.

Although the part of me that belonged to Maziar felt heavy from breaking his heart, the part that was Ben's danced around free and light. I hung onto to it, pushing the broken pieces of me further back into my mind. I had drawn another line in the sand, this time separating myself from Maziar. I was moving on.

"I love you, too."

CHAPTER TWENTY-SIX

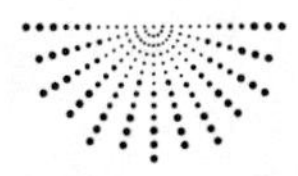

TWO YEARS LATER...

The alarm went off at eight in the morning. I rolled over in bed and grabbed my phone, shutting it off. I lay there a few minutes with my eyes closed, listening to the familiar sounds of home: Mom busily making breakfast in the kitchen, my brother stirring awake, and Dad, no doubt, sitting on the couch reading the paper. I felt a smile stretch across my face as I found peace in the world around me.

I was pulled out of my thoughts as I heard the familiar ping of my text messages. I forfeited the idea of any further sleep, opening my eyes to check my phone. My smile grew wider.

8:05 The day is finally here. We're almost done! Can't wait to see you. Officially starting the BIG countdown! Seven more days...

The familiar fuzzy feeling, that started deep in the pit of my stomach, began to unfurl. I lay on my bed and daydreamed about how handsome Ben was going to look in his cap and gown. Today we were graduating, closing one door in our lives to open another. Even more so, there were only seven more days until we started on our new adventure.

Ben and I were moving to Santa Barbara in a week. With the help of Seti, we had jobs lined up at two different pharmacies. We had placed a deposit on a quaint little two-bedroom apartment, overlooking the ocean. Half of our belongings were sitting in boxes on the living room floor, waiting for us.

My parents had nearly died when I told them what I was planning to do. Mom began to cry, Dad yelled, and Nima did damage control. Ben had insisted that he be there when I told them. He didn't want me to face them alone. He sat quietly on the couch, a pillar of strength for me to lean on. Once they got themselves under control, my parents attempted to sway us on our decision.

"You're not even engaged? What will people think?" Mom asked.

"I don't care what they think. I'm a grown woman," I replied.

"What about your *mamanbozorg*?" she said, more to herself than me. I knew she was dreading telling my grandmother.

"She's just going to have to deal with it, Mom."

"Why are you moving so fast? You guys are just graduating. Why not take some time to work and see where your relationship goes?" Dad reasoned.

"We've been together for over two years, Dad. We aren't moving too fast by anyone's standards," I responded.

After an hour of debating, Mom stormed off to her room. Dad sat on the couch in defeat. I took my spot next to Ben, exhausted.

He turned to Dad, speaking for the first time that evening. "Sir, if I may say something?"

Dad looked up at him, but didn't say a word.

"I know that this isn't common practice in your culture, and it seems like we're doing something wrong. But I wanted you to know that I love your daughter. I'm not playing around or wasting her time. I see a future for us. I'd marry her today if she would have me. We've talked about it, but Sara wants to wait. This is her taking it slow," Ben assured him.

Dad looked weary and tired. He had found himself stuck in this battle of choices for too long. He was not an unreasonable man; he knew that the world had changed since he was young.

"I know that things are different now. You children don't do things the way we did. I appreciate that you love my daughter; I really do. And I respect you for being here today even though you knew we wouldn't be happy. That shows you're a decent man." He paused, taking a deep breath before he continued. "I've always trusted Sara and her decisions. I know she wouldn't be making this move with you if you weren't worthy of her. But it's going to take us some time to get used to. My wife more than myself." He turned toward the hallway, in the direction Mom had stormed off in, defeated.

I lay in bed, replaying that day in my mind. It had been two months since I'd had that conversation with my parents. A few weeks of battles followed, but, somehow, we'd managed to find our center again. My parents realized that I was an adult, twenty-eight years old. I was graduating from pharmacy school and this was how I'd chosen to start the next part of my life.

They also knew me well enough to know that life had changed me. I no longer depended on their guidance or felt the debilitating guilt of going against their wishes. For better or worse, I'd become stronger in making my own decisions. Standing in my way wouldn't stop me—they'd only end up losing me. Reluctantly, they gave in. They began to try to get to know Ben.

I rolled out of bed and got ready for the big day. I threw on a simple, strapless navy blue dress and slid a gold chain around my neck. It held a small, blue eye charm, traditional in my culture to ward off the "evil eyes." Mom had bought it for me and insisted I wear it today. My entire family was coming to my graduation and she was certain that someone would unintentionally jinx me.

The Iranian culture was full of superstitions, the "evil eye" being the most prominently recognized. The concept was being the victim of a curse on someone else's behalf. Iranians tended to be secretive regarding their accomplishments or endeavors for fear that they would fall victim to these curses.

It was referred to as "*Cheshm khordan*," which literally translated into being struck by the eye. The idea behind it was that, if someone's heart longed for something you had, be it your job, your husband, your life, they would project a negative energy onto you, hence causing the curse and the cascade of bad luck to follow. Even if they loved you dearly, they wouldn't be able to control their envy, leading to these misfortunes.

In order to combat the "evil eye," we enlisted the help of anti-evil eye trinkets, usually in the form of a blue eye charm of sorts. In addition, we would burn *esfand*, a type of seed, to ward off the "evil eyes." The seeds were held over the fire until they popped and began to smoke, and then the smoke was circled around the head and the house to rid everyone of the bad eyes.

When I came out of my room, I could already smell the smoke of the *esfand* burning. Mom hurried out of the kitchen with the carrier in hand the moment I stepped into the living room, where Dad and Nima were waiting. She quickly made circles around our heads while saying the traditional chant, then made a lap around the room and went back into the kitchen to put it all away. Once Mom felt she'd efficiently rid us of all the negativity, we headed over to the school. When we arrived, my family went to their seats while I went to staging.

Sandra was the first to spot me and squealed out my name. I laughed and made my way over to her. I was the last to arrive, in true Iranian style, always fashionably late. Ben stood amongst the crowd of our friends. He put his arm around my waist and pulled me into him, placing a gentle kiss on my lips. I smiled up against his mouth, goosebumps spreading across my skin at his touch. He held me close to his side until the ushers separated us by last name.

Once we were all lined up, the music started and we were directed to our seats up on stage. I spotted my family instantly, my mom and aunt frantically waving at me from a few rows back. My grandmother sat beside them, trying to seem as though she wasn't proud of my big accomplishment. I tried to smile at her, knowing none of this was easy for any of us.

The graduation ceremony proceeded as usual, with a few opening words from the dean and speeches by the valedictorian and a guest speaker. Then, they began calling us up row by row. When my name was called, I looked out into the crowd and saw that both my parents were crying.

Along with the excitement of finishing school, there was an air of sadness to the moment. In the next few days, we'd all be going our separate ways. Sandra would be going back up north with her family. Thomas would be going back east.

We'd all promised to keep in touch and visit each other as much as we could, but we knew life would get complicated. Promises would fall by the wayside; time would take its toll on our relationships. The thought of losing them broke my heart. They'd become my second family.

When it was over, we stood up as they pronounced us official graduates. We threw our hats up into the air, cheering. A sea of burgundy and gold rained back down on us. We ran toward each other and spent the next few minutes embracing one another, with tears of joy streaming down our faces. Once we were finished, we reluctantly found our families. We were celebrating the following night before everyone headed home to get on with their lives. The emotional goodbyes, and heartfelt confessions, would have to wait.

I found my parents. They both threw their arms around me at the same time, Mom crying on my shoulder. When she finally let go, Nima hugged me tightly.

"I'm so proud of you," he said, making me cry.

I finally made it to my friends. Leyla and Neda hugged me at the same time, adding their bouquets to my already overflowing arms. Neda looked at me apprehensively when she pulled away. I tilted my head to the side, trying to figure out the source of her discomfort. She slid her hand out of her purse and handed me a card.

"Maziar wanted me to give this to you. I wasn't sure if it was okay, but he insisted," she said unsteadily. She looked down, afraid she'd made the wrong choice by bringing it for me. I took the card from her.

"Thank you," I said, trying to smile reassuringly. I could see the relief wash over her.

Maziar's card proceeded to burn a hole in my hand as I took part in conversations with my family and friends. I wanted to drop all the flowers, run to a private nook, and tear open the envelope to see what he'd written inside. I was overwhelmed by guilt as I watched Ben make his way over to me. I shouldn't care what Maziar had to say.

Ben approached us, his smile in full effect. He turned toward Dad and put out his hand.

"*Mobarak basheh,*" he said in his broken, rehearsed Farsi.

My parents stared at him, not registering it at first. Then, my dad smiled, knowing Ben had put another olive branch in their court.

"*Merci,*" Mom said. She smiled at me, but the corners didn't reach her eyes. She was trying.

Ben's family walked over to us then, and the parents proceeded to congratulate each other. We had plans to go out to lunch with my family, to celebrate after the graduation. Mom leaned in and whispered something to Dad, who then turned toward Ben and his family.

"We're going to get some lunch. Would you like to join us?" he asked.

Ben was thrown back by the offer and didn't respond immediately. June stepped in, having been filled in on my parents' reluctance toward the new move.

"We would love to," she replied.

Once at the restaurant, Maziar's card had faded into the background, locked away in my purse. We all took our seats, Ben sandwiched between Leyla and me in an attempt to somehow protect him from my grandmother. She'd been eyeing him from the moment we got there. Ben ignored her obvious judgments, still making an effort to make conversation with her. I felt bad for him, knowing that his attempts were falling on deaf ears. *Mamanbozorg* was deeply rooted in her ways and no amount of boyish charm was going to change that. He tried anyway.

His mom and stepdad sat at one end of the table with my parents. The dads spoke about work; the moms about family. At one point I overheard June insist that my parents come to Minnesota for a visit. Mom smiled politely and thanked her for the offer. Even though she didn't accept the invitation, she didn't outright refuse it, either—another attempt to evolve on her behalf. All in all, the meal went as well as I could have hoped for.

On the drive home, we all sat in silence for a while. I was staring out the window at the houses flashing by when Mom spoke.

"Ben's parents seem like nice people," she said.

"They are," I responded as I felt a glimmer of hope begin to form in my chest.

Later that evening, I was lying on my bed reading when I heard my phone. As I grabbed my purse to pull it out, Maziar's card slid onto the comforter. I looked at it, surprised; I'd forgotten I had it. My phone rang again with a second message. Both were from Ben. I suddenly felt guilty about not having told him about the card.

9:45 Good night, doll.

9:46 Love you.

I quickly typed a response, turning my attention back to the light blue envelope that sat taunting me. I looked at it reluctantly, afraid to reach out and touch it, as if it would find a way to sear my heart and burn down my defenses. As I contemplated shredding it and throwing it away, a light knock came from the door. I quickly hid it under my pillow, narrowly avoiding its discovery as Dad came in.

"We're about to put a movie on. Do you want to come watch with us?" he asked.

"Sure," I replied. When I realized he was waiting for me, I slid off the bed and followed him into the living room, leaving the card in its hiding spot.

The movie ended close to midnight. I was tired and exhausted from the day's events as I dragged myself back to my room. I climbed into bed and lay there for a few moments, wondering if I should deal with Maziar's card in the morning. When I realized I wouldn't be able to, wondering what he'd written, I reached under my pillow and pulled it out. As I slowly tore open the envelope, my fingers tingled with apprehension against the paper.

The cover had a light gray graduation hat, with pastel confetti surrounding it. It had CONGRATULATIONS written along the top in bold, black letters. I held my breath as I opened the flap. The entire blank side was filled in with Maziar's writing.

Dearest Sara,

Congratulations on finishing pharmacy school! I'm so very proud of you, but I always knew you could do it. Enjoy your day; you deserve it. This isn't how I expected to spend your graduation, alone at home, thinking of where you are and who you're celebrating it with. But then again, a lot of things have come and gone that didn't go how I'd imagined years ago when I first fell in love with you. I know we decided a long time ago to walk away, but I want you to know that not a day goes by that I don't think of you. Not a moment passes when I don't wish things could have been different between us.

Loving you always,
Maziar

I stared at the words in front of me, unsure how I was supposed to feel. I had tried not to think about Maziar for the past two years. I'd convinced myself that we needed to move on and forced myself to do so. I tried my best to wipe him from my memory, not allowing myself a moment of remorse. I knew I needed a clean break, to quit him cold like an addict would. Strangely, a heaviness sat deep in my chest, the sadness of it both heartbreaking and shocking. I suddenly wished he'd never sent me the card.

I ran my fingers over the letters on the paper. I could feel the impressions left by the force of his pen. He'd been holding this card a few hours earlier, and I imagined him sitting at his desk writing. I didn't allow my thoughts to linger long, pushing Maziar back into the box I hid in the far corners of my mind, and turning the key. I slid the card back into its envelope and placed it in the nightstand drawer. I curled up under my comforter, trying to ignore the pain in my chest. Sleep came quickly and I gladly surrendered to it. Although I desperately tried to cling to thoughts of Ben, I dreamed of Maziar that night instead.

CHAPTER TWENTY-SEVEN

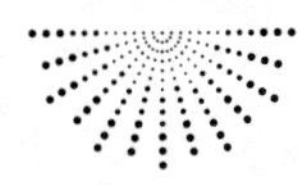

We were meeting at Firefly for dinner and drinks to celebrate our graduation and say our final goodbyes. Everyone was heading home the next day. It was a warm, comfortable night in June. I sat in front of Leyla's house with the windows down, enjoying the breeze as I waited for her.

Dreams from the night before had played in my head all day, making me agitated and uneasy. In the name of nostalgia, I had taken Maziar's necklace out of my jewelry box and slipped it into my purse. I rolled it between my fingers now, wondering why I'd brought it. The cool, familiar touch of the pendant felt comforting even though it shouldn't. I turned it over and stared at our names engraved on the back. The sadness that had started from his card rushed through my chest. I held the heart for a few more moments as if it were a talisman, connecting me to a past I'd long forgotten. I quickly put it back in its hiding place when I saw Leyla coming.

My friends were waiting outside when we pulled up to park. From the street side, the bar was hidden behind a thick cover of vines. All that could be seen was the dark brown steel door of its entrance. It reminded me of a secret passageway.

Once inside, the first room resembled a library with a bar nestled in the far corner. There were book lined shelves and dim red lights that quietly set the room aglow. Beyond the library, the bar opened up into a large seating area with the open sky as its ceiling. There was a big cement fireplace placed in the center of the space and twinkle lights strung across the top, creating a cover of glitter overhead.

We immediately ordered a round of drinks when our table became available. We had one goal in mind for the evening, and that was to get intoxicated. Leyla was my designated driver, allowing me to party without any inhibitions. We drank, we laughed, and at some point Sandra began to cry. There was a DJ spinning music on the upper deck of the building, so we quickly shut her down by dragging her onto the dance floor.

I was covered in the warmth of two cosmos, the third following on their heels, perched clumsily in my hand as I spun around in circles. Without notice, the DJ changed the music and the familiar beats of hip-hop invaded the night.

I stopped spinning, suddenly aware of Ben's eyes on me. He stood a few feet away, the intensity like icicles forming in his blue eyes. The crowd faded as he smiled at me. Before I knew it, Ben stood towering over me with hunger in his eyes.

Our bodies started moving to the music, fitting together like pieces of a puzzle. I could feel his chest up against mine. The warmth of his body radiated through his shirt, grabbing hold of me. I felt myself melt into the familiarity and comfort of him.

We moved against each other with a force that mimicked a lovers' quarrel as the desire escalated between us. I had to resist the urge to steal him away to the bathroom, pushing him up against a stall door. We didn't notice when the song ended, still staring into each other's eyes, silently speaking with our bodies. Sandra placed her hand on my arm and broke us out of our trance.

"Get a room," she said teasingly.

When I got to the table and sat down, I felt my purse vibrate up against the chair. I had missed five calls from Neda and two messages. I didn't think much of it at first, thinking maybe she was drinking and had lost track of how many times she'd called.

11:40 Sara, call me as soon as you get this.

11:45 Sara, I keep trying to call you but you're not picking up. You NEED to call me as soon as you get this. It's an EMERGENCY!!!!

I felt more confused than nervous when I dialed her number. I had no idea that what she was about to say was going to change my life forever.

"Sara, oh, thank God you...me, you need...come to the... Maziar...accident!"

Her phone was breaking up and she was crying. I could barely make out what she was saying, but I heard the two most devastating words: Maziar and accident. I suddenly stood up, knocking over a few empty glasses. They crashed to the floor, interrupting the conversation at the table. Everyone turned to look at me. Leyla was beside me in seconds. Ben was moments behind her. I had one hand against my phone and the other on my left ear, trying to mute out the noises of the restaurant.

"What? What's happened? Neda, I can't hear you. Please slow down. Where are you?" I asked, desperately.

Then, the line disconnected. I moved the phone away from my ear and stared at it as if I couldn't figure out what it was. The world was spinning, and my thoughts felt like they were drowning in a puddle of mud. What was happening?

"What is it?" Leyla asked, when I didn't offer an explanation.

"It was Neda. She was crying. Her phone isn't working," I said, lost.

"Could you make out anything she said?" Leyla replied, trying to urge me forward.

"I think she said Maziar was in a bad accident. She told me to come to the hospital."

Leyla paled, turning toward Ben, who was standing behind her. He thought she was looking for help, but she was just foreseeing the near future, the colossal mess that was about to unfold. I could see her putting the pieces together in her mind. He stepped in and grabbed my arm, helping me out of the chair.

"Let's go outside. It's quieter and maybe Neda is somewhere with better reception now," he directed, guiding me along behind him. Leyla followed.

With shaky hands, I stood in front of the restaurant and dialed Neda's number again. As I listened to the phone ring, I felt like my body was floating and I was frozen in time. I couldn't feel a thing; I was totally numb. I could see the mix of emotion radiating off of Ben, both worry at the state I was in, and anger at my reaction to the news. I turned away from him, incapable of dealing with his feelings at the moment.

This time she picked up on the third ring.

"Sara!"

"Neda, what's going on? What's happened to Maziar?" I sent a silent prayer, hoping her phone would work long enough for her to explain. The uncertainty was more unbearable than the details themselves.

"Where are you? Can you get to the hospital?" she pleaded.

"Wait, what? Neda, slow down. Why do I need to come to the hospital? What's happened?" I couldn't keep my voice steady. My throat suddenly felt dry.

"Sara, he's been in a really bad accident. He was driving home from a party and some drunk driver hit his car. He was almost crushed. I didn't get to see him before they took him."

"Took him where?" I screamed, terror taking over me. What had happened to Maziar? How bad was it? The questions kept swirling around in my head.

"Sara, he's in surgery. The doctor said he's really banged up and it doesn't look good. I don't know all the details. But you need to get here, fast. Can you come?" she pleaded.

I was crying now, and with a whisper I replied, "Yes."

I hung up the phone and looked up. Leyla and Ben were staring at me, both with identical looks of horror across their faces. I just began to sob, the magnitude of what was happening hitting me all at once. Ben reached out and pulled me into his chest, his reluctance emanating off of him. I cried listlessly against him, unable to wrap my head around how my breakdown was making him feel. My face lay against his heart and I could feel the pulse beating wildly in his chest. I knew this wasn't fair, but I couldn't stop myself.

"Sara, what did she say? What's happened to Maziar?" Leyla asked, as she gently rubbed my back.

"He's been in an accident. It doesn't sound good," I said, my voice catching at the end. I pulled away from Ben and could feel him involuntarily take a step farther away from me, putting distance between us.

"Okay, so are we going to the hospital?" she asked, glancing behind me at Ben.

"I need to go," I answered. I didn't turn to see how my words affected him.

She paused for a moment, and even though I knew she felt the betrayal in my words, saw it flash across Ben's face, she nodded.

"Let me go get our stuff."

"No, wait. I'll come with you. I have to say goodbye to everyone. I won't see them again after this." I hadn't imagined my final farewell with my friends would be rushed and under such dire circumstances.

"Okay," Leyla said, heading back toward the entrance.

When we approached the table, everyone looked up at us, worried. I explained what Neda had told me. Sandra's hand flew to her mouth; Thomas shook his head in disbelief. I tried to stay calm, not wanting my last goodbye with them to be about someone else.

"I have to go to the hospital," I said as if it were a fact and not a choice.

"Are you sure that's a good idea?" Sandra asked. Her eyes conveyed her concern, her silence cautioning me.

I knew that, if I went to the hospital, I'd be placing a divide between Ben and me that I wouldn't be able to repair again. I tried to convince myself I shouldn't go, that I should call Neda back and tell her to just keep me updated. But there was a need deep and primal building inside me, propelling me forward. The consequences of what I was doing couldn't even form into an actual thought in my mind. I had to be with him; that was all I knew. There was nowhere else I could be.

"I don't know, but I know I have to be there," I replied, keeping my eyes focused on Sandra so I couldn't see what my words were doing to Ben. She nodded, understanding that my mind had been made up.

"I'm going with you. His family will be there. You shouldn't be alone," Leyla said, leaving no room for debate.

I hadn't even realized I'd have to face his family. They had been so far from my mind that I hadn't recognized I'd be walking into the lion's den. I didn't know if I was strong enough to face their anger. I didn't know if I would crumble or if I would meet them head-on. The only thing I did know was that, if Maziar had any way of knowing I was there, if on some subconscious level we were connected, then I needed to be there for him. I needed him to feel me so he would fight whatever it was he was facing.

"Want me to come, too?" Sandra asked.

"No, you have an early flight tomorrow. I know you, Sandra. You still haven't packed." I gave her a halfhearted smile as she returned it with one of her own. "Keep your phone on you. I'll keep you posted."

She threw her arms around me and we stood there holding each other tight, trying to hang onto what felt like a lifetime.

"I hope you know what you're doing," she whispered in my ear.

"I don't."

"I love you," she said.

"Me too."

We cried, holding each other, not knowing when we would see each other again. I kissed her cheek and squeezed her one more time before letting go. Everyone was gathered around us. One by one I held onto each of them, trying desperately to cling to the life we'd created together for the past four years. We all cried, knowing that things would be quite different in the morning. We said a final goodbye, and then, Leyla and I made our way to the door. Ben followed.

She went to get my car, giving Ben and me time to talk.

"Sara, what are you doing?" His voice sounded tight, as he struggled to keep his frustration under control.

I looked at him, wondering how I was supposed to explain that being by Maziar's side wasn't a choice I was making. It was a necessity as definite as the air passing through my lungs and the blood rushing through my veins. I just had to go.

"I need to be there. I need to make sure he's okay," I said.

"What about us?"

"This isn't about us, Ben. He's been badly hurt and I don't even know whether he'll live or die. I just have to go. Please understand," I pleaded.

Tears silently streamed down my face. I'd lost control. I could feel a sea of emotions circling us again, threatening to take us under. It was too much to endure in one night and I wasn't sure I would see the light of day. He cleared his throat, desperately fighting against his anger.

"Okay. I'm coming with you," he said.

I wanted to say no, to tell him the hospital would be hard enough without him. That I couldn't face it knowing he was watching. I couldn't tell him I had no idea what I was feeling and I was terrified of him seeing something happen that could break his heart. I didn't want to deal with how hurt he would be. But I knew I couldn't, so instead I just nodded and smiled, praying he couldn't see the truth. And when he reached out and took my hand, I let him.

Leyla pulled up then. She sat in the car with it idling at the curb, patiently waiting, knowing that this wasn't a moment that could be rushed. He glanced over at her, then turned his gaze back at me.

"Ready, doll?" he asked.

I felt my heart shatter into a million pieces.

He leaned in, gently kissing me, his lips barely touching mine like the fluttering wings of a butterfly. I looked up into those magnificent blue eyes and could feel the fear floating behind them. I wanted to tell him I was terrified too, but I didn't. Instead, I turned and got into the car.

CHAPTER TWENTY-EIGHT

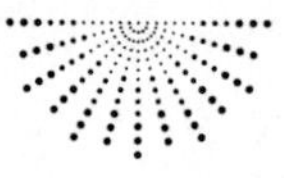

I called Mom on the drive over to the hospital. After I explained what had happened, she and Dad were adamant they meet me there. I knew they were worried that I was stepping into the line of fire and they wanted to be there to shield me from the danger. Having them there, though, would only complicate things further than they already were. I told her as much. After some coercing, she agreed to stay put but made me promise I would leave at the first sign of battle. I agreed, but only to make her feel better; I had no intention of leaving.

The large white building came into view and Leyla turned where the red light flashed EMERGENCY. Neda was waiting for us outside.

I grabbed my red jacket from the back seat and threw it over my clothes. We had come straight from the bar, and although my outfit was modest, I felt naked and exposed. The jacket gave me a false sense of security, as if I were hiding behind protective armor. I had Maziar's necklace wrapped around my fingers, with my hand shoved in my pocket where no one could see. I prayed it would give me the strength I needed to make it through the night.

Neda threw her arms around me and started to cry.

"Sara, I'm so happy you're here. He still isn't out of surgery, and no one's come out to update us. Everyone is freaking out," she said between sobs.

Ben stepped up behind me and placed his hand on my back. His movements startled Neda, who hadn't noticed him standing there. She looked up at him, confused, his presence out of place.

"Hi, Ben," she said, uneasily.

"Hey, Neda."

"Are you ready?" she asked, cautiously turning toward me.

It was obvious the family would not be happy when I walked through the door, but adding Ben to the mix was a recipe for disaster. The message was written all over Neda's face. I turned toward Leyla, eyes pleading.

"Why don't you and I stay down here in the lobby, Ben? I'm sure tensions are high and too many people will just make it worse," she said.

Ben hesitated.

"That may be a good idea. My aunt and uncle are losing it up there," Neda added, trying to sway him.

All the while, I quietly stared at him. He never took his eyes off of me, but he knew I didn't want him to come.

"Okay, but keep your phone on you, Sara," he demanded.

"I will," I said, leaning in to kiss his cheek. He grabbed my waist and pulled me into him.

"I love you," he whispered.

I knew I should say it back, but I couldn't. My feelings were in disarray, nothing quite making sense. I just kissed him again, hoping it would be enough. I squeezed Leyla's hand in appreciation as I passed her on my way to the elevator.

Once we got inside, Neda took us up to the seventh floor. The ride felt like an eternity. I was shaking and I tried desperately to calm down. I didn't want my body to betray me as soon as I walked into the lion's den.

When the doors opened, Neda looked at me. I managed an unconvincing half-smile as we walked out into the hallway. Right before we went into the waiting room, she reached out and grabbed my hand. She might have shown me her vulnerable side a few moments ago, but when it came to her family, she morphed into my protector. I was grateful for her loyalty.

I took a deep breath, trying to find the courage to be strong. The walls I had erected around me all these years were rapidly crumbling tonight, and the broken girl I tried desperately to hide was peeking out from beneath the rubble.

All eyes looked up at us as soon as we walked in. Shock radiated throughout the room, leaving a strangling silence in its wake. It was obvious they hadn't known I was coming, and for a second I wondered why I thought they would have. Neda wouldn't have told them that she was calling me because they would have vetoed it immediately. I could see how she would have thought it better if I just showed up.

Sitting at the far wall directly in front of me were Maziar's mother and his sister. Bita was staring at me, her anger coming off of her in waves. Her green eyes looked like they were actually glowing with hatred. His mother didn't even look up at me. She sat hunched forward, crumbled in on herself with grief. Against the left wall sat his aunt and uncle, and against the right was his father. When I looked over at him, I almost thought I saw the beginning of a smile flash across his lips. But as quickly as it came, it was gone, convincing me I'd imagined it.

"What is she doing here, Neda?" Bita demanded.

"Maziar would want her here," Neda responded, glaring at her.

"No, he wouldn't."

Bita turned her serpent gaze toward me, trying to intimidate me enough to make me leave. I stared back at her, impassive. Where she was fuming, I was the picture of calm, hiding the storm raging inside me. Engaging the devil would do me no good.

"Yes, he would. Who do you think you're fooling? You all know he wants her here!" Neda yelled.

Her frustration bellowed in her voice as it bounced off the waiting room walls. I squeezed her hand, trying to urge her to calm down before things got out of hand. I'd just gotten here.

Whether it was the enormity of the events of the night, or the intensity of Bita's hatred toward me, she laid into Neda and a screaming match began in the middle of the waiting room. All of a sudden, as if she'd been awakened by the noise, Maziar's mother came alive.

"Stop it! Both of you, just be quiet!"

Everyone looked at her, and I could feel my heart drop down to the floor. I steadied myself for what was coming next, but she didn't even look at me. She seemed to slip back into her catatonic daze immediately.

"Neda, I know you think Maziar wants Sara here, but this is a family situation and we're all worried. She only makes it worse," Maziar's aunt said. She turned and looked at me. "You need to leave."

I was not expecting to be thrown out by Lily *Khanoom*, leaving me speechless. Before I could gather my wits, his father jumped in.

"No, Lily, she isn't leaving. I told Neda to call her."

Maziar's mom slowly turned toward her husband, the confusion apparent in her expression. She looked as if his words were swimming through a pool of water and she couldn't understand them. He looked at his wife, the expression on his face softening as he gazed at the woman he'd spent his life with.

"When I was with Maziar, before they took him into surgery," he said, choking up, "he was fighting to stay conscious, Naghmeh. He begged me to call Sara. He said he needed her to be here. Then, they took him away." His face crumbled as tears rolled down his cheeks. He stared at his idle hands sitting in his lap, useless in saving his son. "He told me he loved you before he went unconscious," he said tenderly.

His mother began to cry.

The tears were free-flowing now, down my face and onto the floor. In that moment, I didn't care what his mother or sister thought any longer. I didn't care if they were looking at me as if I were ridiculous or out of bounds. I didn't care if they hated the idea of us. All I knew was that Maziar, in his last moments, was thinking of me. That he mustered up the courage to ask his father to bring me here. And somehow, in all the chaos, Parviz had heard him.

I stared at his father, bewildered by the turn of events. He looked back at me, the kindness apparent now. I hadn't mistaken earlier when I thought I'd seen something other than contempt in him. I could see the change of heart happening in those green eyes, lighter than the vibrant eyes of his daughter, but nonetheless breathtaking. The deep-set lines outlining them crinkled as he gave me the only smile he could manage. He didn't care that it broke his wife's heart to see him give me a little acceptance, or that switching sides enraged his daughter. All he cared about was that he'd managed to get me here as his son had asked.

Maybe love was bigger than circumstance.

"Is he hurt badly? Is he going to be okay?" I asked him, my voice unsteady with fear. Was it possible that I'd never see his face again, hear him laugh, or see him smile?

"He's hurt badly. The other car hit him on his side. The door was pushed in and Maziar was thrown into the passenger's seat. He broke one of his legs and his wrist. But they are more worried about the head injury he sustained. The car folded in on itself and the impact smashed him into the door. He was pretty banged up. By the time they took him into surgery, they said his brain was already swelling from the trauma." He started to sob, barely managing to say, "They don't know if there will be any lasting damage."

I sat down, putting my head in my hands in a vain attempt at privacy. I tried to cry silently, allowing only the sound of my ragged breaths to escape. The pain searing through me was excruciating. It was like nothing I'd ever felt before, bringing me to my knees. I clutched my chest, willing my heart to stop and take me out of this misery. A world without Maziar was a world I didn't want to be in.

I could feel someone looking at me from across the room and I looked up, expecting to see vivid green fury staring back at me. Instead, I found Naghmeh's tear stricken face. I wasn't met with the anger I'd grown so accustomed to, but, rather, she seemed to have just noticed I was sitting there. Before my presence seemed to truly register, the doctor walked in. Everyone's focus turned to him.

"Maziar is out of surgery," he said. "His left leg was broken in three different places. We reset it and put it in a cast. His right wrist was worse off. We think he tried to stop his impact instinctively. The force shattered it. Some of the bones had been broken to dust, so we had to try to put his wrist back together the best we could with what was left. We added screws and plates where we needed. It's going to be a while before he's able to use it."

"How about his head injury?" Parviz asked.

"That's a little more complicated. We were able to drain the fluid and stop the swelling for now. We've had to place Maziar in an induced coma to allow his body to heal itself. We don't anticipate leaving him that way too long, but we'll know better in a few days." The doctor's features softened, alerting that bad news was coming. "His head injury was very bad. The impact was pretty severe. We won't know what we're looking at until he wakes up."

Naghmeh moved forward, grabbing onto her husband's arm to steady herself, and asked the question we were all thinking.

"He will wake up, though, right?"

The doctor reached out for her hand. She allowed him to take it, knowing that any comfort he was giving only confirmed that things were worse than he was letting on.

"We're very hopeful. Unfortunately, we don't know anything for sure. We just need to be patient and wait," he said kindly.

Bita slid back down in her seat and started to sob. Deep moans of pain escaped her lips as her aunt consoled her. His uncle battled the tears filling his eyes as he paced back and forth with nervous energy. His parents stood there staring at the doctor, frozen in the nightmare they'd suddenly found themselves in. My chest burned and I felt like I was suffocating.

I ran to the bathroom, starting to uncontrollably gasp for air. I couldn't see out of my eyes anymore, blackness invading my vision. I was going to pass out and I welcomed it; anything to get me out of this hell I was in, if even for a moment. Neda came in behind me. She placed herself right in front of me, yelling at me to breathe. I fought the darkness and obeyed. Then, I crumbled to the floor.

I prayed while I lay on the cold bathroom tiles, begging God to let Maziar wake up. I made negotiations, promised everything I could think of in exchange for him being okay. Then, I cried because we had wasted so much time apart. Now it might be too late. He might not wake up, or worse, he could wake up and not be the same Maziar I knew. Either way, I would have lost him forever, and that alone was the saddest thing I could think to bear. I couldn't live without him.

If he died here in this hospital, I knew part of me would die with him.

* * *

It had been two hours since I'd arrived at the hospital. I sat in the bathroom, exhausted, the burden of my emotions causing a horrid pounding in my head. I leaned against the wall, the coolness of the tiles soothing. I heard the familiar ring of my phone. I hadn't thought it was possible to feel any more anxiety, but a wave crashed over me, pinning me in place.

Ben was downstairs waiting for me. In the chaos that had ensued from the moment I'd arrived, I'd forgotten he'd come with me. The reality of my situation hit me hard as I pulled out my phone, dreading the next obstacle I was about to face.

12:00 You okay? It's getting late. I'm worried.

I stared at the screen, feeling like I was going to throw up. I wished I could melt away into the floor, to hide from my tangled life. But I knew avoiding Ben would only make an already horrific situation worse.

12:05 I'll be right down.

"I need to go downstairs to talk to Ben," I said as Neda helped me off the floor.

"Okay." Her eyes were full of worry. "Are you leaving?"

"No, but I need to talk to Ben." We looked at each other, both knowing that my struggles had just begun.

"Do you want me to come with you?"

"No," I said, "It's better I go alone."

The ride down in the elevator felt like it lasted another lifetime. When I walked out into the lobby, both Leyla and Ben stood up. I smiled wearily as I approached them.

"Hey, doll," Ben said.

What remained of my beaten and battered heart was crushed under the weight of his hopeful gaze.

"Hi," I replied.

He came up and wrapped his arms around me. I wanted to simultaneously melt into him and push him away. The contradiction of my feelings was jarring. Leyla knew what I was about to do, so she excused herself to the bathroom, giving us privacy. Her arm brushed against my hand as she walked by, giving me strength.

"It's late. I think we should go home," he said.

I just looked at him, wondering what it was I was doing. I knew I was drawing a line, one we could never return from. No matter how hard I tried to convince myself I should leave with Ben, that it was the right thing to do, my body wouldn't obey. I was treading in dangerous waters, but I couldn't persuade myself to stop.

"I'm not going." His eyes widened with surprise. I continued trying to hang on to my nerve before it was drained out of me by his reaction. "He's still in surgery. It's not looking so good. I just need to stay and make sure he's okay," I reasoned.

"Can't Neda call you with an update once he's out?"

"I'd rather stay," I said, pushing forward.

"Sara, it's really late. We have a lot of packing to still do. We're leaving in a few days."

He couldn't keep the pleading out of his voice. I knew it killed him to look so vulnerable when I was choosing Maziar over him, once again.

"I know. I'll get it done. Don't worry. I just need to stay for a few more hours," I responded, maintaining the façade that nothing had changed between us.

"Then, I'll stay with you," he demanded.

I'd been afraid he would say that. I needed him to leave. I couldn't worry about him and Maziar at the same time.

"There's no reason for you to stay. You'd be down here and I'd be upstairs. Go home. Get some sleep. No use in both of us being exhausted."

Leyla walked back toward us. Before Ben had a chance to say anything else, I turned to her.

"Can you take Ben back to his car? I'm going to stay until Maziar is out of surgery."

She could see he wasn't happy, but her loyalties were with me. "Sure. Then, I'll head back to get you."

"That'd be great." I turned toward Ben. "I'll see you later." I leaned in and quickly kissed him, then turned and walked down the hall. I knew he was staring at me but I didn't turn around.

I needed to get back to Maziar.

CHAPTER TWENTY-NINE

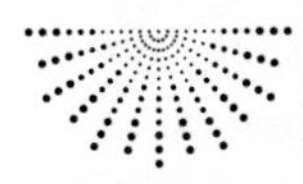

Maziar spent the next few hours in recovery. We all waited impatiently, the walls of the waiting room closing in on us as the minutes on the clock continued to tick by. Naghmeh sat in the corner by herself, periodically bursting into tears. The sound of her wailing had gone from heartbreaking to nerve-wracking as the patience continued to grow thin.

Finally, the nurse came in to tell us that he'd been moved to a private room and that we could see him. They only allowed two people to visit at a time, so naturally his parents went first. I paced back and forth with worry. I needed desperately to go in, but I had no idea if I'd be allowed to, with his mother and sister barring my way.

Parviz walked back into the waiting room. He appeared to have aged in the hour he'd spent by his son's hospital bed. His shoulders hunched forward, the wariness in his gait even more apparent. The fluorescent lights overhead emphasized the gray in his hair, making it appear more dramatic, adding years to his appearance. His face looked gaunt and tired, the wrinkles making irregular patterns on his skin. His eyes were red and swollen, making it obvious that the sight of his son had broken his heart. He told us that his wife refused to leave Maziar's side, so we had to go in one by one. Maziar's aunt, Lily, went in next.

The air rushed out of me and I stood paralyzed with despair. His mother wasn't going to leave the room, which meant I wouldn't be allowed in. I was devastated and angry, with no idea what to do next. Neda stood up and came to my side. She grabbed my hand, breaking me out of my thoughts. I turned and looked at her, terrified at the prospect of not seeing Maziar.

"Don't worry. You'll be able to see him," she said, still staring at her uncle's broken figure as she spoke. "I promise."

I don't know how I expected her to rectify the situation, but in that moment, I wanted to believe her.

The next few hours were a revolving door of taking turns to sit with Maziar. Each person would go in, stay about an hour, then come out to give the next person a turn, while all the while his mother remaining vigilant by his side. I waited patiently, but as each new person went inside, the more consumed I became with worry over how Naghmeh would react. I continued to pace back and forth, trying to dissipate some of the nervous energy that bound my body tightly.

Neda was the last to go in from the family. She only spent about twenty minutes sitting with him. I had the distinct feeling she cut her visit short because she knew I was dying to get in there. When she came back into the waiting room, she looked at her uncle. A silent understanding passed between them as he stood up and walked toward me.

"Sara, let me show you where Maziar's room is," he said.

I was unable to form any words to convey my gratitude. He just gave me a weary smile, letting me know he knew how much it meant to me. I could visibly see Neda relax once he was leading me out of the room, his hand on the back of my arm, guiding me through the door.

We had to take an elevator down to the fifth floor. We stepped out, and he guided me toward the left. He stopped in front of room 515. I suddenly froze, the fear of what I would find behind it paralyzing me. He must have understood what I was thinking because he stepped in front of me and grabbed the door handle, looking me in the eye.

"Be brave. He needs you right now," he said, as he pushed it open. I obediently followed.

Maziar lay on a large hospital bed with wires encircling him, attached to machines that beeped and hummed. They had intubated him. The sound of the inhalation and exhalation of the machine pumping air into his chest had a soothing, rhythmic pattern to it. I could no longer see his lips. They were taped around the tube that made its way into his lungs. He had a white bandage wrapped around his head, covering the skin where they shaved his hair. There was a cast on his right hand reaching past his wrist, and another covering almost his entire left leg, which was propped up on a stack of pillows.

The white sheets, the bandages, and the walls seemed to consume him in a sea of clouds. The lack of color accentuated his beaten and battered body, making his bruises the most prominent feature. He reminded me of a broken angel.

I didn't notice his mother staring at her son's ruined body, or his father standing beside me telling me it was okay. I didn't notice the light above flickering ever so slightly or the nurse who came in to record the numbers on the machine. All I saw was the love of my life lying lifeless on the bed before me, unable to even do something as simple as breathe on his own. I felt a dam inside me break and a sea of emotion engulf me. My heart had no remaining surfaces left to shatter, so it decided to die altogether.

I blindly walked to Maziar's side. I didn't glance at Naghmeh, who hadn't even noticed my presence. I fell into the empty chair beside his bed and reached out to grab the fingers peeking out from his cast. I intertwined them with my own, instantly feeling the familiar electricity flowing between us. I placed my other hand on his chest, making sure that his heart was still beating beneath the sea of tubes surrounding him. I felt its rhythm against my palm, relieved.

"Naghmeh," Parviz said, "you should take a break, *azizam*. You've been sitting here with Maziar for hours. Why don't we go for a walk, get a cup of *chaye?* Sara is with him. He'll be okay."

I looked at Maziar's mother, waiting for her protest. Her husband's voice jarred her and she suddenly looked up, as if she'd just noticed there were people in the room. She still had the confused, flustered expression she wore in the waiting room. She looked straight at me, but her eyes seemed glassy and uncomprehending. I wasn't sure if she actually saw me.

The intensity of her grief had put her in an alternate world, one that only existed around the wires attached to her son. She seemed incapable of seeing anything further than that, including the girl she fought so desperately to remove from his life years before. She stood up as her husband gently coerced her out of the chair and allowed him to lead her out of the room. She never spoke a word.

I turned my attention back to Maziar. I looked at his battered face and could still see the beauty that lay beneath the purples and reds invading his skin. I put my hand against his face, and through my tears, I started to speak. I didn't know if he could hear me but I was sure he could feel me there. I needed to fill the silence. I told him about everything that had led me to this moment, how scared I'd been when Neda had called me, that it was because of his father that I was even there, and that I thought Parviz had officially become our ally.

Then, I begged him to fight.

I don't know how long I held his hand and whispered into his ear, but at some point I felt a presence behind me. I turned around and saw his mother standing in the doorway watching us. She looked at me for a minute, then walked over to the opposite side of Maziar's bed and sat in her chair, placing his free hand in hers. We both held onto him, peacefully coexisting. We stayed that way, neither looking at the other, as we silently prayed for his recovery.

We sat together in the cold quiet of the hospital room for another hour. Shortly after, Maziar's aunt came in and asked if she could get a turn.

"Of course, Lily *Khanoom,*" I said, leaning in and kissing Maziar's cheek. "I'll be back soon," I whispered into his ear.

I walked to the waiting room and saw that within the past few hours more members of Maziar's family had arrived. Pasha and Emanuel were also there, sitting next to Neda, who was looking at me with concern as I walked through the door. I paid them no attention as I made my way toward Parviz. He was standing at the other end of the room talking to his brother and two cousins. They all looked at me as I approached, which prompted him to turn around and face me.

I walked right up to him, tears streaming down my face, and threw my arms around him. He was startled at my sudden show of emotion, standing motionless for a few seconds. Then, he hugged me back.

"Thank you, Parviz *Khan,*" I said.

"You're welcome," he replied, providing a small beacon of light in the nightmare.

Everyone had gone silent, unsure how to interpret what they were seeing. Bita glared at me–surprisingly, the only anger that could be felt within the room. I didn't care what any of them thought; I was just grateful that Maziar's father was able to finally recognize what Maziar and I had. He was able to push past his opinions and old traditions, unexpectedly planting a seed of hope in my chest. I could feel it starting to bloom around my heart.

CHAPTER THIRTY

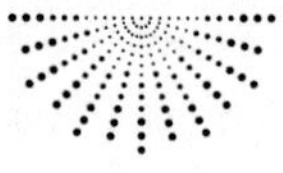

It had been five days since Maziar's accident. The doctors had reduced the amount of barbiturates given to him, taking him out of the coma on the third day.

The coma was only a temporary solution, decreasing the pressure built up on his brain after the impact to minimize any permanent damage on the portions affected. By the third day, the doctors had seen enough reduction in swelling and Maziar's brain waves had normalized. They'd warned us, however, that even though the drugs were going to be reduced and he was going to be taken off the ventilator, he might not wake up immediately. His body was still fighting against the plethora of injuries.

I had sat next to Maziar's bed holding his hand since he had been admitted. I'd left only for a few hours to shower and sleep. And when they took him off the ventilator, I stood next to him, holding my breath with the rest of his family while we waited to see if he'd inhale on his own.

My parents were worried that I'd collapse if I continued at this pace but could see that there was no point in trying to convince me otherwise. The tides had changed over the past week and everyone could see it. I was driven by my dedication to him and fueled by my love. The dam I'd built between us, keeping him at bay, convincing myself that we were better apart, had shattered. I had a newfound purpose, a strength that I'd pulled from deep down in my soul. Even Maziar's family sensed it and I could feel their resolve shaking beneath my force. I didn't care anymore what anyone thought, and everyone knew it.

I had almost lost him. I'd spent the past five days by his bedside, making every deal possible with my maker, begging that Maziar wake up. I'd cried all the tears I had, leaving me anxiety ridden and exhausted.

He hadn't woken up yet. He hadn't twitched an eyelid or flicked a finger. The stress of sitting around waiting for the past two days had worn us all down. They had lifted the two-visitor ban for us and now I sat in the chair to Maziar's right, while his mother sat across from me on the other side of his bed. She would go in and out of her catatonic state, looking up only when someone addressed her directly or urged her to drink something. I had yet to see a definite sign that she even knew I existed.

His father and Bita sat in the far corner on two adjacent seats next to each other, quietly whispering. Leyla had just come back, staying true to her word and only leaving me alone for a few hours at a time. If I had let her, she would have glued herself to my side for the past week.

We all existed quietly in the space between us. The anger and hatred had dissipated, all of us too consumed with worry and exhaustion to engage in any other battles. Parviz had eased into a more comfortable new normal with me. He would smile when I walked in or pat me on the shoulder as he walked out of the room. He would engage in short, polite conversations with me. Bita and I were content to just avoid each other, the natural glares and anger having taken a back seat to our current situation.

I had minimal contact with Ben while in the hospital. He would text me to check in, sending me pictures of boxes he was packing, trying to remain positive about our move. Every time my phone rang, though, I was filled with dread. I wanted to escape, to hide within the four walls of Maziar's hospital room where nothing but he and I existed. Instead of telling Ben I'd changed my mind, I continued to sound invested. I knew it was wrong to lead him on, but I wanted to avoid the inevitable conversation for as long as I could. I had too much already on my plate. Today, though, was the day we were supposed to be heading to Santa Barbara.

I stood up and stretched, needing to shake the stiffness from sitting idly too long out of my limbs. I turned toward Leyla.

"Want to take a walk with me to the cafeteria?"

"Of course," she replied, standing up.

I wondered, at that moment, how I would've ever gotten through life without her. She was as loyal as they came, fierce in protecting me. She'd held my hand throughout my entire ordeal with Maziar, from the moment it began, and now she stood vigilant beside me, daring anyone to try to push me around. I realized how lucky I was to have been blessed in finding a sister like her.

Armed with a little more courage, I turned and faced his mother. She looked up at me through puffy, tired, eyes.

"Would you like some *chayee*? You haven't had much to eat today. Can I get you some food?"

She looked startled for a second, like she had no idea who I was. When she didn't respond, Parviz spoke up.

"Yes, *aziz*, we would love some, if you don't mind."

"No problem," I said, smiling at him.

Her disorientation didn't offend me. It was obvious that the trauma of the past week had taken its toll on her. She was unable to function from the debilitating effects of her grief.

"Bita?" I asked, turning toward Maziar's sister. I didn't flinch as I saw Leyla's jaw drop in my peripheral vision.

"Coffee...please," she stammered. I'd caught her off guard.

"Sure," I said, walking out the door

"Well played, my friend, well played," Leyla said teasingly, once we were out of earshot. "Seriously, what was all that?"

"I don't know. I was just being polite. Plus, I'm so tired of fighting. I don't care if I have to be the one to swallow my pride if it means we can at least stop hating each other. It's exhausting."

"Well I'm proud of you. It takes guts to play with the lions," she said, still beaming at me.

"Thanks."

We walked slowly to the cafeteria, needing a break from the confines of the hospital room. Maziar's lack of consciousness was driving me mad, so I was relishing anything that would allow me a break from the worry and fear at his bedside. We got the coffees and teas and I bought a few cookies and muffins in case anyone was hungry. None of us had eaten or slept much in the past few days. We all appeared gaunt and haggard with dark circles under our eyes and deep lines etched across our foreheads. Sugar would do us all a little good.

On our way back to the room, I felt my phone buzz in my pocket. I handed the drinks over to Leyla as we stopped in the hall so I could check it. I gasped.

1:15 I'm downstairs.

"What is it?" Leyla asked.

"It's Ben," I said, looking at her. "He's here." I could feel the dread coursing through my veins as if it had replaced my blood.

"That's not good."

"No, it's not!" I replied, panicked.

She reached out and grabbed the remaining snacks from my hands, strategically placing them in her arms so she could carry all the goods back to the room herself.

"What are you doing?" I asked, suddenly terrified she was leaving me.

"Well your boyfriend is downstairs in the lobby of the hospital where your ex-boyfriend is staying. You're supposed to be on your way to your new apartment as we speak. Instead, you're here." She looked me in the eye. "I think it's about time you deal with this situation, don't you?"

"I don't want to," I said, shaking my head.

"I don't think that really matters." She gave me a little nudge with her elbow. "You can do this." Then, she walked into the elevator, leaving me alone in the cold, unfamiliar hallway.

I had known this conversation was coming—it was inevitable. But I'd spent the past week in a constant battle of my head and heart. I still wasn't sure what to say. Ben was the reliable choice. We had built a solid future together, and now I was backing out of so many promises. I knew Ben was the better choice.

But hearing that something had happened to Maziar had turned my world on its axis. Feelings I had suppressed years ago had rushed through the walls I'd erected. Now I couldn't turn them off, no matter how much I tried. I was still in love with him. I wasn't sure I'd ever really stopped.

I saw Ben as soon as I walked into the lobby. He was standing at the far wall, staring thoughtfully out the window at something beyond the glass. I could see his profile as I neared him. The dark circles under his eyes were prominent and his cheekbones jutted out more noticeably, as if he'd lost weight in the past few days. He looked tired. He turned instinctively as I approached.

"Hi."

"Hey, doll," he replied. A familiar pang rushed through my chest.

"How are you?" I asked, knowing it was a stupid question. It was obvious in the way he looked.

He didn't respond, just stared at me as if he were trying to come up with the right words to say. The anxiety continued to build, as the silence stretched before us.

"The car is packed. Today is moving day," he said, very matter-of-fact, as if he were making an observation.

"I know," I replied. I forced myself to look him in the eye, despite wanting to stare at the floor.

"Are you coming?" he asked.

"I can't. Not today," I said. He didn't flinch, already knowing my answer. In a futile attempt to rectify the situation, I continued, "But I still have time. We don't start work for another week. I'll be right behind you."

"Please stop lying," he responded. I could see the anger clouding his crystal-blue eyes as he struggled to maintain control. "From the moment Maziar got into the accident, you'd made up your mind that you were going back to him. You're acting as if the last two years meant nothing to you."

"Ben, that's not true."

"Isn't it? You came running over here without thinking how it would affect us. I tried to convince myself that you were just concerned, that you felt some irrational loyalty to him, but I knew better. I've always known better, Sara." His voice had gotten louder, his grip slipping on the fragile strings holding him together. People started to look our way but he didn't notice. "How stupid was I to think you could actually walk away from this guy? You've never been able to leave him behind. That's been your biggest flaw. I should've left you years ago when I had the chance."

The last of his words stung deep.

"Ben, I'm so sorry," I whispered.

"Oh, save it! Don't play the martyr, acting like this is all out of your control, like you have no idea what you've done to me. I'm sick of it. You aren't the victim here, Sara. You chew people up and spit them out when they no longer serve their purpose. You were never going to go with me, were you? Not after Neda's phone call."

He searched my eyes for an answer other than what he knew to be true but came up empty. I just stood there, shocked, tears filling my eyes from the truth of his words.

"Ben, I'm so sorry," was all I could offer him.

We stood there amongst a sea of people, yet we were the only two in the room. I wanted to give him some comfort, find a way to make things right for him because he didn't deserve this, but there was nothing I could do. I'd already done the damage and now I could never take it back.

"I am, too," he said. Then, he turned and walked out the door.

I stared at his back until he became a small dot in my vision, too far to make out the features of his broad shoulders or the lines of the phoenix peeking out through the bottom of his sleeve. I stared at the space he left behind as he turned into the parking lot, realizing our moment in this life was over.

Then, I turned and went back to Maziar's room.

* * *

Everyone was where I had left them. I stood in the doorway watching his family hovering around him, realizing that situations like this had a way of mending even the most broken of bridges and creating a small platform for the possibility of change. I didn't know what would happen if Maziar woke up, whether we'd all continue to grow or return to our old antics. I did know that, years ago, the four of us couldn't sit in the same room together without an explosion.

I took my seat, returning to my post by his side. I sat there holding his hand until the sun had set and night had fallen upon us. It was easy to lose track of hours here, sitting in a tiny hospital room, staring at its four white walls, waiting. At six thirty I stood up to leave.

The breakdown of shifts had gone this way for the past five days. I would leave with Leyla to go home, take a shower, eat, and head back around eight thirty. His family left once I got there, his parents returning at midnight to spend the night in the empty bed beside him. I'd return the next morning and start the cycle all over again.

Parviz and I had written our numbers on a piece of paper beside the phone. There was an understanding between us that at the slightest notice of any change, whoever was here would call the other. I reluctantly stood up, kissing Maziar's head before I left.

A half-hour later, I walked through the door of my house. My parents sat nervously on the couch, pretending to watch television. They were both awaiting my arrival, hoping I had good news about Maziar. I looked at them, and without saying a word, I shook my head no. Dad stared at the floor as Mom's eyes filled with tears.

Maziar and I might have ended a long time ago, but like me, my parents had never stopped loving him. He'd been a part of my family, an image of my future they had allowed themselves to dream about, and only circumstances had severed our ties. If Maziar's parents hadn't been so adamant that we couldn't be together, I knew my parents would have fully been on board with our relationship. Mom would have continued battling my grandmother, if she were the only one standing in our way.

I was tired. My muscles ached as if I'd run a marathon and my head hurt from worry. My eyes drooped from exhaustion and my stomach rumbled with hunger. I could have laid my head down, falling asleep for days. But I couldn't afford to acknowledge my physical state. I had to be strong, to push forward so I could be there when Maziar woke up. If he woke up. The thought felt like a hot knife piercing my stomach.

Mom got up from the couch and put her arm around my shoulders, leading me back to her spot next to Dad. I let my body sink into the pillows, let the warmth her body had left on the fabric cocoon me. Dad placed his arm around me and pulled me into his side. I put my head on his shoulder.

"Ben left for Santa Barbara today," I said wearily.

"He did?" Dad asked. "When will you be heading up there?"

I could almost see Mom hold her breath as she waited for me to answer him.

"I'm not. He's going alone," I said.

Neither of them commented. I knew my parents had both hoped my decision to move with Ben would change, but they never said it out loud. They were trying to avoid any further wars between us. I wanted to be angry that they'd gotten what they wanted, but I didn't have the energy. Instead, I let Dad comfort me with his embrace. His hand unconsciously made its way to my head as he started to play with my hair like he did when I was younger. The methodical movement lulled me, allowing my muscles to relax further into the cushions. I began to doze off.

I wasn't sure how long I slept cuddled up under my dad's arm, but I was roused by the sound of my brother coming down the hall. I smiled behind closed lids, welcoming the normalcy of the moment. When I opened my eyes, I found Dad glaring at him for waking me.

"It's fine, Dad. I have to shower and eat anyway. I need to get back to the hospital," I said, squeezing his arm as I sat up.

"How's Maziar?" Nima asked.

"He's the same. He hasn't woken up."

"He will," he offered encouragingly.

I just smiled past the hopelessness I felt in my heart. Then, I pulled myself away from the couch and into the shower. I walked into the kitchen a half-hour later to find my family sitting around the table waiting on me to eat dinner.

I was struck by the immense amount of love I sensed as they looked at me. I had felt alone this past week, but I realized I hadn't been. They'd been there all along, silently waiting to catch me if I fell. That, in combination with the emotional week, was all it took to unravel me. I started sobbing in the middle of the kitchen.

Mom began to cry as she watched me slowly break under the weight of it all. Dad murmured soothing words to calm me as Nima held me, letting me shower the side of his shirt with my tears. We stood frozen in time, my family giving me the strength I lacked until I had no tears left to cry.

"I'm sorry. I'm fine. I'm just really tired and stressed," I said as I wiped the tears from my face.

"Maybe you should stay home tonight. I know you want to be there, Sara, but you're going to get sick like this. Then, you won't be any good for Maziar," Mom pleaded.

"I can't."

She sighed, knowing I wouldn't budge, and at the same time, understanding why I needed to be there.

"Okay, sit down and eat something at least. I'll make you some tea before you go back. We'll drive you tonight. You can't drive like this."

I didn't protest. I could barely keep my eyes open, so a half-hour later I welcomed the ride.

CHAPTER THIRTY-ONE

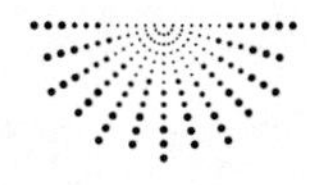

It was eight forty when I walked through Maziar's hospital room door. His family sat in a semi-circle around his bed, each with their hand reaching out to touch him on one of his limbs. All any of us wanted to do was let him know we were there and he wasn't fighting alone.

Parviz looked up at me, his exhaustion covering his face like a mask. He got up and silently gathered his wife and their things, too tired to engage in any conversation. Bita sat in her chair, staring at her brother lying deathly still beneath the white hospital sheets.

I could feel the pain she was experiencing as she watched him. We were worlds apart, but in that one thing, we were two of the same. We both loved Maziar, each praying to her own God that he'd be okay. For a moment, I felt compassion for the girl who had set the ball rolling in ruining my relationship. I realized that the heart was capable of a lot more forgiving than I'd imagined.

Once his parents had all their things, his mom placed her hand on Bita's shoulder, breaking her away from Maziar's bedside. Reluctantly she stood up, running her hand across his foot as her goodbye.

"Sara, we'll be back in a few hours. You'll call us if anything changes?" Parviz asked.

"Of course," I replied, patting the hand he'd placed on my shoulder.

Once they'd left, I pulled my chair closer to Maziar's bed and reached out to hold his hand. I'd run out of new things to say so I started to take us both back in time, recollecting moments from our past together. I reminisced about the day we met, how I could feel the electricity course through my veins from the first time his arm brushed up against mine. I took him back to the secret garden where we danced in the rain. I retold the story of when I told my parents about our relationship and praised him for how swiftly he had Mom eating out of his hand. I kept pulling from my scrapbook of memories, trying to fill the emptiness in the room.

I wanted to feel him, to lie with my hand on his chest like I used to. The hospital rail was creating a barrier, so I crawled over it into the small space beside him. Taking care not to jar any of the tubes that were connected to his body, I lay as close as I could, feeling the rhythm of his heart beat beneath my palm, an unspoken confirmation that he was alive. I dozed off with my head against Maziar's shoulder.

I was startled awake when I felt the bed move. I lay frozen, unsure if I'd dreamed it or if Maziar had actually shifted. I held my breath, too terrified to look at him, worried I would only be disappointed when I saw him still lying there motionless. A minute passed before I lifted my head.

His face was peaceful as if he were just dreaming. The only movement was the rising and falling of his chest as he breathed. I lost the little glimmer of hope that had found its way into my heart just moments ago. I tried to tame my despair, telling myself that Maziar would wake up soon. He had to. I just needed to be patient.

Midnight came sooner than I'd expected. I heard the shuffle of his parents' feet in the hallway. I sat up and moved off of the bed before they made their way into the room. I didn't want them to witness the intimacy I felt lying close to him. I wanted to keep that moment for myself.

* * *

The next morning, I didn't go straight to the hospital. I was filled with the dread of walking through the door only to find Maziar still lying motionless on the bed. I wanted him to wake up so badly it hurt. I decided to take a drive first to clear my head.

Before I knew it, I'd pulled over onto the dirt road leading to the secret garden. As if my body were moving on its own command, I got out and started walking down the trail. The familiar fear of getting lost or stuck was nonexistent this time, even though I was alone. I was propelled forward by the severe need to be hidden under the canopy of its leaves, surrounded by its magic.

I ducked under the archway of branches, stepping into the fairy garden. It was early, and I was alone. I made my way as far down as I could, sitting on the carpet of grass. The peacefulness grabbed hold of me, breathing new life into my lungs. I instantly felt closer to Maziar, as if his spirit had followed me here, watching me from the cover of trees.

I began to pray. As the words came out of me, part Arabic, part English, I looked up toward the sky for a confirmation that someone was listening. There was none, and so I hopelessly returned my gaze back to the stream, finding solace in the lapping water.

"Maziar, if you can hear me somehow, come back to me. I'm sorry I walked away. I'm sorry we wasted so much time. I should have stayed. We should have fought for us. I can't imagine my life without you. Please don't leave me. You have to wake up."

Tears were streaming down my face; the dam erected long ago no longer existent. It felt freeing to let it out, not having to worry about who was watching, or trying to push my emotions back behind locked doors. For the first time in days, I could finally let go.

My phone vibrated up against my leg, startling me. I wiped the tears from my cheeks, reaching into my pocket to grab it. Neda's picture flashed on my screen. I felt a rush of anxiety as I picked it up, bracing for bad news.

"He's awake."

* * *

I came crashing through the door of the hospital room at full speed.

Neda's voice kept replaying in my mind, "He's awake," but I couldn't wrap my head around it. I was terrified I'd get there only to find that it had been a mistake.

I stopped in the doorway, the crowd around his bed blocking my view. I stood frozen to the floor, my heart slamming against my chest. I listened, hearing nothing but the murmur of their voices at first. But then that familiar gravelly sound, scratchy from not having been used, floated through the air. My hand flew to my mouth as I gasped, alerting every one of my arrival. All heads turned toward me, staring. Some glared, some looked confused, but I didn't notice any of them. I cautiously moved toward him, afraid any sudden movements would wake me from this dream.

Lying amongst the mountain of white sheets was Maziar. He was sitting up with his back against the pillows. He looked tired, worn down, but he was awake. He broke out into that beautiful smile and I lost it. I began to cry as I rushed over to his side, with no regard for who was watching. He reached out, pulling me close to him.

"You're here," he whispered, placing his head against mine.

He softly kissed the top of my head. I was so afraid I'd manifested him out of thin air I couldn't look up at him. If I were dreaming, I prayed I'd never wake up. Then, I heard him again, this time saying my name.

"Sara."

Maziar was really awake.

I slowly pulled back to find his familiar hazel eyes staring at me. He managed a smile through the pain and discomfort of his body, trying to reassure me that this was in fact not a dream. I sat back on the bed in disbelief. Then, I began to laugh, crying at the same time. I looked like I'd gone crazy.

"It's okay. I'm okay," Maziar repeated over and over again.

I sobbed with relief, the anxieties and worry of the week having broken me. I reached out to touch his face, still trying to make sure he was real. I lay my hand against it and felt his warm breath tickle my fingers. He turned his head and kissed the inside of my palm.

I had forgotten that anyone else was in the room until I felt Neda place her hand on my shoulder. I begrudgingly pulled away from him, moving off his bed. Everyone was silently watching, and I suddenly felt embarrassed that they'd witness our reunion.

I glanced up and saw his mother staring at me from beside his bed. This time, there was recognition in her eyes. Her vegetative state was long gone, replaced by the familiar anger I was so accustomed to seeing. My stomach jerked as I looked away.

* * *

The next few hours were a whirlwind of visitors and tears. I sat quietly in the back of the room as Maziar's family took turns hugging and kissing him while they cried. His eyes remained fixed on me the entire time. I could see Naghmeh take notice, could feel her anger begin to boil. I dreaded what her reaction meant but tried my best to ignore it.

Finally, the crowd departed, leaving for the night. His mother reluctantly agreed to go home for a few hours, Parviz almost dragging her out of the room. Part of me thought his insistence to leave had something to do with allowing us some time alone.

When they finally walked out the door, Maziar motioned me over to the bed, scooting to one side. I carefully climbed in next to him, wanting desperately to touch him. He leaned his cheek on my head, wrapping his good arm around me.

"When the car hit me, I remember thinking that I was going to die and I'd never see you again." My heart hurt imagining the moment of impact, the fear he must have felt. "Sara, I know you keep telling me this won't work, and I've tried so hard to leave you alone. But I can't. I want to be with you."

"You just woke up. We don't need to talk about all of this right now," I said, pulling in closer to his side, taking care not to hurt him.

"No," he protested. "I don't want to wait to talk about this. Don't you get it? That's all we've been doing, just waiting like something's going to change. But it's not going to, Sara. And I don't want us to be apart anymore. I don't care what my family has to say. I refuse to let them tell me who to love. I want to be with you. That's all that matters now." He looked into my eyes and I could see the child hidden behind them, wounded and insecure. When I didn't speak, he continued, "If you're avoiding it because you don't love me anymore, then just say it."

I looked down at the multitude of tubes connected to his arms, the bruises on his skin, the small tuft of hair growing back on his head, and knew there was nowhere else I could be. He was right; nothing had changed. Judging from Naghmeh's reaction to me tonight, I knew that she would still be a problem for us. The rational part of me understood we were likely doomed, but the part of me that had thought I'd lost him, that had feared being in a world where I'd never hear him say he loved me again, wouldn't walk away. That part of me couldn't, knowing what we had was worth fighting for. I finally refused to allow faith and tradition the power to tear us apart.

"I love you, Maziar, and I don't want to spend another day without you."

I leaned in, and with my hand on the side of his face, gently placed my lips against his. It was the first time we'd kissed in over three years, but the electricity still sparked between us like fireworks. I had no idea how we were going to forge this path together, but I knew in the deepest parts of my soul that we truly couldn't live apart.

I spent the next few hours sitting on his bed, holding his hand. He refused to let go, even when the nurse came in to examine him. He just made her work her way around our intertwined fingers as I took him through the events of the past few days, starting from when Neda had called me.

"And Ben?" he asked, finally addressing the elephant in the room.

"He left for Santa Barbara."

Maziar said nothing. He just leaned back against the pillows and tried to hide his smile.

CHAPTER THIRTY-TWO

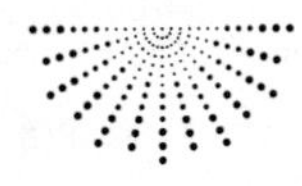

Maziar's recovery was a tedious one, to say the least. He was discharged from the hospital a week after he'd woken up, his vitals and scans receiving approval from the doctors. He couldn't walk so he was equipped with a set of crutches and a wheelchair. It would be some time before he'd be able to move his right hand, as well. Even after his casts were removed, he'd still have to engage in intensive physical therapy. It would be months before he'd be able to walk normally again, and he would never regain full mobility in his wrist. However, much to everyone's delight, there seemed to be no lingering effects from the head injury. We all took that as an overall win.

I had spent every day at the hospital with him. He would reluctantly let me go home at midnight to only be up and waiting for me at six in the morning when I returned. He was like a toddler with separation anxiety, worried he would wake up one morning and find I'd disappeared.

As he became more fixated on me, his mother became more distant and cold. I could see that she was starting to realize her son had finally made his choice, and his family wasn't it. Her inability to influence him infuriated her.

I was the natural target. She avoided speaking to me, and when she did, her answers were short and frigid. I tried to seem oblivious to her attitude, pretending I hadn't noticed, making it easier for me to coexist with her in the same space for so many hours in a day.

Parviz, however, had remained steadfast and kind, not changing his interaction with me at all. I started to feel more confident that he had crossed over to our side permanently, and allowed myself to let down my guard with him. When it was just the three of us in the room, the conversations felt less strained, more natural. I could see Maziar noticing the change in his father as well. Their relationship began evolving because of it, an unspoken closeness blooming between them from his father's acceptance of me.

Bita had gone back to her normal antics, ignoring me for the most part. She'd abandoned her evil ways, but avoided being in the same space as me. When we were forced to be around each other, she would pretend I wasn't there, making her disdain for me that much more apparent to those around us. Again, I took the high road, ignoring it the best I could, focusing my attention on Maziar.

He noticed everyone's behavior, quietly taking mental notes. Instead of putting a wedge between us, all Naghmeh and Bita were succeeding in doing was pushing us closer together. Whenever I was there, he insisted I sit on the bed next to him as he wound my hand tightly in his. He wouldn't allow our physical connection to be severed by anything, be it his family, the nurses, or even the doctors. He hung on to me as if I were a life jacket and he were floating out at sea. The more he put his foot down, the further he shoved his mother away, and the angrier she became.

Maziar had been out of school for the past two years. He'd gotten a position at a prestigious law firm downtown as soon as he'd graduated. He'd moved into a small apartment in Studio City to be closer to work. He'd been there for a year, but when he was discharged from the hospital, his mother insisted that he come home with them. He needed around-the-clock assistance. Since there weren't any good alternatives, he agreed.

We made the forty-minute drive in relative silence. I was worrying over the possible explosion that could occur the minute I stepped into their house. I was going into the lion's den, stepping onto their turf, and it made me uneasy. Despite the solid shield that Maziar had erected around me, I couldn't help but think their disdain could somehow penetrate it if we were in their home field. Being there felt dangerous. He attempted to distract me, but finally realized it was useless. He gave up and resorted to just reaching across the center console and holding my hand.

We pulled up to the iron gates and I punched in the code that automatically opened the doors. I drove down the long driveway, parking my car behind his father's. I turned the car off and sat there staring out the window at the view, trying to calm my nerves. He put his hand underneath my chin and turned my face toward him.

"It's going to be okay. I won't let them hurt you anymore. It's you and me now. You trust me, right?" he asked.

"With everything," I said, trying my best to smile.

I made my way over to the passenger's side of the car. I opened it just as his parents came out to help. As I was easing him out of the seat, Naghmeh came running over to where we were standing, almost pushing me out of the way. Maziar looked up at me as I stepped to the side, anger fuming in his pupils. I shook my head, urging him to let it go, not wanting to start the feud just seconds after arriving. He complied, but I could see the rage nestling in his chest waiting to be taunted. I took a deep breath; this could be a long day.

We settled Maziar in his old bed, propped up against a mountain of pillows as if we were attempting to bubble-wrap him with feathers. He protested, but gave in for our sakes. Once he was comfortable, he ordered me to nestle down beside him, making sure his mother and sister were there to witness his fidelity to me. The look on their faces was classic, a smirk escaping my lips before I could stop it.

The remainder of the day continued in a lazy haze, talking, dozing, and when he had the energy, playing cards. As evening approached, his mother's visits to the room became more frequent. I could feel the urgency in her stride, trying to compel me to leave. Over Maziar's protests, I got up around eight.

"Call me when you get home," he demanded.

"I will."

"I'll walk Sara out," his mother chimed in. She placed her hand on my back rushing me out of his room. She couldn't wait till I left.

We approached the front door and she continued to follow me out. I stiffened with a sinking feeling, realizing that something pivotal was about to happen. She silently walked beside me until I reached my car. As I unlocked the door, she began to speak. I turned to face her, unwilling to let her see my discomfort. The reality was I wanted to crawl into a hole and hide.

"Sara, first let me say thank you for staying with Maziar this whole time. You were very helpful and I know Maziar appreciated it. You're a good girl." I braced myself, knowing nothing good was about to follow. "But this isn't going to work between the two of you. You know that, right?" she asked, looking at me considerately.

I stood there speechless, unsure what I was supposed to say.

"I think it would be best if you break up with my son. Tell him it's because you're going to focus on your work or that you're not ready for a relationship. Or tell him you don't love him and you just want to be friends. It's better if it comes from you. It will cause fewer problems for all of us." She looked at me with a kind, motherly smile while she spoke, as if she hadn't just commanded me to shatter my life into a million pieces for her.

I looked at her, baffled. How could she stand there talking to me like we were friends while she was asking me to break her son's heart? I couldn't speak; my throat was dry and unyielding. My parents had raised me to be respectful to my elders, so telling her off like I desperately wanted to fell dead on my lips before the words could come out. Part of me wanted to cry. The other part wanted to heed her advice and run, realizing they would never leave us in peace, no matter how strongly Maziar stood against them.

I just turned and got into the car.

I drove away, leaving her standing in the large concrete driveway of her castle. I didn't turn to look at the wicked queen, but her words resonated in my mind, filling me with the dread I'd somehow forgotten. I had once again, it seemed, found myself at a crossroads.

CHAPTER THIRTY-THREE

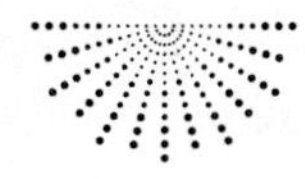

I call Maziar when I got home, as I'd promised him I would. I kept it short, not engaging in the long, drawn-out conversation he was attempting to begin.

"What happened, Sara? Did she say something?" he asked, concerned.

"No," I replied quickly. "She walked me to the door, that's all."

He didn't believe me, but even so, I wasn't sure I wanted to share the details with him. If I were forced again to walk away, would it not it be better to do so without causing a civil war? That would only make things tougher on him.

For the next few days, every time he called, I tried to keep it superficial, dodging conversations that could lead to his family. I wasn't sure how I wanted to handle the situation with his mother. The scared coward in me wanted to turn and run. But the fearless half, which only weeks ago had refused to leave his bedside, was urging me to be brave. I was confused and didn't want to deal with Maziar until I had figured myself out. He kept insisting that I come over, though, but the more excuses I gave, the more irritable and angry he became.

"You need to tell him what that witch said to you," Leyla advised one afternoon as we lay on her bed. "I can't believe you're even thinking about keeping it from him!"

She was appalled at his mother's reaction to Maziar's declaration of love for me. If I had allowed her to, I think she would've gone to his house and torn the woman's head off.

"Okay, but what good would that do if I end up breaking it off with him anyway?" I asked.

"Why on Earth would you do such a ridiculous thing? I can't believe you right now," she yelled. "He loves you. He's willing to choose you and you're thinking of walking away? Are you serious? I want to slap you right now!"

"I know Maziar said he doesn't care what they think, but Leyla, that woman and her evil spawn will not go quietly."

"And? So what if they don't? Maziar will deal with it," she said with confidence.

"Yeah, but that's the problem. What if he can't? What if he does at first, but then the pressure of it all just breaks him and he caves again? This time I'll be too broken to recover."

"That won't happen," she insisted. "Maziar won't cave and he'll never leave you again. But let's just say I'm wrong and it happens. You will not break, Sara. You'll pick yourself up again like you always have, and you'll be just fine. I wish you could see what I see. I don't see this weakling you keep talking about. What I see is a confident, strong woman who's risked it all for love, coming out on the other side still standing. I promise you: you'll be just fine either way," she said tenderly.

I leaned in and wrapped Leyla in a hug. "I love you," I said, because there was no need to say anything else.

* * *

After a lot of thought, I'd decided Leyla was right. I was going to talk to Maziar. I realized that going to his house to have this conversation was not the best of ideas. However, doing it over the phone seemed worse. I called him to see if I could at least set it up that his mother and sister would be out when I arrived. He picked up on the first ring, and by the tone in his voice, I knew he'd been waiting for my call.

"Hey."

"Hi. How are you?"

"I'm okay. Tired of being stuck in this bed. I can't wait till these casts come off in a few weeks," he said, frustrated.

"I bet. I know it sucks. I'm sorry. What have you been doing?" I asked, trying to avoid why I'd really called.

"Nothing, really, since you refuse to come over and keep me company. Are you going to tell me what's going on, Sara, or am I going to have to leave this bed to come find you?"

"I'm sorry. I've just been trying to figure out what I'm supposed to do. I needed a few days to think," I said apologetically.

"Well, have you figured it out?"

"Yes. I need to talk to you, but I don't want to come over when there's anyone but your dad home. Is that happening anytime soon?"

"Why don't you want anyone here?" he asked.

"Because it's about your mother."

* * *

I showed up at his house two hours later. I was greeted by Parviz at the door, who smiled warmly as he let me inside.

"We haven't seen you for a few days. Everything okay?" he asked skeptically, and I wondered if his wife had shared our conversation with him.

"Yes, I've just been busy," I replied, trying to sound convincing. Then, I quickly made my way to Maziar's room, trying to avoid any further questions.

I softly knocked on his already opened door. He was holding a book in his hand and he set it down when he saw me. His face lit up as he smiled, relief taking over his features now that I'd arrived.

I scooted onto the bed next to him. He immediately reached out and pulled my face to his, kissing me gently. It began slow and soft, then was overcome by the fierce desperation that had now permanently settled between us. The fear of each moment being out last, always lingered in the back of our minds since the accident. When I pulled back to face him, he instinctively grabbed hold of my hand, refusing to let me get farther than the range of his reach.

"What's going on, Sara? What has my mother done?" he asked, getting right to the point.

"Okay, before I tell you, you have to promise you won't lose it. It'll only make the situation worse," I pleaded, so nervous I could hear ringing in my ears.

"Sara, tell me," he said, the anger already beginning to brew within him.

"See, you're already getting mad and I haven't even told you anything yet!"

He took a deep breath, trying to center himself. "Okay, I won't get upset. Just tell me. The suspense is making it worse."

I looked at him, knowing the minute the words left my lips, he wouldn't be able to control his fury. I had no idea what he would do next. For a minute, I began to doubt that telling him was the best idea. I knew I would spark the beginning of a war, and I was certain that in the end we would all lose somehow.

"Sara, just tell me. I'll be fine," he demanded.

I steadied my voice as I began to replay the details of the conversation I had with Naghmeh. He sat quietly, listening the entire time, taking care not to interrupt me. I could see the frustration building as I spoke, but I tried to ignore it, telling myself I was doing the right thing by telling him.

"You should have told me right when it happened," he said when I was done.

"I didn't know what I was supposed to do," I replied weakly.

"What do you mean you didn't know what to do? Were you really thinking of walking away again, Sara? I spent the past few days terrified you'd changed your mind about us, going crazy in this jail cell of a room. Now I find out that I was right to be worried, that you were thinking of leaving me just because my mother said you should." He wore his disappointment like armor.

"I know I shouldn't have stayed away, Maziar. I'm sorry. But she literally said this won't work! It scared me."

"Why would it scare you? I told you already that what they think doesn't matter. I want you, and no one is going to change that."

"You say that now, but what if they never leave us alone? What if you can't stand up to them forever? I'm scared that in the end you'll leave," I said, the desperation coating my words.

A tenderness took over his features, replacing the anger that was there just moments ago.

"Come here," he said, as he patted the spot next to him on the bed. I scooted into the pillows, nestling safely beneath his arm, placing my head in the space between his shoulder and neck. "We knew this was going to happen. Just because we've decided that we are going to be together no matter what, doesn't mean the people are going to stop. But I'm never leaving you. I promise you that, Sara. I love you. My mom can't say or do anything to change that."

I knew this was a risk, but it always was when it came to love. I didn't know the future, but I knew that I didn't want to walk away from Maziar. I loved him. I trusted him wholeheartedly, and I decided I would trust in this too. I would believe him when he said he had chosen me.

CHAPTER THIRTY-FOUR

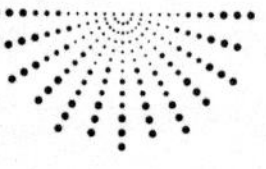

I was sitting at home later that evening when my phone began to ring. I glanced over and saw Maziar's number pop up on my screen, releasing the surge of butterflies that had been waiting in the pit of my stomach. I'd been dreading his call, not knowing what I would hear on the other end. I picked up immediately.

"Hi."

"Hey, baby," he said, calmly.

"Everything okay?"

"It's fine, but I need you to do me a favor. I need you to meet me at my apartment in twenty minutes," he directed.

"Wait, what?" I asked, thinking I hadn't heard him correctly.

"I'll explain everything when I get there," he said. "Pasha is coming to pick me up. Will you meet me?"

"Of course, but I don't understand. You can't even walk," I pointed out worriedly.

"I'll be fine."

Suddenly, I became aware of voices in the background. I could hear yelling and crying, all intertwined with each other. I couldn't make out what they were saying at first but I could identify his mother's voice, matched in equal volume by his father's. Bita must have stepped closer to Maziar because I could clearly hear her when she spoke.

"You're seriously going to leave your entire family for some stupid little bitch!"

The phone became muffled, Maziar undoubtedly covering the receiver. I stood frozen in my room, left dumbfounded by the chaos unfolding on the other end of the line.

"Bita, shut your mouth. You're never to talk about her like that again, do you understand me?" he yelled. I envisioned her cowering away from his wrath.

He turned his attention back on me. "I'll see you in twenty minutes."

"Okay," was all I could muster up my wits to say.

"I love you," he said, before he hung up.

I looked down at my phone, the dial tone still blaring, trying to comprehend what was going on. I shut it off and began looking around my room as if I was searching for an answer within its four walls. Was this all really happening or was I stuck in some horrible dream? I didn't know.

It took me five minutes to break out of my daze and start moving around collecting my things. I continued to walk in a fuzzy haze, out my door and into the kitchen. Mom was busy washing dishes. She looked over her shoulder at me.

"What's wrong?" she asked immediately.

I slid into one of the seats at the kitchen table and she came to sit across from me. The concern was evident in her eyes but she didn't say anything. Just waited.

"I think Maziar just fought with his mom over me. He's moving back to his apartment."

Mom looked shocked, then told me to start from the beginning and tell her everything that happened. I launched into an explanation of the past five minutes. When I was done, a small smile broke out across her face.

"Well, good for him," she said, more to herself than me.

For the first time Maziar had made it abundantly clear that he'd chosen me.

* * *

I made it to the apartment in record time, but he hadn't arrived yet. I picked up my phone and dialed Leyla's number.

"Hey, what's up?" she said in her chipper voice.

"He moved out of his parent's house," I blurted out.

"Wait, what? Maziar? What happened?"

I could hear her interest building on the other end as she tried to patiently wait for me to finish my explanation.

"I'm sitting in my car, waiting for him to show up now," I said, when I was done.

"No shit. Wow." She laughed. "I'm pretty impressed right now. He's definitely a keeper."

"Yeah, he is, isn't he?"

For the first time in a very long time, I let myself toy with the idea that this could actually work. I had to admit, I was pretty amazed myself at how Maziar had put his foot down, making it clear I wasn't going anywhere this time. He'd been saying he had chosen me, but the nagging voice in the back of my mind continued to tell me to tread cautiously. But now, there was no confusing his intentions. I wasn't just proud; I was madly in love with him.

"I've got to go," I said, as Pasha pulled up. I grabbed my stuff and quickly made my way over to his car. "What have you done?" I asked him, as he opened the door.

He reached out and grabbed my outstretched hand as I helped him out of the car. Once he was standing in front of me, he leaned down so his face was inches away from mine.

"I was defending your honor," he said, his breath warm on my lips. Then, he leaned toward my ear and whispered, "I love you."

"I love you, too," I said, shuddering.

Pasha brought the wheelchair over, interrupting us. I instinctively tried to take a step back but Maziar stopped me, instead leaning in and kissing my lips. I blushed with embarrassment as Pasha stood witness to our tender moment.

Once Maziar was settled in his seat, we headed down the walkway to the apartment. Luckily, it was on the first floor, so we didn't have to tackle the problem of the stairs. Maziar handed me the keys, and I pushed the front door open, allowing Pasha to roll him inside. I'd never been to his apartment before.

I stepped in to find a large open space that housed the living room, kitchen, and dining area. To my right, a white L-shaped couch sat up against the wall with a black rectangular coffee table nestled in between it. Across the room was a large flat-screen television with a matching shelf unit underneath, decorated with his books and a few framed photographs.

One of the frames caught my attention. It had a black and white photo of Maziar and me in it from Pasha's party. Azi must have taken it. I couldn't remember what we were talking about, but I was laughing at something Maziar had said. I was leaning into him and we were looking at each other, unaware that the moment was being captured on film. The tenderness in his smile and the way he was looking at me sent chills up my spine.

I wandered down the hallway toward the sound of the two boys from the other room. I passed by two doors on my left, the first opening into the guest bathroom and the second into a small bedroom that Maziar had converted into his office. There was a blue Persian rug thrown on the floor. *How Iranian of him*, I thought to myself as I smiled. To the right was the master bedroom.

Pasha had Maziar situated on the bed, propping his leg up with some pillows. He was moving it every which way, trying to make sure he had it adequately elevated. Maziar took it in stride, never complaining even though I could see his discomfort. When he was done, he stepped back, admiring his work with a boyish grin.

"I have to go pick up my mom," he said, as he glanced down at his watch. "I'll come back after. Should I pick up some dinner on my way?"

"Yeah, that would be great," Maziar responded.

"Who's staying with him tonight?" I asked Pasha, knowing Maziar couldn't be alone. "He obviously can't fend for himself. We're going to have to figure out who's willing to help and come up with some sort of schedule."

"I know. I wasn't really thinking of that part when I stormed out, or should I say, rolled out of my house," Maziar said jokingly, something he always did when he was nervous.

"It's okay, baby. We'll figure it out," I replied, trying to comfort him. I didn't want to make him more anxious by showing him I was worried with the details. "I'll stay the whole time myself if I have to."

"I can take the first shift tonight. I'm sure Emanuel will pitch in as well. I'll call him when I get in the car," Pasha interjected.

"I'm sure Neda will, too," I said.

"Okay that's four. Totally doable. I have to go, but I'll call you when I'm heading back about dinner." He bumped fists with Maziar and kissed my cheek as he grabbed his keys and left the room.

I scooted beside Maziar on the bed when he was gone. He looked tired and worried, despite his best efforts to hide it from me. I reached out and played with his hair. I could see the fatigue take over his body as he sank into the mattress. His eyes began to flutter closed, sleep flirtatiously beckoning him into her cocoon.

"My mom pretty much disowned me and I almost killed Bita," he said, behind closed lids.

"It was that bad, huh? I'm sorry."

"Don't be. It's their fault. They're being unreasonable. My dad was pretty awesome, though."

"Yeah? What did he do?" I said, comforted that at least Maziar hadn't faced their wrath alone.

"He backed me up the whole time, telling my mom that it was my life and that you were a great girl. It was cool." He smiled, eyes still closed.

"That makes me so happy," I told him, leaning in and kissing his head. "Let yourself sleep now. You need some rest."

"No, I don't want to leave you alone while I sleep," he protested.

"I'm not alone. I want you to sleep," I said, gently pushing him back down. "I'm just going to sit here next to you and watch television."

"Are you sure?" he mumbled, exhausted.

"Yes, I'm sure. There isn't anywhere else I'd rather be."

He smiled and turned his head toward me so he was nestled up against my arm. Within minutes, his breathing slowed, and I could see his eyes fluttering behind his lashes. He looked peaceful, all the worry lines on his face relaxing away as he dreamed.

Two hours later, when Pasha showed up with dinner, he woke up upon feeling the mattress shift beneath him as I got up to open the front door. We helped him move onto the couch just as Neda arrived. He seemed more rested and in better spirits than earlier and I was able to relax. I was wound up with worry about whether he'd regret walking out on his family as the day progressed. When he kissed me goodbye that evening, I couldn't find any remorse in his eyes.

My parents had waited up for me. I found them on the couch when I came home. I was tired, but I sat down and explained what had happened between Maziar and his family anyway. When I was done, I told them that I'd be alternating shifts with the others to help care for him until he could better do it on his own.

"I've got the next two nights," I stated.

"Okay, you should help him," Mom said, surprising me. I'd expected her to protest in the name of tradition.

By standing up to his family, Maziar had proven his level of commitment to me in her eyes. Any apprehension she'd felt regarding his intentions had seemed to disappear. She was still upset that Naghmeh was adamantly against us, but the wheels were in motion now, and there was nothing left to do but be supportive.

The following morning, I had breakfast with my family, then drove over to Maziar's apartment to spend the next few days with him. The sun was shining brightly, its warmth laying kisses on my skin through the open window. A subtle breeze was blowing, and birds were soaring on its current through the sky.

I could see something new for Maziar and me balancing on the horizon ahead, the start of the next set of chapters in the story of us.

CHAPTER THIRTY-FIVE

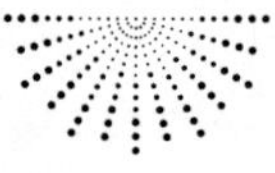

The weeks passed melodically with Maziar and me falling into the comfortable familiarity between us. I spent most of my time at his apartment, leaving only when my position was relieved by the others. He'd become restless, prisoner to his disabilities, so when the day approached that he was to get his casts off, he fluttered about, antsy with the anticipation.

I was in the throes of getting set up to start working, worried about how I would leave him when I did. I'd been hired in the Palisades where I'd originally done my internship. When my trip to Santa Barbara was canceled, I'd reached out to the company regarding a position that was local. Seti had pulled strings with corporate, and I'd been taken up shortly after. I was to start in two weeks.

When the day of Maziar's appointment arrived, we were both relieved. I drove him over to the office and helped him out of the car. As I wheeled him toward the entrance of the doctor's office, his parents suddenly appeared, standing before the double doors. I shook my head, trying to clear it, making sure I wasn't imaging it. He'd kept in touch with his father, but he'd avoided his mother and sister at all costs. It had been weeks since he'd seen them.

The cool façade of indifference settled over his features while the fury of anger burned viciously behind his eyes. I held my breath as I approached them, trying desperately not to stumble over my feet. I was terrified of how the next few minutes would unfold.

"Hi, son," Parviz said energetically, as if it were just another day.

"Hi, Dad," Maziar replied, never breaking eye contact with his mother.

She didn't say anything, just challenged him with her own pride and resilience. His father and I looked back and forth between them waiting for the next move, but none came. Eons passed as they each engaged in their own cause, neither leaving their stubborn posts. The moment was broken only by the sound of the lock on the front doors opening. I was consumed by the anxiety of the silent exchange between them, fidgeting from foot to foot.

"Take me inside, Sara," Maziar demanded, without turning away from her.

I didn't move, afraid that my compliance would only further the riff between his mother and me, something that would not be in the best interest of any of us. Maziar's frustration was palpable as he turned toward me, having to break the staring contest between them.

"Let's go," he said, with such assertions that my legs moved forward on their own.

Parviz held the door open for us as I pushed Maziar inside. I placed his wheelchair at the end of the row of chairs in the waiting area and approached the desk to sign him in. I was glad to have something to do; their animosity was debilitating. I felt sorry for his father, stuck in the middle of this mess.

I busied myself at the desk, trying to stall as long as I could before returning to where Maziar was waiting for me. I sat down in the chair beside him and he immediately reached out and grabbed my hand. I desperately wished the floor beneath us would open up and swallow me so I could hide from his mother's burning rage. The face-off had me petrified.

He was called in a few minutes later. They didn't attempt to follow us in, knowing that Maziar would only veto their entrance. Once inside the examination room, the nurse took Maziar's vitals, then left. I finally exhaled, unaware I'd been holding my breath. He reached out, still in his chair, and held my hand.

"You okay?" he asked.

I just looked at him and wondered how I was supposed to answer that question. His mother hated me and saw me as the prime cause for her son's disappearance. She thought I was tearing her family apart.

I was madly in love with him, but the fear that she would succeed in somehow breaking us up was making its way back up my throat, forming into a scream. He was oblivious to the possibility that our union would prove to be a mistake. I wanted to yell at him, I wanted to cry, I wanted to tell him that in fact I wasn't okay, that I'd turned into a basket case of emotions lying so heavy on my chest that my heart felt like it was going to explode. I wanted to tell him that, despite what I had said, I was still terrified, even after his declaration of love, even after he'd openly chosen me, and even after he told me he would never ever leave me. I wanted to tell him that the terror of losing him was all-consuming and hadn't left a moment of my thoughts.

Instead, I said, "I'm fine," the truth only becoming another obstacle we couldn't face.

The doctor came in a few minutes later. The nurse followed with a tray of equipment that looked like torture instruments rather than medical supplies. Maziar cowered back on the examination table as the doctor reached over and grabbed the saw off the tray. It had a threatening metal blade with pointed teeth, and when it was turned on, it moved back and forth rapidly. The doctor laughed at Maziar's fearful expression, assuring him it would only cut through the plaster and not his skin. Nonetheless, he held my hand and closed his eyes like a child until it was over.

The skin beneath the plaster was paled and dulled in comparison to the darkened skin that spread across the rest of his limbs. His leg appeared slightly smaller than the other, since the muscles had atrophied beneath the cast's confinements. The doctor assured him that the appearance of both his leg and wrist were normal and would resolve with time. As Maziar tried to move them, he was met with stiffness and discomfort in his joints. His frustration was evident even after the doctor told him it would take some time to recover.

When we returned to the waiting room, his parents were still sitting where we'd left them. Naghmeh looked at Maziar and the two of them engaged in another silent conversation, each ruffling their feathers to prove their dominance. Then, without a word, she stood up and walked out the door. Parviz was startled by her abrupt exit and quickly stood up.

"Bye, son," he said, kissing Maziar on the head, then squeezing my hand as he scurried after his wife.

Why had she come all this way only to refuse to speak to her son? I couldn't understand how it was possible for his mother to hang on to her beliefs so tightly, even after Maziar had almost died. It felt wrong on a fundamental level. I knew she thought that things couldn't work between us. In her mind, she might have even thought she was working for her son's benefit by trying to keep us apart. Still, she was choosing to lose him over letting go.

He sat there, in his wheelchair, hard as stone. He portrayed a picturesque vision of calm and cool, as if the riff between them equated to nothing more than breaking a favorite mug. It was upsetting and annoying, but inconsequential. There was no sign of the betrayal and pain I imagined he was feeling in that moment. His performance was Oscar-worthy, so believable that I started to question whether his family truly was unimportant.

Once inside the car, I turned to face him, expecting to find something broken within him. Instead, I was met with a smile that reached the edges of his eyes and a genuine sense of happiness swirling around him. I sat back, confused.

"Are you hungry?" he asked. "Can I treat you to lunch?"

I looked at him, wondering if I were caught in some alternate world. How was he able to so easily move past what had just happened in the doctor's office?

"I just don't want to deal with it right now. Can we pretend none of that happened back there until later?" he said, addressing the bewildered look on my face. "Today was supposed to be a good day. I finally got my damn casts off. I just want to be happy about it for a little while. Enjoy having lunch with my girlfriend. Can we do that?"

I didn't answer, still trying to wrap my head around it all.

"I hate what just happened. I'm angry and hurt by my mom, but I can't give in to her demands. It's my life, she needs to understand that. I just don't want to let her ruin any more days we have together so I'm choosing to let go of those feelings for now. Does that make sense?" he asked, trying to explain his reaction.

As I looked deep into his hazel eyes, I realized he'd decided not to allow his mother any more power over his emotions. Taking away her influence was a way for Maziar to take back control. I could support him in that.

"Yes, it does," I said. "Let's go get some lunch."

CHAPTER THIRTY-SIX

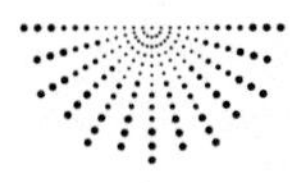

It had been a month since I began my job at CVS. Since the internship, Seti had gotten married and was now five months pregnant with her first baby. We'd spend a few minutes chatting when our shifts ran back-to-back, so she knew how things had gone with Maziar's family.

Weeks passed, but Maziar never attempted to reach out to his mother or sister. At first, Bita made frequent attempts to contact him, but after his persistent refusal to speak to her, it had dwindled. In their absence, the two of us had fallen into a nice rhythm of playing house. I'd head to his apartment after work and we'd spend the rest of the evening together, making dinner and cuddling on the couch like newlyweds. I would sleep at home most nights, though, to keep my parents' reprimanding to a minimum. They were supportive, but still had a tough time accepting that I was spending the night with a man out of wedlock. However ridiculous it was at my age, I tried to keep the sleepovers to a minimum.

Maziar was on his way to healing. With physical therapy, he was able to get around on his own. We still hadn't been intimate since we'd rekindled our relationship, both acting like apprehensive teenagers afraid of rejection. The love between us was obvious, the desire tangible, and I was restless. I eagerly anticipated getting over our newfound shyness.

One Friday night, I'd been working later than usual and was exhausted when I got to his house. I slowly dragged my body out of the car and made the short walk to his door. I was still fumbling through my purse looking for my keys when Maziar opened the door.

He'd been home for a little while, so he was dressed in a pair of black sweats and a white T-shirt, his hair slicked back and wet from his shower. His skin had become even more tanned over the past few weeks, and he shimmered beneath the outdoor light. His eyes sparkled as he flashed me his beautiful smile, making my heart quicken as it always did.

He leaned in and took my bags, gently kissing my lips in the process. I felt a small spark as they touched mine, radiating down my torso and into my fingertips. I buzzed with the closeness of him.

He moved aside to allow me through the door. I was instantly enveloped by the smell of food cooking on the stove. I looked over and saw that he'd set the dining room table, two candles burning in its center. A bottle of wine was already open and sitting on the counter, flanked by two glasses. Maziar came around, placing my stuff on the couch, then walked into the kitchen to turn down the flame.

"Go shower and change while I finish dinner. It'll be done in a few minutes," he ordered playfully, eyes still twinkling.

I walked into the bedroom in a daze, my desire to be wrapped around his body growing by the second. As I stepped under the hot water, I closed my eyes and allowed myself to imagine him beside me, his hand running down the side of my body, his lips laying a path of kisses behind them. I had to breathe to avoid shuddering silently under the water, alone. When I finished, I put on a lacy bra and panties beneath my yoga pants and tank top in hopes that something would happen between us.

When I made my way back to the kitchen, Maziar had poured us two glasses of wine and was now dishing our food onto the plates. He'd made *khoresteh ghaymeh*, split pea stew, and white rice. I didn't know he could make Persian food.

"I've got a few tricks up my sleeve," he said, reading my expression.

He kissed my cheek as he walked past me. "I'm hoping to show you some of the others later tonight."

I felt the heat explode inside me as I saw the desire in his eyes. My face felt hot and I wondered if I were blushing. I walked over to the table and took my seat across from him, grabbing our wine glasses along the way.

He sat down across from me and took a sip, eyes intently burning into me as if he were looking right through my skin. I wondered if my need for him could be seen bursting out of me, a pattern of desire and lust spread across the wall behind me. I couldn't take my eyes off of him. He broke the trance, turning his gaze toward his plate as he grabbed his fork and spoon. I felt hot and flustered, trying to keep the red from invading my cheeks.

"I hope you like it," he said, as he put a spoonful of the stew into his mouth.

I looked down at my plate, fumbling with my own utensils as I tried regaining my composure. He watched me intently loading my spoon as I took a bite, balancing on the edge of his seat like a little kid, waiting to see my reaction. I found it endearing.

"Hmmm, that's good," I said, giving him the approval he so desperately wanted.

The food was actually delicious, and I hadn't realized how hungry I'd been. We spent the rest of the meal enjoying the fruits of his labor while he poured us one glass of wine after another.

When we'd both had our fill, I stood up and started to clear off the table, with Maziar trailing behind me. Once all the dishes were in the sink, I turned on the water and started on the task of washing them. I could hear him cleaning off the table and grabbing the empty wine bottles behind me. Then, he suddenly went silent. Before I could turn around to see what had happened, I felt a familiar heat penetrate my back as Maziar came up behind me. My soapy dish froze midair as his breath rustled my hair, sending chills up my spine. He took one step closer, his chest leaning up against me, the beating of his heart thumping up against the back of my rib cage. I sucked in my breath as he wrapped his arm around my waist and pulled me in, eliminating the faintest space between us.

I could feel his desire hardened up against my lower back and my heart began to beat furiously against my chest. He slowly reached out and eased my arm down, placing the dish I was holding back into the sink. With the water still running, he gently placed his hand under my shirt. I gasped as it slowly inched up my stomach and over the delicate lace of my bra. He moved his fingers into the space between the fabric and my skin, running circles against my nipple. The desire shot through my body like fire, threatening to undo me right there against the kitchen sink. With my breast still in his hand, he reached up with the other and moved my hair aside, placing his lips on the tender skin of my neck. He teased me with a flutter of kisses, barely making contact. A groan escaped my lips. It had been so long since I'd felt his touch, each fingertip sending my body into convulsions.

He pulled my shirt up over my head and cast it to the side. With the hands of an expert, he unlatched my bra while flooding my neck and back with a trail of lips on skin. I could hardly breathe, the heat between my legs boiling with the need to feel him inside me.

I turned in his arms so I could face him, my bare chest brushing against his shirt. No longer able to resist, I pulled it over his head, placing my own trail of kisses over the tight muscles of his chest and stomach. He shuddered underneath my hand, encouraging me forward.

I moved my way back up to his mouth and began to tease him with my tongue. When he couldn't take it any longer, he wrapped his hands in my hair and pulled my mouth to his, crushing me with his lips. The need for each other was as visible as the steam rising off the water running in the sink behind us.

Before I knew what had happened, Maziar had relieved us both of our unnecessary clothing, discarding them onto the floor. He pushed up against me, his desire hard and stiff against my thigh. He grabbed me by the waist and lifted me into the air, placing me down on the kitchen counter to his left. He pushed my legs open, creating a space that outlined his body perfectly. All of a sudden, he pulled back, severing the connections between us. I looked up at him, confused, desperate for more.

"I love you, Sara," he said with such tenderness a knot formed in my throat.

"I love you, too."

I laid my hand against his cheek, and he kissed the inside of my wrist. Then, he eased himself inside of me and slowly made love to me on the kitchen counter. Our bodies ignited with recognition, fitting together like lost puzzle pieces. Each movement felt new, yet old, as we discovered each other once again.

After it was over, we stayed there intertwined, our bodies leaning into each other with the sweet exhaustion that takes lovers afterward. I don't know how long we stayed that way, but we held onto each other in desperation, trying to erase all the years we'd lost.

"I love you," he whispered into my ear again.

"I love you, too."

"Forever?" he asked. There was a fearful, childlike expression in his eyes, and I knew in that moment that I had the power to break him.

"For always."

That night, long after I'd left him standing on the curb as he watched me drive away, I lay in bed thinking about how our lives were intertwined. We truly couldn't survive without each other, two pieces of a whole. The idea of spending another day in this life without Maziar seemed unfathomable. I had found my true love years ago, and fate had given us a second chance. Now I was floating through the fairy tale I'd always dreamed of.

* * *

The next morning, I was still reeling from the night before. I fluttered around getting ready for work, a ridiculous Cheshire smile plastered across my face. Mom looked at me as I buzzed into the kitchen, humming. She raised her eyebrow in question, but didn't say a word, as she sat down to breakfast with me.

When I got to work, Seti was waiting for me with stories of baby registries and itty-bitty items of necessity she'd discovered on her recent trip to Babies-R-Us. She was glowing with her pregnancy, happier than I'd ever seen her. They'd just found out the baby was a girl, so she'd gone crazy adding dresses and tutus to her wish list. She pulled up a chair while I got started on the day's tasks, describing the baby nursery to me in detail.

A few minutes later, one of the techs came over to grab me for a consult. As I walked toward the front of the pharmacy, Seti followed, getting ready to head home. We both stopped abruptly as we approached the window, frozen as if we'd seen a ghost. Seti turned and looked at me just as my brain registered who it was.

Bita.

I stood dumbfounded, unable to wrap my head around Bita's presence in my store. It made no sense, the confusion hindering my ability to form a coherent sentence. I almost expected her to dissipate into a puff of smoke, proving to be only my imagination.

"I'm really sorry to show up like this, but could I talk to you, Sara?" Bita asked, diverting her eyes toward Seti, who was now standing in front of me protectively. "I just want to talk, I swear. I'm not here to cause any trouble," she said, more to Seti than me. "Please."

I continued to just stand there, unable to decide on how to proceed. Seti wasn't convinced by Bita's kind-girl act and took a step forward, breaking me out of my frozen trance. I reached out stopping her, afraid she'd hurl her pregnant body at Maziar's sister.

"It's fine," I said. "I'll be fine," I assured her.

"You know you don't have to talk to her. You don't owe her anything," Seti responded bitterly.

I was facing Bita as Seti spoke, and I noticed an unfamiliar humbleness in her. The fire I'd seen burning in her eyes so many times before was gone, instead replaced by a deep pain that clutched onto the remaining embers of her flame. The confident girl I was used to was nowhere to be found.

She reminded me of a beautiful bird with a fractured wing that had finally realized soaring above the clouds wasn't all that life entailed, and even those who soared too close to the sun could burn. Her family wasn't as invincible as she'd originally believed, shattered apart and thrown to the wind when Maziar drew his line in the sand. I knew I should hate her, that there was an evilness in her that was only masked by her instability without her brother. But the heart in me that wanted to believe people were inherently good still felt compelled to hear her out.

"Come back at lunch," I said, watching relief flood Bita's features.

"Are you crazy? Did you forget what they did to you?" Seti said in protest.

"No, I haven't forgotten. But if it were my brother, I'd hope Maziar would do the same," I replied, keeping my eyes trained on Bita.

"Thank you." She turned and left before Seti had a chance to change my mind.

"Okay, but walk away if it gets ugly. Promise me," Seti demanded.

"I will. Now go home and put those swollen feet up. I'll be fine. I'm a big girl."

"I know. Will you call me after work and tell me what happened?" she asked.

"Yes. Now go," I said, lovingly pushing her toward the pharmacy door.

Once she was out of sight, I leaned against the counter, trying to steady my nerves. One of my technicians came over to ask me if I was okay.

"I'm fine," I said, then excused myself to the bathroom.

I stood staring at my reflection in the mirror, splashing water on my pale face. I was tired, so very tired of dealing with the constant roller coaster ride I felt like I was always on. The past few months without Maziar's family had been amazing, giving us a fair chance for once to explore what we could be. I was terrified that they would rear their heads, causing it all to come crashing down around me again.

I spent the rest of the morning questioning Bita's motives, trying to figure out why she would possibly want to talk to me. I kept staring at the clock, cursing at its snail's pace as the minutes stretched on. The anticipation was killing me.

It seemed like an eternity before my lunch break finally arrived. I grabbed my bag and headed out the door, trying to keep from breaking into a sprint. True to her word, Bita stood outside, waiting. When I saw her, I had the strange feeling that in an alternate world we would have been friends and this could have been a regular Saturday lunch date. But, sadly, that alternate world didn't exist.

She turned toward the double doors as they slid open, alerting her to my arrival. She smiled at me, as if we hadn't spent the past few years as mortal enemies. I felt a sudden surge of hatred course through my veins at her audacity, brushing our history aside as she did. But I swallowed it down, pushing it to the furthest corners of my mind where I'd started a collection of all the things I would deal with later.

"Hi," she said, more timidly than I'd expected.

"Hi."

"I was thinking we could walk down the street to the sushi restaurant on the corner? I remember Maziar telling me that you loved that place. Is that okay?"

"Yeah, that's fine. It's good," I said, wondering what conversation would have prompted that information to be exchanged. I wasn't sure how I was supposed to act around her. This whole thing felt bizarre.

"I know things haven't been great between us," she said, as we walked toward the restaurant.

I just looked at her, raising an eyebrow.

"Okay, so I was a royal bitch to you, I know that. I take responsibility for all of it."

She glanced down at the sidewalk like a child that had been reprimanded. This all felt so foreign to me, Bita open with her feelings, exuding a new-found vulnerability. I didn't know what to do with her.

Once inside the restaurant, she remained quiet until we were seated. She asked the hostess to put us in the back corner of the room to create some semblance of privacy. When we finally sat down, she took a deep breath. Her anxiety surrounded her like a heavy cloak.

"I know you're wondering why I asked you here today." She paused, gathering her thoughts before she spoke again. "I haven't talked to Maziar for over two months now, and I really miss my brother. I know that shouldn't matter to you, but I don't know what to do. I was hoping you might help me. I've tried calling and texting, but he never responds. I've showed up at his work a few times, but he refuses to see me, having his secretary tell me to leave."

She looked down at the table, twisting the chopsticks between her fingers. I could see the pain etched across her face, could feel the sense of loss consuming her. She didn't look like the powerful serpent I had experience so many times before, but instead like a lost, scared little girl. Despite my better judgment, I actually started to feel sorry for her, forgetting for a second all the horrible things she'd done to me. But memories like those are never too far behind.

"Why should I help you? You and your mom decided I wasn't good enough and did everything you could to break Maziar and me up. You didn't even care what that did to us. Now you want me to feel sorry for you because your brother won't talk to you, but you never felt bad for me."

My voice had risen with emotion, winning the attention of a few patrons sitting nearby.

Instead of lashing back at me, Bita sat there staring at her hands, filled with what appeared to be remorse.

"You're right," she said, finally. "You have every right to hate my family. If I were you, I know I would. I don't know what to say other than that I'm sorry. I truly am, Sara, for how everything happened and how that hurt you. We were wrong. I didn't come here today thinking I could make you change your mind about me in an hour. But I'm really not as horrible as I acted. If there was a way to take it all back and start over, I would."

I sat across from Maziar's sister, realizing she was just a girl, broken and deflated by the loss of someone she loved. It didn't matter in what capacity the love was felt, the loss of it could destroy you either way. Their relationship was fractured, and she was asking me to help fix it somehow because she'd run out of options.

I could feel the exhaustion down to my bones. I was tired of this struggle, tired of hating, and weary from always being afraid. I wanted the animosity to end. I had felt hope once, that maybe we could all find a way to be in Maziar's life together. If that was possible, wasn't I obligated out of love to help piece it all back together for him?

I was fearful, though, that if I decided to help his sister, I would live to regret it. I was afraid that I'd go out on a limb, orchestrating a reconciliation, and once he was back in their grasp they would snatch him away from me again.

Bita sat there staring at me, the inkling of hope mingled with the fear and worry that had taken over her features. She'd come here unsure of my reaction, yet she desperately needed my help and was willing to take the risk of being the fool.

"I don't know if I can help you," I said finally. She exhaled, having been holding her breath with hopes of my compliance. "He's really mad at you all. I don't know if my talking to him would even make a difference. I'm not sure what it is exactly that you think I can do."

The spark of hope reignited in her eyes as my words settled on her. I hadn't refused to help her as she was sure I would. I was merely telling her I wasn't sure how I could help her, which meant I might actually be willing to try.

"I was just hoping you could talk to him for me. To tell him how sorry I am about everything. If he would just talk to me, I know we could fix this." She looked at me with eager puppy eyes, waiting for my consent to her plan.

"I'll talk to him. I would've told him that you came to see me anyway. We don't keep things from each other." She sat perched on the edge of her seat waiting for me to continue. "But how do I know you won't go back to the way things used to be the minute you and your brother are fine again? I'm sorry, but I don't trust any of you," I said cautiously.

"I guess you can't know that," she said quietly. "I can tell you that I'll never go there again, that I just want my brother to be happy. I've realized that means being with you. I could tell you that I truly never thought you were a bad person or that you weren't good enough for him, that everything that happened was stupid and unnecessary. My family, myself included, unfairly judged you. I could promise you that if you help me fix things with my brother, I'll have your back forever. I could say I'm sorry a million times." She paused, and then, with a consideration I'd never seen in her, she said, "I could tell you all kinds of things that are true, Sara, but in the end you'd have to make the decision to trust me."

I didn't know it then, as I sat across from Maziar's sister, struggling with my decision to love or hate, to help or hurt, that this moment would define the person I would become. I didn't know that, when I decided to help her, not only did I start to learn the power of forgiveness, but that Bita would learn her own lessons too. She would teach me that people could find the strength within them to change if they wanted to.

"I'll talk to him."

* * *

The rest of my shift dragged on like I was running up a hill in heavy boots, thick with layers of mud. I must have glanced at the clock a million times, trying to will it to move faster. I couldn't take the waiting. I wanted to get the conversation with Maziar over with and deal with the inevitable explosion that was sure to follow. I was hoping that after the initial anger had settled, he'd realize I was actually trying to help him rather than break his heart.

I bounced around the pharmacy like I'd bathed in a pool of caffeine, counting down the minutes till my relief showed up. When she walked through the door, I almost flew to my car.

I called Mom from the car and updated her on what had happened. She was as shocked as I'd been that Bita would have thought to turn to me for help. She agreed, though, that if I could help mend their relationship, then I should at least try.

When I got to his apartment, I stayed in the car, too terrified to move. I frantically grasped at my thoughts, trying to come up with the best way to tell him about his sister. I eventually forced myself to get out, trying to convince myself everything would be fine. When I opened the front door and realized he wasn't home, I breathed in a sigh of relief.

I sent him a text to see when he'd be arriving, so I could be ready. He'd gotten caught up on a project and would be at work for another hour. I decided to start on dinner to keep myself busy. Food and a bottle of wine could help take the edge off of our heavy conversation.

When Maziar finally walked through the door, I was busy chopping vegetables for a salad and stirring the pasta sauce on the stove, singing to myself. I was startled when I turned to find him leaning against the counter, watching me. I hadn't heard him come in.

He came up behind me and put his arms around my waist, losing himself in the crook of my neck as he kissed the tender skin below my ear. I felt the electricity course through my body at his contact.

"Go change. Dinner will be ready in ten minutes," I said.

A few minutes later I heard the shower go on and was tempted to sneak in with him. I thought a quickie might help ease the tension of the coming conversation. I decided, though, that it would be best to talk first, pulling the sex card out afterward to help rectify the damage.

I giggled at myself, thinking how women frequently viewed sex as a tool to relieve conflict in so many situations with their significant others. The usefulness of it was lost on men, as they viewed it just as pleasure. *Simple little birds*, I thought, as I smirked silently to myself in the kitchen.

Maziar walked in just as I finished setting the table. He took the bottle of wine off the counter and poured us each a glass. He brought them over as he sat down, waiting for me to join him.

My nerves were on overdrive and I was afraid my movements looked jerky and spastic. I could feel tingling at the base of my neck from the knots that had formed in my shoulders. I tried to discreetly roll them out when he wasn't looking. I put on my best smile as I approached the table, trying to appear normal, but Maziar was looking at me. His head was tilted to the side and his eyes were squinted in thought. I knew I'd been caught.

"Are you okay?" he asked skeptically.

I wanted to curse at my lack of acting skills. Only a few minutes in, and I'd already been discovered. He knew something was wrong. I thought about trying to deny it but decided otherwise. Now was as good a time as any to get this over with.

"Bita came to see me at work today," I blurted out.

He shifted in his seat at the mention of her name.

"What did she want?" he asked, before I had a chance to continue.

I could see the rigid look in his eyes, challenging me to betray him. I hadn't even started and he was already pissed. My right hand rested on the stem of my wine glass, shaking slightly from the tension. I took a long sip, trying to calm my own nerves. I started to realize that I might not make it through this conversation in one piece if the anger in Maziar's eyes was any indication.

"She came to see me about you," I said, struggling to keep my tone even.

"Obviously. I didn't think she came to take you out to lunch so you could be the sister she's always wished for," he said, each word drenched in his attitude.

I looked at him, shocked at his tone and irritated that he was already directing his anger at me even though I'd only said ten words.

"What is up with the attitude?" I asked. "Why are you so mad right now? I haven't done anything. She came to me. I didn't go looking for her."

I could see his anger dissipate as he looked at me across the table, replaced by a deeper sadness that lay hidden behind his rage. He took a deep breath and let it out slowly.

"I'm sorry. You're right. I'm not mad at you. I'm angry at them. The mention of their names puts me on edge. Don't be upset."

"I'm not. I just don't want you mad at me!" I said, frustrated.

He reached across the table and took my free hand, the other one still clenching the wine glass.

"I'm sorry. Go ahead. Tell me what she said."

I gathered my courage and told him about the afternoon, leaving no details unturned. I quoted his sister as best I could, as I described her distress in words that painted a picture, hoping it would appeal to his softer side. I could see the image taking shape in his mind as he leaned back in his chair, listening.

"She misses you. She wanted me to make sure you know how sorry she is."

As I watched him struggle with my words, I witnessed the walls he'd built around himself slowly fall apart, leaving only his wounded heart exposed. My own heart clenched with his pain, knowing they'd broken him in ways they weren't even aware of. They were so consumed with their own feelings that they'd failed to realize they'd pulled the foundation out from beneath him. All for falling in love with me.

"Why did she come to see you?" he finally asked, as if he'd just realized it didn't make any sense.

"She was hoping I could convince you to talk to her," I said.

He spun the wine glass between his fingers, staring at the swirling red liquid. I sat quietly, waiting. When he looked up at me, his eyes were filled with tears, and the rawness of his emotions felt like daggers shooting through my chest. I wanted to grab him, hold him, tell him I loved him enough to fill the voids they'd left behind.

"I don't know what to do," he said innocently.

I could understand his weariness; he was unsure which direction he should go. It made sense that he would want to mend his relationship with his family, but that he'd be apprehensive because of the effect they could have on us. Unable to stand another minute without touching him, I stood up and took the seat to his right. I reached out and grabbed his hand, bringing it up to my mouth, gently kissing his palm.

"I know, baby."

He held onto my fingers firmly, always worried I would flutter away if he didn't grab on tight. I reached out with my other hand and placed it on his cheek. He leaned into it, a tear escaping his eye and falling onto my fingertips. He lost his resolve then, and for the first time in years, I saw Maziar come undone. Unable to hang on to his emotions any longer, he hung his head and let the tears fall onto the floor as he quietly sobbed, the pain escaping from his broken heart.

I found strength where he couldn't, pulled him close to me, folding him into my arms. I shushed him and swayed, as if he were a child I was calming. He didn't stay vulnerable and fragile for very long, but it gave him relief, lifted a weight off his chest that I hadn't realized was causing him to buckle. When he looked up at me, wiping his eyes, he was smiling.

"I love you," he said, leaning in to kiss me. He wasn't insecure or wounded that I'd just seen him cry. Instead, he seemed relieved and light.

"I love you too."

"So what do you think I should do?" he asked, as he leaned back in his chair.

"I've never seen Bita the way she was today. She seemed really sad that she hadn't talked to you. She actually seemed kind of lost without you. I'm not sure exactly what to make of her, but my gut tells me she was sincere. If it were me, and it were Nima, I'd talk to him," I said truthfully.

"Yeah, but your brother is different. He would never do the things Bita did," he countered.

"Maybe, but she's still your sister. And even if you're mad, you still love her. It obviously isn't easy to stop talking to your family. I know you act like you don't care, but who do you think you're fooling?"

"You mean I'm not as good an actor as I thought I was?" he asked, smiling.

"No, you're not." I laughed. "Besides, what are you afraid of? It's just a conversation with your sister."

"Is it, though? Nothing is that simple with them."

"True, but what's the worst that can happen?" I asked.

"They could cause problems for us again," he replied glumly.

"Okay, but they can't hurt us anymore, right?" I tried to exude more confidence into my words than I actually felt.

I was afraid of the same thing. I was terrified I would lose everything we'd built in the past few months and find myself broken and crippled from the loss of it. But Maziar didn't need to feel my apprehension or worry about my feelings. He needed me to be a pillar in his storm and tell him that everything would turn out fine. I loved him enough to see past myself, to keep from steering him in my own selfish directions. I would be his strength, encouraging him to put his pieces back together, regardless of its cost to me.

"Just talk to her. See what she has to say, then decide what you want to do with it all," I encouraged.

After a few moments of thoughtful consideration, he said, "Okay, but I want you to be there. I need them to know that they can't separate us. I want them to know my decision has been made and I'm not willing to compromise."

"Okay," I said, smiling at his resolve.

Our love exuded strength where we couldn't, becoming a faith that we both deeply believed in. I wondered then how I'd gotten so lucky; how I was living in the dream all little girls dreamed of when they were small? How was I so blessed to have my Prince Charming sitting next to me, so deeply in love with me? I wouldn't let his family break us apart. If they wanted a war, I was ready, and this time I would win.

That night we made love as if it were a declaration to the world that our souls would forever be entwined. If one of us fell, we both did, refusing to endure even a moment apart in this life or the next.

CHAPTER THIRTY-SEVEN

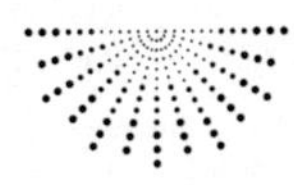

Maziar refused to contact his sister directly. He didn't want to give her the opportunity to strike up a conversation over the phone, avoiding having to meet him face to face. He'd abandoned any feelings of pain, only replacing them with unbidden anger. He was hell-bent on making her squirm, and squirm she did.

Instead, I was enlisted with the task of ironing out the specifics. Still not fully trusting Bita's motives, I resorted to discussing the details via text messages so there would be a trail for proof later if necessary. We were set to meet her at the Starbucks near my house Saturday afternoon.

I was slipping on my shoes just as I heard Maziar ring the doorbell. He was standing in the living room talking to my parents when I walked in. He was dressed in a pair of light blue Levi's and an emerald green T-shirt. It pulled the green specks out of his eyes, burying any hint of brown that was present in them before. It still seemed to surprise me every time I noticed how handsome he was, as if it were the first time I were laying eyes on him. I wondered if the novelty of his looks would ever wear off. I desperately hoped not.

I noticed how Mom held onto him a few seconds longer when she hugged him goodbye. I knew that, in her eyes, he'd done what she felt Dad had failed in doing so many times throughout their own lives. He had chosen me and placed me above his family and their desires. He refused to give into their demands. He would live without them if he had to, but not without me. That had been all that Mom had wanted Dad to do, and although in his mind he had, she'd never felt fully satisfied with his valor. She had now become Maziar's ally. He wasn't even aware of how profound his actions truly were to her.

We arrived at the coffee shop a few minutes later. Maziar was the epitome of calm and collected as we made our way to the door, while I was a mess of nerves and stress in comparison.

"Calm down," he gently urged.

I spotted Bita sitting at the far back corner of the coffee shop and was suddenly hit with the irony of the situation. It had been a lifetime ago when I'd walked through this very door, spotting Maziar in the same chair, as fidgety and rattled as she was, waiting on the conversation that would end us. Now I stood looking at Maziar's sister with the same mixture of dread and hope that her brother had in that very chair. Life did seem to have a way of coming full circle.

Maziar walked ahead of me, grabbing my hand on the way toward the table, breaking me out of my thoughts. Bita looked up as we approached, a hesitant smile across her face. Her brother remained stoic and unaltered.

"Bita," he said by way of greeting, slightly nodding his head as he took his seat.

I could visibly see her body tense in reaction, and she began to furiously tap her leg under the table. It had become quite obvious to me within the first few seconds that Maziar was going to make this as uncomfortable as possible for all of us. I had the sudden urge to pummel him, right there in the center of a rather busy Starbucks.

She looked at me and said, "Hi, Sara," as her brother stared impassively at her.

"Hey," I responded with a little more fervor than was necessary in an attempt to alleviate the tense energy in the air. I earned an eye roll from Maziar and sank back in my seat, having been silently reprimanded.

I realized that this conversation was a battle between siblings, so I decided it would be in my best interest to sit back and stay out of the line of fire. Bita stared at Maziar like a terrified child, trying desperately to maintain some semblance of control in a conversation that had yet to begin, and in a battle she already seemed to have lost. Maziar was the first to break the silence.

"So, why did you ask me to come here, Bita? Are you going to sit there and stare at me, or are you going to say something?" The irritation in his tone was thick and unyielding.

Bita was thrown back by his outright rage toward her. She seemed to become slightly offended in return. She grabbed her coffee cup tighter, eyeing her brother while she took a sip. The battle of wills was about to begin, and I couldn't help but wish I could open a trap door beneath me to escape.

"I've been trying to get a hold of you for months, but you keep ignoring me," she said, with less attitude than I'd expected.

"Obviously you didn't seem to get the hint," Maziar replied, eye roll and irritation in full effect.

I turned and looked at him, appalled by his lack of cooperation. He didn't look back at me or even flinch, but I knew he could sense my disdain. Although I knew he could feel it, I wasn't sure if he even cared because he continued to lay into her.

"I've made it very clear that I'm not interested in talking to either you or Mom. I'm pretty pissed that you would even think it was acceptable to just show up at Sara's work, manipulating her into setting this whole thing up."

"I didn't manipulate her. I just asked for her help," she protested.

Bita looked down at her hands, twisting a napkin furiously between her fingers. I actually felt a pang of sympathy for her, suddenly feeling the need to reach across the table and console her. I sat quietly brewing as Maziar continued to tell Bita how disappointed he was in her and what a horrible person she was.

When he was done, she was nearly in tears. I knew Maziar was warranted in his anger, but he was also upset with his mother, and Bita was paying the price for both. I knew I should hate her, but I wasn't very good at holding grudges, and Maziar's attack had unexpectedly made me her ally. Unable to take much more, Bita excused herself to the bathroom. Once she was out of earshot, I turned on him like a tiger about to pounce on his prey.

"What the hell was that?" I asked furiously.

"What do you mean?" His voice was eerily calm and equally frustrating.

"What do I mean? Are you kidding me?" I said.

"Keep your voice down," he demanded.

There was a hard set to his pupils, and I had to consciously keep my body from recoiling away from him, not allowing him to bully me.

"Why did you even agree to come if all you were going to do was attack her from the moment we sat down? If I'd known you had no intention of actually hearing her out, I wouldn't have agreed to this."

"What exactly would you like me to be doing right now? Should I be crying because my sister has decided that she misses me now, after months of giving me shit and making my life hell? You don't even know the half of it, Sara, because I chose to spare you. You have no idea what battles I had to get into with them over us." His cheeks were flushed with anger, signaling that I was treading on a very thin line.

"I know that. But your mom is also to blame," I said, trying to coerce him off the ledge. "It just feels like she's taking the beating for all of it."

"Yeah, but she didn't have my back. I always have Bita's back, no matter what, when it comes to my parents. I don't always agree with her or what she's doing, but I never let her face them alone. Bita took Mom's side, became a soldier for the enemy. I would never have done that to her," he said, his features softening into the hurt he was trying desperately to hide.

"No one is your enemy. I know it feels that way, but they aren't your enemy," I said.

I reached over and took his hand. I hated that he felt this way, hated that I had anything to do with the fact that his family had shattered him. I wanted so badly to find a way to make it all better for him.

I understood the anger he felt toward his mother and Bita, but I knew those feelings would consume him like a cancer, eating him from the inside out. He needed to let go of the pain and find a way to forgive. Whether I wanted to or not, I knew I had to forgive them first so he could.

When Bita returned to the table, I held Maziar's hand and squeezed as I turned to face her. She sat there, with red-rimmed eyes, evidence of the breakdown she'd just had in the bathroom stall. She took a deep breath and began to speak. Unable to look her brother in the eyes, she stared at an advertisement propped up on the table instead.

"I don't know how we got here, Maziar, I really don't, but I don't need you to tell me that you're disappointed in me because I already know that. I'm disappointed in me. You would never would have acted the way I did." She finally looked at Maziar. "I'm so sorry," she said. Then, she turned toward me. "I mean it, Sara. I'm so very sorry."

A tear slipped from her right eye before she could stop it. I was holding Maziar's hand with my left and, without thinking, I reached over with my right and squeezed Bita's hands from across the table.

"I forgive you," I said, and looked at Maziar.

He just sat there, riddled with emotions that could be seen all over his face, despite his best efforts. He didn't know what to do, how to let his anger go, or how to walk out of the store without forgiving his sister. He was struggling with himself, stuck in a battle of contradictions.

"I'm so mad at you," he whispered. "I would never have left you and backed up Mom and Dad. I would never have abandoned you."

Bita was weeping now, unable to control her feelings in any capacity. My own heart ached for the pain in his voice and the raw emotions he was laying out in front of us.

"I know. I don't know what to do but keep saying I'm sorry, Maziar. Please forgive me. Please."

He looked at his sister, but his eyes were glossed over, and I knew he was no longer seeing her. I imagined he'd taken a trip back in time, to the six-year-old he'd taught to ride a bike, the ten-year-old he used to play shipwreck with, the fifteen-year-old he went homecoming-dress shopping with, despite his protests. Then, he saw the woman she'd become, knowing she had the potential to be much more. He saw the sister, broken and sad before him, lost without her brother, and he reached out and grabbed her hand.

"I can forgive you. I just don't know if I can trust you," he said honestly.

"I can work on that. I'll prove to you that I won't ever take someone else's side over yours, not even Mom and Dad's. We can work on trust. You just need to forgive me first." She smiled at him.

"I'll try," he said, and smiled back at her.

Their hands lay intertwined in the center of the table and I thought to myself that life was amazing. It twisted and turned us in a million different directions, yet in the end, we kept finding ourselves in places that seemed impossible only moments before.

I would never have thought, a few years ago, after Bita and I had drawn our battle lines, that someday we would all be sitting here full of remorse for time lost, forgiveness for mistakes made, and hope for a future filled with love, and not just hate.

CHAPTER THIRTY-EIGHT

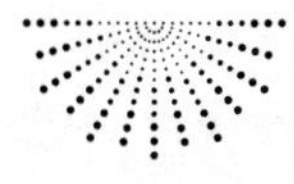

In the weeks to come, Maziar and his sister slowly started to rebuild the tattered pieces of their relationship. Bita began to call her brother every few days. Their conversations mimicked those of acquaintances at first, only encompassing topics two people who were close to strangers would engage in. She was a force to be reckoned with, though.

She remained steadfast, moving forward with the determination of a tornado, never letting Maziar's clipped responses or disinterest deter her. After a while, she began to break down his defenses, brick by brick, placing herself within the confines of his walls. As I stood back and watched them evolve, I began to believe that their falling-out had actually worked in their benefit, creating stronger bonds than before. In the end, their relationship was better for it.

Life propelled them onward, and soon days turned into weeks and phone calls turned into coffee dates. I started to witness the same ease and comfort I felt with Nima mirrored in Maziar's relationship with his sister. Much to my own surprise, I too began to feel comfortable around her. I started to be less apprehensive, letting my guard down when she was around. Time continued to push us forward, healing our battle scars and festered wounds until they became a remnant of the way things were, and not like the way things had become.

About a month and a half after Maziar and his sister had reconnected, I'd spent the earlier part of the day at his apartment. We'd gone on a morning run, then to breakfast. I was tidying up when I heard a knock at the front door. Maziar was getting ready in the bedroom, having lunch plans with his sister. He'd invited me to tag along, but I'd declined, having made my own date with Leyla.

I opened the door, expecting to find Bita. Instead, I was greeted by both his sister and father. Parviz was smiling kindly at me, as he always did now.

"*Salom Aghah*, Parviz. Hey, Bita," I said.

Suddenly, out of the corner of my eye, I caught someone to my left. I instinctively turned and found Naghmeh standing a few feet away from me. My smile faded, overtaken by what I assumed was a look of confusion. I stood there mute, not knowing what to do. I heard Maziar rustling about in the living room.

"Is that Bita?" he asked, as he approached the door. I had only opened it widely enough to frame my body, so he had no idea who I was looking at.

He grabbed the side of the door and swung it open, standing beside me. At first glance, he only saw his sister and father, and immediately smiled.

"Hey, Dad, I didn't know you were coming with us."

"Yes, it was last-minute," his father replied, looking nervously side to side.

Bita bounced back and forth on the balls of her feet. Maziar noticed her anxious energy, and turned his head to the left, in the direction in which I was still frozen.

His body instantly tensed as he saw her. I turned toward him, nervous, and somewhat curious, as to what he would do next. Within a millisecond, his expression had transformed from the warm, inviting one of a moment ago, to a passive, hard mask, hiding his reaction. He stood silent and expressionless, determined to outweigh his mother in pride.

She looked at her son. Beneath the anger and irritation, a deeper longing could be seen. Her features softened ever so slightly as she gazed into his eyes. She was no doubt traveling back in time, to better days, when he was her shadow, with his little hand tightly wound around hers. I could sense how much she had missed him, almost see her hand twitch by her side, aching to reach out and touch him. We stood there in the stillness surrounding us, intruders on her thoughts. It seemed to last an eternity, but she finally took the first step, breaking the silence.

"Hello, son."

We waited, wondering if he would acknowledge her attempt or brush it aside. Maziar reached out and grabbed my hand, once again wordlessly declaring his position.

"Hi, Mom," was all he offered.

"It's good to see you. It's been too long," she said.

Maziar didn't respond, just continued to impassively stare at her, never wavering. She stood looking back at him, equal parts strength and confidence.

I started to feel restless, wanting desperately to flee from the situation before anyone had a chance to say another word. Maziar's father came to the rescue, creating a window for me to bow out respectfully through.

"So, how about we go and get some lunch? I'm hungry." He chuckled, trying to alleviate the tension. He looked at me. "Sara, will you be joining us?"

I finally pulled my gaze away from Naghmeh, who still hadn't graced me with even the slightest acknowledgment.

"No," I said. "I have other plans today. I should actually get going. I'm going to be late."

"Oh, that's too bad. Maybe next time," he replied, politely.

He tried his best to convey a genuine disappointment. Bita met me with the same comforting expression, both working hard to hide their relief that I wouldn't be there to make an already stressful situation worse. I didn't spare his mother another glance when I turned and walked back inside.

I went into the bedroom to grab my purse and get out as fast as I could. I heard Maziar invite his family in, then his footsteps down the hall. My heart froze. I couldn't deal with him. I bustled around grabbing my stuff, trying desperately to keep the fact that I was rattled hidden from his peering eyes. He came up behind me and grabbed my arm, stopping me in the middle of the room. I looked up at him, trying to keep my face expressionless.

"I'm sorry. I had no idea she was coming."

He looked at me, worried that I might bolt out the door and never return. He knew I wasn't ready to see her, wasn't ready to face the reality behind the little fairy tale we'd been living these past few months. Now the truth was coming to haunt us.

I'd just gotten past the doubt that surrounded Bita, had just begun to feel comfortable, able to manage more than an hour in her presence without looking over my shoulder, expecting her to stab me in the back. Then his mother showed up, cold and uncompromising, her sharp eyes poking holes into my flesh, creating weaknesses in my armor. I was hit with the weight of the truth behind her unwavering stance on the two of us, her inability to see past her old ways and her traditions.

I felt a heavy sadness settle in the middle of my chest as he searched my eyes for some semblance of stability, some sureness that I was remaining steadfast and strong in our hold on each other. I looked away, unable to disappoint him when he recognized there was just fear.

"Yeah, I know. It's obvious you didn't know she was coming."

I tried to sound light and easy, but my voice shook on the end of my words. I pulled free from him, the physical connection making it harder to breathe, and busied myself in gathering my things.

I was consumed by the need to get out of the space his mother was occupying, to get as far away as possible from the negative energy that was nipping at me from every direction. I put the last of my things into my bag and finally managed to find my keys.

Maziar stood alone, in the center of the bedroom, helplessly staring at me. I was too overwhelmed with my need to run to worry about his feelings. I resorted to looking everywhere but at him, trying to avoid eye contact. I couldn't bear to see the distress I was causing him. Before I could walk out the door, he reached out and grabbed my arm again.

"Sara, wait," he pleaded.

"I can't. I really have to go. I'm going to be so late. You guys need to leave, too. They're waiting for you."

"I don't care," he said, pulling me into him. "Stop running."

He wrapped his arms around me and forced me up against him. He held me close, his hand cradling the back of my head. I let him comfort me as I melted into his chest. I allowed myself to take in a deep breath of him, letting him fill my lungs with the calm force he was. I granted myself a moment to listen to his heart beat against my ear, relieving an inkling of the ache I felt. I panicked with the thought that they would somehow whisk him away from me again.

"It's going to be okay," he said, sensing my fear.

I desperately wanted to believe him, but like a wound that refused to heal, the voice from long ago was back in my head shouting warnings at me at the top of her lungs. It was too late. I was already allowing her to fill my head with thoughts of his family's plotting and scheming to get me out of his life. I began to doubt Bita's motives, began to wonder if I'd been suckered yet again.

"I know it will," I replied. "I really do have to go." I stood on my tiptoes, placing a quick kiss on his lips, then headed out the bedroom door. He came out behind me, following me into the living room. "Bye, everyone. Have a good lunch," I chirped as I made my way to the front door. I needed to get away.

I didn't glance back at them, only wanting to get as far away as I could. I walked out the door and quickly closed it behind me, not allowing Maziar to follow me out, either. I didn't give myself time to think, just forced myself to walk to the car.

I was an hour early for lunch, sticky and sweaty from our workout, and not even close to being ready. I debated going home first, but I wasn't sure who would be there. Detouring from the original plan would only raise suspicions. It would tip Mom off that something had gone wrong. I wasn't ready for an interrogation. I decided to call Leyla. Luckily, her family was out, so I briefly gave her an update as I headed over to shower and change.

After I'd gotten ready, Leyla was waiting for me on her bed. I was hoping to avoid talking about it altogether, but I knew she wasn't going to let me off the hook. I sat down and began to describe the afternoon, in greater detail than before.

"Sara, nothing has happened yet. Why are you freaking out?" she asked.

"What do you mean why am I freaking out? You didn't see his mother. She's never going to budge. She literally didn't acknowledge my existence. How am I not supposed to freak out right now?" I said, exasperated. "She is obviously going to try to weasel her way back into his life, then cut me out!"

Leyla laughed. "You're so dramatic," she said, rolling her eyes.

"You're not helping." I scowled at her.

"I know. I'm sorry. Do you want my opinion on it?"

"Of course I do," I urged, desperate for help.

"Okay, I think you shouldn't freak out about it yet. Nothing has actually happened. I think you should have some faith in him. I really don't think he's going to cave simply because she's come around. Remember it was Maziar who cut them off. He hasn't reached out to contact any of them, other than his dad, but that's only because he supports you guys. Bita came running after him. Don't worry unless you have to–and I'm telling you, you don't have to."

She always seemed to be the voice of reason in my chaotic mind. I prayed she was right, that Maziar would stay strong in the midst of the storm. We spent the rest of the afternoon talking of other things as I tried to keep my mind off what was happening across town.

A few hours later, Maziar called. I wasn't ready to get an update on what had just gone down between them, so I sent him to voicemail. Leyla looked at me disapprovingly but didn't comment, knowing I needed to do things in my own time.

After lunch, I was supposed to head back to Maziar's so we could rent a movie and relax for the evening, but I lacked the courage to face the afternoon. I'd missed three calls and two text messages from him, urging me to call back. I couldn't gather the strength to call him, so I buried my phone in my purse and decided to go home instead.

I pulled up to my house so deep in thought that I failed to notice the car parked out front. I walked through the door and was startled to hear his voice. He was sitting with my parents on the couch, drinking tea. They were all laughing at something he'd said. I wasn't sure what it was, but from the way Mom was giggling, it was the most hilarious thing she'd ever heard. I looked like a deer in headlights, standing there, watching.

"Hi, *azizam*," Mom said. "*Chayee mekhay?*"

I shook my head, never taking my eyes off of Maziar. Tea would not rectify this situation. He looked back at me with a little smirk playing at the corners of his lips.

"What are you doing here?" I asked.

"You weren't picking up my calls so I decided to come over to make sure you were okay. 'What are *you* doing here?' is the better question," he said, tilting his head to the side in challenge. The smugness danced in his eyes. "I thought we had plans."

I suddenly felt angry, having the urge to throw my water bottle at his head. Mom smiled as I squirmed. I glared in her direction, as her loyalties become very clear. Dad laughed. I felt like I'd walked into the middle of an inside joke and I was the odd man out somehow.

"What is going on here?" I said to all three of them, accusingly.

Maziar stood up, walking over to me. "Well," he said, "you weren't responding to me, so I called your mom to make sure you weren't lying dead in a ditch somewhere. When she said she'd thought you were with me, I had to tell her what happened today with my parents. Both of us agreed that you would likely avoid me, like always. We thought I should come to the house and wait for you, that being the likely place you'd end up." He was looking down at me through long lashes, his sex appeal irritating. "I'm not going to let you run, Sara, no matter how badly you think you want to." He leaned down and kissed my forehead, refraining from showing too much affection in front of my parents. "Can we go get a movie and go back to my place now?"

"Oh Sara, don't give the boy such a hard time," Dad threw in playfully.

What was happening here? How had my parents crossed over to being Maziar's allies, and why was it making me want to flutter around with happiness that they had? I couldn't stay angry very long.

"You're so annoying," I mumbled, swatting him across the arm.

"I know, but that's why you love me."

"It's good to know you have my back, guys," I said to my parents.

"Go have fun," Mom replied, shooing us out the door. "See you later."

By the time we got to his car, the playfulness had left his eyes, replaced by irritation. I was confused for a moment, unsure of what had just happened in the past few seconds to cause his mood change.

"You don't get to avoid me, Sara. That isn't okay. Do you understand?" he said, his anger barely contained beneath the surface. "It's not fair. I already have so much shit to deal with that I can't worry I'm going to lose you every time something happens. I don't know what I have to do to prove it's you and me. No one else matters."

His rage was short-lived as he sat back in his seat, visibly exhausted. My heart broke. I hadn't realized I'd hurt him by avoiding his calls. I was too busy worrying about how I felt to notice that I was now his foundation, and when I hid, I was leaving him alone. I reached across the center console, wrapping my arms around him.

"I'm sorry. I didn't mean to make it harder for you. I'm just really scared," I said apologetically.

"I know, but you don't get to leave. I can't feel like I have to always worry about you, too. It's hard enough. Promise me, Sara: you have to have my back in all this, and that means being there."

"I promise."

* * *

I stood behind Maziar as he fumbled with the keys. I wanted desperately to know what had happened at their lunch, but at the same time, I was terrified of the outcome. I stayed quiet as I followed him inside.

Suddenly, he turned and pushed me up against the door, kissing me deeply. His fingers pressed into my skin as he shoved his body up against mine, pushing us deeper into the wood. He tore at my shirt, frantically pulling it up over my head as if he we were running out of vital time. He teased me with kisses up and down my neck, moving onto my breasts as he unhooked the clasp of my bra.

I was startled at his urgency, a feeling of fear mixing in with the pleasure he was leaving on my skin. I couldn't detach from my thoughts, worried that something worse than I'd expected had happened at lunch, and now he was trying to ease the impact. His need for me was tangible, exuding from his pores, filling the room around us. With knots in my throat and dread in my stomach, I leaned into him, matching his chaos.

I pulled his shirt over his head, laid my own intense path of lips all over his body, feeling the goosebumps rise in my wake. I tore his pants off, discarding them on the floor. I pushed him away from me, took in the perfection of his figure, each muscle creating its own ripple on his chest, his arms, his legs.

His desire stood at attention, making its presence known. I reached out and touched him; he shuddered beneath my fingers. A moan slipped his lips as I teased his ear between my teeth, his manhood between my hands. Suddenly, he hoisted me up and wrapped my legs around his waist, pushing himself deep inside me. I screamed out with pleasure as he took me up against the door.

When it was over, he held onto me tightly as I leaned my head on his shoulder, burying my face in the crook of his neck. He walked over the couch and gently put me down, lying next to me. He pulled me close to him, nestling me under the crook of his arm.

"So, did it go that badly today?" I asked.

"No," he said, reassuringly. "But even if it did, I'm never leaving you, Sara. I know you don't believe that, but I'm going to say it every day until you do."

"I just thought, with how we just made love, that things had gone really badly. Like you were trying to soften the blow before telling me the details."

"No, that was just because I've wanted you all damn day," he confessed, smirking.

"Oh, okay," I giggled. "Well, then, how did lunch go?"

"About that, things didn't go badly, but you have to stay open-minded."

"What do you mean?" I asked.

I pulled myself up on my elbow to look at him, not liking the tone in his voice. My giddiness for his desire was rapidly replaced by dread.

"Well, lunch went as expected. We talked and argued. I put my foot down. My mom tried to push back. I, obviously, didn't budge. She finally gave in, realizing that I'm a package deal. She knows if she doesn't accept you, then she loses me."

"And?" I held my breath, waiting for the punchline.

"She wants to go out to dinner with us next week," he said.

"What?" I asked, horrified.

"She knows I'm thinking forever with you, so she says she wants to get to know you." He reached out and pulled me back to his chest, placing my head down where I could hear the beating of his heart. "This is a good thing, Sara. This means she knows she can't break us up. I think she's going to try."

I lay there, devoid of words as my mind swirled with an avalanche of thoughts. Was she really trying to get to know me, or was this just another ploy in her never-ending plans to sever me from Maziar's life? If this was indeed part of her plan, would Maziar really be able to withstand her advances? They'd had one lunch and he was already convinced she'd changed. As my thoughts crashed into each other, Maziar gently played with my hair, trying to soothe me off the ledge I was standing on.

"How am I supposed to act around her? What do I say?" I asked, terrified.

"Just be yourself. She's the one trying to prove herself, not you."

Maziar seemed happy, convinced this was a turning point. But I knew better. She'd successfully made her way in again over one afternoon, and she wasn't going to allow anyone to push her out a second time. She'd play whatever game he needed her to and then have her way with me. But she'd thrown down the gauntlet and now the ball was in my court. I could do nothing but accept the invitation, readying for the worse while praying for the best.

I rolled myself on top of Maziar and had my way with him again, right there on the couch, trying to consume the last moments of our uninterrupted happiness before his mother stole them away.

CHAPTER THIRTY-NINE

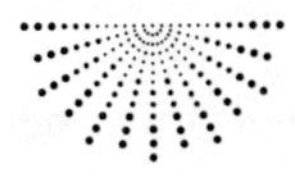

The week preceding the "dinner" flew by. I wanted time to drag on, to stand still, giving me a moment to find the courage I needed to face off with the lioness. I felt small and weak, a mere child facing a dragon, with only sticks and rocks as weapons. It wasn't in my nature to be good at the art of confrontation, even more so with one of my elders. I went through the motions of each day unable to focus, all along my mind preoccupied with the events of the weekend looming before me.

Seti and Leyla had taken it upon themselves to prepare me, throwing every scenario possible in my direction. I felt like a prize fighter in intensive training, readying for the championship. By the time it was Saturday, I felt dizzy from preparations and exhausted from the apprehension. I wanted to flake on the whole thing, throwing my hands up in defeat before the war had even begun.

I spent most of the day hanging out with Mom as she, too, went about preparing me for the battle ahead. She urged me stick up for myself, to say my piece but to do it respectfully to avoid any further issues in an already dramatic situation. I wasn't worried about being rude, but I was scared that I wouldn't have the guts to say anything at all.

I was standing in front of the mirror staring at my reflection when I heard a light knock on my door. I was noticing how the pink of my blazer brought out the rosiness in my cheeks, how the white of my tank top reflected off the deep brown of my eyes, making them look like pools of dark chocolate, the pupils barely discernible. I watched Maziar's necklace sway with each breath I took, moving in unison with the long curls that fell around my face. I took in my tiny frame, lean and hard from my morning runs, outlined by my black pants.

"Maziar's here," Mom said, popping her head in.

"I know. I heard the doorbell. I just need another minute."

"Okay," she said tenderly, knowing I was worried.

I made my way to the living room a few minutes later. Maziar was standing by the doorway talking to Dad. He looked toward me as I walked in, a smile breaking out across his face. I felt my breath catch in the back of my throat as it always did when he looked at me that way.

"You ready?" he asked, knowing I was dreading this dinner.

"Yes." I leaned in to kiss my parents.

"Take good care of my daughter, Maziar," Mom urged.

He stopped and turned to face her. "Of course I will. I always do," he assured her. He leaned in and kissed her cheek. She blushed under his unwavering attention. I was grateful that this was at least one relationship I didn't have to worry about.

His parents had made dinner reservations in Malibu. The drive over was a quiet one as I tried to muster up the courage to face the evening. I hadn't even realized we'd made it until the attendant opened my door. I just sat there staring at him, desperately wanting to remain in my seat. When I didn't move, he reached out his hand so I could take it. I reluctantly let him help me out of the car.

Maziar came over to me and gently kissed the top of my head. "It's going to be okay," he whispered in my ear.

I wished I could believe him, wished we could walk out of here with no war wounds to show for it. But that nagging voice had taken up permanent residence in my head, screaming warnings of danger at me. No matter what I did, I couldn't shake her. I knew this evening was a bad idea.

The hostess walked us over to our table. It was located on the deck overlooking the ocean. The sun had almost set and the sky was aglow with pinks and oranges that swirled around the cotton candy clouds. The waves crashed against the rocks below, their rhythmic pattern soothing in the background. I stared out at the water and wondered how I'd gotten here. How did we go from two kids in a club to Judgment Day at this restaurant? How was I exactly where I'd tried so hard to avoid being?

I fidgeted in my seat as we waited for his family to arrive. I pulled obsessively at a frayed string on the side of my pants, giving my hands something to do other than lie idly in my lap. I hadn't even noticed Maziar ordering us drinks until the waitress showed up with two glasses of wine. I gratefully grabbed mine, taking a long sip.

"I love you," he said reassuringly.

Before I could respond, I spotted Bita walking through the door and my heart dropped. She saw us from across the restaurant and headed toward us, smiling. Her parents were trailing behind her, Parviz in the lead, his arm stretched out behind him, holding his wife's hand. His smile was wide and warm, crinkling the corners of his eyes. It did nothing to calm my nerves, my gaze intently set on his wife.

Naghmeh stood proper and poised, exuding perfection from her pores. Her face was smoothed into an expression of indifference as she set her sights on me. I could feel the icicles forming on my skin from the chill of her stare. My stomach roiled with tension, but I tried to swallow it down, remembering what Mom had told me. The fact that I was falling apart on the inside was irrelevant. I needed to find a way to mask my emotions from the four people sitting at this table. I focused on calming my own features.

We stood up when they approached, as is customary when greeting new arrivals in our culture. Bita came in first, hugging us both. She took the seat directly across from me, trying to position herself in the crossfire, in hopes that she could deflect some of the ammunition shot my way. I saw a silent approval exchanged across the table between Maziar and his sister as she lapped up his validation. His father came in next, shaking his hand, then leaning in to give me a quick hug.

When it was his mother's turn, she wrapped her arms tightly

around her son, glancing at me from over his shoulder with an expressionless face. The dread began to amplify in the pit of my stomach and I had to focus on staying unresponsive to keep her from seeing it. I felt like I was going to throw up. Once Maziar successfully severed himself from her, she reached across the table, grabbing my hand.

"*Salom*, Sara. It's good to see you," she said, disinterested.

"*Salom*, Naghmeh *Khanoom*. It's good to see you too," I answered, mimicking her tone.

We stood there awkwardly looking at each other until Parviz pulled the seat out for her. We all followed suit, sitting down. I grabbed my wine glass, taking another long drink, not caring what judgments were behind his mother's intense gaze. Maziar just smiled, no doubt amused by my sudden disregard for proper Persian girl etiquette. I could hear Mom's voice in my head.

"Sara, it looks like you have no class if you drink like that," was its response to my downing a glass of wine.

Technically, Muslims didn't drink. But we weren't religious. However, Mom's generation had been raised in Iran, a predominantly Muslim country. It was looked down upon to drink during her time, and after the revolution, it became outlawed. Mom didn't drink, and even though she didn't stop me from drinking, she thought I should be mindful about how I appeared when I did. What I was doing at the moment would disappoint her. Even so, I welcomed the alcohol despite how it made me look to Naghmeh, begging it to dull my senses and make the evening bearable.

Parviz began asking each of us about work, trying to find something to fill the void the tension was creating. Bita joined in, the two of them spinning our conversations around in different directions, trying to mask the discomfort that everyone was so obviously feeling.

His mother seemed to be the only person at the table unaffected. She'd voice her opinion on the various topics being discussed but made it a point to stare at me expressionlessly when I spoke. Her eyes, though, bored into me like a claw drill, digging through my layers as if I were upturned earth.

The fear began to dissipate, quickly replaced by the anger flaring in the center of my chest. How dare she make me feel like an impostor in my own world? I was furious that I'd allowed her to make me doubt every word that came out of my mouth. When did she become the gatekeeper, deciding if I was worthy enough for passage?

The truth was that Maziar had chosen me despite her protests. The days of making a good impression were gone, wasted years ago when I'd desperately needed this woman's approval. She hadn't spared me a second thought when she tore us apart, leaving me by the wayside to die.

I tried again to mend our bridges after Maziar's accident. I was willing to see past her malicious ways and forge a relationship with his family. But she couldn't move forward, trying to convince me to leave her son and keep her dirty secret. In the end, her son was unwilling to compromise, and she was the one who'd swallowed her pride and come to him.

If she were smart, she would do her damnedest to work things out with me. If I walked away from this dinner disgruntled, I would still be going home with Maziar. I was the one sleeping with him, which meant I was the one in control.

I was the one he'd follow home.

Maybe it was the wine, or maybe it was the discovery that I wasn't as powerless as I'd felt at the beginning of the night, but I didn't feel as helpless as I did minutes ago. She was watching me intently now. I wondered if she could feel the energy shift around me, the fear dissolve into nothingness. I leaned back in my chair wanting to stay angry.

But, as I watched her glance between Maziar and me, I realized that regardless of how horrible I thought she was, I was sure that she felt that she was doing right by her son. She was convinced that we were doomed, incapable of seeing past her judgment, and her apprehension of change. She was trying to keep him from making what she thought was a big mistake. This wasn't truly about me, not personally. I just didn't fit into the mold of what she'd been raised to think was right.

I desperately wanted to let myself hate her. I wanted to be a royal bitch and then walk out of the restaurant hand in hand with her son, flaunting it in her face. I wanted to prove to her that I could crush her if I really wanted to, weave my voodoo and pull him completely out of her life. I wanted to win, but I knew it would cause us all to lose in the end.

The conversations had quieted, mundane topics having all been used up and worn out. Bita and Parviz looked at each other despondently, knowing the conversation was about to take a turn. Naghmeh slowly took a sip of her water, eyeing the two of us over the edge of her glass.

"Maziar, we asked you here to discuss the situation you've created for yourself," she said.

His father looked at her, appalled at her lead-in to the topic of our relationship. Bita physically sank back in her seat, trying to disappear into the table linens. I just glared at his mother, who was very convincingly pretending I was invisible, furious that she'd just referred to me as a "situation." Before I had a chance to say a word, Maziar jumped in.

"What situation would that be, Mom? Because surely you aren't referring to Sara as a situation," he said calmly, his anger burning a hole into her defenses.

"Oh Maziar, please don't be dramatic. You know what I mean," she replied. She waved her hand in the air, nonchalantly brushing his response aside as if she were talking to a child. "We need to know what your plans are with all of this, because we don't see this working out."

The anger boiled inside me like a tea kettle about to explode. I wanted to say something, to tell her she was out of line, but there was no time. The conversation was moving at the speed of a tennis match, toggling back and forth between the two of them as Maziar met her step for step.

"Well, it's a good thing I didn't ask you if you thought this would work out, now, isn't it? Truth is it doesn't matter what you think."

"How can you say that, Maziar? We're your family. How do you plan on doing this all alone?" she asked, furious.

"My family doesn't seem to be the problem, Mom. You seem to be the only one that has an issue with my relationship. And as far as doing this without you, and anyone who agrees with you," he said, turning to look at his father and sister, "Sara has enough family for the two of us."

She sat there, shocked into silence as if Maziar had reached across the table and slapped her. She hadn't come to this dinner thinking she was going to lose. Not giving her time for a rebuttal, Maziar continued, going for the jugular.

"I thought you wanted to have this dinner because you realized I was serious about Sara. I thought you genuinely wanted to get to know her. I can see now that I was wrong." He steadied his gaze on his mother's wounded face and, without an ounce of remorse, said, "I'm really sorry, Mom, that you're too selfish to care about what it is that I want. I'm also sorry that things have to end this way, but you aren't leaving me any choice. I love Sara. If we want to be together, that's our choice, not yours or anyone else's. It's sad that you can't see past yourself, but I'm done."

"Maziar, think about what you're saying. I'm not saying Sara is a bad girl, but there's no way this is going to work," she replied, an edge of desperation invading her words. She continued by listing all the reasons why we were doomed, hoping a light would go off for her son and she could convince him to walk away.

I pitied her naïveté. She'd come from a generation that didn't accept change. In fact, they shunned it, as if steering away from the crowd was a cardinal sin. She came from a culture that stuck to their ways, putting more emphasis on race and religion than love and compatibility. It wasn't her fault that she felt anxious about the possibility of Maziar and me together. She was a product of her upbringing, incapable of breaking the chains that bound her.

Maziar sat patiently as his mother presented her case. He held my hand the entire time, refusing to let her sever even the smallest connection between us. He maintained his composure, but he was fuming. I knew it took every ounce of his self-control to keep from flipping the table in anger.

I, on the other hand, had my emotions flashing across my face. I went from angry to appalled to sad to shocked, my expressions changing with each of her words. I had abandoned my attempt at wearing a mask, too mortified to hide my weaknesses.

Multiple times during the conversation, I'd wanted to say something, to throw in my own opinion, to yell at her audacity.

However, Maziar was so on point with his responses there wasn't a need for me to stand up for myself. He was successfully doing it on his own. It was better for the fight to come from him rather than me anyway. The future was big; the end result unpredictable.

I was reminded of a saying my grandmother always said: "*Yek seebroh meendazi tooyeh havah, sad bar meecharkheh ta bekhoreh beh zameen.*" When you throw an apple in the air, it spins a hundred times before hitting the ground. You never knew how life would go, turning around in so many different directions before you reached the final outcome. It was better for Maziar to speak on our behalf. His mother could eventually forgive him if they worked things out, but she would never forgive me.

He continued to stare at her with disappointment on his face. He had come to this dinner truly believing his mother had had a change of heart, that she was going to try to get to know the girl he loved. He thought, even if she couldn't fully be on board with what he was planning to do, she was going to at least be supportive enough to find common ground. My heart broke, knowing she'd once again hurt him more than she could have imagined.

Maziar wasn't going to let her see what she'd done to him, though. He wasn't going to appear vulnerable. He had too much pride to let her know she'd broken him.

"I don't have to explain my decisions to you. I had hoped you would come around, but that isn't the case. You've made your choice, Mom, and now I'm making mine," he said in a cold, even tone. "Let's go, Sara."

He stood up, startling us all into attention. I looked at him, eyes pleading for him to reconsider. I knew that walking out of this restaurant meant we were crossing the point of no return. I silently urged him to find a different way to deal with this moment. I was angry too, but I could see the bigger picture. Severing all ties wouldn't lead to a happy outcome. He, however, was resolved in his decision. He was done, and my fears had no bearing.

"Come on. Let's go home," he said, reaching down to help me out of my chair.

"You're going to regret this, Maziar," his mother threatened. It was her last desperate plea to assert some semblance of control.

Maziar didn't respond. He just turned around and walked away. I could hear his father's voice as he reprimanded his wife, his tone low and assertive.

"Naghmeh, that's enough!" he demanded.

"But, Parviz," she began, but he stopped her.

"That's enough. I won't let you do this," he said, pulling his chair out to follow us.

Bita just sat at the table, her head buried in her hands. By the time Maziar had handed the valet his ticket, Parviz was beside him.

"Son, please, don't leave like this," he pleaded.

He turned toward his father, his rage bright in his eyes. "I meant it, Dad. I'm done. I'm not doing this anymore."

"But she's your mother," he desperately reasoned.

I stood there watching the spool of thread unravel. I reached out and put my hand on Maziar's arm, forming a union. I wanted to comfort him, to let him know he wasn't alone. He gave me a wary smile. He looked exhausted, as if he had the weight of the world on his shoulders while he hiked up a mountain.

"Do you feel the same way, Dad?" he asked, no longer able to hide his vulnerability.

I saw Maziar transform into a little boy. He stood there, wide-eyed and innocent, staring at his father, wanting desperately to feel his support. Parviz allowed his eyes to linger on the man before him. Life had moved forward in a flash, and the little boy he once held tightly in his arms was no longer present. He'd grown into a man, one who was now in love with a woman. He needed at least one of his parents to support him as he moved forward in this new chapter of his life.

"No," he said. He reached out and pulled me close to him, placing a kiss on the crown of my head. "No, I don't." He smiled. He then leaned in and wrapped his arms around his son. "I'm proud of you."

I watched Maziar allow himself a moment of weakness in his father's, big, strong arms. I saw the relief spread across his face, saw it in the rise and fall of his chest. I knew his father's approval meant everything. Even the biggest giants needed a moment to hand their troubles off to someone else.

The car came around. Maziar let go of his dad as the valet came to open my door. From the spot I stood in, I could see that Bita and Naghmeh were making their way toward us. Maziar spotted them as well.

"You guys go and enjoy the rest of your night," Parviz said, as he guided us toward the car. "We'll talk later."

Maziar squeezed his father's arm and walked over to the driver's seat. The valet had my door open and I was already inside, shutting it behind me.

"I love you," Parviz said.

"I love you too, Dad," Maziar replied, glancing at his mother, who was now standing by her husband. Without even the slightest acknowledgment, he got into the car, leaving the woman who had raised him behind.

* * *

That night we lay in bed, wrapped in each other's arms, content with the quiet of the dark. Our war wounds from the most recent battle were too devastating to leave us energy for much else. Maziar tried to make light of the situation, throwing in humor where he could, masking the magnitude of what had taken place mere hours ago. Finally, he resorted to just lying in bed with my head on his shoulder, his arms wrapped protectively around me.

A few hours later, when his breath slowed and his body shed the tension of the day, I knew he'd fallen asleep. I envied his escape, as I still lay there twirling the night around in my head. I had no idea how we were going to move forward after this. I was consumed with worry, overtaken by a deep sadness that wrapped itself around the muscles of my heart, constricting with every beat.

I didn't understand how things had unraveled so quickly at dinner. I couldn't fathom how a mother could sever her deepest bond over a disagreement. I knew she truly believed we were doomed, but I'd always thought a mother would follow into the darkness, committing herself to the flames for her child. Naghmeh had cut her bonds, pushing him into the abyss to go at it alone. I knew she loved him.

Maybe she thought the ultimatum would bring him to his senses and back to her? I wasn't sure.

I allowed myself to feel the heaviness of the situation in its entirety. I stared up at the glow of the street lights dancing across the ceiling, allowing myself a moment of pity to feel sorry for how difficult things always seemed for Maziar and me. I'd never thought our love would tear families apart, leaving everything in disarray. I let myself feel bad for the man lying next to me, for the deep void I knew his mother had left him.

As I watched the lights flicker, I finally allowed myself the luxury of crying, in the deep silence of the dark, where no one could see me.

CHAPTER FORTY

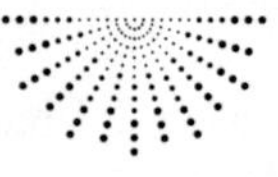

Weeks passed and Maziar refused to discuss what had happened with his mother. If I brought it up, he would shut it down, saying that she was no longer of consequence. I was worried at first, but the more he reiterated that she was meaningless, the more my fears were dulled. Soon I found myself believing him.

I had all but technically moved in with him, Mom having abandoned her doubts of our future once Maziar had renounced Naghmeh. He was the epitome of what she'd always wished Dad would have done for her, creating a unique bond between them. I still came home most nights, but I spent all my waking hours with Maziar, and when I did want to stay, I wasn't met with much hesitation.

With all the recent drama we'd been dealing with and our heavy workloads, Maziar thought we could use a break to decompress. He surprised me with tickets for five days in Cabo, Mexico. We had a beachfront suite at the Esperanza Resort.

The following weeks couldn't move fast enough, both of us itching to get away from our reality. When the day finally arrived, we were both up bright and early from the excitement. Maziar had bribed

Nima into giving us a ride, allowing him to use his BMW in our absence. My brother gladly obliged.

We sat side by side at the airport, trying to kill time before our flight. My book lay open on my lap but I wasn't reading it. I was too busy staring at him, overwhelmed by how much I loved him. At times, I found it terrifying. Somewhere over the past few years I'd started needing Maziar as much as I needed air to breathe. We'd become intertwined like the intricate design of veins and arteries. Separating us would lead to devastating consequences. That was what his mother didn't understand: we hadn't chosen to be together; we needed to be, choices having nothing to do with the situation.

I remember Maziar telling me that in the Jewish religion there was a belief that each soul was broken into two parts and sent to the Earth to find each other. *Besheret*, meaning soulmate, the one person that you're divinely destined to be with. I found the idea beautiful because I was living it. Maziar and I made up the same soul, two equal parts of the same entity. What his mother didn't realize, much to her dismay, was that the other half of her son's soul wasn't Jewish. We had tried to live apart, but it didn't work. We belonged together.

"What?" he asked when he realized I was staring at him.

"Nothing. I just love you; that's all," I said, noticing how the lines around his eyes were more defined now than when I'd met him.

He slipped his arm behind my back, pulling me closer to him. He brushed his lips up against mine, the electricity shooting through my body. I put my hands on either side of his face, kissing him more deeply, careless of what spectators were witnessing.

We were interrupted when our flight was called. We boarded the plane hand in hand.

* * *

Esperanza meant hope. Staring out over the vast views of its beautiful grounds left me with just that. The crashing waves hummed a constant lullaby like subtle background music. The cool breeze blowing through the open lobby left goosebumps as it caressed my skin. The high ceilings and marble pillars gave the hotel an upscale feel, with fancy couches and lounge chairs placed throughout for the patrons.

Maziar went to check us in as I wandered onto the deck to admire the dreamlike scene before me. The sound of the waves mingled with the lapping water in the infinity pool made me feel calm, something I hadn't felt for months. I was so mesmerized by the beauty surrounding me that I hadn't noticed Maziar standing beside me. He placed his hand on my shoulder, startling me.

"Sorry, I didn't mean to scare you," he said apologizing.

"It's okay. Isn't it gorgeous?"

"It's breathtaking," he agreed. "Let's go get settled."

The room was a short elevator ride from the lobby, nestled in the corner of the third floor. The suite opened up to the right, the bed placed in the center of the room under a canopy of white chiffon. It reminded me of fairy wings as it fluttered in the breeze. The far wall was made out of glass that was folded back like an accordion, opening it to the beach below.

The terrace had a wraparound padded bench and an infinity-edge hot tub. Just beyond the terrace was the vast blue ocean. We stood surrounded by the purring of the wind and the crashing of the waves as we watched seagulls dip down into the water. I could feel my body instinctively relax, every muscle unwinding on the way down.

Maziar wrapped his arms around me, kissing the skin below my ear. My body responded with heat through my limbs as I turned to face him, running my fingertips over the exposed flesh of his arm and neck. He shuddered when I wrapped my hand around the back of his head, pulling his mouth onto mine, teasing his lips with my tongue. He pushed his body up against me, making my heart pound uncontrollably against my chest. His fingers grazed my skin as he pulled my shirt off, causing shivers to run up my spine. He leaned down and placed his lips where his fingers had just been, the warmth of his tongue like a drug coursing through my veins. I almost lost myself.

We managed to discard our clothing into a rumpled mess on the floor. He wrapped his arms around my hips and picked me up. I hooked my legs around his waist. He walked us onto the terrace, neither worried about what could be seen from the beach below. He gently laid me down on the cushions, lowering his body onto mine.

For a moment, I was hit with the realization that I was actually with Maziar, that we'd somehow made it through the storm despite our never-ending obstacles. The emotions overwhelmed me, mimicking the force of the waves below. I grabbed onto his back, pouring all of my feelings back into him. He matched the fierceness of my movements. We made love in the cool ocean breeze, ridding our bodies of the tension we'd harbored for the past few months.

When it was over, Maziar carried me over to the bed. We slid in side by side underneath the plush feather blankets, naked. We fell asleep wrapped around each other, nestled together in our little Mexican heaven.

When we woke up again, the sun was setting. We lay in bed and watched it drop behind the ocean, taking the light with it. The sky lit up in patterns of reds and purples like grape and strawberry bubblegum swirls as the sun descended. We lay silent and still, watching in awe.

When the darkness had taken over, Maziar took me again under the glitter of the stars. There was a new freedom in our movements, shedding the layers of skin from the past that had been weighing us down. A cover of peace had settled over us in this foreign land.

I wanted to stay like this forever.

* * *

We spent the next few days relaxing by the pool, flanked by drinks and the vibrant sun. We took long walks along the shore, reminiscing about our easier days when we were still vying for each other's attention, innocent and clueless.

We sat on the beach, digging our toes into the sand, watching the waves crash beneath the bright moon. We got lost in our future, organizing its details as we giggled and argued.

"If we have kids, what do you want to raise them as?" I asked, as we lay on towels staring at the stars. I realized we'd never had this conversation. Although I agreed that inter-religious pairings weren't as dire as my culture portrayed them to be, I knew that the core of the issue was the complication of faith in regards to children.

"Don't tell me you're rethinking your decision now," Maziar joked.

"No, but I get why everyone is all bent up over it. We keep having to defend ourselves, but we've never actually made a decision about this. We should probably talk about it, right? Come up with some sort of plan?"

"Well, what do you think?"

"I think I'd like to raise them with a combination of both. Neither of us is super-religious, so why can't we teach them what we each believe? Isn't that what religion is about? What we believe in and find important as human beings? I think they are all the same at their core anyway."

"So we teach them the cores, then," Maziar replied.

"Yeah," I said, smiling.

He lifted himself up on one elbow so he could look down on me. "Good, because you're kind of stuck with me now anyway," he said, grinning teasingly. Then, he leaned down and kissed me.

We returned to our room in the early hours of the morning, falling asleep under the fairy wings, wishful dreams of our future dancing in our heads.

For the first time in what felt like a lifetime we were able to focus on just ourselves. Gone was the constant static brought about by the never-ending cultural expectations we so readily seemed to break and the aftermath of anger that seemed to follow. Here, we didn't have to prove ourselves, defend our relationship, convince anyone that we belonged together. For the first time ever, we just were.

* * *

When I woke up on the morning of our final day, I lay still in bed listening to Maziar's breathing. I felt a pang of disappointment, knowing the following day things would return to how they'd been. We were leaving paradise to only find ourselves back in the hell we'd escaped from. Maziar kept trying to convince me that his mother's lack of acceptance was meaningless, and to some extent, I believed him. I knew Maziar had chosen me, that Naghmeh no longer possessed the power to change that. I also knew that pushing her aside wasn't as easy as he was trying to make it seem.

I closed my eyes, praying the day would drag on forever so we could stay in this heaven a little longer. I hoped we'd stay this open and free even after we returned to our original story. I prayed Maziar would find a way to be this happy, despite his mother.

He stirred beside me, opening his eyes.

"Good morning, baby," I said, leaning in to kiss him.

"Good morning," he said, with a grin. He threw his arms around me and pulled me on top of him. "I could get used to this," he said, smirking, as he began kissing me more fervently.

I wrapped my body around his and we tumbled between the sheets, taking each other to that sweet spot where the world exploded around us. An hour later, we made our way to the pool, spending the rest of the day in a lazy, intoxicated haze. When the sun lit the sky in a dim orange glow, we returned to our room to get ready for dinner.

We sat at the restaurant completely oblivious to those around us. The conversation never paused, with Maziar making me laugh so hard I was in tears. Before we knew it, we were the last people there, holding up the staff from closing.

Maziar paid our bill and grabbed my hand, guiding us out of the doors. We stepped outside and he paused, pulling me toward him and kissing me tenderly. The emotions wrapped up in his face could have moved mountains, making my heart flutter in response. Then, he grabbed my hand and led us down the pathway.

Moments later, we heard the crash of thunder. Before we knew what was happening, we felt droplets of water falling onto our skin. The rain began with a drizzle, but within minutes, it started to come down in sheets. We began running, trying to make it back to our room.

Halfway there, I pulled on Maziar's arm, stopping him in the middle of the path as I laughed hysterically.

"There's no point in running. We're pretty wet already," I pointed out.

"You're right," he said, grinning. Then, he took a step back and bowed down as if he were a knight. "Would you be kind enough to give me this dance?"

I smiled through the rain cluttering my vision and reached out to him. He took my hand and we began to dance. I don't know how long he twirled me around on the pavement as people around us ran back to their rooms. Three couples stopped when they saw us, and decided to join in on their own waltz in the rain. The eight of us swirled around, careless of the wet clothing sticking to our bodies, or the strands of hair stuck to our faces. Our laughter soared to the sky, taking part in the dramatics of the thunder.

Without warning, Maziar stopped and looked at me, as the others continued to dance around us. His eyes held an intensity I wasn't expecting, causing me to freeze mid-swing. My heart crashed against my chest with the promise of something coming. I wasn't sure what was happening, but I could feel its profoundness. Without a word, he took a few steps back, bending down on one knee. The others stopped abruptly, staring at him.

"Sara, I had this elaborate scene set up in our room with champagne and dessert. There were rose petals, too. But I can't wait another minute to do this," he said.

As his words began to sink in, my heart continued to beat furiously against my rib cage, threatening to stop altogether. I began to shake, and despite the cold rain, I could feel heat flooding my limbs.

"You know how much I love you. I always have. From the moment I saw you, I knew you were special. You were like no one else I'd ever met. I can't imagine my life without you. I know things haven't been easy." He paused, the emotions thick in his voice. I stood there crying as he reached out and grabbed my left hand. "I know you deserve better, but I'm hoping you'll still have me. Will you marry me, Sara?" he asked.

I was crying so hard I couldn't speak. I just nodded. He pulled a ring out of his pocket and gently slipped it on my finger. The light from the lamp caught the diamond as it sparkled against the rain. He stood up, wrapping his arms around me. I kissed him, crying and laughing all at the same time.

* * *

Maziar stood at the door of our room, fumbling in his pocket for the key. I reached out and turned him around, pushing him up against it. The emotions were raging inside me, unable to wait another moment to get close to him. I pressed my body into his, my mouth finding the soft skin of his lower lip, as my fingers dug into the flesh of his forearms.

I wanted him.

One hand was wrapped around my hair, the other trying clumsily to open the door. He blindly placed the key into the slot and heard the familiar click of the lock. Never letting go, he pushed the door open and we tumbled toward the bed, a tangle of arms and legs tearing at each other's clothing. By the time we made the short stretch, we were naked, bodies pressed against each other, fingers tracing a map. He lifted me up, taking the final few steps over to the bed, placing me gently down on the mattress. His body hovered over mine as he looked deep into me, all the love I felt reflected back in his eyes. He brushed a hair off my face, his finger slowly etching a path along my forehead, setting my nerves on fire.

"I can't believe you said yes," he whispered, more to himself than me.

I reached out, lightly pulling him down on top of me. I softly kissed his forehead, then his cheeks, ending on his eyelids.

"I love you," I said.

He kept his eyes trained on me as he gently eased himself inside. As we began moving against each other, gone was the fierceness of moments ago, replaced by a slow-building dance. We were grateful for the length of every second that passed, urging time to stand still, as we lost ourselves to each other. We took our time, enjoying the feel of each other's skin, the desire that washed over our bodies. When we finally reached the end, our bodies slowed, savoring the fall. We shuddered back to Earth in sync, intertwined and connected. We lay enveloped by the crashing waves and our ragged breathing. I settled my head on Maziar's chest, listening to the beating of his heart.

"We're getting married," he said.

"Yes, we are."

CHAPTER FORTY-ONE

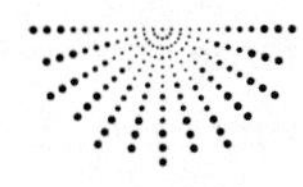

The proposal was an elaborate plan Maziar had set into motion weeks before. Unbeknownst to me, he'd sat down with my parents while I was at work, asking them for their blessings. They'd been thrilled, and sworn to secrecy for the next two weeks.

When we returned from Mexico, we were greeted by a little celebratory get-together with my family. Also, there were Neda and Bita. Missing were Maziar's parents, a small detail everyone noticed.

"Where are his parents?" my grandmother asked. She knew why there weren't there but felt the need to point out the obvious.

"Leave it alone, *Maman*," Mom replied, her eyes icily staring the old woman down.

"Humph. Well, just seems like they should be," she said, unable to resist the last jab.

I just turned and walked away, but the damage was done. I felt the small knot of hesitation instantly magnify in response to *Mamanbozorg's* words. I was already worried about how we were going to proceed with the wedding events in his mother's absence. My grandmother had just made it worse. Maziar, however, just smiled at the old woman, refusing to allow her to get the best of him. He believed we would be fine.

In the Iranian culture, there is a traditional proposal referred to as the *khastegari*. In the old days, when a man was of marrying age, he and his family would seek out an appropriate bride. Once they'd decided on a potential mate, the process began.

It consisted of two various visits in which one or more representatives from the man's family would take part. The first visit was for the parties to become acquainted and didn't include a formal proposal or commitment. If it progressed to a second meeting, a marriage proposal was made by the suitor and his family.

Nowadays, however, the first two *khastegaries* were done in one step. The groom would privately ask the bride's parents for their permission. This was a sign of respect more than necessity. He would then propose to his bride much like how it's done in Western cultures, creating some elaborate fairytale plan he'd come up with. Taking part in the ritual was nothing more than formality, occurring afterward when the two sets of parents sat down to discuss the logistics of the wedding.

Talks quickly began after the engagement on whether Maziar's family would follow through with the tradition. Mom knew of Naghmeh's hesitations, but Maziar had already proposed. He'd set the wheels in motion and now her absence could be viewed as an insult to my family. She began whispering in my ear about her discontent. I became stressed and irritable, finding every reason to snap at Maziar, releasing my frustrations onto him.

"What's wrong with you?" he asked one night, after sustaining my mood all evening. "You've been going off on everything lately. I have a hard time believing you're this angry over where I left my shoes." He just looked at me, annoyed and confused.

I had tried to ward off Mom, arguing with her, trying to make her see our situation was out of the normal parameters. I begged her to drop it, to see past the world of traditions. To her, though, the lack of involvement coming from Maziar's camp was unnerving. She knew our relatives would view Naghmeh's absence as a direct result of her disdain for my family, so her pride wouldn't let it go.

Gone were the days when she thought Maziar choosing me was enough to get us through. Now she wanted the comfort of knowing I would be accepted by the family I was marrying into. She also wanted to prove my grandmother wrong.

"Nothing's wrong," I said, not wanting to deal with it.

He looked at me, hazel eyes boring down on my lie. I'd never been good at lying.

"That's not true," he said, calling my bluff as he scooted closer to me on the couch. "Tell me what's wrong."

I looked at his persistent face and felt the exhaustion come crashing into me. I wanted so badly to spend my days flipping through magazines and surfing the wedding websites. Instead, this chapter of our story was much like the rest, sitting around worrying about the obstacles we needed to overcome. At the same time, I was too overwhelmed to shoulder the weight on my own any longer.

"My mom keeps stressing me out that your parents haven't come over for the *khastegari*. We've been fighting, and it's just getting to me," I admitted.

"Why didn't you tell me what your mom was saying?" he asked.

"Because I knew the situation was already difficult for you. I didn't want to make it worse."

"Yeah, but we're getting married, Sara. You're supposed to talk to me when something is bothering you so we don't end up fighting like this, even if you think I have too much going on. Okay?" he said, trying to convince me.

I wondered how Maziar had become the rational one while I warped into the timid, emotional wreck. I used to feel headstrong and badass; now I just felt tired and worn down. I blamed it on the hell I'd been dealing with the past few years, but I suddenly questioned my own strength. I leaned into him, allowing him to carry my worries as he lay his strength over me like a warm blanket.

"Okay," I said, grateful for his presence.

* * *

I walked down the produce aisle grabbing vegetables for dinner. I was comparing two heads of lettuce when I heard someone say my name.

"Sara?"

My heart stopped, recognizing his voice instantly. I looked up to find Ben.

"Hey," I replied, flustered.

He smiled, flashing his dimples at me. He looked good. He'd gotten a tan, no doubt from the Santa Barbara beaches, causing his crystal-blue eyes to stand out against the bronze backdrop. They twinkled now, as he looked at me.

"How are you?" he asked.

"I'm good. How are you? How's Santa Barbara?"

"It's great. I love it there. I hear you're working with Seti. Do you like it?" I must have looked confused that he knew that information so he threw in, "We talk from time to time."

It hadn't even crossed my mind that they'd stayed friends. Made sense.

"It's great," I said. "What brings you here?"

I suddenly realized I was still holding the lettuce like a moron. I went to place one back on the pile and bag the other. Before he had a chance to reply, the overhead lights caught my ring, causing it to flash across the cart. Ben instinctively looked down at it. *Shit!*

"Congratulations," he said, not skipping a beat.

"Thanks," I replied, uneasily. I unconsciously braced myself for his anger.

"I'm happy for you, Sara." He seemed completely unaffected.

Just then, a blond woman walked up behind him, placing her arm around his waist.

"Are you ready, babe?" she asked, eyeing me curiously.

"Yeah. Sara, this is Liz."

"Hi," I said. "Nice to meet you."

"You, too," she replied, kindly.

He was looking at her while she spoke to me. His face held an expression I recognized well. Then, he turned back towards me. "Okay, we have to go," he said. "It was great seeing you, Sara. Take care." He smiled at me one more time before he turned and walked away with Liz on his arm.

I stared at their backs for a moment, waiting to feel something life-altering, but I didn't. Ben seemed genuinely happy, and all I felt was relieved. I was glad he'd moved on, that he'd found someone else, someone who could give what he wanted.

Good for him, I thought. He deserved it.

I smiled to myself as I turned to finish my shopping.

* * *

I fumbled with the keys, trying to balance grocery bags on my arms. As I walked in, I heard Maziar in the bedroom having a heated conversation on the phone. I couldn't make out any of the words, so I was forced to flutter about anxiously until he finished. He walked into the kitchen a few minutes later, flustered but smiling.

"Ask and you shall receive, beautiful," he said, obviously proud of himself. "I just talked to my dad. We'll be coming to your house next weekend."

"What about your mom? Is she coming?" I asked, the knot of dread now a hard basketball in my gut.

"I'm not sure," he replied, thoughtfully. "My dad said he'd talk to her."

I began to chew my bottom lip as he reached out and pulled me into his arms.

"He knows the tradition. I'm sure he's going to talk to her. If she refuses, then he'll ask my aunt." I felt sick to my stomach, the constant unknown slowly killing me. He held me tighter. "Stop worrying. It's going to be okay."

I looked up at him, wondering if he really was naïve enough to think things would magically fall into place or if he was just putting on a show for my benefit.

"I have to call my mom," I said, frantically.

"No need. I already called her right after I hung up with my dad," he said, smiling broadly.

"You called her?" I asked, shocked. I could barely look his mother in the eye and here he was going head-on with mine.

"Yes. I wanted to make sure Saturday was okay. Plus, I figured she'd be stressing about the whole thing, so I thought I'd save you from the conversation," he said. "At least for tonight."

He constantly amazed me, putting himself in uncomfortable situations so I didn't have to. He dealt with the backlash, put his foot down, got into screaming matches, whatever it took to show the world I was his Number One.

I must've done something right in a past life.

* * *

Saturday arrived and my house exploded into chaos. Mom's anxiety was demanding, consuming everyone in its wake. We ran around cleaning and setting up, trying to make everything as perfect as she needed it to be. There'd been no confirmation that Naghmeh would be attending, and I'd been sick to my stomach for days.

When Maziar's family finally arrived, Mom and I were in the kitchen. We froze simultaneously, glued to our spots on the floor. I had a plate of pastries hanging midair, holding my breath, trying to identify the voices as they came in. Mom was doing the same.

"Welcome, Parviz *khan*. Come in, Naghmeh *khanoom*," we heard Dad say. We gasped in unison.

Did he just say Naghmeh? Had his mother actually shown up? A few days ago, the final verdict was that if she refused to come, Maziar's Aunt Lily would stand in. A smile spread across Mom's face, taking her presence as a victory. I smiled back at her, trying to mimic her enthusiasm, but I was filled with apprehension. I knew she hadn't accepted us, so her presence meant only one thing: there was a struggle ahead.

Mom turned and walked out of the kitchen, urging me to follow. We came in with trays of tea and pastries that she placed on the coffee table. She began the pleasantries, greeting the guest, welcoming them to our home. Maziar's father hugged me affectionately. His mother, however, greeted me coldly. I prayed Mom hadn't noticed, but the subtle crinkle of her forehead told me otherwise.

I looked at Maziar, who had also seen the exchange. Although he remained passive, I could see his protectiveness bubbling to the surface. I took a seat next to him, reached out for his hand, rubbing his palm to calm him. Simultaneously, I looked at Mom, pleading with my eyes for her to let it go. With a little nod, she conveyed that she would. I could hardly breathe, afraid I'd have a heart attack before it was all over.

Dad started the conversation, trying to break the ice. He asked Maziar's parents about their family, tracing their roots back to various cities in Iran, a common practice when meeting for the first time. They talked about old times back home, people and places they shared. Soon the wives were participating a bit as well.

A half-hour in, when all neutral topics were exhausted, the *khastegari* began. The fathers took the lead, each speaking affectionately about the other's child. For a moment, it almost seemed as if things would run smoothly. However, the lioness reared her head, making our house of cards come crashing down.

"I'm sorry, Abbas *khan*. I don't mean to be rude. I think we should discuss the issue at hand, though. Everyone is acting as if we don't have a bigger problem."

The muscles in Maziar's jaw twitched with anger. Both he and Nima moved forward in their seats, my soldiers coming to attention. I braced myself as she continued.

"These kids are young and in love. They don't understand how difficult marriage is, especially when children become involved. I just don't think they understand what they're doing. We come from such different backgrounds." She was careful to choose her words, trying to convey her opinion respectfully. I was thankful for that much.

Maziar sat forward, ready to pounce on her. Mom looked at him, slightly raising her hand to stop him before he could get started.

"What are you referring to, Naghmeh *joon*? Aren't we all Iranian here?" Mom asked, a small smirk playing at the corner of her lips as she forced Naghmeh's hand.

"I was referring to the different religions, Shireen *joon*," she responded, feigning a look of innocence as she waited for Mom to make the next move. The battle of wills had begun.

"There will definitely be some navigating that has to be done because of that. But that said, I think the kids are mature enough to handle it. I don't think they're going in blindly, or taking this decision lightly," Dad replied, jumping in. "The truth is, they're adults who love each other. If they want to spend their lives together, who are we to stop them? We're only here to provide guidance if they ask for it."

"Yes. We need to put our own differences aside. Any arguing we do amongst ourselves only makes things more difficult. Surely we can all find common ground, don't you think?" Mom added.

"We're no longer in the world we grew up in. Times have changed in this country. The youth now falls in love first, then worries about the logistics later. Race and religion don't concern them. Love and compatibility are all that matters," Parviz said. "Maziar and Sara are strong, and it's obvious how much they love each other. I for one am not the least bit worried about them. They'll find a way to make it work."

I was so overwhelmed by the emotions in the room. Parviz's smile filled my eyes with tears. Maziar and Nima's strength hovered protectively over me. My parents' love shined like a beacon in the dark. I couldn't look at Naghmeh.

She was also witnessing all the people willing to come to our aid, despite our differences. I could tell she felt overwhelmed by the wealth of emotions too, but not for the same reasons. She suddenly realized she stood alone.

"What will happen with all our customs? Will we have a Jewish wedding or a Muslim one? Will you come to Shabbat dinners?" she asked, looking wildly around the room for an ally. "And when you have kids, will we have a bris? Or a Bat Mitzvah? Have you even thought about that?"

Gone was the strength of a few moments ago, replaced by a deep desperation in her voice, compelling me to look at her. When I did, I saw that she was staring at me, searching my eyes for an answer. She needed validation that she wouldn't lose her only son. Maziar stepped in, still on the defensive.

"Mom, those are all details that we have to figure out, but we're going to do what works best for us. Everyone is just going to have to deal with it."

I placed my hand on Maziar's leg, knowing that his anger would cause more harm than good. She had legitimate concerns, and if nothing else, they deserved to be addressed. Remaining silent was no longer an option for me. I needed to step up and take control.

"Naghmeh *khanoom*, I understand why you're worried, but you don't have to be," I assured her. "We haven't discussed all the details, but we aren't planning on getting married and just forgetting everything we grew up with. We're going to incorporate as much of both of our traditions as we can. It's something that's important to us." I maintained eye contact as I spoke so she could see the truth in my words. "God is God regardless of his name, and God is love, something both of us have plenty of. That's what we are going to teach our children."

She looked at me for a few moments, trying to read me. I held her gaze, knowing she wasn't completely convinced. Then, she turned toward Mom, and with a weary smile on her face asked, "Shireen, could I have another cup of *chayee*, please?"

A unanimous exhalation passed through the room as everyone acknowledged the change of subject as her admittance of defeat. She had found herself alone, isolated on the island she'd created. She was hoping to find allies in today's meeting, but was met with unexpected resistance. She knew pressing the issue would only cause an explosion between her and her son. The already strained relationship between them teetered on a string, and losing him was the one thing she was trying to avoid.

We looked at each other, neither of us fully convinced of the other's efforts. After a few moments, she gave me a halfhearted smile, her acknowledgment that she'd lost today's battle. I smiled back, extending an olive branch in hopes that it could be the start of some sort of peace treaty between us.

I wasn't sure if she would go home and think things through, having a change of heart, or at least finding some tolerance for Maziar and me. I wanted to believe that her love for him would inspire her to shed her preconceptions. But I had spent so many years facing walls she'd placed around me that I couldn't completely convince myself of the hope everyone else seemed to be feeling.

Too tired to analyze the situation any further, I allowed myself a night where I could pretend Maziar and I were just another normal couple, planning a normal wedding, not some representation of the ongoing conflict in the Middle East. I let my mind wander as those around me spoke of various wedding details.

I avoided looking in Naghmeh's direction. If no one could see the hesitation and frustration emanating from her, I could, and I was too exhausted to allow her to take this night from me as well.

CHAPTER FORTY-TWO

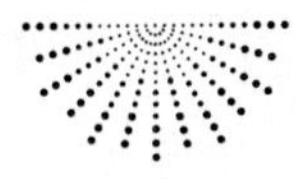

The next few weeks were a whirlwind of various venues and vendors. Maziar and I made our appointments, flanked by our mothers, Bita, and Neda. Due to his sister's persistence, Naghmeh made appearances, but continued to show minimal involvement. The strain on Maziar's relationship with her had progressed from a crack to a fault line, the tension making us all uncomfortable.

Mom had taken it upon herself to establish a relationship with my soon-to-be mother-in-law, a camaraderie to extinguish the stiffness we felt when she was around. She remained cordial but distant where I was concerned. I slowly began to realize that the problem had lost its focus on me and was now stemming from her relationship with her son.

I kept hoping Maziar would stop being difficult and make the first move. If only he would crack the door open for her, I knew she'd take a step inside. He was impossible, becoming agitated and angry every time I brought her up. I was usually forced to back down to avoid a full-fledged argument.

I'd spent sleepless nights pondering over their relationship. I'd concluded that, to rectify the situation, Maziar had to stop rejecting his mother. Even if Naghmeh had begun to regret her position, she wouldn't allow herself to give in when he was ignoring her. She was an Iranian woman, after all, with stubbornness and pride woven deep into the fabric of her DNA. Both of their unyielding natures did not allow for much progress.

I'd been trying to figure out how to talk to him all week. I leaned up against his arm, flipping through a magazine while he worked on his laptop. Although I appeared calm, I was a nervous wreck, trying to figure out how to bring it up without looking like I was siding with her.

"I wanted to talk to you about your mom," I blurted out, realizing I had no good way of approaching the subject. I felt Maziar's body stiffen against my back.

"What about her?" he asked, irritated, patience already running thin.

"Well, I've noticed that you're giving her the cold shoulder and I feel like that may be the reason why she isn't warming up to this wedding," I stammered nervously.

"Well, she's made her choice. I told you–I'm done," he said without even looking up from his screen. The finality in his voice sparked my anger.

"You don't get to just be done," I said, before I could stop myself.

"Excuse me?"

"I know you're mad, but you don't get to make decisions on your own when they affect me," I said, trying to hold my ground.

"What are you talking about? She's *my* mother."

I realized that challenging him would only spur more stubbornness, but I needed progress. I changed my tactics, scooting in closer and grabbing his hand. I felt him recoil, stopping himself before he pulled away. I wanted to be hurt, but I forced myself to keep going.

"Your mom is no longer just your problem; that's where you're wrong. I need her to be okay with this wedding. If you keep being mean, that's never going to happen. Don't you want to give us a chance to have some sort of relationship?"

"Sara, she's made it abundantly clear she doesn't want to know you. You're stuck in some sort of fantasy where everything ends happily ever after." His features softened. "You always see the best in people. It's one of the things I love about you. But I'm sorry, baby. She isn't going to come around."

I wondered if he was right. Was I hoping for the impossible? Should I hate her too? No, I decided. We were all human, and all dealing with big changes. Maybe I did try to see the best in people, but I didn't believe people were inherently evil. Maybe she didn't deserve a chance after what she'd done, but I was choosing to give her one anyway.

"Maybe you're right. Maybe she won't ever come around. But a lot has happened since the beginning and so much has changed. I think if you just give her a chance, she may surprise you."

I moved in closer, trying to use my femininity to compel him. I reached out and ran my fingers through his hair, seducing him with my touch. Maziar had used these tactics against me many times before; now I was flipping the script.

"Could you please try, just for me?" I batted my eyelashes as I leaned in to kiss him. He started to laugh against my mouth. I pulled back and looked at him, a smirk playing on my lips.

"Well played, Sara," he said. "Well played."

He threw the magazine off the couch and pushed me back on the cushions. I smiled against his shoulder, knowing I'd just won this battle.

* * *

Two weeks later, we had an appointment with the florist. As usual, our entourage accompanied us. We sat at the table surrounded by binders full of sample arrangements, busily flipping through pages as we discussed possible color schemes. Maziar had made an effort to be seated next to his mother, a feat only I noticed.

"Mom, what do you think about this one?" he asked nonchalantly as he leaned over toward her with his binder. "I kind of like these deep purple flowers, but this white orchid one is nice too," he said, pointing to the other center piece.

We all froze as jaws fell open in surprise. He didn't falter at our reaction, acting as if they hadn't spent the past few months in silence. Naghmeh just looked at him, tongue-tied for a moment before she gathered her wits.

"I like the purple ones," she said, almost in a whisper.

"Yeah, I think you're right. They're prettier," he agreed, flashing his irresistible smile at her.

The smile she gave him in return resembled the light that shines through the dark at sunrise. He had his charm on full blast, and to secure the deal, he placed his hand on his mother's arm when he pushed the binder toward me so I could see it.

"I think they're beautiful," I said.

Naghmeh just blushed at my response. Bita sat back in awe, giddy at the new development. Mom squeezed my leg under the table, her excitement apparent on her face. I couldn't take my eyes off of Maziar. He looked straight at me as the women around us buzzed with glee and winked.

That was the moment he turned everything around. Throughout the years, he would teach me that love meant seeing past yourself, always putting the other person first no matter what that meant for you. I knew it was hard for him to swallow his pride, but he did it because he loved me. Maziar had put my needs before his so many times through the course of our relationship, and he was doing it again.

I didn't realize I could love him anymore than I already did, but I was wrong.

* * *

As the days progressed, the tension between Maziar and Naghmeh dissipated until it could no longer be felt in the space around them. She still kept her distance when it came to me, but I could see her world had shifted. She would smile at me more often, and when we were all in a discussion, she took part more freely, interacting with me more than before. The hope that things could work out for us began to bloom in me again.

The following month, at Bita's insistence, we had an appointment at a high-end bridal store on the west side. We'd yet to choose a wedding date, but Bita thought that taking part in the time-honored tradition of wedding-dress shopping would be a bonding experience.

We arrived just minutes before the appointment time. Bita, Neda, and Naghmeh were patiently waiting outside. We were quickly taken in, and I was rushed into a dressing room. The next hour become a whirlwind of tulle and lace. I was put into and taken out of one dress after another, making me feel like a Barbie doll. With every new garment, I was pushed out the door to stand on display, greeted by praise, applause, and pictures for Leyla since she couldn't be there, then pushed back in to be on display again moments later. By the time I tried on what felt like the hundredth dress, I had a headache.

The final dress that Neda and Bita brought to the dressing room was a fitted vintage ensemble. The deepest layer was white satin that peeked out from beneath the many layers of lace. It was strapless and hugged my body down to my hips where it began to flare. The lace sat across my bare chest, traveling down my arms in fitted sleeves, as my skin peered out from beneath its pattern. The remainder ran down my body and mimicked the satin, with multiple layers at the bottom that panned out on the floor behind me.

They helped me into it, then stood back gawking at me, Bita's eyes brimming with tears for the first time that morning. Then, they pushed me out onto the little stage so the mothers could look at me. I was staring down at my dress trying to see what the fuss was about when I came out.

There was a collective gasp, snapping my attention back to the mothers. Mom was crying, and Naghmeh was staring at me with a look in her eyes I'd never seen before. Without turning toward Mom, she reached out and grabbed her hand.

"She looks beautiful," she whispered.

Mom placed her other hand on top of Naghmeh's, still crying. The two women turned toward each other and smiled, now both in tears. I stood frozen along with the others, unsure of what was happening. Neither woman was paying any attention to us.

"They're going to be okay," Mom said, patting Naghmeh's hand.

"How are you so sure?" she asked.

"Because we aren't going to let them be anything else," Mom replied confidently.

The two women were locked in a moment that we were intruders in. I wanted to look away, to give them the privacy the moment seemed to demand, but I couldn't tear my eyes off of them. I could see the walls around Naghmeh beginning to crumble, right there in the middle of the store.

She reached over and pulled Mom into an embrace, both of them allowing their emotions to run freely between them. When they pulled away, they were both laughing as they wiped tears off their cheeks. They turned toward our peering eyes and giggled even louder.

Not many words had been exchanged between them, but it was evident that mountains had moved within the silence. Naghmeh turned toward me.

"That's the dress. You look amazing, *aziz*."

The smile on my face stretched so wide my cheeks began to hurt. I hadn't realized it, but my cheeks were wet from tears. She stood up and walked over to me, putting her hands on my shoulders as she pushed me back to get a better look.

"Beautiful," she whispered, then hugged me.

I stood locked in an embrace with a woman who, I'd thought just months ago, was my enemy. No longer could I feel her disdain or hatred, instead replaced with a kindness I hadn't imagined I could feel, but had desperately wanted to.

CHAPTER FORTY-THREE

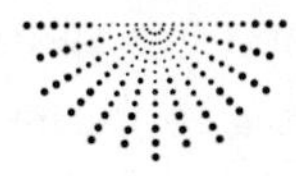

The alarm wakes me at six thirty. I reach over for it in a haze, refusing to allow the calm of sleep to leave me. I roll onto my side and curl around my pillow, welcoming just a few more minutes of darkness behind my closed lids. I can hear the rustling of the other inhabitants in the house as they, too, turn off their alarms and start readying for the day. A broad smile stretches across my face. Today is my wedding day.

Mom shows up, gently knocking before coming in. She thinks I'm asleep and I can feel the weight of her gaze settle on me before she walks over. She gently sits down on the edge of the bed, reaches out and runs her hand across my head, a gesture that reminds me of when I was little.

"Sara, get up, *azizam*. The hairdresser will be here soon," she whispers.

I try to pinch back the tears that spring to my eyes as I realize this will be the last morning I'll be in the same house as her, the last time she'll wake me up. The relevance of the day causes a wave of panic to invade my happiness. I've been an adult for many years now, but for the first time I feel like a grownup.

I roll over and look at my mom, her hand still resting on my head.

She meets me with that special smile that only she possesses, the one with the ability to heal any wound, calm any fear, make any moment more spectacular. It reaches deep inside me. Tears escape my eyes then, landing in a wet puddle on the pillow. She laughs through her own tears, leaning in to kiss my forehead.

"None of that, *eshgham*. Today is a happy day. Now get up or you'll be late to your own wedding!" she teases, as she lifts herself off the bed and leaves the room.

I stare at the spot she stood just moments ago, trying to breathe through the pain that is starting to fill my heart. I spent the past few weeks daydreaming about the life I was about to begin, so I forgot to realize there was a life I was also leaving behind. I have the urge to throw the blankets over my head, going back to the safety of my dreams. Instead, I force myself up on my elbows and swing my feet over the edge. Today was meant to be a good day.

The next few hours are a rush of bodies through the house. The men headed out earlier this morning, suits in tow. They were meeting Maziar, his father, and the groomsmen for breakfast and then drinks and lounging at the apartment until wedding time.

The vibe I imagine at the apartment is far from the chaos buzzing around me. I am ringed by frantic women trying to put themselves together. We have two hairdressers, one working on me while the other cranks out the bridesmaids. We have multiple makeup artists working furiously as they try to get all twenty women primed and primped for the event.

I sit back, armed with a venti latte, watching the scene unfolding before me, and I smile. "I'm getting married today," is the thought that keeps playing on repeat in my mind. Maziar's mother looks at me and winks as she and Mom flutter around filling teacups and handing out pastries in between their own mission to get ready.

I wear my hair up in a loose bohemian bun to accentuate the open back and lace details of my dress. As soon as it's finished, I'm shuffled over to the corner of the room designated for makeup to spend another hour under the aesthetician's hot lights and expert hands. By the time I'm ready to get into my dress, I'm exhausted.

"Shake it off," Mom says. "No time for sleep."

"Give me that," Layla orders, grabbing my empty cup and replacing it with a new one. She's taking her maid-of-honor duties very seriously.

Before I know it, they push me into the bedroom, flapping around me like butterflies as I step into my dress.

"He's here!" Leyla squeals, just as Mom fastens the last button.

I experience an unexpected rush in my stomach. I reach out and grab the edge of the chair, suddenly lightheaded and dizzy. A fog settles over my thoughts. I'm nervous.

I hear the door open from the other end of the house, feel the chatter of the men vibrating off the walls. I try to remind myself to keep breathing, the simple task suddenly becoming difficult. I haven't seen Maziar for three days, wedding details taking up most of my time. I'm dying to see him.

My veil is placed on my head as a light knock comes from the door. Dad peeks in. Once Mom gives him the okay to enter, he squeezes through the space, trying to minimize any visibility from the other side. He walks up to me and immediately begins to cry.

Silence surrounds us, everyone trying to hold back their own tears at the sudden show of emotion from the man standing before me. I look up into the light, rapidly blinking for fear of ruining my makeup.

"Don't cry, Dad. You're going to make me cry," I say as I reach out for him. He throws his arms around me and pulls me into his chest.

"I can't help it. I've dreamed of this day since you were a baby, and now that it's here, I don't know how I'm going to let you go."

He starts to sway with me, dancing to the music of our heartbeats like we used to do when I was a little girl. I give in to my emotions then, and cry on his shoulder, unable to focus on anything but him. How did I fail to realize how difficult this day was going to be? How did I not recognize that, in a way, I'd be leaving them? Mom comes to the rescue, separating us.

"Abbas, go. The photographers are waiting for her to come out and I don't want her pictures to be of red, puffy eyes!"

Dad chuckles and kisses my cheek, then Mom's. "You all look beautiful, ladies," he says, as he heads out the door.

Mom hands me a tissue and I dab my cheeks to rid myself of any residual makeup that may have smudged from my tears. Leyla ruffles my veil, then makes sure the lace of my dress sits perfectly on my bare shoulders. She smiles up at me from under smoky eyelids.

"You ready?" she asks.

"Yes," I say, my heart rapidly fluttering inside my chest.

The bridesmaids position themselves around me as per the photographer's request, and we head out the door for our "first look" pictures. The lights from the flashing cameras blind me and it takes my eyes a few moments to adjust. When they do, I see him.

Standing before me, in his fitted black suit, is the man I've spent my life dreaming of. As he looks back at me, the bodies in the room disappear and the world fades. No one else matters.

I vaguely hear the snapping of photos and the murmur of talking, but I see nothing. I glide toward him on the clouds beneath my feet. He looks down at me, silence enveloping us in its embrace. My heart swells with so much love that I fear it will explode right here in the living room, turning me into a puddle on the floor.

He reaches out and gently runs his thumb down my cheek, a gesture so gentle I feel the tears choking me.

"You look beautiful," he whispers.

"You look beautiful too," I say, and smile.

We are locked in a tender moment that no one can invade, the bodies hovering around us faded into oblivion.

"You ready?" he asks, then adds, "I can't wait to make you my wife."

"I've been waiting for you all my life," I say in response.

He leans down and places a soft kiss lightly on my lips. I feel the surge of electricity his touch always brings. I smile up against him, eyes still closed, filled with a longing I can't describe.

He pulls back, and just like that, our dream fades. I'm suddenly aware of the crowd around me, the flashing lights of the cameras. Mom stands next to Naghmeh, hand in hand with her, smiles on their faces, bright like the sun shining through the window. Nima informs us the limo has arrived. We turn and head out the door, with our entourage of bridesmaids, groomsmen, and siblings trailing us.

Once at the venue, we stand side by side, taking in the beauty of the ceremonial room. Directly in front of us is the platform with the *sofreh aghd*, the traditional Muslim wedding ceremony spread. There is a plethora of items on the table, each with its own meaning. A plush white bench is placed in front of the platform where Maziar and I will be seated as we stare into the mirror set directly in front of us.

Traditionally, the couple looks into the mirror together, representing the light and brightness of their future reflecting back at them. The designer has taken time putting great detail into the various aspects of the *sofreh*, giving it the vintage, classy feel I'd requested. The bread has been designed to resemble flowers, the eggs are dressed in pearls. She's worked deep purple flowers into various locations, pulling in the color scheme of the event. They pop against the pearl and white backgrounds of the platform.

To the left of the *sofreh* is the *chuppah*, the traditional Jewish wedding canopy, symbolizing the home the new couple will build together. All four legs are hidden by the elaborate design of purples and greens from the various flowers being used in the centerpieces. A platform sits in the center as well, with a small table holding the silver chalice of wine and the glass that Maziar will break once the marriage ritual is complete.

The wedding coordinator asks me if everything is as it should be.

"It's perfect," I say, in awe of my very own fairytale.

We'd been adamant that both ceremonies take place in the same room, as a silent declaration to our guests that we place no difference between the two. Both are set up as we'd hoped, and both look beautiful. We are shuffled back into the bridal suite to prepare for the start of the first ceremony.

* * *

I stand before Maziar, staring into his eyes as he whirls me around on the dance floor. The crowd moving around us has faded into the periphery, my husband the only one I can see. That still sounds foreign dancing around in my head. I wonder when it will roll off of my tongue as easily as his name.

Suddenly, from the corner of my eye, I pick up some movement. Maziar has noticed as well. I can see he's distracted as we dance. I have the haze of intoxication playing on the edges of my attention, so I fail to pick up the cautious vibe that is emanating off of him. I nonchalantly turn. I notice bodies rushing out of the big double doors into the foyer at a speed that feels unusual. We stop and stare at the commotion.

Leyla and Sandra are on me within seconds, trying to turn me around, away from the doors and back into the beat of the song. Maziar kisses the top of my head, and before I know what's happening, he rushes out the double doors with half of the guests.

I panic, the anxiety mingling with the alcohol as I try to comprehend the scene unfolding before me. I turn to follow but am blocked by Sandra. She tries to distract me back into dancing. Realizing I'm not going to get past them, I turn and begin to dance, waiting.

The moment I feel their guard falter, I turn and run.

* * *

I stand in the center of the foyer, tears streaming down my face, watching my beautiful wedding fall to pieces around me. There's commotion everywhere.

The group surrounding my cousin has now dissipated. I assume they've ushered him home. I've lost sight of Thomas, now vanished along with Maziar. I see Dad yelling in the corner, frustrated and angry, Mom trying desperately to calm him down. Some guests have retired back to their tables; others are saying their goodbyes. I find myself suddenly worrying that someone may step on the broken glass and hurt themselves, or worse yet, get spilled wine on their expensive dresses. And the flower petals. They are still strewn all over the floor, now crushed beneath designer shoes, leaving purplish red smudges on the marble tiles. It looks like blood. I find the resemblance nauseating.

Suddenly, Leyla materializes before me, the sight of her an angel in the darkness.

The weight of the panic is crushing, my chest burning with it. She wraps her arms around me and pulls me close, protectively. I close my eyes and breathe, on the verge of hyperventilating.

"My wedding," I say through desperate tears.

"Was beautiful," she responds.

"But look, it's ruined."

She gently laughs. "No it isn't. It's been a fantastic night. This isn't changing anything. Just think of what an awesome story we can tell in ten years."

I can't help myself, I laugh through the tears. She always has a way of doing that, making me smile in the most morbid of situation. For a moment, she's successfully taken me out of the chaos I've found myself in.

My grandmother stands in the far corner whispering to my aunt. Our eyes lock for just a moment, but I can feel her disappointment cross the distance. I can hear her voice rumbling in my head.

I told you so, I imagine her saying, and for a brief second, I wonder if she was right.

I brush it aside, scanning the room looking for Maziar. I can't find him anywhere. The panic returns. I turn and find Bita standing beside me.

"Where's your brother?" I desperately plead. She looks as shocked and exhausted as I feel.

"He's outside with Nima."

I don't wait for any further information, just pick up my dress and head out the door, leaving her and Leyla behind. I step out onto the balcony. He stands a few feet away from me, laughing with my brother and Neda. I experience a wave of relief at the sight of him. But then I notice Nima holding an ice pack against his knuckles and I become confused.

The tapping of my heels announces my arrival as they turn to look at me. My brother's expression seems apologetic, and slightly scared. I'm further confused by his reaction.

"What happened to your hand? Are you okay?" I ask him.

"I'm fine," he says, as I walk up to him to examine it closer.

"What?" I ask. They are all looking at me with strange expressions. I find it frustrating.

"Oh, God, she doesn't know," Neda whimpers.

I feel like I've walked into an inside joke and I've just missed the punch line.

"What don't I know?" I say, eyeing her.

She bounces back and forth on her toes with nervousness. Maziar jumps in to rescue her.

"So our Nima here was apparently protecting Neda's honor this evening," he says with a grin.

It takes me a minute, but I finally put the pieces together.

"Wait, you started this entire thing?" I ask.

I begin to lose hold on my anger and he slightly cowers away from my gaze.

"He didn't start anything. Your cousin Ardeshir did. Nima just came to Neda's rescue," Maziar says, walking toward me, hands out like he's approaching a rabid animal.

I look at my brother expectantly. He picks up on my cue and begins to explain.

"Ardeshir was bugging Neda all night. He kept trying to hit on her but she wasn't interested. He wouldn't take the hint. I came out to get a drink and walked in on them. She was yelling and he wouldn't let go of her arm. I was trying to defuse the situation. I told him to leave her alone," Nima said, shaking his head. "He started spewing nonsense. He was drunk and it turned into more than it should have. We ended up in a fight. Next thing I know, *Amoo* is there, so is Dad, and they're about get into it. If it weren't for Dad's friends, they would've fought too. Everyone got caught in the crossfire." He watched me apologetically as he continued. "He started to say some really *offensive* stuff, Sara."

I could see the pleading look in my brother's eyes begging me not to make him repeat it. I suddenly realize Ardeshir turned it religious.

"Oh no," I say, mortified. "He didn't."

"He did," Nima confirms sadly.

"Where is he? I'm going to kill that son of a bitch!" I turn to head back inside, but Maziar reaches out and stops me.

"He's already gone. Your uncle left with him a while ago. He was ashamed and embarrassed by his son's behavior and apologized profusely to my father and me on the way out. Besides, Nima already took care of it," he replies, grinning.

I turn to my brother.

"Tell me he looks worse than you."

"He had a black eye by the time he walked out," Maziar says, laughing.

"Good! I didn't get a good look at him, but if I'd known, I would have punched him in the other eye," I admit angrily.

We walk back into the foyer to find it's almost empty. The clock now reads two in the morning and the guest have all gone home. My friends are still there, helping Mom and Naghmeh grab the remaining centerpieces and gather all the gifts. Leyla looks at me as I walk up to them.

"You okay?"

"Yeah, I'm fine. Just tired." I give her a weary smile, suddenly feeling drained from the emotional roller coaster of the evening.

Mom comes up behind me and kisses my head. "We're all tired. It's been a long day," she says.

Naghmeh is beside me. She reaches out and squeezes my hand. "Long but perfect," she adds, letting me know that the events of the night haven't altered anything between us. "You and Maziar go home. We can handle it from here."

Maziar comes up from behind and wraps his arms around my waist. "The limo is waiting downstairs to take us home," he informs me.

I look at both mothers as they shoo us away.

"Are you sure?" I ask, feeling guilty leaving them with the mess.

"We got this. You guys go," Leyla says.

I smile at the women surrounding me, so fiercely grateful for their presence in my life.

"Okay. I'll see you all tomorrow morning?" I ask. Mom's having an after-wedding brunch.

"Yes," they reply in unison.

"Love you guys," I say as Maziar and I turn and walk away.

* * *

I lie next to my husband in the early hours of the morning. My body is wrapped around his and I'm lulled into a dreamlike state by the rising and falling of his chest as he breathes.

We arrived at the apartment, both giddy that we were "home." He lifted me up into his arms and carried me through the door. He had spread arrangements throughout the apartment, creating a flower-like haven around us. He took me straight to the bedroom where we slowly undressed each other and indulged in the first night of being husband and wife.

As I rest my head against his chest, the idea of being married still swirls around my mind. I'm in disbelief that we've actually made it. I realize I never really believed it would happen. I'd convinced myself years ago that I would always love Maziar, but we were destined to be pieces of a past we desperately wanted but couldn't have. After some time, I wouldn't allow myself to even toy with the idea of a miracle happening to bring us back together, allowing for us to now be spending our lives together.

I know in the deepest parts of me that none of this would have happened if not for the intensity of Maziar's love. Despite all our obstacles, it had no limits, and he kept pushing against the traditions that held us apart. If I allowed myself to remember the years that fell between us, I would be overwhelmed with the sadness that seemed to have loomed in the corners of my life. To love him, but know I couldn't be with him, was devastating.

I'm grateful for the man lying beside me, for his perseverance, refusing to admit defeat. If his love did not encompass the eternity of strength that he'd shown, I would be lying in my own bed tonight alone.

I curl up closer to him, drinking in the warmth of his body. I indulge in the idea that he is now mine forever. He instinctively holds me tighter as he feels my chest up against him. He turns and lays a kiss on the top of my head, and I know I've finally found my way home.

EPILOGUE

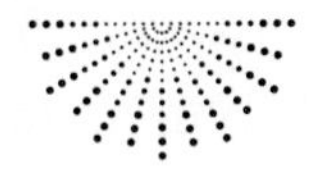

The pain reeling through me is excruciating, tearing through my insides, surely taking me to my death. I stare up at the florescent lights flashing above my head as the wheels beneath me spin rapidly. Maziar is beside me, the look of concern on his face only adding to the ever-building anxiety within me.

I woke up a few hours ago to a sharp pain swimming around my lower back. This had happened before and resulted in an unnecessary trip to the emergency room, only to find out I was experiencing false labor.

When I woke up early this morning, I thought it was the same thing. I stood up, drank a glass of water, and paced around the living room for a little while waiting for it to subside. Maziar woke up an hour later and joined me, walking with me while he held hand. The pain only got worse, and in his panic, he decided to wake the doctor at four in the morning despite my protests.

She advised us that this could be the real thing. Assuring me I had time, with the contractions still fifteen minutes apart, she told me to gather my things and meet her at the hospital. Somewhere between the phone call and the hospital my contractions sped up and I began what I presumed meant I was dying. Maziar nearly had a heart attack.

I lie curled up on the labor and delivery bed clutching my stomach, praying the anesthesiologist shows up soon. They tell me I'm already six centimeters dilated and quickly increasing, my window for an epidural rapidly closing. I silently curse the woman having a C-section down the hall, occupying my only chance at relief. I'm in so much pain that the tears are mingling with my sweat.

Maziar, unsure of what to do, is diligently rubbing my back and murmuring encouraging words, trying to pass his strength telepathically. I don't have the heart to tell him he isn't helping, so I try to focus on the repetitive motion of his hand while I breathe like they taught me in Lamaze class.

Mom stands on the other side, rubbing my shoulders, Naghmeh at the edge of the bed with Bita, hands idly lying on my legs. So many people are touching me that I want to scream, but I'm too exhausted to do anything about it. The fathers come in and out of the room, lost and useless. Nima isn't coming near me, out in the hall waiting in the safety of its confines.

Another surge of pain runs through my body and I scream out in desperation. I look up at Mom, sobbing.

"I'm going to die," I cry as she brushes the hair out of my face.

"Oh baby," Maziar whispers, his face crumbling.

The doctor walks in, cheery and peppy. I get the sudden urge to kick her as she moves Bita and my mother-in-law out of the way so she can check how dilated I am. They both go outside, giving me some privacy.

"I need an epidural," I plead. "Is the anesthesiologist coming?" I desperately look at my doctor as her arm is God-knows-how-deep inside me. She looks at me sympathetically.

"Sorry, honey. Looks like we're doing this the old-fashioned way. He's coming."

I hear Mom quietly sob with excitement, feel Maziar falter beside me beneath his mountain of fear. I look at the doctor and think, *I'm going to die, and now I have to do it in excruciating pain*. I'm suddenly angry.

"What do you mean? I don't want to do this naturally. I want an epidural!" I scream.

Bita and Naghmeh pop their heads back in at the sudden rise of my voice, both looking terrified.

"I know you didn't plan on doing it like this, Sara. I understand you're tired and it hurts, but we have no choice. He's coming. I can already feel his head." She smiles but I don't find it comforting. "You have no choice now, mama. You have to push." She calls out a few directions to the nurses and gets geared up.

Maziar is stroking my head and I turn to him, crying. He meets me with his own tears.

"You can do this, baby. You got this."

I just sob, the pain tearing through me only getting worse. "I can't. I really can't."

"Yes, you can, Sara," Mom encourages.

The nurses usher my in-laws out into the hall and shut the door. The doctor places herself between my legs; I scoot up on the bed. I look back and forth between my husband and Mom, grab hold of their hands, and begin to push.

Moments or hours later, all having turned into a blur of pain, they place an amazing pink baby on my chest. He's got thick dark hair on his head and glowing hazel eyes like his father. He's covered in a layer of mucous, but he stares up at me wailing, unbelievably beautiful.

Maziar is pulled in close, running his finger across the baby's cheek, tears flowing down his face. Mom has his foot in her hand, marveling at his tiny toes. Maziar is pulled over to cut the cord.

The nurses whisk the baby away, cleaning, weighing, and testing him. Maziar goes to the end of the room with him, already so protective of our little addition. I can feel Mom's need to follow, but she decides to stay beside me as the doctor finishes. She strokes my head and the two of us whisper with excitement about my son.

The baby and I are finally cleaned up. Maziar carries our little burrito back over to me. I take him into my arms and for the first time feel what love truly means. The three of us are lost in our little bubble of infatuation when the rest of the family is ushered inside.

He gets passed around from person to person, with not a dry eye in the house. I sit back on the cushions, utterly exhausted, taking in the immense love filling the room. Maziar beams at his son as his mother holds him.

"What are you naming him?" Nima asks.

"Milad," Maziar and I respond in unison.

"How fitting," Mom says.

"Why?" Nima asks.

"Because it means, 'new beginning.' Our little gift," Naghmeh says, staring into her grandson's eyes.

I look around at the people in my room, feeling grateful for my family, as they coo at the baby. The road leading to this moment has been tedious and long, with days when it seemed impossible. Somehow, by fate and the strength of the love between Maziar and me, we created the family before us. Now we have a son, a new little person binding us together even more strongly.

What I feel at this moment for my baby, and the beautiful man holding him, knows no bounds.

THE END

Thank you for reading! Find book 2 of the FORBIDDEN LOVE novels coming soon. For more about Negeen Papehn find her across social media.

Website: www.negeenpapehn.com

Twitter: twitter.com/NegeenPapehn

Facebook: www.facebook.com/NegeenPapehn/

Instagram: www.instagram.com/NegeenPapehn/

* * *

Please sign up for the City Owl Press newsletter for chances to win special subscriber-only contests and giveaways as well as receiving information on upcoming releases and special excerpts.

All reviews are **welcome** and **appreciated**. Please consider leaving one on your favorite social media and book buying sites.

For books in the world of romance and speculative fiction that embody Innovation, Creativity, and Affordability, check out City Owl Press at www.cityowlpress.com.

ACKNOWLEDGMENTS

When I wrote this book, it was purely a passion project, something to do in the little time I could find between the kids, husband, and the day job. It was a way to tap into a creativity I had long ago lost sight of. I never in a million years thought I'd be writing an acknowledgment page. Trying to sum up the tribe of people that helped me get here seems impossible, but here it goes...

To all my beautiful friends that eagerly and excitedly agreed to be my betas. Alex, Azi, Teri, Allison, Ally, Eynav, Renee, Shab, Jennifer, and my dental girls. I thank you for putting up with my stalking as I pestered you to finish, for the million questions I tirelessly threw your way, and for the multiple "book club" discussions you engaged in with me. I could never have done this without you.

A special thanks to Leyla for always being the head of my fan club, Tara for being my "editor," Pat for being my muse, James and Barry for being my "man view," and Shoe for always believing in me even when I couldn't believe in myself.

Ann, Margi, Magda, despite coming onto the scene after the fact, your excitement of all things in this madness of publishing and your encouragement as you rooted me on, helped me stay grounded. You three will always be my writing gurus.

To my editor Amanda, thank you for taking a chance on me. Your efforts and encouragement have shaped this book into its best version and I couldn't have done it without you. Tina, thank you for always putting up with me and my tireless questions. My City Owl Press family, you are amazing! Thank you for helping me share my story with the world.

Mom, Dad, Nav and Oms, I don't have words to explain how your support in this, and all things, means to me. Thank you. Nahal, thanks for always making me feel like a rock star. Jen, thanks for tearing this book apart and overwhelming me with your critique, then encouraging me to do the rewrite. It obviously paid off. I love you all.

Bijan, Minoo, and Mahsa, thank you for being nothing like the characters in my book. You are wonderful and I couldn't have asked for a better family to marry into. I love you guys.

To my husband Mike, thank you for never letting me stop writing despite how I worried that this story may make people think this was our life. "It's fiction" you said, and pushed me to move forward. Your encouragement is what gave me the courage to put it all on paper and see what could happen.

And last but never least, to my two amazing boys, Elijah and Noah. I did this for you. I want you to know that nothing is impossible, so always reach for the stars because you never know what you may find. The nights I felt like throwing my laptop (and my dreams) out the window, your excitement at the number of pages I'd written and the idea that your mom may actually have a book on a shelf somewhere that you could hold in your hands, kept me going.

I love you both to space and back. You are everything...

ABOUT THE AUTHOR

NEGEEN PAPEHN was born and raised in southern California, where she currently lives with her husband and two rambunctious boys. She wasn't always a writer. A graduate of USC dental school, Negeen spends half of her week with patients and the other half in front of her laptop. In the little time she finds in between, she loves to play with her boys, go wine tasting with her friends, throw parties, and relax with her family.

Website: www.negeenpapehn.com

Twitter: twitter.com/NegeenPapehn

Facebook: www.facebook.com/NegeenPapehn/

Instagram: www.instagram.com/NegeenPapehn/

ABOUT THE PUBLISHER

City Owl Press is a cutting edge indie publishing company, bringing the world of romance and speculative fiction to discerning readers.

www.cityowlpress.com

CPSIA information can be obtained
at www.ICGtesting.com
Printed in the USA
FSOW01n0149080118
43146FS